ALFRED HITCHCOCK PRESENTS:

THE MASTER'S CHOICE

ALFRED HITCHCOCK

Presents:
THE MASTER'S CHOICE

⌂ Random House, New York

Acknowledgments

SHE FELL AMONG THIEVES by Robert Edmond Alter. Copyright © 1964 by Popular Publications. Reprinted by permission of Larry Sternig Literary Agency.

THE HILLS BEYOND FURCY by Robert G. Anderson. First published in *Alfred Hitchcock's Mystery Magazine*. Reprinted by permission of Larry Sternig Literary Agency.

A GUN IS A NERVOUS THING by Charlotte Armstrong. Reprinted by permission of Coward, McCann & Geoghegan, Inc., from *The Albatross* by Charlotte Armstrong. Copyright © 1957 by Charlotte Armstrong.

SEE HOW THEY RUN by Robert Bloch. Copyright © 1973 by Davis Publications, for *Ellery Queen's Mystery Magazine,* April 1973. Reprinted by permission of the author and his agents, Kirby McCauley Ltd.

NOTHING SHORT OF HIGHWAY ROBBERY by Lawrence Block. First published in *Alfred Hitchcock's Mystery Magazine*. Copyright © 1977 by Davis Publications, Inc. Reprinted by permission of the author.

PUPPET SHOW by Fredric Brown. Reprinted by permission of the author and the author's agents, Scott Meredith Literary Agency, Inc.

DE MORTUIS . . . by John Collier. Copyright 1942 by *The New Yorker*. Copyright renewed 1969 by John Collier. Reprinted by permission of the Harold Matson Company, Inc.

SNOWBALL by Ursula Curtiss. Reprinted by permission of Brandt & Brandt from *The Lethal Sex*. Copyright © 1959 by Mystery Writers of America, Inc.

HERE, DAEMOS! from *Legends in the Dark* by August Derleth. Reprinted by permission of the author and the author's agents, Scott Meredith Literary Agency, Inc.

THE COOKIE LADY by Philip K. Dick. Reprinted by permission of the author and the author's agents, Scott Meredith Literary Agency, Inc.

THE WAGER by Robert L. Fish. First published in *Playboy* Magazine. Copyright © 1973 by Robert L. Fish.

SCREAM IN A SOUNDPROOF ROOM by Michael Gilbert. First published in *This Week Magazine*. Permission granted by the author and his agent, Curtis Brown, Ltd.

RETURN OF VERGE LIKENS by Davis Grubb. Reprinted from *Collier's*. Permission granted by the author and his agent, Elaine Markson Literary Agency.

The Editor gratefully acknowledges the invaluable assistance of Harold Q. Masur in the preparation of this volume

Introduction

Good evening.

I trust you have enjoyed a pleasant dinner. You have? Good. Then you are now ready for dessert. I have gathered together in this collection a group of macabre pastry chefs and they have prepared a number of alarming concoctions. Not only for your hedonistic gratification, but for the more sensitive gastronomes a nougat or two that will nourish your soul.

When I delivered this feast to my publishers I was greeted with a ukase. (If you do not have a dictionary handy, a ukase is an imperial decree.) I was directed to hatch up an introduction. Something original, they said. Stimulating. Provocative. Something to prod bookstore browsers into loosening their purse strings.

It gave me pause. I was for a moment somewhat disenchanted. I have always thought of publishing as a noble enterprise, transcending the profit motive. I do not collect these stories with commerce in mind. I collect them because I wish to share my pleasure. Currency of the realm does not intrigue me. I can manage to survive quite nicely without a publisher's meager royalties. You can see from my ample silhouette that I do not suffer from malnutrition.

Nevertheless, on closer inspection, I can understand the publisher's concern. Books must be sold so that more books can be published. I know, too, that money ranks near the top of all human priorities. And with that in mind, you must certainly be aware of a murderous inflationary spiral. Economists call it an erosion of buying power. So that no matter what you pay for this volume, that sum a few years hence will be worth approximately seven cents.

Think of it. Seven cents. Such a trifling sum for a collection of extraordinary stories culled from a cast of thousands. By any standard, a bargain.

Well, no matter. I have done my duty.

It is up to you.

Contents

ALFRED HITCHCOCK PRESENTS:

THE MASTER'S CHOICE

She Fell Among Thieves

Robert Edmond Alter

Our six Trans-Jordan boys were spading back the hard, cindery earth crusted over a formation of flat, snug stones. Either they were uncovering an old, worthless, stone floor or they were uncovering an old, old, sunken, stone roof. Which might mean there was something under the roof. Something of archaeological value.

I was sitting on a broken bit of wall just above them, supervising the job. Tanner, my partner, was in his tent with the shakes. He had been suffering from intermittent fever for the past few days.

It was an old complaint with him. He'd had malaria in Cambodia. But that was before I knew him.

Twilight was flowing over the ironbound Jordan hills and the first fat drops of the long-awaited rain were just beginning to splat on the bone-dry dirt. They were widely separate at first, each silvery pear-shaped drop striking the earth like a tiny ripe fruit. I wished the boys would hurry—before the rain turned to buckshot.

The headman, Hassin, straightened up and grinned at me. He was very thrifty with his English words. If a grin would suffice, he always had one ready.

"Very good," I said.

They had uncovered the total area of the stone flooring or roofing. The stones formed a rectangle of, say, twenty by fifteen. I hunkered down for a closer inspection. The light was dimming rapidly.

It was a roof, all right, formed by overlapping courses of masonry crowned by hewn capstones. Couldn't be any doubt of it. So—was it possible that we had uncovered the first room of a lost city, or was it merely an old cellar? One way or another, the long-gone artisans who had laid this roof had put it together to last, to endure through centuries of dust-submerged oblivion.

Why? What was housed in the space under the old roof?

"Good," I said to Hassin. "Remove one of the cornerstones."

He translated the order and the Arabs went to work with crowbars, prying up one of the fair-sized slabs. A rectangle of black, hollow space appeared.

"Bring the ladder and the flashlight," I said.

Waiting for them, I fished out a stub of candle and lit it. A cold, black, unwholesome odor rose from the hole in the roof. I tested the air with the candle, to insure against poisonous gases. Then the boys sank the ladder in the opening and Hassin handed me the flashlight.

"You and the men stay up here," I said. "Understand? Give them cigarettes."

He grinned and nodded.

Tanner had taught me not to trust them. What they saw, they talked about, and Tanner was the type of digger who preferred to keep his findings to himself—unless they were the usual run-of-the-mill artifacts. I started down the ladder.

The place itself was not truly clammy. It was the cold, dark air that gave the suggestion. I started to shiver. The pregnant raindrops followed me down the rungs.

I played the torch over the old stone walls, seeing here and there a faint white filigree of mold. The flooring was the earth itself and it was as black as sin.

The figure of a naked white female stood in the halo of light.

It took me so by surprise, that for an absurd moment, I almost blurted, "Excuse me." Then I had to laugh at myself. It was only a life-sized marble statue. It glowed, pale and cold and glorious, like moonlight. I went closer.

It was the most remarkable statue I had ever seen. The detail of the female was astounding. Her hair, eyelashes, fingernails, everything. She stood with her legs slightly apart, her torso turning at the hips, her head looking back over one shoulder.

It was the expression on her face that held me. It was enigmatical. Was it surprise, horror or ecstasy? At what strange sight was she staring? Involuntarily, I threw a mechanical glance over my own shoulder. Stupid!

Who had been the sculptor? How had the statue come here? How long ago? Excitement beat in my ears, slopped and slushed around in my brain like warm, heady wine. I was dead certain that I had made an exceedingly valuable discovery. I went up the ladder and dismissed the work crew. Hassin grinned at me as he turned away. Had he seen? Had he peeked through the roof?

I hurried through the rubble of our digging to Tanner's tent. The rain was coming down like wet bayonet points.

"You've never dreamed of a statue like this," I told Tanner. "She —she's beautiful! And that's a weak word. The look on her face. That enigmatic expression!"

Tanner grunted and threw a quinine pill into his mouth. He was a squat, powerful man. Bald. He was a free-lancer. Had to be. There wasn't a reputable archaeological group in the world that would touch him with a ten-foot pole. His methods were shady.

The Mexican Government was down on him for smuggling artifacts out of Yucatan; he had been run out of Cambodia for the same business, and the Greeks threw up their hands in horror at the mention of his name. I was new in the game and this was my first jaunt with Tanner. I didn't especially like the man, but I admired his professional knowledge. It seemed to me that I could learn quite a bit about the financial end of archaeology—the rewards— from a man like Tanner.

"I didn't think you could find statuary of this kind in this region," I said.

Tanner trembled with his fever and smiled wryly. "Neither did I —after the way you describe her. But there could be a hundred reasons how she came to this place. Let's have a look."

In raincoats, with topees on our heads, we went out into the rain-lashed night. It was turning torrential. On our left we heard it machine-gunning the dark, salty surface of the Dead Sea.

Tanner took one look at the white statue and went into a spasm of trembling. "G-god, she's f-fantastic, Miller! Ge-get the Coleman lit."

I ignited the two meshy little bags and raised the lantern for another look at the statue. Tanner prowled around her like an Arab chieftain contemplating a marketable female slave.

"Fantastic! The exquisite d-detail of her!" He shivered violently, hugging his upper arms. "She's old, old, old. My boy you have no idea how old. She's not Greek or Roman. Hell, even their greatest sculptors couldn't capture a facial expression like that. L-lord, you can practically see the pores in her skin!"

Her face had me again—that enigmatical backward look. What had she seen? I pulled my eyes away.

"Look at her coiffure," Tanner said. "The sculptor used a Jewess for his model. Miller, I'll stake my reputation she dates back to the Old Testament."

I wondered to which reputation he was making reference. Then I found out. He turned to me and, in that sepulchral place, with that pale, cold female standing by us, his fever-bright eyes looked wild.

"Miller—do you have any idea what she's worth?" he asked, his eyes greedy.

I shook my head, staring at him, knowing what was coming.

"She's worth the thirty years I've spent grubbing in this business. Twelve times I've tracked around the world searching for her—without even realizing that she, or something as magnificent as she, existed! This"—he gestured toward the glowing female object—"is the treasure hunter's dream. This is the bonanza!"

I said, "You have more to say."

"Oh, yes. Oh, my God, yes! Much more. There's thousands in her, Miller. I know the right people. Two of them are in Paris. No questions asked. No mention of our names, ever. Nothing on paper. And no taxes. Right down the middle, boy. Fifty-fifty. If . . ."

"If I help you smuggle her out of the country," I said.

He laughed, his eyes leaping from my face to her face.

"There's no other way to work it. You know there isn't. That greasy governor of this district is as grabby as a fish net strung with hooks. We're damned well lucky if he'll let us keep the worthless potsherds and beads we turn up. Do Hassin and the boys know about her?"

"I don't think so. I came down here by myself. But who ever knows about Hassin? He might have peeked when my back was turned."

Tanner nodded, shivering. "If he knows, he'll run right to the authorities. Not a doubt of it. Miller, we're getting her out of here to-night. Now."

I argued with him. Sure. For a minute, half-heartedly. But I was already caught by the infectious aura of his excitement. And we both knew it. I would be rich. Or, if Tanner failed to turn up the right buyer, I would at least be famous.

"You're certain of her age and value?" I'd accept any assurance.

"I know my business, don't I? She's not listed in any catalogue, I know. Her true worth will be any connoisseur's guess. But you can leave that part to me. All you have to do is help me get her out."

"To where? And how?"

He was sweating now.

"To Israel. That's the first move. I know an influential Jew there who'll help us for a little payola. Let's see. . . . We'd have to find and steal some kind of craft to cross the Dead Sea. And those damned Arab patrol boats would probably catch us halfway over. No. We'll take the truck and follow the shore down to Ein Hatseva. The barbed wire ends about fifteen miles below Sodom. All right?"

I nodded. "Right."

We had to rig up the block and tackle to get her out of the pit. She was heavy, but not as heavy as I thought marble would be.

"What do you think she is—chalcedony?" I asked as we hauled and shoved and strained in our own sweat, with the blinding torrent of rain pouring down on us. "You notice how she seems to have a certain sparkle about her in the light?"

"Could—could be just the moisture," Tanner grunted. "After eons of dampness down in that cellar."

Maybe. But the cellar had seemed as hermetically sealed as King Tut's tomb.

We swayed her up into the rain and the dark and Tanner said, "Get the truck. Hurry! For God's sake hurry!"

Our vehicle was an archaic old wreck, with tall, metal sides around the bed and an open top. I backed her up to the opening and trotted around to drop the tail gate. Tanner, holding onto the swaying statue in the tackle, watched me balefully. The gate came down with a rusty screech, like an ecstatic banshee busting loose. Cold, black water gurgled out of the bed. Tanner was shivering so violently that his teeth actually chattered.

"All right. G-get her b-by the sh-sh—*n-not by the head*, man! G-good God, be careful! B-by the shoulders!"

Grunting, heaving, shoving up, we jockeyed the gleaming woman-sized statue into the truck bed, Tanner hissing like a frantic boa constrictor. "Easy n-now! Careful! D-don't chip her!"

She was in, on her back with the rain peppering her body, her head slightly turned over her left shoulder, staring with that strange, fixed expression. At what? I slammed up the tail gate.

"I'll d-drive," Tanner said, and he gave me a shove.

Frowning with apprehension, I squelched around to the passenger side and climbed into the cab. Tanner slammed the door on his side, and for a long moment, he clung to the wheel with the shakes.

"My God, Tanner. You're in no shape for this. You'll kill—"

"Shut up! I've been through worse than this in Brazil and Cambodia. And for less—far less. W-what you want me to do? Crawl into my tent w-with my pills for a week? And let that damned governor snatch her away from me! I'll be all right, I tell you."

He turned her over and dumped her in gear and we jolted out of the mud with a tire spin and a neck-snapping leap and went lurching for the road.

"*Easy!*" I yelled.

"Shut up!" he snapped.

The old truck slid onto the road, careening slightly, found traction and went rolling into the gold-streaked blackness.

Outside, it rain, rain, rained. Inside it dribbled, the moisture seeping around the door frames and the seams of the windshield. The truck skidded, swerved, slewed around, the tires treading for the ground, finding it, digging in and going forward again, and Tanner shivering and chattering and hunching down over the wheel.

And suddenly it all seemed crazy to me—this pellmell race into the night, down a muddy, nameless road, in a blinding rain, the fever-ridden, obsessed man clutching the swerving wheel at my side, and that pale, cold, wet female statue riding behind me, with her head turned over her shoulder and staring, staring. . . .

"Tanner," I said. "This is all wrong."

"Shut up! Damn it, Miller, shut up! Can't you realize what I've got in the back of this truck? It's my life. My entire life! Thirty years of searching and dreaming. Never honestly believing that she or anything like her would actually appear. And now she has. She has! And I've got her, and I'm going to get her out, and there's no power on earth can stop me!"

His heavy usage of the first-person possessive concerned me: *I've, I'm, me, my.* . . . Did he still consider me his fifty-fifty partner? Was it the fever or the statue that was destroying his rationality?

A crystalline white eye materialized ahead of us, far down the road and coming on. It brodied around to a static, knifing stop and then a second, smaller light appeared and began to wigwag at us.

"That's a motorcycle," I said. "Someone signaling us with a flashlight to stop."

Then I realized that Tanner meant to drive right over the man and his cycle.

I slashed at his brake foot with my left boot. "You fool! You can't kill him!"

The truck went into a mad skid, the rear end skittering halfway around in a muddy pivot.

"Goddamn you!"

"Will you, for crapsake, take it easy!" I yelled at him.

A rain-coated Arab was picking his way toward us, slipping in the muck. He was one of the shore patrolmen and he carried an old World War II machine pistol in the cradle of his arm. He came up to Tanner's side and tapped the muzzle of the weapon against the streaming window. Tanner silently rolled it down.

"Your identification," the Arab said. "Where are you going?"

We dug out our wallets and showed him our ID cards. "Al Mazra," Tanner said in a quiet, almost dreamy, voice.

"You can see we're archaeologists," I said. "We move from place to place, searching for Dead Sea scrolls."

"So?" the Arab said. "Let me see your permits, please."

"You have them," Tanner said. "They're in our wallets."

"Yes? And what are you carrying in this truck?"

"Only our equipment," I said.

"So? We will have a look."

Tanner reached down between his legs. The gesture had no meaning to me at that moment. I was in a panic to get out my door and meet the Arab at the back of the truck. I knew these people. They could be bribed.

The rain hit me like a break in a dike. I squelched to the back of the truck. The Arab came around the other end.

"Open up," he ordered.

The truck bed must have been like a bathtub. Rainwater was

pouring out of every crack and hole. I put my hand on the right-hand bolt and smiled at him. "Look here . . ." I started to say.

Tanner's silhouette appeared behind the Arab and I saw his right arm swing up. The wrench literally bounced off the Arab's head and the machine pistol roared *babap bap* straight in the air as the senseless man dropped into the mud.

"*Tanner!* You crazy idiot! We could have bribed him!"

Tanner said nothing. He threw the wrench aside and yanked the machine pistol free of the Arab. Then he said, "Drag him into the *karoo* shrub. Hurry!"

I stooped over the prostrate man, but in the night and the rain, I couldn't tell how badly he was hurt. He didn't seem right to me, though. Not at all.

"Tanner, he's badly hurt or dead."

The muzzle of the machine pistol tapped me coldly, jarringly, under the chin, then retreated. When I looked up, Tanner was aiming at my chest.

"Drag him into the bush."

"Tanner, listen to me. What if he's not dead? What if he's badly hurt? We can't leave him out here in—"

"Get him into the bush."

It wasn't necessary for him to say "or." I knew where I stood. Either I dragged the sad-apple Arab into the bush, *or* I joined him in the muddy road.

"You drive," Tanner said. And there were no ifs about that, either. Not with that gun aimed at my navel.

He herded me around through the passenger side and followed me into the cab. I released the brake and put her in gear and started to ease around the parked motorcycle. Tanner kept the gun at my right side.

"We could have bribed him, Tanner," I said again.

"No. He knew about us," Tanner insisted. "The governor sent him."

"Damn it, he *didn't* know about us! You hit him for no reason!"

"Shut up and drive!" The barrel nudged me in the ribs.

I was scared—sick-stomach scared. I could still hear the *bappity-bap* of that gun ringing in my ears. Those slugs would plow through me like darning needles through warm butter. I shut up and drove.

It poured rain. Tanner went in and out of the shakes. We passed through the district of Moab, then through sleeping Al Mazra. In less than an hour, we skirted Khinzirah and headed for As Safiyah. Another ten miles and we could cut west and aim for Beersheba, in Israel.

Tanner was starting to mutter to himself. ". . . so old she might go into the reckoning of millenniums. Tell you, she's of no known period. Might even belong to Abraham's time. Seems impossible, and yet . . . and yet . . ."

And yet, she lay back there in the bouncing truck bed, alone in the wet night, as we droned on through the pouring darkness.

It never let up, the rain, not for a moment. It seemed to cover the night land as Noah's deluge had once done.

Tanner figured we were past the barbed wire barricades which separated Jordan and Israel, and he said, "Take the first turnoff west." He was burning up again. When I looked at him, he was swabbing sweat from his face with his left hand.

Maybe I could have slammed the brakes then and jumped him as he spun off balance. Maybe I could have gotten that gun away from him. But I didn't. I don't know why not. I didn't. I just drove on.

Tanner was wrong. The Arabs had extended the Jordan line. The road we were on ran us smack into a frontier outpost. We were on top of it before I could do anything about it.

The white-and-red barricade was down, stabbing across our path, and an armed sentry was waving us to halt with his torch. There was a guardhouse, and an officer came through the door swathed to his eyes in a khaki-colored *cheche*.

I hit the brakes and we went into a mud-creaming skid. Tanner said one very old, very short Anglo-Saxon word and swung up the machine pistol. I grabbed at the barrel in a panic.

"Don't! There's a whole guardhouse of them. And look over there!" I pointed to the south of the sentry box.

Tanner hesitated, staring. Barbed wire entanglements coiled off into the murk on either side of the road. A sandbagged sap squatted on top of the shallow bluff where the road curved down into No Man's Land. We could see a three-man crew hunkering around a light machine gun. The nest commanded the road.

"They'll cut us to shreds," I said.

Tanner sucked his breath as the armed Arab officer came squelching noisily through the mud.

Tanner relaxed with a soul-weary sigh. "I had it," he muttered. "I had the answer for at least one man's purpose of existence in this stupid damn world. And now . . ."

The officer, followed by the sentry who carried an old Lebel rifle, came up on my side and the sentry swung the barrel of the Lebel toward me significantly. I rolled down the window, still clinging tightly to the barrel of Tanner's gun with my right hand.

"*Bism' Allah*," I said to the officer, a lieutenant.

"Where do you think you're going?"

"We're American archaeologists. We want to cross over to Beer-sheba."

"From where are you coming?"

"Upper Moab."

"Why didn't you cross at Sodom?"

Good question. I tried a bluff in assimilated anger.

"We're sick and tired of bribes. We thought if we came far enough south, we could cross over without having to pay tribute to every son of Allah who stood in our way with a gun at our heads."

The lieutenant laughed.

"You thought that, eh? What are you carrying into Israel?"

"Nothing."

He turned slightly without taking his eyes from me. "Keep your rifle at his head while I check the truck."

I stared blankly at the aimed Lebel rifle while my world turned slowly upside down. It wasn't just the trouble we would be in for trying to smuggle the statue out of the country; it might also be murder. Which would mean a firing squad.

I turned and looked at Tanner. He was trembling again and his eyes were sideslipping in his moist face, like a ferret caught in a trap. He still hadn't quite made up his mind.

"Don't," I whispered. "We'll never get through alive."

His sick eyes looked into mine.

"She's mine," he said hoarsely. "They can't take her away from me. I'd rather die than give her up!"

Then he snatched the barrel of the machine pistol from my hand. The Arab lieutenant came slogging back.

"All right," he said. "You may pass." I stared. Then I said, "Thank you."

Tanner looked stunned. He gawked at the lieutenant. I put the truck in gear and let out the pedal and we shivered forward a few feet. Another sentry worked on some sort of gear in the dark and the white-and-red pole rose slowly into the raining sky.

I pressed the gas and we rumbled through the barricade and into the waiting blackness of No Man's Land. I didn't get it. I couldn't understand. True, I hadn't heard the tail gate drop, but surely the Arab officer had looked into the truck bed. Certainly, he had climbed up on the rear bumper and investigated the back of the truck with his torch.

So why hadn't he seen the statue? Why hadn't he arrested us as smugglers?

"Stop the truck," Tanner said.

"What?"

"Stop! I want to look back here. Something's wrong."

"No," I said. "Not here. We're only a hundred yards from the Israel barricade. At this point, they can both see us."

"But something's wrong, Miller! What?"

"Wait! Damn it, can't you wait? The Jews are right ahead."

The armed Israelites came out from behind their barricade to meet us. I stopped the truck. This time it was a Jewish lieutenant who stepped up to the cab window.

"Who are you and what are you bringing into Israel?"

I don't know why I said it but I did. "Nothing. We're American archaeologists."

"We'll see," the lieutenant said. "You realize that if you enter Israel now, you will not be permitted to re-enter Jordan?"

"That's all right by us," I said.

"We'll have to check the back of your truck," he said.

Tanner was already out his door. I shot out mine. The three of us met at the back of the truck.

The lieutenant looked at us with raised, wet eyebrows. "Something wrong?"

"That's what we want to find out," I told him.

Tanner and I unbolted the tail gate and let it drop with its usual screak. We stared into the rain-whipped truck bed. Water poured out of it like a miniature Niagara.

That's all there was—draining water. Nothing else.

"Stolen!" Tanner screamed. "My God, they stole her!"

"No!" I grabbed at his arm. "They didn't have a chance. We would have heard the tail gate. The Arab lieutenant was only back there for a few seconds by himself. He *couldn't* have gotten her out by himself. She weighs far too much."

"Then where?" Tanner wailed. "Where's she gone to? Oh, my God! *She's dissolved!* The rain! The filthy rain!"

He turned away from the open truck bed, away from me and the bewildered-looking lieutenant. And he started to laugh. The high mounting rocking laugh of insanity. He sat right down in the mud and roared with laughter until his breath failed him, and then he went into hiccupping, giggling sobs.

"Very nice," the lieutenant said to me. "Very nice what you've brought us. As if we didn't have our fair share already. All right. Let us get him into the infirmary. We'll have to strap him down."

The lieutenant and I left Tanner with a Jewish medic. We went outside and over to the barbed wire to have a smoke. The rain had petered to a sullen mist. I had nothing to say. I had only one question and it wasn't anything the lieutenant could answer.

Where had she gone? How? And when?

The medic came out and accepted a cigarette from the lieutenant.

"I gave him a shot to calm him down," he told us. Then he looked at me and jerked his thumb back at the infirmary shack. "Religious fanatic, eh?" he said.

"Who? Tanner? No. Why?"

"Because he keeps raving about Lot's wife," the medic said. "About how she looked back at the destruction of Sodom and Gomorrah even though God had warned her not to. And so she was turned to a pillar of salt."

The Hills Beyond Furcy

Robert G. Anderson

The party had passed its peak. Tienne, the tall, enigmatic exchange student from Haiti, surveyed the half dozen couples, college classmates all, who were gyrating tiredly in various versions of the Swim, the Jerk, or the Gorilla.

Dave Grayden's apartment was crowded, filled with body heat and hazy with smoke, a contrast to the February wind which lashed at the windows. Tienne stood in a darkened alcove, aloof, remote; his intense gaze riveted on Carol Braun—no—Carol Mason, now that she and Roger were married.

The Roger Masons, guests at this informal discotheque, were to leave in two days on a delayed honeymoon to the Caribbean; delayed because of Roger's graduation. But it had been worth waiting for, because even before his graduation in the top ten of his class in chemical engineering, job offers had poured in on him. He finally chose Fraser Oil, which offered an excellent starting salary, plus the chance for rapid advancement. They also had given him a generous bonus for signing, plus a month's grace before reporting for work.

Someone turned the record player down and called out in a thick voice, "Tienne, how about some of your voodoo? You know, that ol' black magic."

A flicker of annoyance darted across the dark, handsome features of the Haitian. He tried to ignore the request, but others took it up; they were tired of dancing.

"Show us some magic; show us some voodoo from Haiti."

The dancing stopped altogether, and the record player turned itself off. The group eyed him expectantly, hoping he'd respond.

Chick Melardi, bold and brash as always, scoffed, "Voodoo! That mumbo-jumbo! Jumping around the place and killing chickens; oh, brother!"

But he was the lone dissenter; the others hooted him down. Chick's words stung Tienne and his lips tightened. The fact that he had one too many of Dave's Specials also made him a little reckless. A wry smile played about his lips. He shrugged and held up a hand.

"All right, what do you want?"

He stepped to the middle of the room, and the couples fell back into a ragged circle. Tienne stood alone, a bold, striking figure in a dark business suit. His eyes held darting yellow lights in their depths, lights which lashed like the tail of a wild thing.

Carol and Roger pressed forward with the rest, and Roger's thoughts went back two years, to when Tienne had first arrived at the university. From the day when he had accidentally dumped a bowl of bean soup into Carol's lap in the crush of a busy cafeteria, they had formed an unusual triumvirate on campus. It was Carol who had taught the Haitian student the intricacies of American slang, and how much catsup and/or mustard was proper on a Campus-Union hamburger, the real "in" things.

Carol's courses were in the humanities, far removed from the scientific chemical engineering of Roger and Tienne. She told Roger that, surprisingly, Tienne had a remarkable insight into poetry and philosophy. If Roger felt a twinge of jealousy at this, he was comforted by the knowledge that he and Carol would be married just as soon as he graduated. They did get married, and although Tienne knew how it was with them, he continued to gaze at her with his wise, old, young, sad, adoring eyes.

Carol was the target of Tienne's eyes now, as he stood alone, the air charged and electric about him. Carol turned her eyes away.

Impish little Donna Lennart, wobbling and giggling, suggested, "I'll tell you what, Tienne. Get Dave here to shut up, for a starter. He's been bending my ear all evening about his canoe trip in British Columbia last summer; what a bore!"

"Hey, you can't say things like that about your boyfriend. Besides, I've got so much money that everything I say should be fascinating."

There was laughter at this, but Tienne held up a hand again, and the room quieted by stages. His voice was commanding.

"You!" He indicated Morrie Day, a devotee of the bongos, "Take this beat!" He rapped a staccato series on the edge of a side table. To the others, "Be quiet, and observe."

Morrie carried the pair of bongos from a corner, sat down and clasped them between his knees. Soon the room was pervaded with a sound like the thumping of a wild heart; even the compulsive whisperers were stilled.

From an inside pocket, Tienne took a small package wrapped in what looked like a dirty rag. Carefully he unrolled it and revealed three dried chicken bones, several short, hollow sticks, and a few white feathers. The feathers were dotted with dark blots. Dried blood? The wild drumming subsided to a hum, and Tienne placed the bundle on the floor and began a slow shuffle around it. There was an intense look on his face as he began an unintelligible chant, a curious mixture of French patois and African. Roger caught the word, "Malele," recurring time and again.

Once Tienne stopped his shuffling dance, and squatting, quickly and accurately drew a portrait of a man on the rug by dribbling sand from his fingers. It was a likeness of Dave. As he finished, Tienne drew a final line across the throat of the picture. Then he straightened, resuming his shuffling dance and chant. The spectators were engulfed in rhythm as his voice rose and fell, the words weaving around the drumbeats. The throbbing grew and Tienne shuffled faster, his lips moving in exhortation. Both he and Morrie were perspiring freely now. Tienne's dark face gleamed. Morrie's features were contorted with his efforts on the drums.

Suddenly, the drumming and chanting stopped as if a door had slammed on it. Tienne sank into a chair. Wearily he took out his handkerchief and wiped his face. He bent forward and scooped up the white bundle. Gradually his face resumed its impassive mien.

The couples remained as they were, shaken and awed. There was something intangible vibrating in the air about them, retreating now.

Dave, panic in his eyes, gesticulated wildly and tried to talk, but no sound came. And although the buzzing spectators may have thought for a moment that it was a joke, there was no mistaking the fright on Dave's face. Even Donna became concerned. Tienne got up and thrust his hand into his pocket, withdrew some leaves, and crushing them between his fingers, massaged the powdered remains against Dave's throat. Dave burst into a torrent of words.

"I really couldn't talk! Did you think I was kidding? I thought someone had taken hold of my neck and squeezed." He grabbed Tienne by the lapel. "What did you do to me?"

"Just call it a form of hypnotism," he answered, and shrugged Dave's arm away. For some time Tienne listened to the chorus of "How did you do it?" and "Show me how it's done," but finally, he was able to work free of the press around him. The groups argued heatedly among themselves, forgetting him for the moment. When they looked for him later, he was gone. There were a few more drinks consumed and attempts made to renew the conversation, but the party soon broke up.

Carol sat quietly beside her husband in the taxi going home.

"That was quite a show Tienne put on—a new side to him. What did you make of it?" Roger asked.

"I—I don't know. It was all so bewildering. He has power."

"So did Houdini and Thurston," Roger said lightly.

"Don't laugh; I *felt* this."

"Agh, just sleight of hand, some new wrinkle of an old trick; there's probably a simple scientific explanation. As for Dave, anyone can hypnotize him when he's half stoned."

Should she tell him, Carol asked herself, about the little voice beating insistently against her eardrums during Tienne's chant. "I love you—I love you—you are mine—you are mine—," like a drumbeat? No! It would only reopen the wound made by that ugly scene only two weeks ago, just a few days after she and Roger were married. Roger had come home tired from his long hours of intensive lab work, to find her and Tienne laughing and listening to her records of little French songs.

"You just can't come here all hours of the day, Tienne, and visit with my wife when I'm not home," Roger had blurted. "We're married, and it's different now. Call it jealousy, but it doesn't look right."

Carol had been crushed, and Tienne retreated into his reserve. Never before had it been necessary for them to weigh their actions so carefully. Roger was tempted to end the strain with a jocular quip but decided it was better to have it understood from the beginning.

"Perhaps you are right," was Tienne's stiff reply. With a short, "I'm sorry, I'll not trouble you again," he left, and they had not seen him until tonight at the party.

As a result of that showdown, Carol and Roger had had their first spat, although it was mostly hurt silence on her part. She was filled with compassion toward Tienne, but she could see Roger's point, also. But now she could never tell him of the poem—a poem of Tienne's—recited to her in a voice of quiet ardor in the university library:

> "In the hills beyond Furcy
> The sky is blue and high,
> And the sea curls beneath our feet.
> My love will trust me
> With her hand in mine
> We will soar with the eagles."

And now, married, it was Roger and Carol who would soar with the eagles.

They had their tickets for a cruise of the Caribbean, including several days at Port-au-Prince. At Roger's hesitation at this part of their trip, Carol used her powers of persuasion, searching the depths of his eyes with her own pleading, serious look.

"Please—for friendship's sake—for Tienne's friendship with both of us. Remember how close we all were? He told me a long time ago, a honeymoon in Haiti would be perfect. The fragrance of pine on the heights—the flowering poinsettia plants, tall as a man, blooming scarlet along the roads—I feel I know it. It should be especially beautiful this time of year, and he said the island will cast a magical spell around the heart. Please, for old times' sake?"

To further convince him, Carol added, "Remember when I moved from the apartment on Beall Street and you both helped? Will we ever forget the sight of Tienne walking down the sidewalk with my bright dresses draped over one arm, a dozen books in the other, balancing my orange bed-lamp on his head, with the cord tangling his legs?"

That brought laughter from both of them, and Roger gave in.

They sailed from Miami on a Thursday afternoon. Moving in an unbelievable sun-drenched world, the bright water and soft air beguiling them, they resisted the shipboard activities just to laze and relax on deck. At night the stars in the deep, dark sky winked at them as they stood catching a breeze and watching the phosphorescent wake.

Roger and Carol stepped out onto the dock at Port-au-Prince, into the melee that was Saturday on the Magic Island. At last, Carol thought, the evergreen land that Tienne had praised so gloriously! The waterfront and the city itself teemed with vivid life and color. They went through customs, showed their smallpox vaccination certificates. Roger barely had time to check on their luggage when Carol wanted to know where she could shop for handbags.

"Later," Roger protested. "Later, we'll have time for that. Let's get to the hotel and freshen up. I could stand a drink of that famous rum, too."

They hailed a taxi and were off down Truman Boulevard to the Grand Seigneur Hotel.

It was eight o'clock. Resting in their rooms at the Grand Seigneur, they felt a delicious weariness after their tour of the city. No broken bones were evident as a result of their careening rides in the local camionettes and taxis, although tomorrow might show a few bruises. Surveying the city and bay from the heights of Petionville, they had descended to the Museum to view the anchor purported to be from Columbus' Santa Maria. At Carol's urging, they had prevailed on their slaphappy, suicide-bent taxi driver to take them to the colorful Iron Market where she had run wild, purchasing a handbag, sandals, a stunning handrubbed mahogany jewelry box—and best of all, a complete Haitian girl's costume. It consisted of apricot blouse, green skirt, endless strings of bright beads, and a yellow, mannish straw hat with a broad orange brim.

When Roger had lightly protested, she laughingly waved her hand. "Easy come, easy go. Don't be a scrouge, darling, this stuff is really marked 'Courtesy of Fraser Oil.'" Then, half dreamily, "Wasn't it wonderful they gave you that fat bonus for signing, and time for this—" She waved out over the city and the sparkling bay.

Roger smiled indulgently. "We're not spending a whole month in Haiti—only four days. There are other places, after all. Besides, you know what Mr. Anker of Fraser Oil said. 'Take the month off for a honeymoon, and here's a bonus. But when you report for work, we're going to start taking our pound of flesh.' "

"Bosh!" She hugged him tight. "They know they hired a genius."

Roger held her close. "We're so lucky. Here we are, the girl from Ohio and the Nebraska boy, honeymooning in Haiti. I can't believe it."

"I know how you feel, darling. I have to remind myself twenty times a day, but won't it be fun telling about this to our grandchildren?"

"Well, come on now, enough of this dreaming. Change, or whatever you are going to do. I'm going down to the bar and have a Barbancourt. That's real rum!"

He paused at the door. "Say, about tonight, let's take in the night life at some of these cabarets. We'll eat at a good restaurant and make the rounds. OK?"

"Fine. Now shoo out of here. I'll join you in a few minutes, and maybe we can have a snack at the hotel dining room. I'm starved."

Later that night, at Buteau's, they sat at a little table in a secluded corner of the terrace which afforded an excellent view. Carol was radiant in blue linen with white accessories. It set off her shining hair and healthy, suntanned skin with casual crispness. As a concession to Carol, youth, and the tropics, Roger wore a flame-red dinner jacket. They ordered langouste "flambee," the specialty, and found it delicious.

Laughing and talking honeymoon foolishness, they finished their meal and, leaving Buteau's, went on a round of the cabarets. They finally found themselves squeezed into a small club with a minuscule table holding them apart. The insistent drum beat, together with the flash and color of the place, brought home to them the exotic, vibrant life of the island. Carol's eyes were everywhere—so many laughing brown faces. Did everyone look like Tienne?

They ordered drinks, and watched the sinuous dancing of the Haitian girl in the spotlight, a tall, bronze girl in a green and white dress and cerise turban. Her movements were liquid and languorous. She began to chant. The drums sank to a low throbbing, and the crowd quieted somewhat. At intervals, Roger caught the word "Malele."

"Carol, isn't that the same thing Tienne was saying at Dave Grayden's party, remember?"

"Why yes, it does sound familiar."

Roger looked around. Almost sitting on their laps were a middle-aged couple, tourists from the States like themselves. The man appeared distinguished, prosperous and amused.

"Pardon me," Roger addressed the man, "but can you tell me what she is chanting?"

The man was glad to be friendly; he suggested they push their tiny tables together. He ordered another round of drinks. There were quick introductions.

"Strange that you should ask me," he told them. "Before we took our first trip, Betty and I boned up on Haitian history, and especially voodoo. We've been fascinated by it ever since. In this chant, she is seeking the help of Malele—the turnabout goddess—the capricious one. Malele is also called the 'Old One,' since one of her manifestations is in the guise of an old hag—a gray-haired crone."

"You called her capricious," Carol prompted.

"Yes," the man continued, "Malele is the only voodoo goddess who can substitute herself for a real human being; then the spirit of the one she replaces is set free. For a favorite houngans, or voodoo priest, she can do this, but he must be powerful. Several times, back in the hills of Haiti, I understand it has been accomplished. But it always ends the same. First the victim, then Malele disappears—when she wishes." He laughed a little self-consciously.

Seeing the grave look on both the young people's faces, the man said, "Come, come, be gay! There's life and color and singing all about us. Don't take all this too much to heart."

Carol's gaiety increased and Roger played along. They plunged headlong into the joyousness of the night. The couple, the Raddisons of St. Louis, stayed with them for a short time, but tired early and left.

In the late hours, they found themselves carried along in the colorful stream of traffic. It had been a hectic evening; their heads still throbbed with the beat of drums. They were bushed.

"Let's go back to the hotel," Roger suggested. "But first we'll get some honest-to-goodness bacon and eggs at the Saint Marc."

Carol nodded, "Then we'll call it a night."

They felt better, a little more clear-headed, after they had eaten, but when they got back to the hotel they went straight to bed, weary but happy.

About an hour later, Roger woke. Aware of the subtle influence of the tropical night, he felt for Carol. She was gone. He got up and went into the next room where a vague luminescence from some far-off light filtered in at the window. Carol was at the mirror, her face serene, as if she wcre asleep—or drugged. Yet her voice was plaintive as she argued softly with two shadowy figures in the glass. One was a squat, hideous old hag; the other a tall, handsome male Haitian. Tienne!

"Carol!" Roger cried, his voice hoarse.

The images misted, faded away, leaving the mirror blank. Carol lifted an indecisive hand to her forehead and shuddered, wrenching herself free from some bewildering embrace.

"Where—what am I doing here?" She fell into Roger's arms, sobbing almost soundlessly. "Hold me," she whispered. "I had a dream about Tienne, and a horrible old woman."

"I know—I saw them."

"You saw!"

"Yes, damn him. This is Tienne's work."

His voice was angry and frustrated; he patted Carol's head while many emotions fought within him. Then it hit him. He led her gently to a chair, then crossed over to a lamp and snapped it on. Next, he dragged out all their luggage.

It was in one of her small overnight cases that he found it, wedged cleverly between the blue satin lining and the outer shell, and when he pulled the small white bundle from its hiding place, the chicken bones and hollow sticks fell out and clicked upon themselves as they dropped to the floor. The few dirty white feathers drifted like snowflakes to the rug.

"How did they get in there?" Roger demanded.

Carol was bewildered for a moment, then her eyes widened in remembrance. "It must have been the night before we left! Tienne came over to say goodbye and to wish us luck, he said. I didn't tell you for fear you'd be angry with him. I was packing and was in the room all the time—no! The phone call! It was to the travel agency, and I made it from Clarice's apartment across the hall because ours was disconnected."

"That was it; that was all he needed to put that devilish thing behind the lining of your case. You see what he's doing, don't you? And he's on *his* ground!"

Roger's eyes lit with quick fury, then softened, and he said, "We'll get out of here, first thing in the morning. Hang the rest of this trip! We'll fly back to the good old U.S.A."

Carol nodded dumbly and curled up against him, shivering.

"Let's go back to bed now, get a few hours sleep, anyway," he said. "Things will look different in the morning." Exhausted, they fell into an uneasy sleep, her golden head resting on his outflung arm.

The air which drifted in at the window was laden with the fragrance of jasmine and mimosa. Outside, the tropical night held even the bird peeps in thrall. One, two hours crept by.

Then downstairs, just before dawn, the heavy-lidded night clerk at the desk watched the last straggling revelers. He saw the blond girl cross the lobby. Dressed in Haitian girl costume of sisal shoes, bright apricot blouse, straw hat—strings of beads swinging—she opened the outer door as in a dream, her lovely face expressionless.

She paused a moment outside, then approached the ancient jeep parked at the curb. A proud young Haitian, his mouth wide in a gay smile, stood beside it and held the door for her. She got in.

"Where are we going?" she asked tonelessly, not looking at him.

He jumped in beside her, started the motor. Glancing down protectively he answered, "To the hills beyond Furcy."

The jeep chugged away.

Inside the Grand Seigneur, several floors up, Roger smiled faintly in his sleep, for the pressure of her head on his arm was reassuring. He gave an involuntary hug; nor did the stiff, scraggly gray hairs against his skin disturb his dreams.

A Gun Is a Nervous Thing

Charlotte Armstrong

Down in the heart of the California town a police officer—James Lord was his name—bent over a hospital bed and listened intently. The woman's bruised and swollen lips shaped sounds with difficulty, but he heard enough. At last he snapped erect, and went out into the corridor.

To the cop who was waiting there he said, "Can't tell you all of it now. Woman says her husband beat her up after their kid was shot. Says he's out gunning for the boy's teacher now—thinks she let him die. Ames is the teacher's name. Miss Eve Ames. Get on it quick. We are"—he glanced at his watch—"an hour and forty-five minutes late already."

At that moment Eve Ames stood at the window of a solitary hillside house, looking down over the darkening town. Behind her she heard her hostess, Frances Connor, say, "I'm afraid this thing *is* stiffening up," and Eve turned to look at the older woman, whose stout right leg with bandaged ankle was thrust out before her, resting on a kitchen chair.

"Hadn't I better call a doctor, Miss Connor?" Eve asked.

"Small chance to find a doctor in at six o'clock on a Saturday evening—even if I had a phone." Frances Connor was fifty and, as a school principal, used to authority. She spoke cheerfully and decisively: "It's nothing, my dear; I only scraped the skin. . . . I must get rid of that debris in the yard. Those concrete blocks are a menace to life and limb. I stumbled over one of them."

Eve Ames glanced back out the window. This little house was so new that the paper label still clung to the windowpane. Now that it was getting dark, the narrow yard, all raw earth and builder's litter, was obscured. Across the newly made street—it was only a scratch upon the hill and still rutted and dusty as the bulldozers had left it —the land fell away.

They were high upon the rim of the jeweled fan that the town resembled. The handle of the open fan rested, Eve fancied, in the sea, in the cove; and the town lay tilted, glittering, upon the rimming hills. Below, the main coast highway threaded the fan's fabric like a brilliant living ribbon.

"I'd better dress it again before bedtime," Frances Connor was saying. And Eve caught at her wandering attention.

"We left the extra gauze and tape in the car," she said. "Shall I get them?"

"No hurry. You may have to prepare dinner, Eve—fine hostess that I am."

"Are you hungry, Miss Connor?"

Eve, herself, was not hungry. She was reluctant to stir from her sad reverie, but her hostess was becoming impatient with it.

"Come and sit down, Eve," Frances Connor said. "But first, please put the screen across the window. Without draperies at night, this room is a goldfish bowl, and I don't altogether like it."

Eve Ames did as she was told. She was a tall, slender young woman in her mid-twenties, and she moved with unconscious grace. She sat down, let her breath out in a heavy sigh, and tried to smile.

Frances Connor's brown eyes, in her pouched and sagging face, were kind. "I'm a tough old bird, Eve," she said, lifting her white head to attack directly the younger woman's trouble. "I'd like to help you. Perhaps I can. Sometimes," she said austerely, "there is absolutely nothing you can do with a brutal, tragic fact but meet it with brute courage."

"I can't forget—he was only nine years old." Eve bit on her lip.

"We tried not talking about it," said Frances, "all day long. Let's go over all the 'if's' once more, and be rid of them."

Eve Ames folded her hands in her lap and considered how swiftly the whole terrible event of yesterday had exploded out of an ordinary Friday. She had been sitting in the schoolyard at the noon hour, supervising the children who were eating their lunches at the picnic tables. The schoolyard was a noisy place, a tangle of screams and shouts rose up all around, but her teacher's ears found this normal and not in the least alarming. By the same token, those trained ears caught the wrong note when a boy's high voice came loud close behind her.

Terry Lord, one of her own fourth-graders, was speaking: "Not supposed to point a gun at people—you're not supposed to, you dummy!" His voice was full of strain and even desperation.

Eve had had time to consider the word "gun" just long enough to assume he spoke of a toy. She'd seen the tiny gun that looked very much like a toy, and realized that Danny Mariot must have been pointing it directly at her own back. She'd caught Danny Mariot's eye.

Then Danny had said scornfully, in quick self-defense, "Aw, you're chicken. It's not even loaded. Lookit; I'll show ya." Then he had turned the gun upon himself.

The sound had not been loud enough to disturb many of the children. Eve, kneeling beside Danny on the blacktop of the playground, had said firmly, "Terry, go in at once and bring Miss Connor, please. Children, go quietly to your home rooms, all of you."

She'd known they were obeying because the screaming died off gradually as some of the older ones herded the rest. Then Frances Connor's voice had said, "Is he hurt?"

"He's dead," Eve had said.

All she had been able to see was Danny Mariot's eyes, that last look, soul to soul. His eyes frightened, and then cunning with a child's cunning. He had wanted to lighten his punishment by proving no serious intent.

Now she twisted her hands, helplessly.

Miss Connor was speaking calmly and relentlessly: "What happened was this: The boy found the intriguing little gun in his own kitchen. He smuggled it to school in his lunch box. He showed it off. In the classic phrase, 'He didn't know it was loaded.' Now, Eve, there's no validity to that one. He most certainly would not have taken it out while you were looking, and you know that."

"I know that. I'm all right, Miss Connor."

"Then, if Danny's mother had got herself out of her bed to get his breakfast and prepare his lunch, she'd have seen the gun and put it away. And here's another: If Danny's father, rising at 3 A.M. to go off hunting with his pals, hadn't planned to take the little gun to show for a curiosity, if he hadn't forgotten to take it, and, even worse, if he hadn't left a bullet in it in the first place . . ."

"Poor man," Eve said. "I wonder if he's back."

"Sure to be by now. Did you know him? Or Danny's mother?"

"Mrs. Mariot wasn't a PTA type."

Eve thought of the woman, a short, dumpy, youngish person with wild pale hair. "I've never met her, never met either of them."

"Poor people, pity them," said Frances Connor. "There are more 'if's' yet. If Terry Lord hadn't been properly taught how to behave with a gun, and hadn't spoken up, *you* might very well have got that bullet, Eve."

"I know."

"And again, if Danny Mariot *had* been properly taught, or had paid attention—"

"I can't say that," said Eve. "I cannot. It does not serve him right. He was only nine."

"I never said it wasn't a tragedy," said the older woman gently.

"The thing that bothers me, Miss Connor," said Eve earnestly, "is that Danny was a bit of a bully. The children were a little afraid of him. Now every parent in town is going to be saying, 'See what happens to wicked little boys,' and I wish—I wish the whole thing weren't going to seem to the children exactly like the villain getting his just deserts at the end of the program."

"You wish you could teach them," said Frances Connor affectionately, "an understanding of intricate chance and multiple blame that's beyond their years, I know."

They were silent in the raw little room with the bare floor and the empty, unpainted shelves.

"Don't you think," said Miss Connor, "that you might better take the car and go call Geoffrey? Let him take you to some glamorous eating place. I can manage perfectly well, Eve. After all, I can hobble."

"I'd rather stay," Eve said, almost abruptly.

But Frances Connor persisted: "Maybe you've turned the subject in your mind long enough. I'm afraid that I, a spinster school principal," she continued with perfect good nature, "don't represent much in the way of comfort. Whereas your beau—"

"Shall I start dinner?" Eve interrupted.

"Let's wait a little," Frances said. "It's all we have to do all evening." Her face was thoughtful.

Eve raised her eyes, good gray eyes, set deep in her well-boned face. "Miss Connor, you were wonderful with that poor, stupefied mother. You are good for me, too. You see, this whole part of my life, my job, the children. This is all foreign to Geoffrey. He doesn't . . ." She faltered to a stop.

"My dear," said Frances Connor, pleased, "I think you are a fine teacher, although perhaps sensitive above and beyond the call of duty."

Eve was smiling for the first time in some hours because of the praise. "Which reminds me," she said more cheerfully, "six fifteen— it's Grif Griffin time. Can you bear it?" She reached over to turn on the radio. "You see, my fourth-graders think the sun can't set without Grif Griffin, and how am I to know what's in their minds?"

"You really listen every day?"

"Most days I try to, and it is a help. The other day there was an epidemic—everybody tapping his teeth with his thumbnail. Now, if I hadn't listened to Grif Griffin, I'd never have known what it was."

"What was it?"

"Griffin-eze." Eve's face was animated now. "That means, 'I have important news to tell.' "

"Signals, eh? You interest me," said Frances Connor warmly. "What's Grif Griffin like?"

"You'll see. I'd say he's a nice blend of Sherlock Holmes and Douglas Fairbanks, Sr."

During the commercials, Miss Connor watched her young colleague's face. A lovely girl, she thought; conscientious, fine-boned, fine-grained.

Frances Connor wished for her young friend the deepest and most complete happiness: a husband, children of her own, the full life. It had looked these past few months as if all this was on the horizon for Eve, ever since Geoffrey Taggart had begun to take her out. He was a part-time businessman, the owner of a flourishing shop where artists' materials were sold. The other part of his time Geoffrey, himself, tried to be a painter. He was the right age; he had both money and good taste; he was a most civilized man. Frances Connor, in the back of her mind, had already made the match.

Last evening, after the tragedy at school, Geoffrey and Frances, together, had kept Eve company in her apartment. Geoffrey had been concerned about Eve and most kind. It was possible that he did not, could not, see Eve's full problem; that she had more than her private shock and grief to overcome, that she must face the children Monday morning in some way that would best help *them*. How could a bachelor understand, thought Frances, when even parents scarcely realize how much more than the book lessons a teacher teaches?

"Grif's trailing the man in the blue suit," said the doom-fraught voice of Dusty.

"What's he want us to do?" piped Smallfry, the boy aide.

"Keep down," said Dusty; "it's dangerous. Didn't you hear Grif sneeze three times?"

Eve was listening with only half a mind. It was a local program that sponsored local stunts and contests, and the town kids were entranced with it. A game, Eve thought. Checkerboard moves. Black against white. And the gun was power. Last man on the scene with a gun in his hand was top man, always. She shivered.

Never in her life before had she met brutal tragedy. She wondered whether she had the brute courage to match it.

When the Grif Griffin program was over, the news came on. Lost in her thoughts, Eve heard none of it until she caught her name:

"Alarm is felt for the safety of Miss Eve Ames, a fourth-grade teacher at Jefferson Elementary School."

Eve jerked erect, tingling. The voice went on:

"Martin Mariot, 33, whose nine-year-old son, Daniel, was accidentally shot and killed yesterday on the school playground, went berserk at 4 this afternoon. Mariot beat and critically injured his wife, Susan, in their canyon home. Neighbors who heard the woman's cries, summoned police. Mrs. Susan Mariot, 30, was taken to the hospital unconscious, but Mariot eluded capture and is still at large.

"Mrs. Mariot regained consciousness at 5:45 long enough to tell police officer James Lord that her husband vows vengeance on the boy's teacher, Miss Eve Ames. The man believes that the teacher's delay in calling a doctor resulted in the boy's death. His wife says he has a gun, a twin to the small 22-caliber hand gun with which the boy shot himself yesterday during the lunch hour. It is believed the father, who was out of town when the tragedy took place, has become unbalanced by shock and grief. Lieutenant Lord says the boy died instantly with a bullet in his heart, but according to the injured woman, the distraught father will not believe this to be a fact.

"Ironically, Lieutenant Lord's nine-year-old son, Terry, was a witness to the death of the Mariot boy yesterday. Police rushed to Miss Ames's apartment on Hermosa Street, but failed to find her at home. Her whereabouts are not known. Police request anyone knowing where Miss Eve Ames is now, to contact them immediately.

"The man, Martin Mariot, is armed, and in his distraught state may be dangerous. He is 5′ 9″, wiry, dark hair, dark eyes, has upper joint of left index finger missing. Anyone seeing this man, please notify police at once. Your own station, KYOS, will stand by to give you latest developments."

Eve was on her feet.

"They'll be here any minute," Frances Connor said crisply. "The police, of course. Geoffrey will tell them."

"I lied to him," Eve said. "He doesn't know I am with you. I told him I definitely wouldn't be."

"Oh, Eve! And I have no phone yet—"

"I couldn't tell him," Eve said. "I wanted to be let alone, to think it all through. I didn't want to hurt his feelings."

"Yes, I see. But the police will have to know where you are."

"Yes, I know. I—don't want to have to deal with that—poor man," Eve said gasping.

"He is guilty," Frances Connor said. "His 'if's' are too many. He must know it."

Eve nodded.

Frances began to struggle up. "Well, we can't have you shot, Eve. We'll go to the grocery store down the hill."

"You needn't go, Miss Connor. Is the store still open?"

"Open till seven. Better hurry." Frances Connor settled her stout body back into her chair. "You'll go faster alone. Go on, then. Quickly."

Eve snatched up her coat and purse and the keys to Miss Connor's car. It was absurd that anyone should want to shoot her! She had only to drive downhill less than a mile, call the police from the phone in the little grocery store, and then perhaps stay there until protection came. She could do it. She wouldn't think about Martin Mariot at all.

But she was thinking of him just the same. She was thinking, "A man with a gun, and I understand. I pity him. But what good will understanding and compassion do me? I must go for the police, who have guns, too."

She stepped out the door and ran to Frances Connor's car. She backed it into the road and put its nose ready to go downhill. She was fumbling to find the way to switch the headlights full on. She had lit the dash and was peering at it, concentrated within the car, when the man's voice said hoarsely, "Miss Connor?"

She heard herself say, "Yes?" very sharply and impatiently. After all, she was in a hurry. She had no time for this man, standing in the road looking in at her, mumbling.

"The wife said you'd just built this place up here. I thought—"

"Who are you?" she said, flinging up her chin and speaking loudly. But she knew. Because his left hand grasped the window sill on the car's right side, and the first joint of the index finger was missing.

"Don't matter who I am," he mumbled, and his right hand came up into her sight. Sure enough, he had a little gun. His face was full of odd shadows and hollows, lit as it was from underneath by the dash light.

"Where's Miss Ames?" he demanded harshly. "She's your friend. Where is she? You better tell me, Miss Connor."

Only then did Eve realize that he had taken her for Frances. He'd called her Miss Connor before, and she'd said, "Yes," in a kind of reflex.

"I don't know," she said. "Excuse me, I'm just leaving." But she thought, her brain working with uncanny swiftness, "If I fool him and do drive on, and he finds Miss Connor, he may think she's Eve Ames." This seemed intolerable.

"Wait a minute." He was looking past her. Eve realized he could see a small portion of the room around the edge of the screen. What could he see?

"There's a dame in the house," he said. "Don't kid me. Old lady with a bum leg. Who is that?"

"My mother," said Eve promptly and haughtily, as if he should have known as much. "What's the matter with you? Do you want a lift?" She said this, pretending not to have seen the gun, because it occurred to her strangely detached brain that she was telling lies, and Frances Connor would have no clue to them. She could not leave him in the road outside this house. She was safe as long as he didn't know her. Once at the store . . .

"I need a lift," he said suddenly, and opened the door and got in. "Get going, Miss Connor," he suggested almost mildly. "No need for the old lady to start looking out the window."

So Eve let the brake off. There was nothing else that she could think to do. The car moved along the short level portion and dived down around a curve.

"I need a car," the man said loudly. His voice volume seemed to wax and wane, eccentrically. "The cops took mine."

"The cops?" she said with difficulty.

"You might as well know. I killed my wife this afternoon. I got nothing to lose. I'm going to kill your friend, Miss Ames."

The road dipped deep in a fold of the land, and it was dark and lonely. But just below was the store on the traveled canyon road.

"Do—" she swallowed. "Do you expect me to help you?" Her voice was breathy and light.

"Yeah," he said. "I gotta gun."

Her brain lost its clarity. Her thoughts began to dart now like frightened birds. Could she talk to him? Calm him? Explain to him? Coax him to the hospital? Or try to get the gun and be top woman?

It seemed to her that the steering wheel was shaking, not her hands. They were suddenly on level land, running between houses only a short way from the grocery store.

"Where was you going?" he said abruptly.

"I—to telephone." Her voice came out all right, only a little frightened.

"You got no phone up there in the house?"

"No."

"Wait a minute. Pull up. I gotta figure something."

So the car shuddered and stopped at the edge of the road. Eve let go the wheel and put her icy hands to her cheeks. A few yards ahead was the store, still lit, still open, and on the road cars passed them, going about their normal business.

"Hold on, now," he said. "Don't move." The gun in his right hand was pointing at her across his body. "Where is there a phone?"

"S-store," she stammered, making a gesture.

"This Miss Ames. She lives this side of the coast road, don't she? 1215 Hermosa?"

"Y-yes."

"She there, you think?"

"I don't know."

He turned his head warily.

"It was on the radio," Eve said.

"About me? The cops, I guess." He seemed to accept this. "That's how you knew me?"

"Your finger."

"That so?" he murmured. "And so it's on the air."

"Mr. Mariot," said Eve tensely. "You didn't kill your wife this afternoon. She's alive in the hospital; at least, she was able—"

"She talked," he said immediately. "So they know I'm going for Miss Ames—that right? I saw you come tearing out." Now she felt him relax. "I thought you wasn't too surprised," he said.

He might seem relaxed, but he was shrewd. His brain, Eve divined, was running smoothly and freely, separate from his broken heart. So she could die. She'd better be careful. He was terribly dangerous, she knew.

But Eve said as calmly as she could, "Mr. Mariot. *Why?*"

"Shut up," he said. "I'm thinking." The hand with the gun called attention to itself. "So the old lady's got no phone, and no car, and a bum leg," he said. "So she's not going to tell the cops you're missing."

"M-missing?"

"Listen, Miss Connor," he said somewhat drearily. "Miss Ames being your friend, probably you don't want me to do this, but you're going to help me just the same. I could throw you out right here, and I could fix it so you couldn't talk real soon. I could do that, see? But I need a car, and I maybe need you to get me through to her. Nobody knows I'm gonna be in your car. And I think I need you for a phone call. That's a good idea."

"Phone call?"

"I want you to go in that store and call Miss Ames's place and see if she's there. But you ain't gonna warn her about me, because I'll have my gun on you. Now, the phone in there's in a booth, isn't it?"

"No, it's just a wall phone."

"No booth?" He seemed dashed.

Eve shook her head. She thought of something. This couldn't last. Not another five minutes. The trouble was that Mr. Johnson, the grocer, knew her perfectly well. He had a daughter in her class. The moment she stepped inside that store, he'd sing out, "Hiya, Miss Ames," and what would this man do then? The man with the gun. Now silently pondering his problem.

She said desperately, "Mr. Mariot, I was there yesterday, and really, Miss Ames—"

"I know," he said harshly. "I know exactly, so don't talk to me about it."

But she'd set him talking, and he couldn't stop:

"That Miss Ames, she don't want a fuss. Little kid's hurt, and he's fallen down. But she decides no fuss should be made. So she calls no doctor to help the kid any. She calls you. I heard it was you who finally did call the doc. By then it was too late. I know what happened. I got it out of Sue. And if I didn't kill my lazy slob of a wife—"

Now Eve could see the bitter cruelty on his mouth.

"—let her live with her memories," he said. "But I'm going to kill that Ames woman, and I don't care what happens to me. No more, see? No more. I got this one thing to do, that's all. And I'll do it. I don't care too much what happens to you, either. So shut up, will ya?"

He seemed to think she was keeping the talk going. His voice rose to an ugly shrillness:

"She could have got the doctor to him, and she didn't do it. It was murder! Now she's gonna get a bullet in her, and nobody's going to call no doctor. So shut up."

Eve shut up. She could not, dared not, try to say that the boy was instantly dead. You couldn't contradict an obsession. So she sat in the half-dark, speechless.

What could she do about Mr. Johnson? He was a nice, genial chap. He might get a bullet, too. . . . "No, he won't. And I won't, either," her mind cried. "Not if I can help it." Courage came to her without having been called. This obsessed, sickhearted man must be outwitted, somehow. He mustn't kill anybody. She'd have to use everything she had, every brain cell, every ounce of self-control to prevent it.

"So they know?" the man demanded. "And now I gotta do it with the cops knowing?"

"They know," she said calmly.

"On the air, was it?" he said.

"Yes, it was."

He made a kind of animal grunt; then he pushed the button on the car radio. There was no news on. In a moment, music played. Eve found it strange to be sitting beside the man who intended to kill her, here in the soft dark.

Then she saw the figure of a woman come out of the store and start to cross the road ahead of them. There was no mistaking that waddle or the chicken-stretch of the neck, forward, of those fat shoulders. It was Mrs. Peasley, a power in the PTA. She was already blinking and shielding her eyes from their headlights, and she was never one to walk past a parked car without peering in. Mrs. Peasley prided herself on remembering names, too. She'd say, "Good evening—Miss Ames, isn't it?" in her treacly voice.

Eve was paralyzed. She saw a vision of her own body tumbling out of Miss Connor's car, and the car careening in flight. She dismissed it. That wasn't going to happen. She refused to imagine it.

"Start the car," Mariot said in her ear. "Turn left. Get going."

Her hands and feet jumped to the controls. The car skittered past Mrs. Peasley, whipped in a left turn, and headed away from town back into the canyon.

"Easy now," Mariot said nervously. His mouth was so close to her shoulder, she could feel his breath. "Easy. There's a gas station coupla miles out this way, closed by now. Outside phone booth on the place. I don't see," he added with strange candor, "how I coulda kept the gun on you in the store without looking funny."

"How close was I to the bullet then?" thought Eve. But it wasn't a helpful thought, and she thrust it down.

"Besides," said Mariot savagely, "that Mis' Peasley knows me."

"She—knows you?"

"Nosy old bag was on my draft board," he said with pure exasperation.

A giggle came into Eve's throat, and she choked it down. Escaped by a hair's breadth. What looked like disaster had turned to temporary salvation. But she realized she couldn't afford to think back at all; she must think only forward. Well, then, she'd telephone, and no one would answer. After that she did not know, but it would give her a little time. And Mrs. Peasley might have seen something . . .

Geoffrey Taggart walked up the outside stairs in some haste and knocked at Eve's door. The door opened swiftly and a strong male hand yanked him inside.

"Who are you?" said Lieutenant Lord belligerently.

"Taggart's my name, friend of Miss Ames. She here?" said Geoffrey in his pleasant, cultivated voice.

"Didn't you tell me on the phone," said Lord, "you don't *know* where she's gone?"

"I didn't say that, exactly," said Geoffrey. "I simply knew I wanted a date and she said no."

He was a lean man, in his thirties. James Lord, with his hard-planed face, his matter-of-fact air, seemed stolid beside Geoffrey's high-strung slenderness.

"What made you think she was here, then? If you got any news, spit it out," said the lieutenant.

"I thought she might be washing her hair," blurted Geoffrey. "What I mean to say—"

"Well, she's not washing her hair *here*," drawled Lord. "You think of any other girl friends, for instance? Listen, Taggart; this girl's in bad trouble, and I mean bad." Lord's eyes were cool and steady.

Geoffrey winced. "I know. I'm worried. That's why I came."

The lieutenant had turned his back as if he had given up hoping for anything useful. Geoffrey said, "I know she's not with Frances Connor, just as I told you. But Eve may have gone to San Diego. She has relatives—"

"Who and what address?" The lieutenant turned.

"An Aunt Marie. That's all I—" Geoffrey's voice trailed off and he shrugged helplessly.

"This aunt's a blood relative? Married, is she?" The lieutenant was very quick and precise, and he asked for precision.

Geoffrey said, "I believe so."

"Then we don't have the name."

"Eve didn't say anything about going to San Diego. She may just be out having a bite," said Geoffrey. "After all, it's dinnertime."

"I hope so," the lieutenant said.

"This building is being watched, I suppose?"

"Yeah, it's being watched. That's right. If you want to wait here, keep quiet. Our man may be around here, now. If he hasn't got her already."

"But surely you—" Geoffrey sputtered.

"Surely, surely," said Lord, a little bleakly. "But he's on foot, he could slip through small places. Excuse me. Lie low till I come to let you out."

The lieutenant went out Eve's door and closed it. Geoffrey Taggart looked around, blinking. Eve's curtains were tightly drawn. The place was closed, airless, empty. Geoffrey sat down.

Outside, Lord walked without visible urgency around the corner. He stopped to light a cigarette, and spoke to a shadow in a slot between two houses: "No show?"

"Nope."

The lieutenant looked at the sky.

"Nice person, Miss Ames. My kid likes her fine."

"How could he have got her if we can't find her?" said the soft voice from the shadow.

"Maybe that's why we can't find her," said Lord. "What time is it?"

"6:55."

The lieutenant swore softly. . . .

In Eve's apartment, the telephone rang. Geoffrey Taggart, startled, stared at it a moment. He rose and took the telephone off the cradle gingerly. "Yes?"

"This is Frances Connor," a voice said rapidly.

"Oh, Frances," said Geoffrey with great relief. "Then you've heard! Where is Eve? Do you know? She isn't with you, is she?"

"No. Isn't she there?" The voice was strained.

Naturally, thought Geoffrey; his own voice showed strain, too. "No. Nobody knows where she is, at all. Where could she have gone?" He didn't wait for an answer. "Frances, do you know where this aunt of hers lives in San Diego?"

"No, I—"

"I thought perhaps she'd gone there. I knew she wasn't with you. Fool that I am, I came around hoping she'd decided to wash her hair. All females—" He remembered this was no time to be witty. "I wish I knew what I could do. The police think she may be in some restaurant." He was talking to a deadness on the line. "Where are you, Frances?"

"In a telephone booth at—" The voice stopped.

The voice seemed to return from far away: "You say the police are there?"

"Oh, yes. Not in the room, but they are watching. He's on foot and very slippery, they say. He may try to get in here. Are you alone, Frances?" Again he did not wait for an answer. "Will you be coming here? Maybe you and I could join forces."

"You think she'll be coming along, then?" the voice said.

"Can't be sure. We hope so."

"I may come."

"Good. Good."

"Goodbye, Adam," the voice said, suddenly louder and different. She hung up abruptly. Geoffrey hung up, frowning.

He put his hands in his pockets. *Adam.* It wasn't like Eve to have told Frances Connor that. If a man kids a bit with a girl named Eve and suggests that he may be her Adam some day, it's an intimacy. Not something to giggle over with a female confidante. Still, possibly Frances Connor was like a mother to her. Geoffrey tried to put the injury out of his mind. No time to be petty. Eve was in trouble —bad trouble, the lieutenant said.

There was nothing that he, Geoffrey, could think to do about it. The whole situation was so violent and so—strange. There seemed to be no way to take hold of the problem, to find her, save her. What could he—or, for that matter, the police—do but wait. He moved restlessly in the still, empty place.

Eve slammed the phone on its hook in case Geoffrey reacted to that "Adam" hint. She was jammed into the booth with a man and a gun. There had been a bad moment, after Mariot had put the dime in, when she, confident of getting no answer, had heard Geoffrey's voice. But now she was thankful; thankful that her own voice had been husky and strained, thankful Geoffrey had not given her away, thankful he'd said he knew she wasn't with Frances. Mariot should be all the more convinced that she *was* Frances.

And she was thankful to have been in touch with a friend on her side. Or had she been? Oh, Geoffrey must catch on! The name, Adam, would tell him plainly whom he had been talking to. But what good would it do when he did catch on? She hadn't been able to tell him anything very useful, with the gun sharp in her side, and

Mariot's ear so close to her own that they were almost cheek to cheek.

She was glad to get out of that booth and into the air. The car was parked near the gas pumps, silent since Mariot had turned the music off. Nobody going by had paid any attention to it. Nor to the phone booth with its door held ajar so that the light stayed off. She and the man and the gun had been jammed together in semi-darkness and were now in semidarkness walking close, shoulder to shoulder, back to the car. Traffic rolled by. No motorist looked away from the furthest reach of his headlights. Then they were in Frances Connor's car again, and the police—from what Geoffrey said—were looking for them both to be on foot.

Still, Eve was not afraid any more. She went docilely to the car and into the driver's seat, counting her chances. There was Frances, who would begin to fret and who would stir. There was Geoffrey, who would catch on. There was still Mrs. Peasley, and even per-haps Mr. Johnson, if he had happened to look up and see Miss Con-nor's car lurch so wildly by. A whole series of little points of contact that would connect, and sooner or later the police would know. Time was on her side. Eve sat quietly with her hands lightly resting on the wheel.

Mariot said, "I gotta get into her place." He was single-minded. Everything for him hung on one straight line. Within his purpose, he was shrewd and even cool.

"Why?" said Eve gently. "If she's not there?"

"I'll be waiting for her."

"The police are there."

"Nuts to the police. So it's a trap. I get her first, then who cares?" He shifted in the seat from side to side. "I gotta get past them just once, that's all. She got a garage?"

"She doesn't own a car."

"Every place has got some kind of garage," he said angrily.

"There is a garage," Eve admitted. "Her apartment is over a double garage."

"Yeah," he said with satisfaction. "Inside stairs?"

"There's a stairway." The door from the garage to her apartment was always locked for her protection. She didn't know whether to say so.

"Cars kept in the garage?" he demanded.

"One," she admitted.

"So you'll drive this one in there."

"I'd be stopped," she gasped.

"You'll yell out who you are. This guy thinks you're coming, don't he? You'll get by."

"It's impossible!" she protested. "What if the doors aren't open? What if—? No, it's impossible."

To her surprise, he saw the point she was making almost as if they were collaborators. "Okay. Then we hang around, parked some place nearby, and when she does come—"

Eve did not speak, but he seemed to hear her alarm, to read what was in her mind.

"*You'll* know her," he said. "You know what she looks like."

"I?"

"And you'll tell me," he said. He was smiling cruelly.

"She might never come," said Eve faintly. "She may be in San Diego."

He said, "Get going."

So she started the car and drove toward town.

"What—" she began.

"Yeah?"

It was an odd thing, but they did seem to be on the same side, now and again, chewing on the same problem. Perhaps it was because she had to fill her mind with something besides her own identity. She feared his intuition. She made herself try to follow what he was thinking.

"I was going to say," she told him, "what about the man who answered the phone?"

"Nuts to him," said Mariot.

Mariot wasn't afraid. He was beyond that. He brushed the idea of Geoffrey out of his mind. He had a gun. Then Geoffrey, she realized, would be in danger, too. She thought of Geoffrey's slender figure, his thin, intelligent face. Would he have brute courage to meet brute danger? Was there anything else? Was there any way she could reach past this man's dangerous despair?

"Mr. Mariot," she said musingly, "didn't you think your wife was hurt already? Didn't you think she was grieving?"

A shock of energy seemed to come into his body. "She'd better grieve," he said, and cursed monotonously for a while. They went along the canyon past Mr. Johnson's store, now closed and dark. "If she had got up out of the warm hay," he raved, "but not her!

Not with me away! So the kid gets his own meal—what does she care?"

"Did she get up and cook when you left?" asked Eve a trifle tartly.

"Yeah, three o'clock," he snarled, "because I made her."

"Did you?" Eve thought. "But it isn't necessarily fatal to a nine-year-old to get his own meal for once. It wouldn't have been—except for *your* carelessness, and, oh, you know it!"

She didn't say anything.

"That don't rate her the whole morning in bed," he rasped. "She shoulda took care of the kid. She didn't do it. She didn't take care of the kid. And I *called* her—" His voice broke. "I even called her on the phone as soon as I got up there to Jasper's place. I seen I didn't have my little gun, so I called her, and it wasn't too late yet, Miss Connor. It wasn't too late."

"What time was it when you called her, Mr. Mariot?" said Eve softly.

"One o'clock, just after noon. Only one o'clock, that's what it was. And she says, sure, she's got everything under control. She was just getting out of the sack, see? But she didn't want me to know that. And it wasn't too late yet."

He drew a heavy, sobbing, anguished breath.

"But it was," Eve thought, "unhappy soul! It was already too late. And you know that, too."

"Boy, when this gets to me, did I let her have it. I let her have it, all right. I wish I'd killed her," he said tiredly.

Eve had a vision, then, of his energy running out on him, and his crazy purpose with it. If the pressure would go. The more she could get him to talk, perhaps the more pressure would blow off.

"Maybe you *have* killed her," she said. "The radio said your wife was critically injured."

"Yeah?" He didn't seem to care.

Eve said wonderingly, "Isn't that enough?"

But he was shifting from side to side again in that desperate restlessness. "I went out with the guys. Hunting. I never even got the message till ten o'clock that night. We're in a joint, drinking a few beers. I went outa my head, Miss Connor."

"I can imagine," Eve said, and her voice trembled, her throat ached, she was so sorry for him.

"They tell me to rest," Mariot cried. "Who can rest? Twelve o'clock, midnight, I can't take no more. I start driving back."

"It's a long trip?"

"Ten hours."

"Ten hours there and ten hours back? You must be tired."

"Yeah, tired, all right."

They seemed very close. He seemed to feel at least a little of her genuine sympathy.

"Isn't there a place you could sleep?" she suggested. "A few hours."

But he said solemnly, shockingly, "I'll sleep in my grave. Or in jail—it doesn't matter. Now step on it, Miss Connor," he said sternly. "We ain't getting there."

"I doubt if we'll make it," said Eve primly. "I'm afraid we're nearly out of gas."

"Hold up, then. Stop. Over there against the vacant lot." He was rough and peremptory. A fresh problem seemed to jolt and stimulate him.

Eve managed to get to the curb. They were under some trees. He leaned forward, staring at the gas gauge. One hand, his left, the one with the missing finger joint, groped on the seat behind him. He looked into her face, and his expression was full of cunning. She met his eyes docilely, innocently.

"Miss Connor," he said, "I don't trust you. You're making out to help me too much. Never mind, I figured how to keep the gun on you so you will anyway. Use this, and we can get some gas."

He held up the box of gauze and the adhesive tape that had been destined for Frances Connor's foot.

"Go on," he said. His right hand pointed the little gun straight at her. "Bandage it. The whole hand, the gun and all. It's going to look like a splint or something, but my little gun's going to be in there, and my finger on it. Though nobody's going to know it but you. And don't try pulling anything too tight now, or getting tricky, Miss Connor. Remember, I can get along by myself, probably. And this vacant lot would do for you."

They were well within the town, on a street of little shops, none open. And no movie theaters in this section; nothing to attract, no people walking.

Eve took the box of gauze, the tape.

"I can't trust you," he said, almost regretfully. "You're not going to help me kill Miss Ames. Nobody's going to help me, but I'm going to do it, just the same."

"I'm no nurse," said Eve tartly. "I'm probably going to make a clumsy mess of this."

He fell silent. The hand was as much like metal as the gun, hard and steady, while she began to bandage them both loosely over. Then, with his free hand, he turned the radio on, and hunted along the dial for news.

On KYOS the 7-o'clock spot news was almost over. The newscaster finished a sentence: . . . "nicely dressed, genteel-appearing." He took a breath. "Anyone seeing a woman answering this description, contact Police. Repeat: Anyone knowing the whereabouts of Miss Eve Ames, please contact Police at once. And that's the news from your own station." Music swam in.

Mariot swore. "They woulda told me what she looked like!"

Eve, using both hands to tear off some tape and hide their trembling, said, with a nervous snap, "You should have gone to a PTA meeting once in a while."

She thought the sudden sound in his throat was close to laughter. She looked straight into his eyes. But they could hold no laughter. Never any more. In fact, they fell.

"Come on," he grumbled. "Don't be so fussy."

"It's after seven," Lord said. "You want to stay here or get out?"

Geoffrey stood up. "Miss Connor was driving in to meet me. I spoke to her on the phone. If there's anything the two of us could do—"

"What kind of car does she drive?"

"Two-door sedan." He knew the make but not the year. "Dark blue."

"Okay, she'll hit the roadblock. We're stopping every living soul who tries to get into this block."

"Is there any point in my staying here?" said Geoffrey. "Is there anything at all that I can do?"

"I dunno what," said Lord, not without sympathy.

"I've got to get out of here," muttered Geoffrey.

"Okay, just go down the stairs, quick, and without commotion. Drive away to the north. They'll let you out that way."

"Yes. You don't mind if I circle back? I ought to meet Miss Connor. She's taking a long time."

"Go ahead. Circle back," said Lord wearily.

"I'm going out of my mind," Geoffrey admitted. "I feel so help-less. Things like this—I suppose we have to leave it up to you pro-fessionals. Will you be frank with me? How much hope have you?"

"Do our job if we can," the lieutenant said.

When he had watched Geoffrey to his car, the lieutenant stepped back from the window. He rubbed the back of his neck. Do his job. Sure. But that didn't guarantee success. Crazy man would try to come here, wouldn't he? Should the lieutenant put it on the air that Miss Ames was at home? Or would that be too obvious?

Where the deuce was the girl? Nice girl. He'd guarantee there wasn't a woman walking down a street in this town who hadn't been checked out. But if she was scared and safe and hiding some place, why didn't she let them know? Somehow, the lieutenant thought she would have let them know. He didn't think she was so safe. Unless she *had* gone to San Diego. But he couldn't call every-body named Marie in San Diego. And even from down there, Miss Ames should have heard, should have called . . .

With her heart in her mouth, Eve drove into the gas station and pulled up handy to the pump. The attendant looked in. She swal-lowed. He was no one she knew.

But was he one who had heard her description on the air? She'd been casting up her chances either way. The local station, the chil-dren's hours—how many adults would have been listening? And was all this detail on a national network? She thought not. Rather, hoped not, in fact. Because if the attendant were to say, "Aren't you that teacher they're looking for?" she hadn't much doubt the gun would go off.

Of course, if the man had any control and recognized Mariot, too, he wouldn't say this. But Mariot's mutilated hand had the fingers all curled inward. Mariot was sitting quietly with his band-aged right hand resting on his left forearm. He was utterly concen-trated and tense. The gun was in a perfect position to hurt her cruelly.

The attendant said cheerfully, "Fill 'er up?"

"Please."

The attendant went around to the rear of the car.

"You pay him," Mariot growled. He mustn't show his hand.

Eve picked her purse off the seat between them. In her wallet, she realized suddenly was her death warrant: her identification, her driver's license.

She opened the wallet flat, turning the edge up, with the license, in its plastic slot, away from the man. She slipped a ten-dollar bill out, closed the wallet nervously, dropped it in her lap, and sat twiddling the money. If Mariot had had the use of both hands, he might long ago have rooted about in her purse. . . . No "if's," Eve! No shuddering over old risks past.

How could she use her name and address to communicate? Show it to the attendant? He might not see any significance. He might see too much. She couldn't risk it. She had no card to say Mariot was a killer, with a gun. Let the wallet fall out, then? Leave it behind? No, not here. The attendant would see it too soon and come crying after them.

"Check your oil, folks?"

"Never mind it," Mariot said. He was as tense and hard as metal. "Skip the windshield, too."

"Whatever you say, folks."

Eve gave over the bill.

As the attendant made change, he said cheerfully to Mariot, "Hurt your hand?"

"Broke it," Mariot said.

"Hey, tough!"

"Yeah."

Eve took the change and dropped it loose into her bag, her hands quick and nervous.

"Okay, let's go," said Mariot in a low voice.

She started the motor. The bag slipped off her right thigh and lay between them again, but the wallet was still in her lap, hidden by the edges of her coat.

The car moved. Just as its nose was half out from the canopy, Eve lifted her foot from the accelerator, for she saw Geoffrey Taggart. He was in his black convertible heading out into the canyon, driving fast. The whole pose of his body proclaimed his state of urgency. He was looking for her, of course. He didn't see her. She didn't know whether to be glad or sorry.

"What's wrong?" Mariot said. He was so concentrated, tuned so close to her thoughts.

Eve fogged her own mind and forgot about Geoffrey. "I wish

you'd turn your bandaged hand," she wailed. "Look; I'm n-nervous. My foot slipped."

Mariot made no response at all. The car moved. Then she was at the sidewalk, forced to wait for an opening in traffic.

"That gas-station man," she said, with her eyes on the rear-view mirror, "is looking after us."

Mariot had to cast a look behind. She rammed the wallet down between the door panel and the seat cushion.

"My coat's caught in the door," she said irritably. "It's driving me crazy."

"Yeah," said Mariot, snapping his head back suspiciously. "You better not think about getting out of this car. Not now. Watch it."

"If I could free my coat," she said quietly. "Please."

"We're just about four blocks from where we're going, and that's where we're going, and I need you."

"Please." She lifted both hands from the wheel.

"All right, quick. The light's changing, and you can turn out into the street."

She took her foot off the brake. The car rolled a little. She opened the door with her left hand, and yanked at her coat skirt with her right. The wallet fell out on the sidewalk. She slammed the door quickly shut, grabbed the wheel, and turned out fast to the right, throwing her passenger with the violence of the turn.

"Break my neck!" he growled. "Woman driver. Now, listen."

Eve didn't pay any attention. She was reckoning chances.

Geoffrey was going to Frances, so he would find out soon that she was in Frances's car. And the police would have that information. So this car would be—what was it called? Hot. And her wallet would be found and would place her in town. All this was good—so she nervously hoped.

What, in the meantime, was going to happen when they neared her apartment, she could not foresee. If, indeed, she managed to run the car into the garage, and Mariot found himself trapped with no exit.

She thought, "No. It wouldn't be feasible. We'll park somewhere in the dark and wait and watch for Eve Ames to come walking along. We never will see her. That's all."

"Turn right," Mariot said.

She obeyed, waiting for a pedestrian quite helplessly. Nobody looked at a driver's face in the dark. The units were automobiles, not people; headlights were eyes, and hoods were noses. "What's that car going to do?" you said to yourself.

She made the turn. They climbed a little, going north on a street a block in from the main highway. Her apartment was only three blocks off.

"Listen to me," Mariot said urgently. "Make a smooth turn to the next left, and run into the parking lot behind that diner on the highway."

"What?"

"*Do it.* Cops!"

Eve did it.

As she did, she caught a glimpse under the street lights of two police cars drawn up ahead of them so as to narrow the street. At the same time, her automatic glance into the mirror, as she turned, showed her a motorcycle cop who was immediately behind them. He remained in that position. He also turned. ·

Eve kept to the right, driving slowly and cautiously. The cop was in no hurry and did not pass. She couldn't imagine how the cop could get to the gun or even realize where it was, all in a flash. She simply tried not to think about it.

"Turn into the lot," said Mariot. He knew the cop was there.

Eve swung right over the sidewalk into the parking space behind the diner. Mariot directed her to a spot in the farthest corner against a high fence. Eve found herself shaking as the motor died. The cop had turned in after them.

Mariot put his left arm up on the seat back, and then around her shoulders. He drew her close. The gun, hard under the gauze, rammed into her ribs painfully. Mariot's rough face rasped on hers, his left hand kept her head from recoiling.

The cycle cop trundled slowly along the perimeter of the lot. He was leaving to his right, and he peered past them as if looking for holes in the fence. To their silhouetted embrace, he paid no heed. Then he was beyond them, inspecting the recesses under the legs of the billboard at the highway's margin. In a very short time, he was gone.

Frances Connor's car wasn't "hot" yet.

Eve felt exhausted. She lay relaxed, her cheek against her killer's chin. His body became less hard, the gun less painful. For a space of two minutes, they were propped against each other in a spent heap, and it was peaceful.

"It's just too much," thought Eve. "I'm tired out—and so must *he* be! He'll have to give it up. I'll just lie here like this until it's over."

Back at the gas station, a man waiting for his tires to be checked sauntered casually into the exit lane. He picked up Eve's wallet, did not look at it. It went into his pocket.

When the car was ready, he drove off. He was alone. He hit the red light at the coast highway. Waiting there, he opened the wallet and took the money out. It wasn't much. A five and three ones. He shrugged, and stuffed the bills into his coat. The light changed, and he turned south. As he ran out of town, he tossed the rifled wallet out of his car.

Geoffrey Taggart's jaws ached from tension. *Adam!* Too late, he perceived the possible significance of that word. Could it have been Eve, herself, on the telephone? He no longer believed it was Frances Connor. He had not met her on the road. She was not driving to meet him. Too much time had gone by. So he was hurrying to Frances's house.

He raced along the canyon road. He sent the car zooming up the hill, and as he reached the flat upper end of the road, his headlights illuminated Frances Connor, her coat thrown around her like a cloak, hobbling along in the ruts. He braked.

"Geoffrey! It's about time. She's all right, is she?"

"Nobody knows, Frances." He was out and supporting her, his heart in his boots. "What's happened to you?"

Frances said, "Scraped my foot. It's nothing. What do you mean, nobody's found her? She left here more than an hour ago. I thought she'd sent you to let me know."

"Left here? Eve!"

"Why, yes. We heard the radio. She went to call the police."

"Then *she* called me."

"Called *you?* Where was she? What did she say?"

"I didn't recognize her voice. Frances, for some reason she pretended to be you."

He gave her the substance of that phone call. All but the word "Adam." That he couldn't tell; he felt too sick with guilt about it. But he hadn't been prepared for cryptic signals, for deadly masquerade.

"It must have been Eve," Frances said in bewilderment when he'd finished.

"But why did she lie to me?" said Geoffrey, irritable with the strain. "And if she was at a phone, why didn't she call the police? What's happening to her?"

Frances said, "I don't understand it, either. But we're wasting time."

"She hasn't called the police." He went on worrying at it. "They hadn't heard anything. Why should she—?"

Frances said, "Help me into your car, and turn it around."

Geoffrey turned the car. "I had understood," he said, a trifle sadly, "that she *wasn't* coming here." This hurt. Eve, for some reason, had left him out.

"Doesn't matter," murmured Frances Connor. "I'm just afraid she ran into Mariot. Let's go down to the grocery store."

"It's closed."

"Then we'll rouse Mr. Johnson."

Geoffrey's imagination suddenly came up with an explanation: "Frances, what if this Mariot was in the grocery store when she got there? What if she didn't dare give her own name—or be heard calling the police?" . . . "Then you failed her," his own mind answered, inexorably.

"In that case, we may not be able to rouse Mr. Johnson," said Frances grimly, "or Eve, either. Sorry." She glanced at his set face. "Let's hurry."

The little store was shut and silent, and the door was locked. Frances Connor shouted, and someone stirred in the upstairs apartment.

"Mr. Johnson? Come here."

"What's the matter?"

She wouldn't say, so he came. Lights went up, and he opened the store.

No, Miss Ames had not been in, but he'd seen her in Miss Connor's car. "She went back up the canyon, in a hurry, too. I saw her turn. Made me wonder."

"What on earth? *Up* the canyon?"

"That's right, Miss Connor."

"Tell him what's wrong," said Frances to Geoffrey, who stood appalled, "while I get the police."

She put a coin in the phone. Her heart was jumping.

Geoffrey stuttered out the news, and the grocer said, shocked, "She wasn't alone in the car. I don't know who it was. I couldn't see. A man, I think. *Somebody* was with her."

"Police?" said Frances Connor into the phone. "Have you found Miss Eve Ames yet?"

"No, ma'am," said a weary voice.

"She's in my car."

"Wait a minute!"

A different voice came on: "Lieutenant Lord speaking. Who is this calling?"

"Frances Connor, principal of Jefferson School. Eve Ames left my house, at 115 Plum Terrace, over an hour ago, in my car. She was going to call you from this grocery store. The grocer says he saw her turn up the canyon, and that somebody was with her."

"Can he describe the person?"

"No. He believes it was a man."

"They didn't go up the canyon far," Lord said. "Her wallet was just picked up south of town on the coast highway. There was no money in it. Rifled, probably."

Frances breathed in hard. "What does that mean?"

"She may have tried—" said Frances. "Some woman called Mr. Taggart and gave my name. It wasn't I."

"When was this? Where did he take the call?"

"At her apartment."

"What did she say? He didn't tell me." His voice was curt with exasperation.

Frances explained.

"She said she was going to her apartment?" said Lord. "I don't get it."

"There's been time," said Frances feebly.

The lieutenant said sharply, "Give me a description of your car." Frances did so, crisply.

"Thanks," said Lord. "It's a pleasure to talk to you. What was Miss Ames wearing?"

"Her brown topcoat, no hat, dark-green wool dress, brown pumps, brown handbag."

Lord said, "Hang on." After a full minute his voice came back on the line. "I was told she was *not* with you," he said rather severely.

"Lieutenant—she told a social lie," said Frances.

"I understand," he said, somewhat grimly. "Thank you, Miss Connor. We'll do all we can." He hung up.

"A social lie," said Geoffrey. He was trembling. "Eve didn't want me around. That's why—Where is she now?"

Frances touched him. "We'll look for her everywhere," she said gently. . . .

"So," said the officer beside the lieutenant, "maybe she takes off for San Diego alone in a panic. But why does she lie to Taggart? Why would she throw her empty wallet away? And if she wasn't alone, who took her? Mariot?"

"Maybe Mariot was in earshot when she made that call. She was going to try to get to her apartment, but in the meantime he got her."

"And he went south alone," said the other man.

"So we look for a body in a brown topcoat, maybe up the canyon."

"Pretty dark up there," the other one said.

"She was—quite pretty," said Lord, fiddling with a pencil. "I used to talk to her at PTA, about my kid, Terry."

"*You* go to PTA meetings, Lieutenant?"

"Have to," the lieutenant said, "since Alice died." He rose. "Better call some of the men off that apartment."

"How many, Lieutenant?"

"Leave enough to cover," said Lord abruptly. "Leave plenty to cover."

"You think maybe Mariot *didn't* get her?"

Lord said, "I got the distinct idea from his wife that he wasn't interested in getting away safe."

"Get the teacher and then commit suicide, huh? Or give himself up? That's what you mean? That's what you're saying."

"The guy's got nothing to live for," said Lord, "so you tell me why he wants her money."

Back at the diner in the far reaches of the parking lot, cars came and went, but in fewer numbers all the time. The dinner rush was waning. One car stayed, and the couple inside had not moved much.

Eve embraced the steering wheel, with her head lying upon her arms. To the left, the rush of cars on the coast highway was constant. Yet here, in the back corner of the parking lot, was absolute quiet. The man beside her was motionless and remote. He might even have fallen asleep. She wondered if he had, and what chance this would give her. To move, to open the door, to click the handle and slide out seemed an enormous project.

"Mr. Mariot," she said very quietly at last.

"Yeah?" He hadn't been asleep.

"Why don't you take the car and go? Go to Los Angeles. They won't find you. I won't say—"

"They'll find me," he said listlessly. "That's okay." He wasn't interested.

"Mr. Mariot." She tried another tack: "Wouldn't you like to know about your wife? Wouldn't you like to call the hospital? Or let me?"

"Why?" he said.

"Because if she isn't dead, if she's better, then—"

He began to shift restlessly again.

"I was trying to think of some way out for you," she said.

He didn't speak.

"What's good about revenge," said Eve musingly, "when you get to it? I have often wondered. You don't feel good, do you, because you hurt your wife?"

"Yes, I do," he said childishly.

"And after you kill Miss Ames," said Eve slowly. She let her voice go very flat. "So what? She'll only be—dead."

"Now," he said, almost with pity, "don't do that. You been pretty good, Miss Connor. You don't want to start trying to talk me out of it."

"I wish I could," she said forlornly.

"You been pretty good," he repeated. "Sue said you was a right nice lady, and I guess that's so."

"Have I done it?" thought Eve, galvanized. "Have I touched him? Does compassion work? Will it save me? And him, too?" She felt a moment of exultance and awe. Here, in the quiet, had all his pressures gone? Did he know that she was essentially on his side?

Mariot said, "I guess you're pretty well thought of in this town."

"Please—" She lifted her head, and she was smiling, although tears were in her eyes.

"So I can use you for a shield, all right," said the man with the gun. "No cop's gonna want to hurt you."

Her heart made sick circles downward.

"I'm thinking we could get out of the car and walk up the street, and when we get to the cops, I can keep you between me and them, and probably I'd get through. Trouble is—" he said.

"Trouble?" said Eve, a trifle cynically and sarcastically.

"I don't know she's there yet." He turned his head impatiently. "She wouldn't be in that diner, would she?"

"No," said Eve stonily.

It was the truth. The diner was a greasy-spoon type, strictly for the transients on the coast highway. She'd never been inside. But— oh, why hadn't she lied, and said "Maybe"? Some human being inside that diner might help her.

Mariot was looking at the time.

"Well?" said Eve, suddenly willing for anything but this. "What are you waiting for?"

"Waiting for the 7:30 news," he said.

"The news! That's stupid," she said recklessly. "Do you think they're going to tell you where she is? So you can get her?"

"They'll say if they don't know where she is yet," he informed her patiently, "and that'll tell me she ain't home, won't it? Or maybe they'll say if she is in San Diego. Coupla minutes." He punched the button. A program was ending with a commercial.

But Eve's mind had fled his problem in panic. They *didn't* know where she was. Nobody knew. Therefore the description, her description, would be repeated. And even if, by remote chance, Mariot's tortured mind didn't connect it with her, there was something else. Frances and Geoffrey were together by now. It would be said on the air that she, Eve Ames, was in this car! That would penetrate! That would tear it! Then he'd know!

"I wish I had a cup of coffee," she said loudly over the radio's jabber. "They're not going to tell you where she is." Her voice went on without conscious urging from her brain: "But I can find out for you whether she is in San Diego. Listen." Boldly she pushed the Off button on the radio and turned to face him. "I remember."

"Yeah?"

She could see that he was blinking as if to clear fatigue from his eyes.

"I remember her aunt's name and address. That's all you need to call Long Distance."

"Yeah?" he said rather feebly. "So what?"

"So Miss Ames could be down there. I can call up her aunt and find out."

"Where can you call from?" he said almost mechanically.

"From the diner."

He was thinking, slowly perhaps, but craftily. She could sense that.

"And if she is in San Diego," said Eve, with a note of triumph, "you couldn't get her, could you?"

"Why not?" he said, immediately and truculently. "This car can get as far as San Diego, can't it? In a coupla hours."

He rubbed his chin with his left hand. The stub of his index finger lingered along his lips.

"You don't have to be afraid," she said hastily, "to go into the diner. Why can't I bandage that finger tip, too? Then nobody would know. *You* could use a cup of coffee, by the way," she said rather crossly.

"Yeah, do that," he said suddenly, and held out his left forefinger.

She went to work eagerly. So long as she worked on his left hand and his right was bound to the gun, he couldn't turn the radio on. But if he commanded her to turn it on, how could she avoid it?

"I hope she *is* in San Diego, you know," she babbled. "And, poor thing, she was so terribly upset, that may be exactly where she's gone. Naturally, a person would go to the family. You keep calling her my friend, I know, but a friend is never so close as family."

"It'll do," he said.

"Wait," she said, thinking he meant the bandage. "It needs more tape than that."

She could see, now that his left hand hung free, how it was shaking.

"Mr. Mariot," said Eve, putting both her hands around his trembling one, daring at last to try, "there's only one thing I wish you knew." She tried to push out sympathy, tried, with her heart bursting, just to reach him. "We *loved* the little boy," she said. "Nobody meant him to die. Not anyone."

"Shut up!" He was hot with anger again. The sore spot was too raw. She shouldn't have tried to touch it.

"You talk about revenge," he said bitterly, "and you said, yourself, 'So she'll only be dead.' I said that, too. *I'm* going to die. In one hour. Two. And it's nothing. So maybe Miss Ames ought to live with her memories. Like my wife."

She sighed a long, shuddering sigh.

"All right," Mariot went on, "we go in the diner, we have a cup of coffee, and you call up this aunt. But if she's in San Diego," he said, "it's a long haul. And, like you said, I'm tired. And *you'll do*."

"I?"

"You're her friend," he said. "She'll feel bad. She'll know what grieving is!"

Eve was holding his hand, still. She simply stared at him.

"And maybe that's good enough," he said, snatching his left hand backward. "Now get out. Move!"

Now he sounded rushed and confused. "If she's not in San Diego, we'll do what I said. Start up the street. I'd rather get to her in a way, but if I don't—" His mouth was cruel. "I'd like to think there's some chance she's watching, that she'll see you get it—just like she watched Danny die."

She could feel the tide flow into him. The death of the child, that unspeakable outrage, was the wellspring of his anger and his energy.

Eve saw through his mind that she was not supposed to be a person, but a counter or a symbol. But she said quietly, because she had to try it, and she might not have another chance, "Danny died instantly. There was nothing anyone could do."

"Don't lie to me!" he yelled. "Don't give me that cover-up! Shut up!"

Eve waited quietly, convinced she was about to receive however many bullets were in the little gun.

Then he said furiously, "*Move!*"

So she moved, getting out of the car. But she thought, "He doesn't want to kill me, not really. He's confused, he's wavering. If I am quiet, plain weariness and despair may stop him in time."

She, herself, did not despair. There was the car; someone might see it. There was her wallet; they'd be looking for her in town. There would be people in the diner; she might be recognized by one of them. The man's bandaged hands would attract attention, too. Injury to both hands was a bit odd, and he could be recognized as soon as she. The police were not far, only two blocks up, one over. If anyone suspected, they could be called very quickly. And finally—when the little gun went off, it might not kill her.

So she had hope. She'd keep hope. And, by sheer hope, she might wear him out.

The low diner sat cater-cornered on the lot. They walked around to the entrance. Eve was sure that whatever happened to break her strange captivity would happen very fast, like an explosion. She braced herself as best she could. She knew Mariot glanced at her face almost with curiosity. He batted the door open with an elbow. They were in the light.

The air in this place was heavy with smoke and food odors. There was no one sitting at the counter, no one in any of the small booths along the wall. No customer at all. The counterman was reading the sports section of a newspaper. He looked up at them with no particular welcome. No recognition lit his gaze. He showed no curiosity.

Frances Connor said to Geoffrey, "Don't drive so fast."

"This is no good," said Geoffrey in despair. "I'm afraid it's a police job, Frances."

"I know my car better than they possibly can," the woman said.

"We ought to be near a phone."

"Turn up here, Geoffrey, and slowly, please. It's quite dark under those trees."

"We really ought to stay by a telephone," he insisted.

"What can a telephone do for us?" said Frances bluntly. "I don't insist on being the first to hear she's safe—just so she is safe."

"Don't say that." He ground his teeth.

Neither of them had enjoyed their ride out into the canyon, where beside any fence post, horror might hide against the ground. Horror might wait in the car, for all they knew, parked, abandoned.

"The police, with their prowl cars and their wireless communications," said Geoffrey bitterly. "That's what we depend on. It's futile for you and me—mild people, kind, well-meaning people, to be creeping about the town, peering into shadows on dark streets."

"It would be helpful," said Frances grimly, "if I could spot my car."

"Your car may be a hundred miles away."

"True."

He licked his dry lower lip. "Shouldn't we face it, Frances? There's no defense against uncontrolled violence. What chance has a delicate girl like Eve against a madman with a gun?"

"Maybe she's tougher than you think," said Frances angrily. "And we do not know, yet, that there is no hope."

"We're kidding ourselves," said Geoffrey, painfully.

Eve meant to look around the diner for a telephone, but Mariot had his left hand under her right elbow and his hard fingers compelled her to the counter. They sat up to it, he on her right, and the gun came to rest in the crook of his left arm. She could feel the line the bullet would take across the little space between them.

"What'll it be?" said the counterman. He was looking at that bandaged hand.

"Just coffee," said Mariot briskly. "Black for me. You?"

"Black," Eve said faintly.

The counterman turned to reach for cups. "Bust your hand, fella?" he said cheerfully. "Howja do it?"

"Fell," Mariot said in a tone of disgust. "Darned near busted the both of them."

Now he moved his left hand, and the bandaged finger was revealed.

The counterman's brows sailed up obligingly.

Eve could tell that a cook or some person in white was in the diner's kitchen. A middle patch of him was visible by way of the low-arched, counter-high opening through which food could pass. His head, however, was high. Estimating angles, she judged that he could see only the inner edge of the counter, if as much. Not her. Not Mariot.

The counterman set thick cups before them. Eve looked sideways at Mariot's face. It was the first time she'd seen it in full light. He had thick lashes that concealed his eyes. His whole face had a gaunt, drained look now, almost a look of peace. He took the mug up clumsily in his left hand.

"Pretty slow, this time of night," he said, and there was something pathetic in this commonplace. He was on vacation from tension, on detour from his drive to his own destruction. She felt a pang of pity and a pang of hope. Sometimes an assumed attitude solidifies and becomes a real one. As a forced smile in a fit of blue starts the low mood swinging away.

"Never can tell," said the counterman amiably. "You just driving through?"

Mariot shrugged.

"Piece of pie to go wid?"

"No, thanks."

Eve tasted the hot liquid. It was comforting. She thought that for Mariot it would be relaxing. Also, it was ordinary, a detail of daily life, a little pointer back.

"Shall I phone?" she asked easily.

"Wait a while," he answered. "I was trying to figure."

The counterman took this for ordinary private talk and removed himself to a polite distance.

"When did you last see her?" asked Mariot in a low voice.

For a bewildered moment Eve couldn't think whom he meant. "Oh," she said, "you mean Miss—"

"Yeah." He cut her off. "When?"

"I guess it was this morning."

"She say anything about San Diego?"

"No, but if she's not in town—" Eve fumbled.

"How'd she go? You say she's got no car. She go on the bus?"

"I guess so."

"What I'm trying to figure is if she's had time—"

"To get there? Plenty of time, I should think," Eve said absently. "All day."

She had to figure what she might accomplish with the phone call. Aunt Marie might recognize her voice, and give everything away. Or she could call a wrong number and gain time. But what good would time do?

The counterman was immersed in the sports pages of his paper. He wasn't paying any attention to them. There must be someone.

Then, through the opening to the kitchen, Eve saw a face, and her heart jumped. It was a face at the level of the counter, chin just high enough to reach. There was a child in there. A little boy. And he was watching her!

Eve picked up her coffee and scalded her mouth with a swallow. "Oof!" she said. "Oh, dear." She'd spilled some.

Mariot's eyes were sharp upon her. She could feel him tensing. She knew he was looking around to see what had startled her, and then he saw. A little boy!

His whole body took the shock. He, too, gulped coffee and spilled some. He put the cup down. "We better get out of here," he said.

Eve was trying to think. She had seen this child. He was not one of her fourth-graders, but he had seen her on the playground. He must have. But did he know her name? And had he listened to Grif Griffin tonight and left the news on? Maybe not the news, because the small face was watching without much expression. But most probably he knew Grif Griffin. And Grif Griffin had signals! All the kids knew the signals.

Mariot said harshly, "Drink the coffee, and we'll get out of here."

"You don't want me to phone at all," said Eve in a fluster.

"No. No good," he growled.

She saw his haunted eyes glance toward the child's face. Then his head began to shift from side to side, evading, denying. He began to talk to her rapidly and low, looking at the counter.

"A call would just tip her off, I'm saying she's *there*. In San Diego. What you said about the family, I think you got it. So we'll go to San Diego."

"But—"

"Okay," he said in that rapid undertone. "She hadn't been found here, half an hour ago. And she shoulda been, if she's in town. Even if she is," he added, "the cops aren't going to put her in the apartment."

Eve swallowed. She thought, "That's true."

"But you got her aunt's name and address," Mariot said, "and nobody else has! We can make it. And she won't be expecting me, in San Diego." Mariot ground his teeth. "I want to see her. *She's* the one got it coming. Make it snappy," he said angrily.

Eve thought, "He was ready to kill me—this me—just a few minutes ago. Now he won't deprive me of my cup of coffee."

She thought she couldn't go out on the open highway with this man, couldn't keep this up much longer. How much more time in this diner? A minute? Seconds, anyhow.

Then, what signal could she give to the one human being who was aware of her at all, the child? She couldn't remember Grif Griffin's signals. Now, of all times, the whole code she had thought she knew fairly well fled completely out of her memory. She grasped at only one. The one she'd so recently spoken of to Miss Connor. To tap your teeth meant, "I have news."

Eve put her cup down and, as if she were nervous, made a grimace that bared her teeth, put up her right hand, clicked the thumbnail.

"Too hot," she murmured, not daring to look at the child.

Mariot didn't move. He did not dare look at the child, either. A little boy. Just Danny's age. Mariot was staring at the counter. It gave Eve a chance.

But she couldn't remember any more of Grif Griffin's signals. There had been something to do with danger, on the air just tonight. What meant danger in Grif Griffin's code? She simply did not know. And her seconds were going by.

She glanced up at the boy and she put both hands flat, palm to palm, fingers pointing upward. It wasn't Grif Griffin's code. It was only an ancient human signal. It meant prayer. It meant, "Help me." Would the modern child, for he was watching her with great interest now, understand this classic signal? Was this a child who had ever prayed?

Eve couldn't tell whether he recognized any message. She broke her hands apart and seized the cup again. Drinking, she curled up her left hand, and held the fist it made beside her left ear. *Telephone, little boy! Telephone somebody! Tell!* Suppose he'd never heard of prayer. Certainly he knew about the telephone.

But she dared not glance at him again. She, too, stared at the counter. They must look, she thought, like two miserable sinners, staring sightlessly down, side by side.

Mariot said, "I can't wait here no longer."

She looked up, and the child was gone.

The little boy's name was Gino. He left the diner by the back. No use trying to talk to his uncle, the cook there. Uncle Joe was kinda crabby; he worked too hard, Pa said. But Gino lived in a house on the side street just two doors beyond the parking lot, and his father was in the front yard looking at his ruffled petunias along the entrance walk by a band of light that streamed out the house door.

"Pa, something's the matter."

"Hi, kid, 'bout time you came in. I was looking around for you."

"Pa, there's one of the teachers from my school in the diner with a man, Pa. And she needs somebody to help her."

"Watcha talking, kid?" The father rumpled the child's black hair affectionately.

"It's a teacher, Pa, honest." Gino hopped. "Look—she did like this, Pa. Look."

"Ah, you're dreamin' something up, as usual. Better get inside."

"No, Pa," Gino said, in such a voice that the father reached and pulled the boy forward until his solemn face was in the light.

"What is this?" he said, half kidding, half seriously.

"She was meaning me to notice," Gino said. "I *know* she was." He couldn't explain all about Grif Griffin in two minutes. He couldn't go into that.

"Pa!" he cried. "I think the man musta had a gun on her."

"Ah, Gino." The man relaxed. His white teeth showed in laughter.

"Pa, if we don't do something, and something bad happens . . . ?"

The father felt the young shoulder, and it was trembling, so he considered. The kid was serious, never mind what the truth was. And to the kid, he, the father, was strength, was help, was wisdom. He didn't want to laugh the kid off too fast. A kid should come to his father. Who else? he thought proudly.

So, for the kid's sake, he said, "I'll take a walk down there, okay?" and heard the sigh of faith triumphant.

Then, the boy's hand was pulling his cuff. "Pa, if he's got a gun, you wanta call the cops, maybe? I think she wants us to call the cops. And, anyhow, you don't want to get hurt, Pa."

The father saw the love in his boy's eyes. "We'll take a look before I go calling any cops, kid," he said. "Maybe it's nothing. You didn't *see* a gun, did you?"

Gino said honestly, "No." They were walking in the street now and, ahead, the diner shone. The parking lot was practically empty. Not many in there. The father was thinking, "Crazy ideas kids get, but I'll talk to Joe a coupla minutes, kid'll be satisfied."

He was a stocky, tough-muscled, but peaceful man. He walked in dignity, as wisdom should, not hurrying . . .

Mariot paid for the coffee and turned Eve off her stool with his left hand on her right elbow. He slid around to be on her right. She would not be out of the power of the gun. That power was real, she conceded.

Real, too, was a breaking in Mariot. He could stand no long drive to San Diego. The sight of the boy, perhaps, had poised his great guilt ready to fall on him and smash him. Even though he denied it, he must know it was there. He could hold it off only by violence. Somewhere out on the highway, he would break. He would either go to pieces or go violent. And the violence would fall on her, even if, in his mind, she was only second best. They must not get away.

She opened the diner door herself, helpless to do otherwise. They stepped outside. She saw the two figures on the sidewalk, a man and a boy. She thought Mariot might have seen them, too, because he raked her shoulder blade with the gun.

"Get to the car," he said harshly.

Now he was in a tearing hurry. She took quick, short steps and stumbled a little.

The father stood still, pressing his hands protectively upon the boy.

"They're getting away," Gino said.

"Quiet," the father said.

The father watched this couple go in what certainly looked like guilty flight, the girl stumbling, the man too close in an odd way, across the pavement of the lot. Saw them reach a car. Now he was worried. It wasn't enough suspicion to call the cops on. But it looked funny, all right. The father owed his child wisdom, and what was wise?

"Start up," Mariot said. "Come on; get out of here."

Eve, sliding under the wheel, knew that the boy *did* understand! (Oh, wonderful little boy!) Now she had hope, and someone suspicious. She thought, "I can't leave here in the car, can't be lost again. Let it be now. If he is going to use the gun on me, let it be here! He could have done it already a hundred times. He didn't. He hasn't yet." So she put her will and her wits against his will that they should depart.

Headlights slashed into this dark end of the lot as a car rolled up over the sidewalk, coming in from the street.

"Out the way we come," said Mariot. "Side street. Can't make a left turn into the coast road."

Eve had the motor running. She backed up; her head was turned over her shoulder. She knew that Mariot's head turned, too, in reflex. Then she was ready to go forward. She should wait for this car, which was coming toward them, to let it by. But her left hand darted under the dash and yanked on the hood-release. At the same time she stepped hard on the accelerator. The car jumped. Mariot was jerked in the seat. The hood flew up as the car leaped. The front of the car gaped like an alligator.

Mariot yelled. Around the open hood, Eve couldn't see. Nor

could Mariot. So Eve, with a bit of nice, blind calculation, hit, with a glancing, fender-crushing blow, the incoming car.

"Oh, I'm sorry!" she cried. "I'm sorry, I'm sorry!"

Her skin crawled. Her very bones cringed together. Mariot might shoot. Or he might only slip harmlessly out his side and run away free into the shadows. She wished . . .

He did neither. His hard fingers on that left hand dug into her thigh, and the gun was steady, pointing at her heart. His forehead looked dampish. His eyes were strained and startled in the sockets.

But he said, "Take it easy; I'll talk. Don't worry. We'll get away."

Eve thought, bewildered, "Doesn't he know I opened the hood?"

Mariot didn't seem to know. He seemed to accept an accident that had happened to them both. He was ready to drop with fatigue, of course. Only his purpose could hold him up.

Out of the tail of Eve's eye, she saw the man and the boy pass the corner of the diner. They had not come, as naturally they would have come, to size up the little collision. Instead, they had gone into the diner. So she had hope.

The driver of the other car was at her left, saying the usual: "Look what you're doing, why can't you?" He had a round, smooth face. His pudgy mouth was prim with indignation.

"Nobody's fault the hood's loose," Mariot said. "Take it easy. Not much damage, is there?"

The man walked and put one foot on his front bumper and stood on it. Something jarred free.

"It's nothing much, is it?" Mariot called, "Say, shut that hood down, wouldja, mister?"

"The crust," said the stout man. "The crust." But he reached for the hood and banged it down into place.

"Back off, back off," he yelled angrily.

Eve backed off.

"Hold it," the man said.

"How's our headlight?" Mariot called.

The stout man looked sharply back at him as if to say, "Why don't you get out and look for yourself?"

"Pull ahead, honey," he called to his wife, then stood deliberately in front of Miss Connor's car while his own moved in nervous jerks past it. Then he came to Eve's side again.

"Name, address, license number, insurance company," he

snapped. "I'll give you mine." He had a notebook and pencil. "But you're to blame, and don't forget it."

"Let the insurance companies fight it out," Mariot said, with frantic impatience. "How's our headlight?"

The man gave him a glare. "Okay," he growled, "and I got a notion to kick it in. What about it, lady?"

Eve had to speak. "I don't have a p-pencil," she stammered. "I don't have my license," she said in a panicky voice, because her license was in her wallet, long gone from this car. Good luck? Bad luck? She couldn't tell. "I'm terribly sorry," she said, and pulled herself together. "I was nervous," she said loudly, hoping he would wonder.

"No license," he said. "Is that so? You insured? This your car?"

"Yes, it is. Yes, I'm insured. The Farmers," she guessed wildly.

"Name?"

"Frances Connor."

He wrote it down. "Address?"

"115 Plum Terrace."

Now he peered in at the registration slip wrapped around the steering column. Eve trembled. What was on it? She couldn't remember. Would it say, "Frances Connor, age 50, hair white"? But the stout man seemed satisfied with a mere glance.

"Driving without a license, hey?" he said nastily. "Boy, I wish there was a cop around."

Eve thought wildly, "There are swarms of them just around the corner."

"She didn't say she's got no license," said Mariot. "She hasn't got it with her."

"Oh, yeah?" said the stout man. "I heard that before, too."

He moved to the front of the car, standing with his fat legs wide and stubborn, and slowly and carefully copied the car's number plate. Mariot cursed softly. The man was taking all the time he could.

Inside the diner, in the storeroom at the back, the cook and the boy's father were watching through a small, dark slit in the wall. The little boy, Gino, said, "Pa! What're they doing, Pa?"

"Nothing looked funny to you, Joe?" the father said. "About them two?"

"I couldn't see 'em. Probably the kid's nuts. Harvey didn't see no sign of a gun."

"It's Miss Ames," Gino said. "I know her. She knows me, too. She did this. See?" His small hands showed them prayer. "And she did something else." The boy faltered. He couldn't explain Grif Griffin in one paragraph to these two grown men.

"What do you say, Harvey?" The father turned.

Harvey, the counterman, said, "*Miss Ames!*"

"Sure, she's a teacher at my school," said Gino.

"Listen," the counterman said. "We *better* call the cops. There is a feller after her with a gun. I heard folks talking. The cops are looking all over for this Miss Ames."

"Hurry up—call," the father said.

He took the boy by the shoulder and held the little body close before him. A man has got to be wise when his son believes that he is. Should he go out there and stop those people? Go against a gun? Now, what was it to be wise?

Outside in the parking lot the stout man finished copying the number plate and moved aside.

"Move," Mariot said to Eve.

She let the car begin to move. She saw no help coming.

Lieutenant Lord was in the police car in sixty seconds flat after the message came. They swooped.

"Siren, sir?"

"No, don't get him nervous."

It was going to be mighty touchy, Lord thought. This man had a gun and had the girl. Sometimes a police officer has just one chance to do the right thing. What was it?

"Frances," Geoffrey said, in weary patience, "if your car was this close to Eve's apartment, surely the police would have spotted it."

"I suppose you're right," Frances said dispiritedly. "Shall we telephone, then?" She felt tired and old.

"Where's there a phone, I wonder?" he said.

She peered ahead. "Isn't that a diner, at the end of the block?"

Geoffrey saw the diner squatting on the corner. He felt he could bear no more of this nightmare, this aimless shuttling to and fro on the streets of the town. Insane, to continue. There would be no sight of Eve, living, moving, walking on a sidewalk. It was preposterous to hope so. Maybe the world was full of wild coincidences, of happy chances, of stray encounters. But these always happened to somebody else.

No, Eve was lost. To madness, to evil, to violence. Maybe, even now when they telephoned they would hear some awful finality.

"Let's try a bar," he said suddenly. "I need a drink."

Eve began to pull away. The exit to the side street was to their left. Along the street, Eve suddenly saw Geoffrey's convertible coming—Geoffrey's bare head under the street light and Miss Connor's white one beside it. Surely they'd see her if she took Frances's own car out into their path! But when they saw her, they'd call her name.

Anyhow, she couldn't stop. Mariot was tense and hard. The gun was close under her right breast. She couldn't change direction. She didn't know what to do but go on, out into the street. And Geoffrey would brake his car and shout, and the gun would shoot!

Suddenly the stout man began to yell. "I'll call the police!" he was shouting.

"Hold it," Mariot said to Eve. "What's the matter with you now?" he snarled at the stout man.

In the street, the convertible slid by. The heads did not turn. They did not glance into the dark lot nor notice a strange drivers' argument. Besides, the stout man had his head at Eve's window.

"She isn't going to drive off right in my face without a license," he fumed. "Not if I know it! Who does she think she is? Doesn't she know there's a law?"

"Oh, for—" Mariot was vibrating like a plucked string.

"You gotta license, mister," the fat man said hotly, "I'm telling you, you better drive, or I'm calling the police. And I got your license number. All the crust!"

"Shift over," Mariot said to Eve angrily. "This fool—"

"Fool, am I!" the stout man raged at them. "You'll find out. What's the idea of breaking the law?"

Mariot's face was black as thunder. The right hand moved. Eve thought, "This stout man will get a bullet, too."

"It's his hand," she gasped. "Can't you see I had to drive because he's broken his hand?"

"That so?" said the stout man, jolted. His round eyes took in the bandages.

"Yeah," snarled Mariot, "and this lady—" He choked. "I'll drive, though, if you insist. Now, go soak your fat head."

"Listen, I'm sor—"

But Mariot heaved his body over Eve, and she slid under him on the seat, feeling as if decision was out of her hands forever. Mariot put his feet on the controls. He pushed at the gear lever, clumsily reaching over with his left hand. His right lay on the seat between them, and his wrist was cocked unnaturally because, bound within and rigid to the hand, was the gun.

Again, they were moving. And what would he do? Where would he go? The police car came swooping in, and Eve saw Lieutenant Lord, who knew her well. He'd call, "Miss Ames!" . . . Then she could die. For Mariot, deceived and, in a way, betrayed, would plunge—oh, how gladly at the sound of her name!—into the final violence which he longed for.

She thought, "He mustn't kill me now. When he's so tired, when he is almost ready to fall, when a little more time, a moment to relax, would keep him from my murder." She felt, not fear, but a great sorrow. She put her own left hand on the steering wheel.

She said, "If you turn sharp left, we might make it."

So the car kept moving, and Mariot believed her. It seemed the truth because it was the truth. She, too, wanted them to get away. Together, they heaved on the wheel. The car heeled about. In pure reflex, Mariot's right hand came up to help them turn the wheel.

When Eve saw it come up, and the gun point at the windshield, she knew she must betray him. With both hands she pounced and pinned the bandaged hand and gun against the rim of the wheel with all her strength. The car kept turning, hit the curb.

Lieutenant Lord, who had called no name at all, but leaped nimbly out of his car, was there on the left, yanking the hand brake, holding a gun in his other hand.

The lieutenant said to Eve quietly, "Are you all right?"

Mariot shriveled and faded.

"Yes, I'm fine," she said. "Oh please, someone, *help him!*" Her eyes met the lieutenant's eyes. Lord's strong left hand was recognizing the little gun under the bandage.

"Try and take it easy, Mariot," he said. "You'll be all right." Then, quietly, "Get out of the car, Miss Ames."

Mariot's eyes turned. "Miss Ames?" he said, almost politely, as if they'd just been formally introduced, or as if he'd known this, too, for a long time. All the energy was out of him. There was another thing he'd known for a long time.

"But it's happened before," Eve cried to him, almost as if she loved him. "People have borne it, somehow. Terrible things happen in this terrible world. Other people have left a loaded gun and had their children die."

"That's what I did," he said soberly. Anguish fell in on him.

Lord said gently, "Just get out, Miss Ames. We'll take over. Someone will help him. . . ."

They were in Eve's apartment.

"Never felt so helpless," Geoffrey said. His eyes were dusty with fatigue. "I don't know, Eve, why you didn't scream your head off the moment you saw him."

"If we'd known you were in the car a little sooner," said Lord, "we might have spared you some of it."

"I'm not so sure," Eve said. "He'd have killed somebody. It took time to—to wear on him."

Geoffrey frowned. But the lieutenant nodded.

"His wife's recovering, is she?" Frances put in. She sat with her foot propped up again.

"It's partly her state of mind," Lord said, "but I think she'll make it."

"Poor people," Frances said.

"I can't pity him so much," Geoffrey said sternly. "Going around beating and shooting. He'll stay locked up, won't he?" He looked angry. The whole affair had been an outrage.

Lieutenant Lord paid no attention. "Pretty tight rope," he said to Eve, "and good balancing. Beautiful job of balancing."

"Well," she said, "*you* didn't call my name."

They seemed to understand each other.

"Dumb instinct. I didn't know he'd taken you for Miss Connor. But it isn't always so smart to yell at a man with a gun," said Lord, smiling. "A gun is a nervous thing. Sometimes you have to try to get at what's *behind* the gun. You were just fine."

"She's a tough one," said Frances Connor proudly.

"Terrible experience!" Geoffrey said.

The lieutenant's eyes flicked. He began to move toward the door.

"Lieutenant Lord," Eve said.

"Yes, Miss Ames?"

"Who gave the broadcaster my description?"

"Why, I did." He flushed.

" 'Genteel,' " said Eve thoughtfully.

"I started to say 'gentle,' " he said, a little sheepishly, "and then—well, I couldn't. If you didn't like it, I'm sorry."

Their eyes seemed locked.

Geoffrey said, "Eve, if the officials are through with you, I think what you need is some solid food and soft music."

Eve kept looking at the lieutenant. "Solid food and gentle music," she murmured. "What a nice combination." Then she found herself blushing.

"I'll see you," the lieutenant said, flushing too. "I'm not—" His glance went to Geoffrey, and then back to this brave and dainty girl, who hadn't lost her head, who hadn't given up, who had met and survived the experience of evil—who had, for his taste, the kind of courage you had to have in this world. "I'm not exactly *through* with you," he blurted.

"Any time at all," Eve said sweetly. "Good night, Lieutenant."

"Eve, poor girl," Geoffrey said, "you must be exhausted."

"Oh, be still a minute, Geoffrey," said Frances Connor quite crossly.

But she didn't look cross. Geoffrey Taggart wasn't following. To him the terrible experience was over now. Wasn't it? They went back, didn't they, to everything just as it had been before? He perceived no gain, no value. But Eve was leaning on the inside of the door. She didn't look exhausted. She looked radiant.

"Children," Eve said dreamily. "How I love little boys."

"Well, of course—Gino," began Geoffrey. "He was a hero straight out of a comic strip, wasn't he?"

But Frances Connor said complacently, "Terry's a good kid."

"Terry who? Do you know you've lost me?" said Geoffrey, intending to be humorous.

The women looked at him with faint little absent-minded smiles.

See How They Run

Robert Bloch

April 2nd

Okay, Doc, you win.

I'll keep my promise and make regular entries, but damned if I'll start out with a heading like *Dear Diary*. Or *Dear Doctor,* either. You want me to tell it like it is? Okay, but the way it is right now, Doc, beware. If you've got any ideas about wading in my stream of consciousness, just watch out for the alligators.

I know what you're thinking. "Here's a professional writer who claims he has a writer's block. Get him to keep a diary and he'll be writing in spite of himself. Then he'll see how wrong he is." Right, Doc? Write, Doc?

Only that's not my real problem. My hangup is the exact opposite —antithetical, if you're looking for something fancy. Logorrhea. Verbosity. Two-bit words from a dime-a-dozen writer? But that's what they always say at the studio: writers are a dime a dozen.

Okay, so here's your dime. Run out and buy me a dozen writers. Let's see—I'll have two Hemingways, one Thomas Wolfe, a James Joyce, a couple of Homers if they're fresh, and six William Shakespeares.

I almost said it to Gerber when he dropped me from the show. But what's the use? Those producers have only one idea. They point at the parking lot and say, "I'm driving the Caddy and you're driving the Volks." Sure. If you're so smart, why aren't you rich?

Call it a rationalization if you like. You shrinks are great at pinning labels on everything. Pin the tail on the donkey, that's the name of the game, and the patient is always the jackass. Pardon me, it's not "patient," it's "analysand." For fifty bucks an hour you can afford to dream up a fancy word. And for fifty bucks an hour I can't afford not to word up some fancy dreams.

If that's what you want from me, forget it. There are no dreams. Not any more. Once upon a time (as we writers say) there was a dream. A dream about coming out to Hollywood and cracking the television market. Write for comedy shows, make big money in your spare time this new easy way, buy a fancy pad with a big swimming pool, and live it up until you settle down with a cute little chick.

Dreams are nothing to worry about. It's only when they come true that you've got trouble. Then you find out that the comedy isn't funny any more, the big money disappears, and the swimming pool turns into a stream of consciousness. Even a cute little chick like Jean changes to something else. It's not a dream any more, it's a nightmare, and it's real.

There's a problem for you, Doc. Cure me of reality.

April 5th

A little-known historical fact. Shortly after being wounded in Peru, Pizarro, always a master of understatement, wrote that he was Incapacitated.

Damn it, Doc, I say it's funny! I don't buy your theory about puns being a form of oral aggression. Because I'm not the aggressive type.

Hostile, yes. Why shouldn't I be? Fired off the show after three seasons of sweating blood for Gerber and that lousy notalent comic of his. Lou Lane couldn't get a job as M.C. in a laundromat until I started writing his material and now he's Mr. Nielsen himself, to hear him tell it.

But that's not going to trigger me into doing anything foolish. I don't have to. One season without me and he'll be back where he belongs—a parking attendant in a Drive-In Mortuary. Curb Service. We Pick Up and Deliver. Ha, ha.

Gerber gave me the same pitch; my stuff is getting sour. We don't want black comedy. It's nasty, and this is a family-type show. Okay, so maybe it was my way of releasing tension, getting it out of my system—catharsis, isn't that the term? And it made me come on a little too strong. Which is where you get into the act. Blow my mind for me, put me back on the track, and I'll get myself another assignment and make with the family-type funnies again.

Meanwhile, no problems. Jean is bringing in the bread. I never figured it that way when we got married. At first I thought her singing was a gag and I went along with it. Let the voice coach keep her busy while I was working on the show—give her something to do for a hobby. Even when she took the first few club dates it was still Amateur Night as far as I was concerned. But then they hit her with the recording contract, and after the singles came the album, etc. My little chick turned into a canary.

Funny about Jean. Such a nothing when I met her. Very good in the looks department but aside from that, nothing. It's the singing that made the difference. Finding her voice was like finding herself. All of a sudden, confidence.

Of course I'm proud of her but it still shakes me up a little. The way she takes over, like insisting I see a psychiatrist. Not that I'm hacked about it, I know she's only doing it for my own good, but it's hard to get used to. Like last night at the Guild screening, her agent introduced us to some friends of his—"I want you to meet Jean Norman and her husband."

Second billing. That's not for me, Doc. I'm a big boy now. The last thing I need is an identity crisis, right? And as long as we're playing true confessions, I might as well admit Jean has one point —I've been hitting the bottle a little too hard lately, since I got canned.

I didn't mention it at our last session, but this is the main reason she made me come to you. She says alcohol is my security blanket. Maybe taking it away would fix things. Or would it?

One man's security blanket is another man's shroud.

April 7th

You stupid jerk. What do you mean, alcoholism is only a symptom?

First of all, I'm not an alcoholic. Sure I drink, maybe I drink a lot, everybody drinks in this business. It's either that or pot or hard drugs and I'm not going to freak out and mess up my life. But you've got to have something to keep your head together and just because I belt a few doesn't mean I'm an alcoholic.

But for the sake of argument, suppose it does? You call it a symptom. A symptom of *what?*

Suppose you tell me that little thing. Sitting back in that overstuffed chair with your hands folded on your overstuffed gut and letting me do all the talking—let's hear you spill something for a change. What is it you suspect, Mr. Judge, Mr. Jury, Mr. Prosecuting Attorney, Mr. Executioner? What's the charge—heterosexuality in the first degree?

I'm not asking for sympathy. I get plenty of that from Jean. Too much. I'm up to here on the oh-you-poor-baby routine. I don't want tolerance or understanding or any of that phony jive. Just give me a few facts for a change. I'm tired of Jean playing Mommy and I'm tired of you playing Big Daddy. What I want is some real help, you've got to help me help me please please help me.

April 9th

Two resolutions.

Number one, I'm not going to drink any more. I'm quitting as of now, flat-out. I was stoned when I wrote that last entry and all I had to do was read it today when I'm sober to see what I've been doing to myself. So no more drinking. Not now or ever.

Number two. From now on I'm not showing this to Dr. Moss. I'll cooperate with him completely during therapy sessions but that's it. There's such a thing as invasion of privacy. And after what happened today I'm not going to lay myself wide open again. Particularly without an anesthetic, and I've just given that up.

If I keep on writing everything down it will be for my own information, a matter of personal record. Of course I won't tell him that. He'd come up with some fancy psychiatric zinger, meaning I'm talking to myself. I've got it figured out—the shrinks are all authority figures and they use their labels as putdowns. Who needs it?

All I need is to keep track of what's happening, when things start to get confused. Like they did at the session today.

First of all, this hypnotherapy bit.

As long as this is just between me and myself I'll admit the whole idea of being hypnotized always scared me. And if I had any suspicion the old creep was trying to put me under I'd have cut out of there in two seconds flat.

But he caught me off guard. I was on the couch and supposed to say whatever came into my head. Only I drew a blank, couldn't think of anything. Emotional exhaustion, he said, and turned down the lights. Why not close my eyes and relax? Not go to sleep, just daydream a little. Daydreams are sometimes more important than those that come in sleep. In fact he didn't want me to fall asleep, so if I'd concentrate on his voice and let everything hang loose—

He got to me. I didn't feel I was losing control, no panic, I knew where I was and everything, but he got to me. He must have, because he kept talking about memory. How memory is our own personal form of time travel, a vehicle to carry us back, way back to earliest childhood, didn't I agree? And I said yes, it can carry us back, carry me back, back to old Virginny.

Then I started to hum something I hadn't thought about in years. And he said what's that, it sounds like a nursery rhyme, and I said that's right, Doc, don't you know it, *Three Blind Mice.*

Why don't you sing the words for me, he said. So I started.

> Three blind mice, three blind mice,
> See how they run, see how they run!
> They all ran after the farmer's wife,
> Did you ever see such a sight in your life
> As three blind mice, three blind mice?

"Very nice," he said. "But didn't you leave out a line?"

"What line?" I said. All at once, for no reason at all, I could feel myself getting very uptight. "That's the song. My old lady sang that to me when I was a baby. I wouldn't forget a thing like that. What line?"

He started to sing it to me.

> They all ran after the farmer's wife,
> She cut off their heads with a carving knife,

Then it happened.

It wasn't like remembering. It was happening. Right now, all over again.

Late at night. Cold. Wind blowing. I wake up. I want a drink of water. Everyone asleep. Dark. I go into the kitchen.

Then I hear the noise. Like a tapping on the floor. It scares me. I turn on the light and I see it. In the corner behind the door. The trap. Something moving in it. All gray and furry and flopping up and down.

The mouse. Its paw is caught in the trap and it can't get loose. Maybe I can help. I pick up the trap and push the spring back. I hold the mouse. It wiggles and squeaks and that scares me more. I don't want to hurt it, just put it outside so it can run away. But it wiggles and squeaks and then it bites me.

When I see the blood on my finger I'm not scared any more. I get mad. All I want to do is help and it bites me. Dirty little thing. Squeaking at me with its eyes shut. Blind. Three Blind Mice. Farmer's wife.

There. On the sink. The carving knife.

It tries to bite me again. I'll fix it. I take the knife. And I cut, I drop the knife, and I start to scream.

I was screaming again, thirty years later, and I opened my eyes and there I was in Dr. Moss's office, bawling like a kid.

"How old were you?" Dr. Moss said.

"Seven."

It just popped out. I hadn't remembered how old I was, hadn't remembered what happened—it was all blacked out of my mind, just like the line in the nursery rhyme.

But I remember now. I remember everything. My old lady finding the mouse head in the trash can and then beating the hell out of me. I think that's what made me sick, not the bite, even though the doctor who came and gave me the shot said it was infection that caused the fever. I was laid up in bed for two weeks. When I'd wake up screaming from the nightmares, my old lady used to come in and hold me and tell me how sorry she was. She always told me how sorry she was—after she did something to me.

I guess that's when I really started to hate her. No wonder I built so many of Lou Lane's routines on mother and mother-in-law gags. Oral aggression? Could be. All these years and I never knew it, never realized how I hated her. I still hate her now, hate her—

What I need is a drink.

April 23rd

Two weeks since I wrote the last entry. I told Dr. Moss I quit
keeping a diary and he believed me. I told Dr. Moss a lot of things
besides that, and whether he believed me or not I don't know. Not
that I care one way or the other. I don't believe everything he tells
me, either.

Hebephrenic schizophrenia. Now there's a real grabber.

Meaning certain personality types, confronted with a stress situation they can't handle, revert to childhood or infantile behavior
levels.

I looked it up the other day after I got a peek at Moss's notes,
but if that's what he thinks, then he's the one who's flipped.

Dr. Moss has a thing about words like flipped, nuts, crazy. Mental disturbance, that's his speed.

That and regression. He's hung up on regression. No more hypnosis—I told him that was out, absolutely—and he got the message.
But he uses other techniques like free association, and they seem to
work. What really happens is that I talk myself into remembering,
talk my way back into the past.

I've come up with some weirdies. Like not drinking a glass of
milk until I was five years old—my old lady let me drink that formula stuff out of the bottle and there was a big hassle over it when
I went to kindergarten and wouldn't touch my milk any other way.
Then she clouted me one and said I made her ashamed when she
had to explain to the teacher, and she took the bottle away. But it
was her fault in the first place. I'm beginning to understand why I
hated her.

My old man wasn't any prize, either. Whenever we had company
over for dinner he'd come out with things I'd said to him, all the
dumb kid stuff you say when you don't know any better, and everybody would laugh. Hard to realize kids get embarrassed, too, until
you remember the way it was. The old man kept needling me to
make stupid cracks just so he could take bows for repeating them
to his buddies. No wonder you forget things like that—it hurts too
much to remember.

It still hurts.

Of course there were good memories, too. When you're a kid,

most of the time you don't give a damn about anything, you don't worry about the future, you don't even understand the real meaning of things like pain and death—and that's worth remembering.

I always seem to start out that way in our sessions but then Moss steers me into the other stuff. Catharsis, he says, it's good for you. Let it all hang out. Okay, I'm cooperating, but when we finish up with one of those children's hours I'm ready to go home and have a nice, big drink.

Jean is starting to bug me about it again. We had another hassle last night when she came home from the club date. Singing, that's all she's really interested in nowadays, never has any time for me.

Okay, so that's her business, why doesn't she mind it and let me alone? So I was stoned, so what? I tried to tell her about the therapy, how I was hurting and how a drink helped. "Why don't you grow up?" she said. "A little pain never hurt anyone."

Sometimes I think they're all crazy.

April 25th

They're crazy, all right.

Jean calling Dr. Moss and telling him I was back on the bottle again.

"On the bottle," I said, when he told me about it. "What kind of talk is that? You'd think she was my mother and I was her baby."

"Isn't that what you think?" Moss said.

I just looked at him. I didn't know what to say. This was one time when he did all the talking.

He started out very quietly, about how he'd hoped therapy would help us make certain discoveries together. And over a period of time I'd begin to understand the meaning of the pattern I'd established in my life. Only it hadn't seemed to work out that way, and while as a general thing he didn't care to run the risk of inducing psychic trauma, in this case it seemed indicated that he clarify the situation for me.

That part I can remember, almost word for word, because it made sense. But what he told me after that is all mixed up.

Like saying I have an oral fixation on the bottle because it represents the formula bottle my mother took away from me when I was a kid. And the reason I got into comedy writing was to reproduce the situation where my father used to tell people all my funny

remarks—because even if they laughed it meant I was getting attention, and I wanted attention. But at the same time I resented my father taking the credit for amusing them, just like I resented Lou
Lane making it big because of what I wrote for him. That's why I
blew the job, writing material he couldn't use. I wanted him to use
it and bomb out, because I hated him. Lou Lane had become a father image and I hated my father.

I remember looking at Dr. Moss and thinking he has to be crazy.
Only a crazy shrink could come up with things like that.

He was really wild. Talking about my old lady. How I hated her
so much when I was a kid I had to displace my feelings—transfer
them to something else so I wouldn't feel so guilty about it.

Like the time I got up for a drink of water. I really wanted my
bottle back, but my mother wouldn't give it to me. And maybe the
bottle was a symbol of something she gave my father. Hearing
them was what really woke me up and I hated her for that most of
all.

Then I went into the kitchen and saw the mouse. The mouse
reminded me of the nursery rhyme and the nursery rhyme reminded me of my mother. I took the knife, but I didn't want to kill
the mouse. In my mind I was really killing my mother—

That's when I hit him. Right in his dirty mouth.

Nobody talks about my mother that way.

Apr 29

Better this way. Don't need Moss. Don't need therapy. Do it myself.

Been doing it. Regression. Take a little drink, take a little trip.
Little trip down memory lane.

Not to the bad things. Good things. All the warm soft memories.
The time I was in bed with the fever and mother came in with the
ice cream on the tray. And my father bringing me that toy.

That's what's nice about remembering. Best thing in the world.
There was a poem we used to read in school. I still remember it.
"Backward, turn backward, O time in your flight, make me a child
again just for tonight!" Well, no problem. A few drinks and away
you go. Little oil for the old time machine.

When Jean found out about Dr. Moss she blew her stack. I had
to call him up right away and apologize, she screamed.

"To hell with that," I said. "I don't need him any more. I can work this thing out for myself."

"Maybe you'll have to," Jean said.

Then she told me about Vegas. Lounge date, three weeks on the Strip. All excited because this means she's really made it—the big time. Lou Lane is playing the big room and he called her agent and told her it was all set.

"Wait a minute," I said. "Lou Lane set this up for you?"

"He's been a good friend," Jean told me. "All through this he's kept in touch, because he's worried about you. He'd be your friend, too, if you'd only let him."

Sure he would. With friends like that you don't need enemies. My eyes were opening fast. No wonder he squawked to Gerber and got me off the show. So he could move in on Jean. He had it set up, all right. The two of them, playing Vegas together. Jean in the lounge, him in the big room, and then, after the show—

For a moment there I was so shook up I couldn't see straight and I don't know what I would have done if I could. But I mean I really couldn't see straight because I started to cry. And then she was holding me and it was all right again. She'd cancel the Vegas date and stay here with me, we'd work this out together. But I had to promise her one thing—no more drinking.

I promised. The way she got to me I would have promised her anything.

So I watched her clean out the bar and then she went into town to see her agent.

It's a lie, of course. She could have picked up the phone and called him from here. So she's doing something else.

Like going straight to Lou Lane and spilling everything to him. I can just hear her. "Don't worry, darling, I had to beg off this time or he'd get too suspicious. But what's three weeks in Vegas when we've got a whole lifetime ahead of us?" And then the two of them get together—

No. I'm not going to think about it. I don't have to think about it, there are other things, better things.

That's why I took the bottle. The one she didn't know about when she cleaned out the bar, the one I had stashed away in the basement.

I'm not going to worry any more. She can't tell me what to do. Take a little drink, take a little trip. That's all there is to it.

I'm home free.

Later

She broke the bottle.

She came in and saw me and grabbed the bottle away from me and she broke it. I know she's mad because she ran into the kitchen and slammed the door. Why the kitchen?

Extension phone there.

Wonder if she'll try to call Dr. Moss.

Aprel 30

> I was a bad boy.
> The Dr. come. he sed what did you do.
> I sed she took the bottel away.
> He saw it on the floor the knive
> I had to do it I sed.
> He saw blood.
> Like the mouse he sed.
> No not a mouse. A canarry.
> dont look in the trash can I sed
> But he did.

Nothing Short of Highway Robbery

Lawrence Block ·

I eased up on the gas pedal a few hundred yards ahead of the service station. I was putting the brakes on when my brother Newton opened his eyes and straightened up in his seat.

"We haven't got but a gallon of gas left if we got that much," I told him. "And there's nothing out ahead of us but a hundred miles of sand and a whole lot of cactus, and I already seen enough cactus to last me a spell."

He smothered a yawn with the back of his hand. "Guess I went and fell asleep," he said.

"Guess you did."

He yawned again while a fellow a few years older'n us came off of the front porch of the house and walked our way, moving slow, taking his time. He was wearing a broad-brimmed white hat against the sun and a pair of bib overalls. The house wasn't much, a one-story clapboard structure with a flat roof. The garage alongside it must have been built at the same time and designed by the same man.

He came around to my side and I told him to fill the tank. "Regular," I said.

He shook his head. "High-test is all I got," he said. "That be all right?"

I nodded and he went around the car and commenced unscrewing the gas cap. "Only carries high-test," I said, not wildly happy about it.

"It'll burn as good as the regular, Vern."

"I guess I know that. I guess I know it's another five cents a gallon or another dollar bill on a tankful of gas, and don't you just bet that's why he does it that way? Because what the hell can you do if you want regular? This bird's the only game in town."

"Well, I don't guess a dollar'll break us, Vern."

I said I guess not and I took a look around. The pump wasn't so far to the rear that I couldn't get a look at it, and when I did I saw the price per gallon, and it wasn't just an extra nickel that old boy was taking from us. His high-test was priced a good twelve cents a gallon over everybody else's high-test.

I pointed this out to my brother and did some quick sums in my head. Twelve cents plus a nickel times say twenty gallons was three dollars and forty cents. I said, "Damn, Newton, you know how I hate being played for a fool."

"Well, maybe he's got his higher costs and all—being out in the middle of nowhere and all, little town like this."

"Town? Where's the town at? Where we are ain't nothing but a wide place in the road."

And that was really all it was. Not even a crossroads, just the frame house and the garage alongside it, and on the other side of the road a café with a sign advertising home-cooked food and package goods. A couple of cars over by the garage, two of them with their hoods up and various parts missing from them. Another car parked over by the café.

"Newt," I said, "you ever see a softer place'n this?"

"Don't even think about it."

"Not thinking about a thing. Just mentioning."

"We don't bother with nickels and dimes no more, Vernon. We agreed on that. By tonight we'll be in Silver City. Johnny Mack Lee's already there and first thing in the morning we'll be taking that bank off slicker'n a bald tire. You know all that."

"I know."

"So don't be exercising your mind over nickels and dimes."

"Oh, I know it," I said. "Only we could use some kind of money pretty soon. What have we got left? Hundred dollars?"

"Little better'n that."

"Not much better though."

"Well, tomorrow's payday," Newt said.

I knew he was right but it's a habit a man gets into, looking at a place and figuring how he would go about taking it off. Me and Newt, we always had a feeling for places like filling stations and liquor stores, 7-11 stores and like that. You just take 'em off nice and easy, you get in and get out, and a man can make a living that way. Like the saying goes, it don't pay much but it's regular.

But then the time came that we did a one-to-five over to the state pen and it was an education. We both of us came out of there knowing the right people and the right way to operate. One thing we swore was to swear off nickels and dimes. The man who pulls quick-dollar stick-ups like that, he works ten times as often and takes twenty times the risks of the man who takes his time setting up a big job and scoring it. I remember Johnny Mack Lee saying it takes no more work to knock over a bank than a bakery and the difference is dollars to doughnuts.

I looked up and saw the dude with the hat poking around under the hood. "What's he doing now, Newt? Prospecting for more gold?"

"Checking the oil, I guess."

"Hope we don't need none," I said. "'Cause you just know he's gotta be charging two dollars a quart for it."

He did a good job of checking under there, topping up the battery terminals and all, then he came around and leaned against the car door. "Oil's O.K.," he said. "You sure took a long drink of gas. Good you had enough to get here. And this here's the last station for a whole lot of highway."

"Well," I said, "how much do we owe you?"

He named a figure. High as it was, it came as no surprise to me since I'd already turned and read it off of the pump. Then as I was reaching in my pocket he said, "I guess you know about that fan clutch, don't you?"

"Fan clutch?"

He gave a long slow nod. "I suppose you got a few miles left in it," he said. "Thing is, it could go any minute. You want to step out of the car for a moment I can show you what I'm talking about."

Well, I got out, and Newt got out his side, and we went and joined this bird and peeked under the hood. He reached behind the radiator and took ahold of some damned thing or other and showed us how it was wobbling. "The fan clutch," he said. "You ever replace this here since you owned the car?"

Newt looked at me and I looked back at him. All either of us ever knew about a car is starting it and stopping it and the like. As a boy Newt was awful good at starting them without keys. You know how kids are.

"Now if this goes," he went on, "then there goes your water pump. Probably do a good job on your radiator at the same time. You might want to wait and have your own mechanic take care of it for you. The way it is, though, I wouldn't want to be driving too fast or too far with it. Course if you hold it down to forty miles an hour and stop from time to time so's the heat won't build up—"

Me and Newt looked at each other again. Newt asked some more about the fan clutch and the dude wobbled it again and told us more about what it did, which we pretended to pay attention to and nodded like it made sense to us.

"This fan clutch," Newt said. "What's it run to replace it?"

"Around thirty, thirty-five dollars. Depends on the model and who does the work for you, things like that."

"Take very long?"

"Maybe twenty minutes."

"Could you do it for us?"

The dude considered, cleared his throat, spat in the dirt. "Could," he allowed. "*If* I got the part. Let me just go and check."

When he walked off I said, "Brother, what's the odds that he's got that part?"

"No bet a-tall. You figure there's something wrong with our fan clutch?"

"Who knows?"

"Yeah," Newt said. "Can't figure on him being a crook and just spending his life out here in the middle of nowhere, but then you got to consider the price he gets for the gas and all. He hasn't had a customer since we pulled in, you know. Maybe he gets one car a day and tries to make a living off it."

"So tell him what to do with his fan clutch."

"Then again, Vern, maybe all he is in the world is a good mechanic trying to do us a service. Suppose we cut out of here and fifty miles down the road our fan clutch up and kicks our water pump through our radiator or whatever the hell it is? By God, Vernon, if we don't get to Silver City tonight Johnny Mack Lee's going to be vexed with us."

"That's a fact. But thirty-five dollars for a fan clutch sure eats a hole in our capital, and suppose we finally get to Silver City and find out Johnny Mack Lee got out the wrong side of bed and slipped on a banana peel or something? Meaning if we get there and there's no job, then what do we do?"

"Well, I guess it's better'n being stuck in the desert."

"I guess."

Of course he had just the part we needed. You had to wonder how a little gas station like that would happen to carry a full line of fan clutches, which I never even heard of that particular part before, but when I said as much to Newt he shrugged and said maybe an out-of-the-way place like that was likely to carry a big stock because he was too far from civilization to order parts when the need for them arose.

"The thing is," he said, "all up and down the line you can read all of this either way. Either we're being taken or we're being done a favor for, and there's no way to know for sure."

While he set about doing whatever he had to do with the fan clutch, we took his advice and went across the street for some coffee. "Woman who runs the place is a pretty fair cook," he said. "I take all my meals there my own self."

"Takes all his meals here," I said to Newt. "Hell, she's got him where he's got us. He don't want to eat here he can walk sixty miles to a place more to his liking."

The car that had been parked at the café was gone now and we were the only customers. The woman in charge was too thin and rawboned to serve as an advertisement for her own cooking. She had her faded blonde hair tied up in a red kerchief and she was perched on a stool smoking a cigarette and studying a *True Confessions* magazine. We each of us ordered apple pie at a dollar a wedge and coffee at thirty-five cents a cup. While we were eating, a car pulled up and a man wearing a suit and tie bought a pack of cigarettes from her. He put down a dollar bill and didn't get back two dimes' change.

"I think I know why that old boy across the street charges so much," Newt said softly. "He needs to get top dollar if he's gonna pay for his meals here."

"She does charge the earth."

"You happen to note the liquor prices? She gets seven dollars for a bottle of Ancient Age bourbon. And that's not for a quart either. That's for a fifth."

I nodded. "I just wonder where they keep all that money."

"Brother, we don't even want to think on that."

"Never hurt a man to think."

"These days it's all credit cards anyways. The tourist trade is nothing but credit cards and his regular customers most likely run a monthly tab and give him a check for it."

"We'll be paying cash."

"Well, it's a bit hard to establish credit in our line of work."

"Must be other people pays him cash. And the food and liquor over here, that's gotta be all cash, or most all cash."

"And how much does it generally come to in a day? Be sensible. As little business as they're doing—"

"I already thought of that. Same time, though, look how far they are from wherever they do their banking."

"So?"

"So they wouldn't be banking the day's receipts every night. More likely they drive in and make their deposits once a week, maybe even once every two weeks."

Newt thought about that. "Likely you're right," he allowed. "Still, we're just talking small change."

"Oh, I know."

But when we paid for our pie and coffee, Newton gave the old girl a smile and told her how we sure had enjoyed the pie, which we hadn't all that much, and how her husband was doing a real good job on our car over across the street.

"Oh, he does real good work," she said.

"What he's doing for us," Newt said, "he's replacing our fan clutch. I guess you probably get a lot of people here needing new fan clutches."

"I wouldn't know about that," she said. "Thing is I don't know much about cars. He's the mechanic and I'm the cook is how we divvy things up."

"Sounds like a good system," Newt told her.

On the way across the street Newt separated two twenties from our bankroll and tucked them into his shirt pocket. Then I reminded him about the gas and he added a third twenty. He gave the rest of our stake a quick count and shook his head. "We're getting pretty close to the bone," he said. "Johnny better be where he's supposed to be."

"He's always been reliable."

"That's God's truth. And the bank, it better be the piece of cake he says it is."

"I just hope."

"Twenty thousand a man is how he has it figured. Plus he says it could run three times that. I sure wouldn't complain if it did, brother."

I said I wouldn't either. "It does make it silly to even think about nickels and dimes," I said.

"Just what I was telling you."

"I was never thinking about it, really. Not in the sense of doing it. Just mental exercise, keeps the brain in order."

He gave me a brotherly punch in the shoulder and we laughed together some. Then we went on to where the dude in the big hat was playing with our car. He gave us a large smile and held out a piece of metal for us to admire. "Your old fan clutch," he said, which I had more or less figured. "Take hold of this part. That's it, right there. Now try to turn it."

I tried to turn it and it was hard to turn. He had Newt do the same thing. "Tight," Newt said.

"Lucky you got this far with it," he said, and clucked his tongue and heaved the old fan clutch onto a heap of old metallic junk.

I stood there wondering if a fan clutch was supposed to turn hard or easy or not at all, and if that was our original fan clutch or a piece of junk he kept around for this particular purpose, and I knew Newton was wondering the same thing. I wished they could have taught us something useful in the state pen, something that might have come in handy in later life, something like your basic auto mechanics course. But they had me melting my flesh off my bones in the prison laundry, and they had Newt stamping out license plates, which there isn't much call for in civilian life, being the state penal system has an official monopoly on the business.

Meanwhile Newt had the three twenties out of his shirt pocket and was standing there straightening them out and lining up their edges. "Let's see now," he said. "That's sixteen and change for the gas, and you said thirty- to thirty-five for the fan clutch. What's that all come to?"

It turned out that it came to just under eighty-five dollars.

The fan clutch, it seemed, had run higher than he'd thought it would. Forty-two fifty was what it came to, and that was for the part exclusive of labor. Labor tacked another twelve dollars onto our tab. And while he'd been working there under the hood, our friend had found a few things that simply needed attending to. Our fan belt, for example, was clearly on its last legs and ready to pop any minute. He showed it to us and you could see how worn it was, all frayed and just a thread or two away from popping.

So he had replaced it, and he'd replaced our radiator hoses at the same time. He fished around in his junkpile and came up with a pair of radiator hoses he said had come off our car. The rubber was old and stiff with little cracks in the surface, and it sure smelled like something awful.

I studied the hoses and agreed they were in terrible shape. "So you just went ahead and replaced them on your own," I said.

"Well," he said, "I didn't want to bother you while you were eating."

"That was considerate," Newt said.

"I figured you fellows would want it seen to. You blow a fan belt or a hose out there, well, it's a long walk back, you know. Course I realize you didn't authorize me to do the work, so if you actually want me to take the new ones off and put the old ones back on—"

Of course there was no question of doing that. Newt looked at me for a minute and I looked back at him and he took out our roll, which I don't guess you could call a roll any more from the size of it, and he peeled off another twenty and a ten and added them to the three twenties from his shirt pocket. He held the money in his hand and looked at it and then at the dude, then back at the money, then back at the dude again. You could see he was doing heavy thinking, and I had an idea where his thoughts were leading.

Finally he took in a whole lot of air and let it out in a rush and said, "Well, hell, I guess it's worth it if it leaves us with a car in good condition. Last thing either of us wants is any damn trouble with the damn car. This fixes us up, right? Now we're in good shape with nothing to worry about, right?"

"Well," the dude said.

We looked at him.

"There *is* a thing I noticed."

"Oh?"

"If you'll just look right here," he said. "See how the rubber grommet's gone on the top of your shock-absorber mounting, that's what called it to my attention. Now you see your car's right above the hydraulic lift, that's 'cause I had it up before to take a look at your shocks. Let me just raise it up again and I can point out what's wrong."

Well, he pressed a switch or some such to send the car up off the ground, and pointed here and there underneath it to show us where the shocks were shot and something was cutting into something else and about to commence bending the frame. "If you got the time you ought to let me take care of that for you," he said, "because if you don't get it seen to you wind up with frame damage and your whole front end goes on you, and then where are you?"

He let us take a long look at the underside of the car. There was no question that something was pressing on something and cutting into it. What the hell it all added up to was beyond me.

"Just let me talk to my brother a minute," Newt said to him, and he took hold of my arm and we walked around the side.

"Well," he said, "what do you think? It looks like this old boy here is sticking it in pretty deep."

"It does at that. But that fan belt was shot and those hoses was the next thing to petrified."

"True."

"If they was our fan belt and hoses in the first place and not some junk he had around."

"I had that very thought, Vern."

"Now as for the shock absorbers—"

"Something sure don't look altogether perfect underneath that car. Something's sure cutting into something."

"I know it. But maybe he just went and got a file or some such thing and did some cutting himself."

"In other words, either he's a con man or he's a saint."

"Except we know he ain't a saint, not at the price he gets for gasoline, and not telling us how he eats all his meals across the road and all the time his own wife's running it."

"So what do we do? You want to go on to Silver City on those shocks? I don't even know if we got enough money to cover putting shocks on, far as that goes."

We walked around to the front and asked the price of the shocks. He worked it all out with pencil and paper and came up with a figure of forty-five dollars, including the parts and the labor and the tax and all. Newt and I went into another huddle and he counted his money and I went through my own pockets and came up with a couple dollars, and it worked out that we could pay what we owed and get the shocks and come up with three dollars to bless ourselves with.

So I looked at Newt and he gave a great shrug of his shoulders. Close as we are, we can say a lot without speaking.

We told the dude to go ahead and do the work.

While he installed the shocks, me and Newt went across the street and had us a couple of chicken-fried steaks. They wasn't bad at all even if the price was on the high side. We washed them down with a beer apiece and then each of us had a cup of that coffee. I guess there's been times I had better coffee.

"I'd say you fellows sure were lucky you stopped here," the woman said.

"It's our lucky day, all right," Newt said. While he paid her, I looked over the paperback books and magazines. Some of them looked to be old and secondhand but they weren't none of them reduced in price on account of it, and this didn't surprise me much.

What also didn't surprise us was when we got back to find the shocks installed and our friend with his bag hat off and scratching his mop of hair and telling us how the rear shocks was in even worse shape than the front ones. He went and ran the car up in the air again to show us more things that didn't mean much to us.

Newton said, "Well, sir, my brother and I, we talked it over. We figure we been neglecting this here automobile and we really ought to do right by it. If those rear shocks is bad, well, let's just get 'em the hell off of there and new ones on. And while we're here I'm just about positive we're due for an oil change."

"And I'll replace the oil filter while I'm at it."

"You do that," Newt told him. "And I guess you'll find other things that can do with a bit of fixing. Now we haven't got all the time in the world or all the money in the world either, but I guess we got us a pair of hours to spare, and we consider ourselves lucky having the good fortune to run up against a mechanic who knows which end of a wrench is which. So what we'll do, we'll just find us a patch of shade to set in and you check that car over and find things to do to her. Only things that need doing, but I guess you'd be the best judge of that."

Well, I'll tell you he found things to fix. Now and then a car would roll on in and he'd have to go and sell somebody a tank of gas, but we sure got the lion's share of his time. He replaced the air filter, he cleaned the carburetor, he changed the oil and replaced the oil filter, he tuned the engine and drained and flushed the radiator and filled her with fresh coolant. He gave us new plugs and points, he did this and that and every damn thing he could think of, and I guess the only parts of that car he didn't replace were ones he didn't have replacement parts for.

Through it all, Newt and I sat in a patch of shade and sipped Cokes out of the bottle. Every now and then that bird would come over and tell us what else he found that he ought to be doing, and we'd look at each other and shrug our shoulders and say for him to go ahead and do what had to be done.

"Amazing what was wrong with that car of ours," Newt said to me. "Here I thought it rode pretty good."

"Hell, I pulled in here wanting nothing in the world but a tank of gas. Maybe a quart of oil, and oil was the one thing in the world we didn't need, or it looks like."

"Should ride a whole lot better once he's done with it."

"Well, I guess it should. Man's building a whole new car around the cigarette lighter."

"And the clock. Nothing wrong with that clock, outside of it loses a few minutes a day."

"Lord," Newt said, "don't you be telling him about those few minutes the clock loses. We won't never get out of here."

That dude took the two hours we gave him and about twelve minutes besides, and then he came on over into the shade and presented us with his bill. It was all neatly itemized, everything listed in the right place. All of it added up and the figure in the bottom right-hand corner with the circle around it read $277.45.

"That there is quite a number," I said.

He put the big hat on the back of his head and ran his hand over his forehead. "Whole lot of work involved," he said. "When you take into account all of those parts and all that labor."

"Oh, that's for certain," Newt said. "And I can see they all been taken into account all right."

"That's clear as black and white," I said. "One thing, you couldn't call this a nickel and dime figure."

"That you couldn't," Newton said. "Well, sir, let me just go and get some money from the car. Vern?"

We walked over to the car together. "Funny how things work out," Vern said. "I swear people get forced into things, I just swear to hell and gone they do. What did either of us want beside a tank of gas?"

"Just a tank of gas is all."

"And here we are," he said. He opened the door on the passenger side, waited for a pickup truck to pass going west to east, then popped the glove compartment. He took the .38 for himself and gave me the .32 revolver. "I'll just settle up with our good buddy here," he said, loud enough for the good buddy in question to hear him. "Meanwhile, why don't you just step across the street and pick us up something to drink later on this evening? You never know, might turn out to be a long ways between liquor stores."

I went and gave him a little punch in the upper arm. He laughed the way he does and I put the .32 in my pocket and trotted on across the road to the café.

Puppet Show

Fredric Brown

Horror came to Cherrybell at a little after noon on a blistering hot day in August.

Perhaps that is redundant; *any* August day in Cherrybell, Arizona, is blistering hot. It is on Highway 89, about 40 miles south of Tucson and about 30 miles north of the Mexican border. It consists of two filling stations, one on each side of the road to catch travelers going in both directions, a general store, a beer-and-wine-license-only tavern, a tourist-trap-type trading post for tourists who can't wait until they reach the border to start buying serapes and huaraches, a deserted hamburger stand, and a few 'dobe houses inhabited by Mexican-Americans who work in Nogales, the border town to the south, and who, for God knows what reason, prefer to live in Cherrybell and commute, some of them in Model T Fords. The sign on the highway says, CHERRYBELL, POP. 42, but the sign exaggerates; Pop died last year—Pop Anders, who ran the now deserted hamburger stand—and the correct figure should be 41.

Horror came to Cherrybell mounted on a burro led by an ancient, dirty and gray-bearded desert rat of a prospector who later gave the name of Dade Grant. Horror's name was Garvane. He was approximately nine feet tall but so thin, almost a stick-man, that he could not have weighed over a hundred pounds. Old Dade's burro carried him easily, despite the fact that his feet dragged in the sand on either side. Being dragged through the sand for, as it later turned out, well over five miles hadn't caused the slightest wear on the shoes—more like buskins, they were—which constituted all that he wore except for a pair of what could have been swimming trunks, in robin's-egg blue. But it wasn't his dimensions that made him horrible to look upon; it was his *skin*. It looked red, raw. It looked as though he had been skinned alive, and the skin replaced raw side out. His skull, his face, were equally narrow or elongated; otherwise in every visible way he appeared human—or at least humanoid. Unless you count such little things as the fact that his hair was a robin's-egg blue to match his trunks, as were his eyes and his boots. Blood red and light blue.

Casey, owner of the tavern, was the first one to see them coming across the plain, from the direction of the mountain range to the east. He'd stepped out of the back door of his tavern for a breath of fresh, if hot, air. They were about 100 yards away at that time, and already he could see the utter alienness of the figure on the led burro. Just alienness at that distance, the horror came only at closer range. Casey's jaw dropped and stayed down until the strange trio was about 50 yards away, then he started slowly toward them. There are people who run at the sight of the unknown, others who advance to meet it. Casey advanced, slowly, to meet it.

Still in the wide open, 20 yards from the back of the little tavern, he met them. Dade Grant stopped and dropped the rope by which he was leading the burro. The burro stood still and dropped its head. The stick-man stood up simply by planting his feet solidly and standing, astride the burro. He stepped one leg across it and stood a moment, leaning his weight against his hands on the burro's back, and then sat down in the sand. "High gravity planet," he said. "Can't stand long."

"Kin I get water fer my burro?" the prospector asked Casey. "Must be purty thirsty by now. Hadda leave water bags, some other things, so it could carry—" He jerked a thumb toward the red-and-blue horror.

Casey was just realizing that it *was* a horror. At a distance the color combination seemed only mildly hideous, but close up—the skin was rough and seemed to have veins on the outside and looked moist (although it wasn't) and *damn* if it didn't look just like he had his skin peeled off and put back on inside out. Or just peeled off, period. Casey had never seen anything like it and hoped he wouldn't ever see anything like it again.

Casey felt something behind him and looked over his shoulder. Others had seen now and were coming, but the nearest of them, a pair of boys, were ten yards behind him. *"Muchachos,"* he called out. *"Agua por el burro. Un pozal. Pronto."*

He looked back and said, "What—? Who—?"

"Name's Dade Grant," said the prospector, putting out a hand, which Casey took absently. When he let go of it it jerked back over the desert rat's shoulder, thumb indicating the thing that sat on the sand. *"His* name's Garvane, he tells me. He's an extra something or other, and he's some kind of minister."

Casey nodded at the stick-man and was glad to get a nod in return instead of an extended hand. "I'm Manuel Casey," he said. "What does he mean, an extra something?"

The stick-man's voice was unexpectedly deep and vibrant. "I am an extraterrestrial. And a minister plenipotentiary."

Surprisingly, Casey was a moderately well-educated man and knew both of those phrases; he was probably the only person in Cherrybell who would have known the second one. Less surprisingly, considering the speaker's appearance, he believed both of them.

"What can I do for you, sir?" he asked. "But first, why not come in out of the sun?"

"No, thank you. It's a bit cooler here than they told me it would be, but I'm quite comfortable. This is equivalent to a cool spring evening on my planet. And as to what you can do for me, you can notify your authorities of my presence. I believe they will be interested."

Well, Casey thought, by blind luck he's hit the best man for his purpose within at least 20 miles. Manuel Casey was half Irish, half Mexican. He had a half-brother who was half Irish and half assorted-American, and the half-brother was a bird colonel at Davis-Monthan Air Force Base in Tucson.

He said, "Just a minute, Mr. Garvane, I'll telephone. You, Mr. Grant, would you want to come inside?"

"Naw, I don't mind sun. Out in it all day ever' day. An' Garvane here, he ast me if I'd stick with him till he was finished with what he's gotta do here. Said he'd gimme somethin' purty vallable if I did. Somethin'—a 'lectrononic—"

"An electronic battery-operated portable ore indicator," Garvane said. "A simple little device, indicates presence of a concentration of ore up to two miles, indicates kind, grade, quantity and depth."

Casey gulped, excused himself, and pushed through the gathering crowd into his tavern. He had Colonel Casey on the phone in one minute, but it took him another four minutes to convince the colonel that he was neither drunk nor joking.

Twenty-five minutes after that there was a noise in the sky, a noise that swelled and then died as a four-man helicopter sat down and shut off its rotors a dozen yards from an extraterrestrial, two men and a burro. Casey alone had had the courage to rejoin the trio from the desert; there were other spectators, but they still held well back.

Colonel Casey, a major, a captain and a lieutenant who was the helicopter's pilot all came out and ran over. The stick-man stood up, all nine feet of him; from the effort it cost him to stand you could tell that he was used to a much lighter gravity than Earth's. He bowed, repeated his name and the identification of himself as an extraterrestrial and a minister plenipotentiary. Then he apologized for sitting down again, explained why it was necessary, and sat down.

The colonel introduced himself and the three who had come with him. "And now, sir, what can we do for you?"

The stick-man made a grimace that was probably intended as a smile. His teeth were the same light blue as his hair and eyes.

"You have a cliché, 'Take me to your leader.' I do not ask that. In fact, I *must* remain here. Nor do I ask that any of your leaders be brought here to me. That would be impolite. I am perfectly willing for you to represent them, to talk to you and let you question me. But I do ask one thing.

"You have tape recorders. I ask that before I talk or answer questions you have one brought. I want to be sure that the message your leaders eventually receive is full and accurate."

"Fine," the colonel said. He turned to the pilot. "Lieutenant, get on the radio in the whirlybird and tell them to get us a tape recorder faster than possible. It can be dropped by para— No, that'd take longer, rigging it for a drop. Have them send it by another helicopter." The lieutenant turned to go. "Hey," the colonel said. "Also 50 yards of extension cord. We'll have to plug it in inside Manny's tavern."

The lieutenant sprinted for the helicopter.

The others sat and sweated a moment and then Manuel Casey stood up. "That's a half-an-hour wait," he said, "and if we're going to sit here in the sun, who's for a bottle of cold beer? You, Mr. Garvane?"

"It is a cold beverage, is it not? I am a bit chilly. If you have something hot—?"

"Coffee, coming up. Can I bring you a blanket?"

"No, thank you. It will not be necessary."

Casey left and shortly returned with a tray with half-a-dozen bottles of cold beer and a cup of steaming coffee. The lieutenant was back by then. Casey put the tray down and served the stick-man first, who sipped the coffee and said, "It is delicious."

Colonel Casey cleared his throat, "Serve our prospector friend next, Manny. As for us—well, drinking is forbidden on duty, but it was 112 in the shade in Tucson, and this is hotter and also is *not* in the shade. Gentlemen, consider yourselves on official leave for as long as it takes you to drink one bottle of beer, or until the tape recorder arrives, whichever comes first."

The beer was finished first, but by the time the last of it had vanished, the second helicopter was within sight and sound. Casey asked the stick-man if he wanted more coffee. The offer was politely declined. Casey looked at Dade Grant and winked and the desert rat winked back, so Casey went in for two more bottles, one apiece for the civilian terrestrials. Coming back he met the lieutenant arriving with the extension cord and returned as far as the doorway to show him where to plug it in.

When he came back, he saw that the second helicopter had brought its full complement of four, besides the tape recorder. There were, besides the pilot who had flown it, a technical sergeant who was skilled in its operation and who was now making adjustments on it, and a lieutenant-colonel and a warrant officer who had come along for the ride or because they had been made curious by the *request* for a tape recorder to be rushed to Cherrybell, Arizona, by air. They were standing gaping at the stick-man and whispered conversations were going on.

The colonel said, "Attention" quietly, but it brought complete silence. "Please sit down, gentlemen. In a rough circle. Sergeant, if you rig your mike in the center of the circle, will it pick up clearly what any one of us may say?"

"Yes, sir. I'm almost ready."

Ten men and one extraterrestrial humanoid sat in a rough circle, with the microphone hanging from a small tripod in the approximate center. The humans were sweating profusely; the humanoid shivered slightly. Just outside the circle, the burro stood dejectedly, its head low. Edging closer, but still about five yards away, spread out now in a semicircle, was the entire population of Cherrybell who had been at home at the time; the stores and the filling stations were deserted.

The technical sergeant pushed a button and the tape recorder's reel started to turn. "Testing . . . testing," he said. He held down the rewind button for a second and then pushed the playback button. "Testing . . . testing," said the recorder's speaker. Loud and clear. The sergeant pushed the rewind button, then the erase one to clear the tape. Then the stop button.

"When I push the next button, sir," he said to the colonel, "we'll be recording."

The colonel looked at the tall extraterrestrial, who nodded, and then the colonel nodded at the sergeant. The sergeant pushed the recording button.

"My name is Garvane," said the stick-man, slowly and clearly. "I am from a planet of a star which is not listed in your star catalogs, although the globular cluster in which it is one of 90,000 stars is known to you. It is, from here, in the direction of the center of the galaxy at a distance of over 4000 light-years.

"However, I am not here as a representative of my planet or my people, but as minister plenipotentiary of the Galactic Union, a federation of the enlightened civilizations of the galaxy, for the good of all. It is my assignment to visit you and decide, here and now, whether or not you are to be welcomed to join our federation.

"You may now ask questions freely. However, I reserve the right to postpone answering some of them until my decision has been made. If the decision is favorable, I will then answer all questions, including the ones I have postponed answering meanwhile. Is that satisfactory?"

"Yes," said the colonel. "How did you come here? A spaceship?"

"Correct. It is overhead right now, in orbit 22,000 miles out, so it revolves with the earth and stays over this one spot. I am under observation from it, which is one reason I prefer to remain here in the open. I am to signal it when I want it to come down to pick me up."

"How do you know our language so fluently? Are you telepathic?"

"No, I am not. And nowhere in the galaxy is any race telepathic except among its own members. I was taught your language for this purpose. We have had observers among you for many centuries—by *we*, I mean the Galactic Union, of course. Quite obviously, I could not pass as an Earthman, but there are other races who can. Incidentally, they are not spies, or agents; they have in no way tried to affect you; they are observers and that is all."

"What benefits do we get from joining your union, if we are asked and if we accept?" the colonel asked.

"First, a quick course in the fundamental social sciences which will end your tendency to fight among yourselves and end or at least control your aggressions. After we are satisfied that you have accomplished that and it is safe for you to do so, you will be given space travel, and many other things, as rapidly as you are able to assimilate them."

"And if we are not asked, or refuse?"

"Nothing. You will be left alone; even our observers will be withdrawn. You will work out your own fate—either you will render your planet uninhabited and uninhabitable within the next century, or you will master social science yourselves and again be candidates for membership and again be offered membership. We will check from time to time and if and when it appears certain that you are not going to destroy yourselves, you will again be approached."

"Why the hurry, now that you're here? Why can't you stay long enough for our leaders, as you call them, to talk to you in person?"

"Postponed. The reason is not important but it is complicated, and I simply do not wish to waste time explaining."

"Assuming your decision is favorable, how will we get in touch with you to let you know *our* decision? You know enough about us, obviously, to know that *I* can't make it."

"We will know your decision through our observers. One condition of acceptance is full and uncensored publication in your newspapers of this interview, verbatim from the tape we are now using to record it. Also of all deliberations and decisions of your government."

"And other governments? We can't decide unilaterally for the world."

"Your government has been chosen for a start. If you accept, we shall furnish the techniques that will cause the others to fall in line quickly—and those techniques do not involve force or the threat of force."

"They must be *some* techniques," said the colonel wryly, "if they'll make one certain country I don't have to name fall into line without even a threat."

"Sometimes the offer of reward is more significant than the use of a threat. Do you think the country you do not wish to name would like your country colonizing planets of far stars before they even reach the moon? But that is a minor point, relatively. You may trust the techniques."

"It sounds almost too good to be true. But you said that you are to decide, here and now, whether or not we are to be invited to join. May I ask on what factors you will base your decision?"

"One is that I am—was, since I already have—to check your degree of xenophobia. In the loose sense in which you use it, that means fear of strangers. We have a word that has no counterpart in your vocabulary: it means fear of and revulsion towards *aliens*. I—or at least a member of my race—was chosen to make the first overt contact with you. Because I am what you would call roughly humanoid—as you are what I would call roughly humanoid—I am probably more horrible, more repulsive, to you than many completely different species would be. Because to you I am a caricature of a human being, I am more horrible to you than a being who bears no remote resemblance to you.

"You may think you *do* feel horror at me, and revulsion, but believe me, you have passed that test. There *are* races in the galaxy who can never be members of the federation, no matter how they advance otherwise, because they are violently and incurably xenophobic; they could never face or talk to an alien of any species. They would either run screaming from him or try to kill him instantly. From watching you and these people"—he waved a long arm at the civilian population of Cherrybell not far outside the circle of the conference—"I know you feel revulsion at the sight of me, but believe me, it is relatively slight and certainly curable. You have passed that test satisfactorily."

"And are there other tests?"

"One other. But I think it is time that I—" Instead of finishing the sentence, the stick-man lay back flat on the sand and closed his eyes.

The colonel started to his feet. "What in *hell?*" he said. He walked quickly around the mike's tripod and bent over the recumbent extraterrestrial, putting an ear to the bloody-appearing chest.

As he raised his head, Dade Grant, the grizzled prospector, chuckled. "No heartbeat, Colonel, because no heart. But I may leave him as a souvenir for you and you'll find much more interesting things inside him than heart and guts. Yes, he is a puppet whom I have been operating, as your Edgar Bergen operates his—what's his name?—oh yes, Charlie McCarthy. Now that he has served his purpose, he is deactivated. You can go back to your place, Colonel."

Colonel Casey moved back slowly. "*Why?*" he asked.

Dade Grant was peeling off his beard and wig. He rubbed a cloth across his face to remove makeup and was revealed as a handsome young man. He said, "What he told you, or what you were told through him, was true as far as it went. He is only a simulacrum, yes, but he is an exact duplicate of a member of one of the intelligent races of the galaxy, the one toward whom you would be disposed—if you were violently and incurably xenophobic—to be most horrified by, according to our psychologists. But we did not bring a real member of his species to make first contact because they have a phobia of their own, agoraphobia—fear of space. They are highly civilized and members in good standing of the federation, but they never leave their own planet.

"Our observers assure us you don't have *that* phobia. But they were unable to judge in advance the degree of your xenophobia, and the only way to test it was to bring along something in lieu of someone to test it against, and presumably to let him make the initial contact."

The colonel sighed audibly. "I can't say this doesn't relieve me in one way. We could get along with humanoids, yes, and we will when we have to. But I'll admit it's a relief to learn that the master race of the galaxy is, after all, human instead of only humanoid. What is the second test?"

"You are undergoing it now. Call me—" He snapped his fingers. "What's the name of Bergen's second-string puppet, after Charlie McCarthy?"

The colonel hesitated, but the tech sergeant supplied the answer. "Mortimer Snerd."

"Right. So call me Mortimer Snerd, and now I think it is time that I—" He lay back flat on the sand and closed his eyes just as the stick-man had done a few minutes before.

The burro raised its head and put it into the circle over the shoulder of the tech sergeant.

"That takes care of the puppets, Colonel," it said. "And now, what's this bit about it being important that the master race be human or at least humanoid? What is a master race?"

De Mortuis . . .

John Collier

Dr. Rankin was a large and rawboned man on whom the newest
suit at once appeared outdated, like a suit in a photograph of
twenty years ago. This was due to the squareness and flatness of his
torso, which might have been put together by a manufacturer of
packing cases. His face also had a wooden and a roughly con-
structed look; his hair was wiglike and resentful of the comb. He
had those huge and clumsy hands which can be an asset to a doctor
in a small upstate town where people still retain a rural relish for
paradox, thinking that the more apelike the paw, the more precise
it can be in the delicate business of a tonsillectomy.

This conclusion was perfectly justified in the case of Dr. Rankin.
For example, on this particular fine morning, though his task was
nothing more ticklish than the cementing over of a large patch on
his cellar floor, he managed those large and clumsy hands with all
the unflurried certainty of one who would never leave a sponge
within or create an unsightly scar without.

The Doctor surveyed his handiwork from all angles. He added a
touch here and a touch there till he had achieved a smoothness altogether professional. He swept up a few last crumbs of soil and
dropped them into the furnace. He paused before putting away the
pick and shovel he had been using, and found occasion for yet another artistic sweep of his trowel, which made the new surface pre-

cisely flush with the surrounding floor. At this moment of supreme concentration the porch door upstairs slammed with the report of a minor piece of artillery, which, appropriately enough, caused Dr. Rankin to jump as if he had been shot.

The Doctor lifted a frowning face and an attentive ear. He heard two pairs of heavy feet clump across the resonant floor of the porch. He heard the house door opened and the visitors enter the hall, with which his cellar communicated by a short flight of steps. He heard whistling and then the voices of Buck and Bud crying, "Doc! Hi, Doc! They're biting!"

Whether the Doctor was not inclined for fishing that day, or whether, like others of his large and heavy type, he experienced an especially sharp, unsociable reaction on being suddenly startled, or whether he was merely anxious to finish undisturbed the job in hand and proceed to more important duties, he did not respond immediately to the inviting outcry of his friends. Instead, he listened while it ran its natural course, dying down at last into a puzzled and fretful dialogue.

"I guess he's out."

"I'll write a note—say we're at the creek, to come on down."

"We could tell Irene."

"But she's not here, either. You'd think *she'd* be around."

"Ought to be, by the look of the place."

"You said it, Bud. Just look at this table. You could write your name—"

"Sh-h-h! Look!"

Evidently the last speaker had noticed that the cellar door was ajar and that a light was shining below. Next moment the door was pushed wide open and Bud and Buck looked down.

"Why, Doc! There you are!"

"Didn't you hear us yelling?"

The Doctor, not too pleased at what he had overheard, nevertheless smiled his rather wooden smile as his two friends made their way down the steps. "I thought I heard someone," he said.

"We was bawling our heads off," Buck said. "Thought nobody was home. Where's Irene?"

"Visiting," said the Doctor. "She's gone visiting."

"Hey, what goes on?" said Bud. "What are you doing? Burying one of your patients, or what?"

"Oh, there's been water seeping up through the floor," said the

Doctor. "I figured it might be some spring opened up or something."

"You don't say!" said Bud, assuming instantly the high ethical standpoint of the realtor. "Gee, Doc, I sold you this property. Don't say I fixed you up with a dump where there's an underground spring."

"There was water," said the Doctor.

"Yes, but, Doc, you can look on that geological map the Kiwanis Club got up. There's not a better section of subsoil in the town."

"Looks like he sold you a pup," said Buck, grinning.

"No," said Bud. "Look. When the Doc came here he was green. You'll admit he was green. The things he didn't know!"

"He bought Ted Webber's jalopy," said Buck.

"He'd have bought the Jessop place if I'd let him," said Bud. "But I wouldn't give him a bum steer."

"Not the poor, simple city slicker from Poughkeepsie," said Buck.

"Some people would have taken him," said Bud. "Maybe some people did. Not me. I recommended this property. He and Irene moved straight in as soon as they was married. I wouldn't have put the Doc on to a dump where there'd be a spring under the foundations."

"Oh, forget it," said the Doctor, embarrassed by this conscientiousness. "I guess it was just the heavy rains."

"By gosh!" Buck said, glancing at the besmeared point of the pickaxe. "You certainly went deep enough. Right down into the clay, huh?"

"That's four feet down, the clay," Bud said.

"Eighteen inches," said the Doctor.

"Four feet," said Bud. "I can show you on the map."

"Come on. No arguments," said Buck. "How's about it, Doc? An hour or two at the creek, eh? They're biting."

"Can't do it, boys," said the Doctor. "I've got to see a patient or two."

"Aw, live and let live, Doc," Bud said. "Give 'em a chance to get better. Are you going to depopulate the whole darn town?"

The Doctor looked down, smiled, and muttered, as he always did when this particular jest was trotted out. "Sorry, boys," he said. "I can't make it."

"Well," said Bud, disappointed, "I suppose we'd better get along. How's Irene?"

"Irene?" said the Doctor. "Never better. She's gone visiting. Albany. Got the eleven-o'clock train."

"Eleven o'clock?" said Buck. "For Albany?"

"Did I say Albany?" said the Doctor. "Watertown, I meant."

"Friends in Watertown?" Buck asked.

"Mrs. Slater," said the Doctor. "Mr. and Mrs. Slater. Lived next door to 'em when she was a kid, Irene said, over on Sycamore Street."

"Slater?" said Bud. "Next door to Irene. No."

"Oh, yes," said the Doctor. "She was telling me all about them last night. She got a letter. Seems this Mrs. Slater looked after her when her mother was in the hospital one time."

"No," said Bud.

"That's what she told me," said the Doctor. "Of course, it was a good many years ago."

"Look, Doc," said Buck. "Bud and I were raised in this town. We've known Irene's folks all our lives. We were in and out of their house all the time. There was never anybody next door called Slater."

"Perhaps," said the Doctor, "she married again, this woman. Perhaps it was a different name."

Bud shook his head.

"What time did Irene go to the station?" Buck asked.

"Oh, about a quarter of an hour ago," said the Doctor.

"You didn't drive her?" said Buck.

"She walked," said the Doctor.

"We came down Main Street," Buck said. "We didn't meet her."

"Maybe she walked across the pasture," said the Doctor.

"That's a tough walk with a suitcase," said Buck.

"She just had a couple of things in a little bag," said the Doctor.

Bud was still shaking his head.

Buck looked at Bud, and then at the pick, at the new, damp cement on the floor. "Jesus Christ!" he said.

"Oh, God, Doc!" Bud said. "A guy like you!"

"What in the name of heaven are you two bloody fools thinking?" asked the Doctor. "What are you trying to say?"

"A spring!" said Bud. "I ought to have known right away it wasn't any spring."

The Doctor looked at his cement-work, at the pick, at the large

worried faces of his two friends. His own face turned livid. "Am I
crazy?" he said. "Or are you? You suggest that I've—that Irene—my
wife—oh, go on! Get out! Yes, go and get the sheriff. Tell him to
come here and start digging. You—get out!"

Bud and Buck looked at each other, shifted their feet, and stood
still again.

"Go on," said the Doctor.

"I don't know," said Bud.

"It's not as if he didn't have the provocation," Buck said.

"God knows," Bud said.

"God knows," Buck said. "You know. I know. The whole town
knows. But try telling it to a jury."

The Doctor put his hand to his head. "What's that?" he said.
"What is it? Now what are you saying? What do you mean?"

"If this ain't being on the spot!" said Buck. "Doc, you can see
how it is. It takes some thinking. We've been friends right from the
start. Damn good friends."

"But we've got to think," said Bud. "It's serious. Provocation or
not, there's a law in the land. There's such a thing as being an ac-
complice."·

"You were talking about provocation," said the Doctor.

"You're right," said Buck. "And you're our friend. And if ever it
could be called justified—"

"We've got to fix this somehow," said Bud.

"Justified?" said the Doctor.

"You were bound to get wised up sooner or later," said Buck.

"We could have told you," said Bud. "Only—what the hell?"

"We could," said Buck. "And we nearly did. Five years ago. Before ever you married her. You hadn't been here six months, but we
sort of cottoned to you. Thought of giving you a hint. Spoke about
it. Remember, Bud?"

Bud nodded, "Funny," he said. "I came right out in the open
about that Jessop property. I wouldn't let you buy that, Doc. But
getting married, that's something else again. We could have told
you."

"We're that much responsible," Buck said.

"I'm fifty," said the Doctor. "I suppose it's pretty old for Irene."

"If you was Johnny Weissmuller at the age of twenty-one, it
wouldn't make any difference," said Buck.

"I know a lot of people think she's not exactly a perfect wife," said the Doctor. "Maybe she's not. She's young. She's full of life."

"Oh, skip it!" said Buck sharply, looking at the raw cement. "Skip it, Doc, for God's sake."

The Doctor brushed his hand across his face. "Not everybody wants the same thing," he said. "I'm a sort of dry fellow. I don't open up very easily. Irene—you'd call her gay."

"You said it," said Buck.

"She's no housekeeper," said the Doctor. "I know it. But that's not the only thing a man wants. She's enjoyed herself."

"Yeah," said Buck. "She did."

"That's what I love," said the Doctor. "Because I'm not that way myself. She's not very deep, mentally. All right. Say she's stupid. I don't care. Lazy. No system. Well, I've got plenty of system. She's enjoyed herself. It's beautiful. It's innocent. Like a child."

"Yes. If that was all," Buck said.

"But," said the Doctor, turning his eyes full on him, "you seem to know there was more."

"Everybody knows it," said Buck.

"A decent, straightforward guy comes to a place like this and marries the town floozy," Bud said bitterly. "And nobody'll tell him. Everybody just watches."

"And laughs," said. Buck. "You and me, Bud, as well as the rest."

"We told her to watch her step," said Bud. "We warned her."

"Everybody warned her," said Buck. "But people get fed up. When it got to truck-drivers—"

"It was never us, Doc," said Bud, earnestly. "Not after you came along, anyway."

"The town'll be on your side," said Buck.

"That won't mean much when the case comes to trial in the county seat," said Bud.

"Oh!" cried the Doctor, suddenly. "What shall I do? What shall I do?"

"It's up to you, Bud," said Buck. "I can't turn him in."

"Take it easy, Doc," said Bud. "Calm down. Look, Buck. When we came in here the street was empty, wasn't it?"

"I guess so," said Buck. "Anyway, nobody saw us come down cellar."

"And we haven't been down," Bud said, addressing himself forcefully to the Doctor. "Get that, Doc? We shouted upstairs, hung around a minute or two, and cleared out. But we never came down into this cellar."

"I wish you hadn't," the Doctor said heavily.

"All you have to do is say Irene went out for a walk and never came back," said Buck. "Bud and I can swear we saw her headed out of town with a fellow in a tan roadster. Everybody'll believe that, all right. We'll fix it. But later. Now we'd better scram."

"And remember. We was never down here," Bud said. "So long."

Buck and Bud ascended the steps, moving with a rather absurd degree to caution. "You'd better get that . . . that thing covered up," Buck said over his shoulder.

Left alone, the Doctor sat down on an empty box, holding his head with both hands. He was still sitting like this when the porch door slammed again. This time he did not start. He listened. The house door opened and closed. A voice cried, "Yoo-hoo! Yoo-hoo! I'm back."

The Doctor rose slowly to his feet. "I'm down here, Irene!" he called.

The cellar door opened. A young woman stood at the head of the steps. "Can you beat it?" she said. "I missed the damn train."

"Oh!" said the Doctor. "Did you come back across the field?"

"Yes, like a fool," she said. "I could have hitched a ride and caught the train up the line. Only I didn't think. If you'd run me over to the junction, I could still make it."

"Maybe," said the Doctor. "Did you meet anyone coming back?"

"Not a soul," she said. "Aren't you finished with that old job yet?"

"I'm afraid I'll have to take it all up again," said the Doctor. "Come down here, my dear, and I'll show you."

Snowball

Ursula Curtiss

The cottage had had a gingerbread look in the last of the afternoon light: snow in a steep frosting on its tilted roof, frost rimming its small windowpanes. I remember now that we knocked, both secretly knowing the absurdity of it, and that walking into that livingroom was as shocking as opening a Christmas card to find an obscene verse inside.

It wasn't only the blood on the floorboards, or the brass gleam of the poker standing primly at attention on the hearth. Part of it was the table set for tea at the shadowy end of the room—napkins folded, teapot in a quilted cosy, crusts of bread in a savage litter on the braided rug. And on the window sill in the alcove, like a travesty of domestic comfort, the cat, Snowball.

Beside me, Madden called in his high irritable voice, "Charles?" and in the same split second I shouted, "Anne?"

That was symbolic. Both of us knew that only one of the Jethros could possibly answer, the one who had killed the other.

It's hard to explain about the Jethros. Even Madden, who had been Charles Jethro's literary agent for eighteen years, confessed himself baffled. Maybe that was because each of them had two separate personalities, which made a total of four people living together for twenty years.

You may have read some of Jethro's essays, or attended one of the gatherings at which he was in constant demand as a speaker.

He was a big man, about fifty, and handsome in a craggy disarming way. He was sensitive about his failing eyesight and never wore his thick glasses in public, but somehow he contrived a keen and twinkling air when he spoke at what must have been an indistinguishable blur. He had made two successful departures into the field of verse. *Broiled Offerings*, a sizzling parody of the obscurist school of poetry, was followed by *Puzzles in Smoke*, which the enlightened public bought with great anticipation and the critics circled as warily as a strange dog, because it might or might not be another parody.

That was the Charles Jethro who sparkled at select cocktail parties and wrote witty inscriptions in his books for favored friends. You had to have known him a long time to be even acquainted with the brutal, vindictive, incredibly foul-tempered man who shared the same skin.

His wife Anne, who was perhaps five years younger than he, was his right hand, his amanuensis, his quietly unerring critic. Someone had been unkind enough to call her his seeing-eye bitch; I often wondered if Jethro himself had thought that up. She was one of those willfully neglected-looking women, with tweeds that never quite fitted and tan hair trained back into a knot. Somewhere in her family there had been an admixture of some surprising blood; her mouth was heavy and her eyes as unfathomable as black bean soup. She did Jethro's typing—he would trust it to no one else—and kept him to deadlines and defended him from nuisances like a tigress when he was working.

But the steadiness and the constancy had its other side. No one could bear a grudge as implacably as Anne Jethro, or seethe as long, with the lid on tight, like some dangerous stew. When her hand was forced there was usually a hatpin inside—like the time when Jethro had insisted on her entertaining a trio of visiting Englishwomen at tea, and she had docilely cut watercress sandwiches and plum cake. Opened up, the dainty little napkins revealed, in indelible ink, an unrepeatable phrase about Jethro.

"Charles?" called Madden again from the foot of the stairs, and turned back to me. He said, as though he could hold something at bay by his disapproval, "I don't like this at all, I believe I'll have a look upstairs. I wish that damned cat wouldn't sit there like that."

The cat, Snowball, was a pledge of Jethro's malice towards his wife just as certainly as a diamond pin was a pledge of another man's affection. Anne hated and feared cats with the same violent reaction women usually reserve for rats, and I had seen her driven from the room more than once by this one. Jethro had taken it in as a stray, and named it sardonically—if he had adopted a dog he would have insisted on calling it Fido—and while he caviled at Anne's housekeeping expenditures he fed it on salmon and sardines. He took a perverse delight in its greed and selfishness and haughty tail-switchings, for the simple reason that the cat repelled and frightened his wife.

Because the Jethros hated each other.

Why did they stay together? Their few close friends advanced various theories. They were used to each other, they were actually stimulated by their weird domestic battles, Charles needed Anne emotionally and Anne was financially dependent on Charles—and so forth.

Madden was much too clever to say anything that might be quoted behind his back, but I had always thought it was *because* at bottom they hated each other, and were bound in a mutual pact of revenge. Charles twisted Anne's wrist in one of his ungovernable tempers, and Anne—silent, implacable—hid his glasses for a week while he begged piteously for them. Or Charles hid his glasses himself as an excuse for not making out a cheque for Anne's housekeeping money, and Anne marched off to the nearest pawnshop with his mother's heirloom silver.

People who knew them laughed over these colorful irregularities—"Did you know Jethro hit Anne with one of those baked-bean casseroles?" "No, really? I thought she smashed them all the night those people from Boston came to dinner"—and any uneasiness they felt was slight. Charles could somehow emerge from one of these sessions at his blandest and wittiest, and Anne, sometimes nursing a wrist or a shin, would be calm and helpful with autograph seekers.

But then they had moved to Byfield, the two of them—or the four of them?—into the snows and the silences and the confines of a cottage deep in the country, on the estate of a friend of Jethro's. The move had been partly Madden's idea, to coax out an evaluation of Joyce: Jethro on Joyce, he said in an authoritative squeak, would set the literary world by the ears.

But—the snows, the silence, the very aloneness. No friends dropping in, no convivial engagements outside to break into that tiny, too closely-bound world. Anne and Jethro both had the profoundest respect for Jethro's ability, but that wasn't enough. There was nothing to stimulate Jethro into being bland and witty, or Anne into shelving her grudges; nothing to check the outbreak of rage, and everything to feed it. I had visited them once for an hour or two on the way down from Boston, and I went away feeling as though I had gotten out of a lion's cage. Bare trees and frozen shrubs in burlap and the whistling bitter wind aren't for people who hate each other, with no one to see what they do about it. It was as if something had begun to snowball.

The cat—had Jethro named her more originally than he thought? —watched me complacently as I started out of the living room. Upstairs, Madden was clumping about with the heavy tread common to small men who want to make their weight felt. I walked into the tiny old-fashioned kitchen, but there was nothing there to tell me anything, even if the dusk hadn't begun to close in. The surfaces were bare, the wooden cabinets closed and blank; the black stove Anne had joked about was cold when I touched it.

That would make it—how long since Anne had killed Charles, or Charles had killed Anne?

Madden came downstairs again, tiptoeing solemnly. In spite of his superbly cut cashmere suit and his glowing foulard tie he looked old and cold and worried; for all his petulant squeakings and his ruthless determination to get a book out of his client, he had been fond of Jethro—and Jethro guilty of murder would be in almost as bad a pickle as Jethro dead. He said irritably, "Turn on a light, will you? I suppose we'll have to call the police."

"You'll have to call very loudly then," I said, as jumpy as he was. "The lights are out and so is the phone. All this white stuff is a blizzard, Madden. They get them in the country. We'll have to drive into the village."

"You go," said Madden, making a large gesture for so small a man. "There are candles somewhere, I suppose, and I'll know where to look for his notes and manuscript and things. My God, we don't want the manuscript impounded. Poor Charles."

"Or poor Anne," I said.

The car wouldn't start. I suppose cars never do under such circumstances, although this wasn't entirely coincidental; Madden, whose car we had driven up from New York in, had in his agitation left the ignition on and the battery was dead.

I scuffled back to the cottage in almost complete darkness, trying to keep to the track we had trampled through the snow when we first arrived. Somewhere under the unmarred surface on either side there had to be other footprints—Jethro's, plunging deeply as he carried Anne's body, or Anne's as she had dragged Jethro's—but snow couldn't be peeled back in layers like blankets.

Madden had found candles when I returned, and set them up on the neat, ghastly tea table. The flickering light reached out to the bloodstains, turning them black and caught a knowing wink from the poker. I told him about the car and he said absently, "Oh," and then in a queer voice, "The manuscript is gone, and all his notes. Eight months' work. She might at least," he said bitterly, "have left us that."

"Jethro may have taken them himself, as—insurance. Anne would have killed the cat," I said. "Jethro wouldn't have."

Snowball watched us noncommittally.

Madden wet his lips. "Anne was probably afraid to kill it, afraid it might spring at her."

"If she killed Jethro she would have killed the cat. As," I said uncomfortably, "part of Jethro. If you follow that."

"I can't say that I do, quite," said Madden snappishly. "The thing is—when?"

What he meant was, how far had one of them gotten with the Joyce manuscript and the notes with which to finish it? Madden had wired Jethro two days ago about an offer from *Harper's* for a series of essays on modern poetry; it was the kind of thing that Jethro would have jumped at, and when a further telephone call— that must have been before the wires went down—produced no response, Madden had gotten worried enough to call me and propose a trip to Byfield.

I suppose an expert could have told from the appearance of the bloodstains how old they were; we were only certain of what they had to mean. But the cat hadn't been ravenous enough to finish the crusts of bread on the floor beneath the tea table, or thirsty enough to overturn the cream jug, so that it must have been fed the day before. Unless—

"You're sure," I said to Madden over a brief stomach-turning, "that there's *nothing* upstairs?"

"I don't know what you mean by nothing," began Madden crossly, engrossed in his own problems, and looked at Snowball, washing her whiskers with a satisfied air, and turned pale. "My God, how can you even—no, of course not."

So that placed the time of death—Anne's, or Jethro's—at just before tea time yesterday. With the snow falling, it would have been dark then, and the electricity had been off. And still there had been blood spilled, the poker wiped and put back—all in the dark?

The candles Madden had found in a drawer were new, just now beginning to form shaky threads of wax. There were no kerosene lamps in the house. I stood up, following the vaguest of thoughts, and Snowball moved too.

Madden recoiled at the sudden soft thump. The cat sniffed at a crust and spurned it, and then stalked in a horribly intent way across the floor towards the bloodstains. When she was nearly there she turned around and began briskly to sharpen her claws on one of the small braided rugs with which the living room was furnished.

And the rugs slid. As Snowball sharpened away, the bloodstains disappeared under the twisting pattern. An instant later I noticed the candles in the sconce on the inside living room wall, pale yellow in a black iron holder, and burned almost halfway down.

Those candles, then, had provided the light for murder. With the rug in place over the stains, anyone entering the cottage as a matter of neighborly concern might think that the Jethros had merely gone away for a few days.

Except for the cat. For Anne, it must have been a symbol of hatred. Jethro, on the other hand, would have left it food and water enough to last it until he could come back—or would he, once it had served its purpose?

I heard Madden saying with the waspishness of deep worry, "Well, what is it?" but I went on staring at the right-hand candle. They both leaned a little out from the wall, but the frozen waterfall of wax on that one was *facing* the wall. So it had been taken out of the sconce.

We stayed in the cottage that night, partly because the only alternative was a four-mile walk through the freezing dark, mostly because the place held a curiously pending air. Possibly that was

Snowball, back on the window sill, staring expectantly out at the night.

Madden had a flask in his luggage and we shared a couple of moody drinks. With the first shock gone the Jethros became again not killer and victim, but friends of long years' standing. Madden's concern was largely for Charles; I kept remembering what intelligent good company Anne could be when she wasn't simmering.

The cottage was bitterly cold, but by mutual consent we kept away from the hearth and the poker. In the kitchen we found more candles, and in the black depths of the refrigerator the remains of a ham. The half-loaf of bread was faintly stale but we were both hungry; Madden, a dedicated gourmet, fell upon his sandwich as though it had been snails in his favorite sauce.

Snowball miaowed angrily in the doorway, and although I had seen Madden gazing speculatively at a can of sardines I put them in a saucer on the floor. When the cat had eaten and retired a short way to wash her face I said, "I suppose we'd better let her out."

"I wouldn't do that," said Madden. He didn't like cats but he had a semi-superstitious respect for them. "I think we ought to be able to see where she goes when she does go out."

There was something frightful in the suggestion of the cat sniffing her way daintily to the corpse, and although it was plain that Madden didn't like it either he said stubbornly, "Didn't Charles have a run for her when they first moved out here?"

There was a short wire-enclosed run behind the cottage; I remembered, on an earlier visit, seeing Snowball batting at the fluffy white flowers on a bush that grew beside it. I opened the kitchen door and ushered her out, and before the wind blew the candle out I saw her vault lightly into the enclosure. She didn't care for the cold or the snow, and she scratched at the door before Madden had finished his second sandwich.

After that there was nothing to do but go to sleep. It didn't occur to either of us to occupy the Jethros' beds. We retired to chairs, covered ourselves with our overcoats, and smoked a final cigarette.

"You know," said Madden suddenly, in the slightly lowered tone we had both used unconsciously ever since entering the cottage, "there wasn't much daylight left to look around in. Maybe there's a note."

I couldn't help but stare. "Out burying body, back soon?"

"It was just a thought," said Madden, looking offended, and blew out the candle.

But there was, after all, something to the suggestion. If the braided rug had been pulled over the bloodstains and the poker and the candle replaced in order to conceal the crime from a casual eye, mightn't there be a note?

Anne was meticulous over details; she would never have put the candle into its holder backwards, so that the flow of wax ran the wrong way. *But nearsighted Charles wouldn't have noticed the way.* Or had Anne thought of that, and acted accordingly?

And was that why Snowball was alive?

It occurred to me on the edge of sleep that, barring the fingerprints which the merest child knew enough not to leave around, it was going to take a little while, even for the police to figure out which of the Jethros was dead and which to spread a dragnet for. They were the same blood type; that had come out years ago when Charles needed a transfusion after a severe operation. Unless there were hairs on the poker, long tan ones, or grey-tipped black—

I closed my eyes in the darkness, trying to wipe out the vision that summoned up, and when I opened them the room was blue with early daylight.

There was no note; Madden looked for one while I made instant coffee with cold water, achieving an indescribable effect. We were both chilled and stiff and edgy, and there was a short sharp discussion over which of us would walk into the village to get the police. Madden won, or lost, whichever way you look at it, and he had his hand on the doorknob when we suddenly stared at each other, struck by one of those weird communications of thought.

I said, "Had you better check the nearest hospital first?"

"My God . . . of course. They got cabin fever, and she hit him—"

"Or he hit her—"

"—and realized that this time it had gone too far," interrupted Madden, waving an impatient hand, "and called a doctor and went off to the hospital. It's as simple as that. What idiots we've been, they've been doing this for years on a minor scale. Maybe it's a good thing, teach them both a lesson. I suppose it's all over the front page of the local paper, but that can't be helped. Well, I'm off, I'll be back as soon as I can."

All this didn't explain the missing manuscript, or the fact that the poker and the candle had been put back so tidily, but it did clear up the pending atmosphere, the presence of the cat and, most important of all, the disappearance of *both* the Jethros. Charles could have carried Anne's body, and Anne could have dragged his, but what to do with it then?

It would have been impossible to dig a grave in that frozen ground even if there had been tools to work with, and the property wasn't furnished with any convenient wells or ravines, or even woods, at any handy distance. It was flat and park-like, with a tree here and there and a scattering of winterized shrubs. There were no masses of rhododendrons or pines to offer any kind of concealment.

An embargo had been lifted, and I let Snowball out and followed her into the brilliant morning. Maybe Madden was right and this would be a lesson to the Jethros, like delirium tremens to a drinker or an accident to a careless driver. It should certainly teach them to stick to bean casseroles instead of pokers.

Snowball jumped up on the kitchen steps and began a protracted bath; she paused briefly to measure a distant sparrow and then went back to her plumy tail. Beyond her was the wire run, the wrapped bush that bore white flowers in the spring, and a lot of greyish twiggy growth. Bayberry? I knew that it grew around here; Anne was fond of it.

It wasn't bayberry, and it wasn't growing. It looked at first like a tree bough blown down by the wind, but it wasn't that either because the end had been sawed cleanly through.

I suppose I knew what it was then, and why the cat had been allowed to live. The burlap was knotted firmly around the base of the bush when I dug down through the snow, and in the end I had to go back into the cottage for a knife. For me, the pending air was gone, the savage message delivered.

The burlap kept its shape grotesquely in the icy air when I lifted it off. It was the arched and appalling shape of Charles Jethro, frozen wrists tied to frozen ankles, both lashed securely to the base of the bush that had borne the fat white flowers. The snowball bush.

Here, Daemos!

August Derleth

Martin Webly was not the best choice for the parish at Millham, in the south country: a bustling, officious man of medium height, better than medium weight, with a glint in his eye and determination apparent in the set of his jaw. The parish, however, had been spoiled almost into oblivion by the kindly ministrations of old Dr. Williamson, Webly's predecessor; that he had left finances in a deplorable state was not to be held against him, however much of a problem this might afford the new vicar. Indeed, there were certain people in the parish who held that a problem of this magnitude might be a good thing to help make smoother the edges of the Reverend Mr. Webly. Some regret was manifest.

However, there he was, and there in Millham he meant to stay.

He was not married, but he had a housekeeper, a gardener, and occasionally hired a chauffeur. He took complete possession of the vicarage, and within a fortnight conducted himself as if he had always lived there. Within that fortnight, too, the vicar had got himself thoroughly informed in regard to the financial problems of the parish. He was not pleased and said so in his next sermon; moreover, he said, "something must be done," speaking with such a positive air that several of his listeners were rudely jolted from their lethargic acceptance of the status quo. After due consideration of the enormity of the problem, coupled with a knowledge of the ina-

bility of the parish to raise funds, they settled back again to wait
for the Reverend Mr. Webly's solution to the problem.

They were kept waiting a scant ten days before the vicar announced his solution.

He had come upon certain old papers, he said, which indicated
that a treasure had been buried in the tomb of Nicholas Millham,
posthumously knighted three centuries ago, and he proposed to investigate the tomb forthwith, beginning the second Monday following, and he preferred that his assistants should come from the
parish.

It was an unheard of and impossible solution. In the first place,
everyone had been aware of this legend for a long time, and no one
had ever done anything about it. Why not? demanded the vicar.
Because of the belief in certain local legends, for one thing; because it was thought irreverent for another; because there was a
reasonable doubt about the supposed treasure. Martin Webly was
adamant; he thrust forth his jaw, beetled his eyes, and said that he
would tolerate neither superstition nor any other nonsense, and the
parish had better understand that from the start.

On the following Sunday, old Sir Basil Hether, who was the local
authority on everything from pottery to astronomy, was shown into
the vicar's study. He was faintly apologetic, but rather more distant
in his manner than apologetic.

"I came to see you about the Millham tomb," he said.

"We begin Monday week," said the vicar cheerfully.

"So I heard. But of course, you can't do it, you can't open it, you
know very well there's a curse on it."

The Reverend Martin Webly fingered his jaw patiently and then
took up some old papers which lay not far from his elbow on his
desk. "Yes, yes," he said, a little scorn in his voice. "That curse. Let
me see, I believe it's here somewhere—a copy of it, that would be.
Yes, here it is."

Hether extended his hand for it and opened it slowly, carefully,
with a certain respect for old things. He peered attentively at the
script. "It seems properly clear," he said thoughtfully. "The Latin
is easily translated, and you are warned that any disturbance of the
tomb will give you grievous trouble."

The Reverend Mr. Webly took the old paper back and looked at
it with pursed lips and narrowed eyes out of which his skepticism

showed plainly. "I'm glad you find it so clear," he said. "I fail in that. 'Who dares disturb this tomb releases unto death my companion and now his,'" he read. "That's a free translation, isn't it?"

Hether nodded. "And clear enough, too, I should say."

Webly made no comment. He put the paper down and crossed his hands on his paunch, eyeing the old man with ill-concealed impatience. "Nevertheless, Monday we begin work. I don't anticipate that it will take us very long. And if the men make any kind of trouble about this superstition, I'll take a hand myself."

Hether brightened visibly. "That might not be so bad, then," he said reflectively. "As I understand the curse, it applies only to the disturber of the grave; so you are not really loosing any menace upon the parish."

Webly ignored this thrust and asked about the legends which existed about Nicholas Millham. He had heard hints, of course, but few people wished to speak of the old man. What was there about him?

Hether, however, had no inhibitions. He could say quite readily what there was about Sir Nicholas Millham. The old man had preached demonology, and there were any number of queer events which had been attributed to him in the absence of any other explanation. And then there was, of course, the matter of his death; he had apparently had some foreknowledge of that, and had had the tomb erected and the curse put on it just a week before he was killed in an accident.

Webly had some difficulty restraining himself. He reminded his visitor that this was, after all, the twentieth century, not the dark ages. "But you've said nothing about Millham's companion to which he so cryptically alludes," he went on. "I presume he did have a companion—or is that presuming too much?"

If Sir Basil Hether was aware of the vicar's sarcasm, he chose to overlook it. "Oh, yes, several. But his favorite was a large black dog, named Daemos, and the story goes that on dark nights the villagers could hear the old man's voice calling his dog—'Here, Daemos! Here, Daemos!'"

"What a queer name for a dog!"

Hether rose to go. "Oh, not at all," he said benignly. "When you consider the root of it in the Greek, and its subsequent use in our own language: *daimon* to *daemon* or *demon*. I dare say Millham had a sense of humor."

The Reverend Mr. Webly mentally reserved to include Sir Basil Hether among those destined to receive the benefit of his prayers and showed him out, unmindful of the old man's dubious mutterings and head shakings. The vicar was a practical man; he permitted Hether's "I really wouldn't do it! I wouldn't sanction it!" to pass from his mind even more swiftly than the old man passed from his sight down the lane to where his car stood waiting.

On Monday week the work was begun, everyone exercising the utmost care, so that no damage might be done. The vicar told himself and his parishioners that he was not a vandal. Nevertheless, he had to import workmen from outside; without saying so in so many words, old Hether had given him to understand that he would have difficulty with local workmen, and he had been right. The vicar got outside help, preached a sermon on the evils of superstition, and devoted his attention to the matter of the Millham tomb. He was eager to discover now how great the treasure would be, and whether it would pay the parish's debt, which would please his superiors very much and make his own chances for advancement so much greater. He did not at the moment consider the possibility of his advancement to another plane.

By Wednesday, the coffin was ready for its opening, and the vicar, true to his word, came from his study and opened it. He revealed Sir Nicholas Millham's remains, a small casket of jewels, and a thick mass of musty dust, which slithered like a cloud of fog over the edge of the coffin and vanished. One glance at the jewels was enough to convince the Reverend Mr. Webly that the parish's financial problem had been solved for the time being. He could not keep from returning to his study and telephoning old Hether to impart something of his triumph to him.

Sir Basil was not enthusiastic. Indeed, he was curiously restrained, so that the vicar had the uncomfortable impression that he was talking to a listener who sat annoyingly waiting for the end of a story which had already patently ended.

The vicar's triumph, however, was not to be dampened. He announced a special thanksgiving service for that evening, and preached a long sermon on the ways of Providence, despite the fact that the majority of his parishioners were not present. Old Hether was there, and several strangers, summoned no doubt by the unusual ringing of the bells, and curious about the whispered tales already making their way over the countryside about the vicar's find. The vicar had a few uneasy moments, until he could reassure himself that the jewels were safely locked up where no strangers were likely to find them; the only individual who might demand more information than he cared to impart to his parish was the tax collector for the Crown, and he was certainly not among those present.

Being practical and methodical, the vicar made a conservative estimate of the treasure's worth, and reckoned that, with care, there might be a small fund left over after the parish debt had been paid. It was while he was doing this late that night in his study that the telephone rang and old Hether's voice came over the wire to inquire whether the vicar was still all right.

"Of course, I'm all right. What do you mean?"

"Forgive my curiosity," murmured Sir Basil. "I told you I was superstitious. By the way, if you should need me—my telephone is next to my bed."

The vicar made short work of him; he was not kind. When he put down the telephone he was convinced that he had better plan to give an entire series of lectures upon the evil effect of superstition. If he had been irritated by the curious, stolid refusal of his parish workmen to assist at the opening of the tomb, he was even more disquieted and angered by the persistent stupidity of a man like old Hether, who ought to be about setting a good example rather than upholding the error of these country ways. The vicar, clearly, was from the city; he had come out of Whitechapel, which was not a savory environment. Having seen a good deal of the rawer side of life, he had a natural tendency to be irate about those needless beliefs which always work to make the lot of a poor yokelry more difficult.

When he put out the light and went to bed, the vicar's mind was occupied with sonorous and rather pompous lines deriding the folly of superstition.

He was awakened in the night by what he thought at first was rain against the window pane; but, as he came more fully to his senses, he recognized it as a *snuffling* sound—the kind of sound an animal might make. At the same time he was conscious of a veritable bedlam in the village; it seemed to him that every dog in the countryside was barking furiously, madly, as if something frightened or angered them. He turned over on his side and listened intently; the snuffling sound was repeated.

It was manifestly ridiculous that any kind of animal could be snuffling at his window. The vicar slept on the second floor, and the walls went straight down to the ground, with not even a vine up which something might crawl, much less the roof of a veranda. Yet, there it was, a peculiar, persistent snuffling, accompanied from time to time by an oddly muted whine or growl, and set all the time against that wild barking in the background. He got up at last, irritated, and went over to the window.

The window looked out upon the lane and the corner street-light. Almost the first thing he saw was a man standing there; he stood a little in the shadow, and yet his face was clearly visible—a long, dark, saturnine face, with dark pools for eyes, not exactly a young man, and yet not seeming old except in the curious parchment-like quality of his gaunt features. It was not someone the vicar knew.

While he stood looking, the vicar observed that the stranger under the light was not alone; a large dog bounded out of the vicarage yard and came quietly to his side. It seemed to the vicar with a curious kind of thrill that man and dog both turned and looked for a moment intently at the window from which he peered outward before they turned and vanished in the dark direction of the churchyard.

"What a strange thing!" murmured the vicar.

He stood there a little longer and was conscious presently that the bedlam of barking ceased. It did not occur to him that the barking had stopped in approximately the time it would have taken the watcher and his dog to reach the churchyard. In some respects, the vicar was unimaginative; if he had thought enough of old Hether to give him a ring on the telephone, he might have spared himself.

It was maddening, but from that evening, everything seemed to go wrong. The bishop took him to task for opening the tomb without first investigating every other avenue of raising money and without having the parish convinced of the right to open it. "A form of desecration all the more deprecated since it was done purely for material gain," wrote the bishop. There went the Reverend Mr. Webly's chance for immediate advancement. Before noon, his gardener quit, coming into the study and putting his case very solidly.

"Seein' as how the dogs do bark, and you know what that means, Reverend Zur."

"Why, no, what does it mean?" demanded the vicar truculently.

"Strange dogs about, there be, zur."

"Indeed!"

The vicar paid him and sent him off, not without rancor. It was being borne in upon him painfully that a man even of his standing could not educate people hidebound by all manner of legend and lore simply by denying the existence of their beliefs.

And before the day was out, there was, as might have been expected, old Hether. The vicar was obviously in no mood to see him, but there he was, coming as if he expected to be welcomed by open arms.

"Hear the dogs last night?" asked Hether.

"Who didn't?"

"Thought you might have heard 'em. So did I. Thought it might put you to thinking a bit."

" 'What fools these mortals be!' " quoted the vicar pointedly.

"Quite so," agreed Sir Basil cheerfully producing an old leather book. "Brought you a book I thought you'd like to see. Picture of old Millham in it."

The vicar took the book, glancing at its title: *South Country Demonology*. He opened it to the picture and gazed at the countenance of Nicholas Millham. He had instantly the singular sensation of looking upon someone familiar, but he could not place him. He frowned briefly before handing the book back.

"That black dog beside him was supposed to be his familiar. Of course you're aware of the legend about practitioners of the black arts and their demon companions, who took odd forms, but quite often that of a black dog," old Hether went on.

"I've seen that face somewhere before," said the vicar.

"Then you've seen the book, too, eh?"

"Oh, no."

"Must have. This is the only place Millham's portrait occurs. Never been reprinted, as far as I know, and the book's rare."

Their conversation was not pleasant.

It was not until Sir Basil had gone that the vicar remembered where he had seen that strange gaunt face before—it was the face of the nocturnal watcher under the street-light in the lane!

"What a curious coincidence!" he thought. It was a pity that the vicar was conditioned to think in platitudes.

That evening he made the mistake of working late in the church; though the work he had to do there could have been done any time, it was possible that the vicar obstinately pursued this course because Sir Basil Hether had none too subtly hinted that it might be well if the vicar stayed inside after dark.

When he came out, on his way to the vicarage, he was immediately aware of the wild barking of the Millham dogs, the same mad volume of sound which had assaulted the usually quiet country darkness on the previous night. Looking around him from the comparative security of the church steps, he made out a figure standing at the entry to the churchyard just beyond. He thought briefly of old Hether's ridiculous hints, and reflected that in any case, it was rather late to be considering them.

He went down the steps and up the lane to where the lights of the vicarage shone out. A man's voice was raised in a shout behind him, and he thought with a warm pleasure how pleasant it was to hear the familiar voices of countrymen in the deepening darkness of nights—men in the fields, men on their way home, men with lanterns looking for lost lambs or calves. Even as he thought this, he was aware suddenly of the words that reached his consciousness. He could not believe the evidence of his own ears—a man's voice calling insistently, with a strangely ominous quality: *"Here, Daemos! Here, Daemos!"*

Frightened now, he turned.

He had a fleeting glimpse of a great black hound with red eyes bounding toward him, its mouth slavering, its outline no less distinct than the aspect of earth seen dimly through its dark body— and behind it, coming swiftly as the wind, the tall black-coated stranger, his face demoniac in its saturninity, the face of the dead Nicholas Millham. Then the hound was upon him, and he went down with the furious wild barking of the village dogs still ringing in his ears.

One of the vestrymen found him shortly after midnight. The vicar was not a pleasant sight, with his throat torn out, and many lacerations apart from the severing of his jugular. At the inquest, the coroner's jury decided that the Reverend Mr. Webly had come to his death in an unfortunate encounter with a stray dog, "of some considerable size."

Sir Basil Hether, however, took no chances. Having satisfied himself that the curse on the Millham tomb applied only to the opening of the tomb itself, and not to the removal of the jewels, he nevertheless repaired to the proper quarters and had an elderly gentleman publicly in very bad odor as the practitioner of certain unmentionable acts come down from London and seal the tomb again, with incantations and exorcisms.

Being a man with a healthy regard for country lore, he did not forget to have the Millham curse put back upon the tomb for any future Webly who might dare to show his scorn for the beliefs of the local yokelry.

The Cookie Lady

Philip K. Dick

"Where you going, Bubber?" Ernie Mill shouted from across the
street, fixing papers for his route.

"No place," Bubber Surle said.

"You going to see your lady friend?" Ernie laughed and laughed.
"What do you go visit that old lady for? Let us in on it!"

Bubber went on. He turned the corner and went down Elm
Street. Already, he could see the house, at the end of the street, set
back a little on the lot. The front of the house was overgrown with
weeds, old dry weeds that rustled and chattered in the wind. The
house itself was a little grey box, shabby and unpainted, the porch
steps sagging. There was an old weatherbeaten rocking chair on
the porch with a torn piece of cloth hanging over it.

Bubber went up the walk. As he started up the rickety steps he
took a deep breath. He could smell it, the wonderful warm smell,
and his mouth began to water. His heart thudding with anticipation,
Bubber turned the handle of the bell. The bell grated rustily on the
other side of the door. There was silence for a time, then the sounds
of someone stirring.

Mrs. Drew opened the door. She was old, very old, a little dried-
up old lady, like the weeds that grew along the front of the house.
She smiled down at Bubber, holding the door wide for him to come
in.

"You're just in time," she said. "Come on inside, Bernard. You're just in time—they're just now ready."

Bubber went to the kitchen door and looked in. He could see them, resting on a big blue plate on top of the stove. Cookies, a plate of warm, fresh cookies right out of the oven. Cookies with nuts and raisins in them.

"How do they look?" Mrs. Drew said. She rustled past him, into the kitchen. "And maybe some cold milk, too. You like cold milk with them." She got the milk pitcher from the window box on the back porch. Then she poured a glass of milk for him and set some of the cookies on a small plate. "Let's go into the living room," she said.

Bubber nodded. Mrs. Drew carried the milk and the cookies in and set them on the arm of the couch. Then she sat down in her own chair, watching Bubber plop himself down by the plate and begin to help himself.

Bubber ate greedily, as usual, intent on the cookies, silent except for chewing sounds. Mrs. Drew waited patiently, until the boy had finished, and his already ample sides bulged that much more. When Bubber was done with the plate he glanced towards the kitchen again, at the rest of the cookies on the stove.

"Wouldn't you like to wait until later for the rest?" Mrs. Drew said.

"All right," Bubber agreed.

"How were they?"

"Fine."

"That's good." She leaned back in her chair. "Well, what did you do in school today? How did it go?"

"All right."

The little old lady watched the boy look restlessly around the room. "Bernard," she said presently, "won't you stay and talk to me for a while?" He had some books on his lap, some school books. "Why don't you read to me from your books? You know, I don't see too well any more and it's a comfort to me to be read to."

"Can I have the rest of the cookies after?"

"Of course."

Bubber moved over towards her, to the end of the couch. He opened his books, World Geography, Principles of Arithmetic, Hoyte's Speller. "Which do you want?"

She hesitated. "The geography."

Bubber opened the big blue book at random. PERU. "Peru is bounded on the north by Ecuador and Colombia, on the south by Chile, and on the east by Brazil and Bolivia. Peru is divided into three main sections. These are, first—"

The little old lady watched him read, his fat cheeks wobbling as he read, holding his finger next to the line. She was silent, watching him, studying the boy intently as he read, drinking in each frown of concentration, every motion of his arms and hands. She relaxed, letting herself sink back in her chair. He was very close to her, only a little way off. There was only the table and lamp between them. How nice it was to have him come; he had been coming for over a month, now, ever since the day she had been sitting on her porch and seen him go by and thought to call to him, pointing to the cookies by her rocker.

Why had she done it? She did not know. She had been alone so long that she found herself saying strange things and doing strange things. She saw so few people, only when she went down to the store, or the mailman came with her pension check. Or the garbage man.

The boy's voice droned on. She was comfortable, peaceful and relaxed. The little old lady closed her eyes and folded her hands in her lap. And as she sat, dozing and listening, something began to happen. The little old lady was beginning to change, her grey wrinkles and lines dimming away. As she sat in the chair she was growing younger, the thin fragile body filling out with youth again. The grey hair thickened and darkened, color coming to the wispy strands. Her arms filled, too, the mottled flesh turning a rich hue as it had been once, many years before.

Mrs. Drew breathed deeply, not opening her eyes. She could feel *something* happening, but she did not know just what. *Something* was going on; she could feel it, and it was good. But what it was she did not exactly know. It had happened before, almost every time the boy came and sat by her. Especially of late, since she had moved her chair nearer to the couch. She took a deep breath. How good it felt, the warm fullness, a breath of warmth inside her cold body for the first time in years!

In her chair the little old lady had become a dark-haired matron of perhaps thirty, a woman with full cheeks and plump arms and legs. Her lips were red again, her neck even a little too fleshy, as it had been once in the long forgotten past.

Suddenly the reading stopped. Bubber put down his book and stood up. "I have to go," he said. "Can I take the rest of the cookies with me?"

She blinked, rousing herself. The boy was in the kitchen, filling his pockets with cookies. She nodded, dazed, still under the spell. The boy took the last cookies. He went across the living room to the door. Mrs. Drew stood up. All at once the warmth left her. She looked down at her hands. Wrinkled, thin.

"Oh!" she murmured. Tears blurred her eyes. It was gone, gone again as soon as he moved away. She tottered to the mirror above the mantel and looked at herself. Old faded eyes stared back, eyes deep-set in a withered face. Gone, all gone, as soon as the boy had left her side.

"I'll see you later," Bubber said.

"Please," she whispered. "Please come back again. Will you come back?"

"Sure," Bubber said listlessly. He pushed the door open. "Goodbye." He went down the steps. In a moment she heard his shoes against the sidewalk. He was gone.

"Bubber, you come in here!" May Surle stood angrily on the porch. "You get in here and sit down at the table."

"All right." Bubber came slowly up on to the porch, pushing inside the house.

"What's the matter with you?" She caught his arm. "Where you been? Are you sick?"

"I'm tired." Bubber rubbed his forehead.

His father came through the living room with the newspapers, in his undershirt. "What's the matter?" he said.

"Look at him," May Surle said. "All worn out. What you been doing, Bubber?"

"He's been visiting that old lady," Ralf Surle said. "Can't you tell? He's always washed out after he's been visiting her. What do you go there for, Bub? What goes on?"

"She gives him cookies," May said. "You know how he is about things to eat. He'd do anything for a plate of cookies."

"Bub," his father said, "listen to me. I don't want you hanging around that crazy old lady any more. Do you hear me? I don't care how many cookies she gives you. You come home too tired! No more of that. You hear me?"

Bubber looked down at the floor, leaning against the door. His heart beat heavily, labored. "I told her I'd come back," he muttered.

"You can go once more," May said, going into the dining room, "but only once more. Tell her you won't be able to come back again, though. You make sure you tell her nice. Now go upstairs and get washed up."

"After dinner better have him lie down," Ralf said, looking up the stairs, watching Bubber climb slowly, his hand on the bannister. He shook his head. "I don't like it," he murmured. "I don't want him going there any more. There's something strange about that old lady."

"Well, it'll be the last time," May said.

Wednesday was warm and sunny. Bubber strode along, his hands in his pockets. He stopped in front of McVane's drug store for a minute, looking speculatively at the comic books. At the soda fountain a woman was drinking a big chocolate soda. The sight of it made Bubber's mouth water. That settled it. He turned and continued on his way, even increasing his pace a little.

A few minutes later he came up on to the grey sagging porch and rang the bell. Below him the weeds blew and rustled with the wind. It was almost four o'clock; he could not stay too long. But then, it was the last time anyhow.

The door opened. Mrs. Drew's wrinkled face broke into smiles. "Come in, Bernard. It's good to see you standing there. It makes me feel so young again to have you come visit."

He went inside, looking around.

"I'll start the cookies. I didn't know if you were coming." She padded into the kitchen. "I'll get them started right away. You sit down on the couch."

Bubber went over and sat down. He noticed that the table and lamp were gone; the chair was right up next to the couch. He was looking at the chair in perplexity when Mrs. Drew came rustling back into the room.

"They're in the oven. I had the batter all ready. Now." She sat down in the chair with a sigh. "Well, how did it go today? How was school?"

"Fine."

She nodded. How plump he was, the little boy, sitting just a little distance from her, his cheeks red and full! She could touch him, he was so close. Her aged heart thumped. Ah, to be young again. Youth was so much. It was everything. What did the world mean to the old? *When all the world is old, lad.* . . .

"Do you want to read to me, Bernard?" she asked presently.

"I didn't bring any books."

"Oh." She nodded. "Well, I have some books," she said quickly. "I'll get them."

She got up, crossing to the bookcase. As she opened the doors, Bubber said, "Mrs. Drew, my father says I can't come here any more. He says this is the last time. I thought I'd tell you."

She stopped, standing rigid. Everything seemed to leap around her, the room twisting furiously. She took a harsh, frightened breath. "Bernard, you're—you're not coming back?"

"No, my father says not to."

There was silence. The old lady took a book at random and came slowly back to her chair. After a while she passed the book to him, her hands trembling. The boy took it without expression, looking at its cover.

"Please read, Bernard. Please."

"All right." He opened the book. "Where'll I start?"

"Anywhere. Anywhere, Bernard."

He began to read. It was something by Trollope; she only half heard the words. She put her hand to her forehead, the dry skin, brittle and thin, like old paper. She trembled with anguish. The last time?

Bubber read on, slowly, monotonously. Against the window a fly buzzed. Outside the sun began to set, the air turning cool. A few clouds came up, and the wind in the trees rushed furiously.

The old lady sat, close by the boy, closer than ever, hearing him read, the sound of his voice, sensing him close by. Was this really the last time? Terror rose up in her and she pushed it back. The last time! She gazed at him, the boy sitting so close to her. After a time she reached out her thin, dry hand. She took a deep breath. He would never be back. There would be no more times, no more. This was the last time he would sit there.

She touched his arm.

Bubber looked up. "What is it?" he murmured.

"You don't mind if I touch your arm, do you?"

"No, I guess not." He went on reading. The old lady could feel the youngness of him, flowing between her fingers, through her arm. A pulsating, vibrating youngness, so close to her. It had never been that close, where she could actually touch it. The feel of life made her dizzy, unsteady.

And presently it began to happen, as before. She closed her eyes, letting it move over her, filling her up, carried into her by the sound of the voice and the feel of the arm. The change, the glow, was coming over her, the warm, rising feeling. She was blooming again, filling with life, swelling into richness, as she had been, once, long ago.

She looked down at her arms. Rounded, they were, and the nails clear. Her hair. Black again, heavy and black against her neck. She touched her cheek. The wrinkles had gone, the skin pliant and soft.

Joy filled her, a growing, bursting joy. She stared around her, at the room. She smiled, feeling her firm teeth and gums, red lips, strong white teeth. Suddenly she got to her feet, her body secure and confident. She turned a little, lithe, quick circle.

Bubber stopped reading. "Are the cookies ready?" he said.

"I'll see." Her voice was alive, deep with a quality that had dried out many years before. Now it was there again, *her* voice, throaty and sensual. She walked quickly to the kitchen and opened the oven. She took out the cookies and put them on top of the stove.

"All ready," she called gaily. "Come and get them."

Bubber came past her, his gaze fastened on the sight of the cookies. He did not even notice the woman by the door.

Mrs. Drew hurried from the kitchen. She went into the bedroom, closing the door after her. Then she turned, gazing into the full-length mirror on the door. Young—she was young again, filled out with the sap of vigorous youth. She took a deep breath, her steady bosom swelling. Her eyes flashed, and she smiled. She spun, her skirts flying. Young and lovely.

And this time it had not gone away.

She opened the door. Bubber had filled his mouth and his pockets. He was standing in the center of the livingroom, his face fat and dull, a dead white.

"What's the matter?" Mrs. Drew said.

"I'm going."

"All right, Bernard. And thanks for coming to read to me." She laid her hand on his shoulder. "Perhaps I'll see you again some time."

"My father—"

"I know." She laughed gaily, opening the door for him. "Good-bye, Bernard. Good-bye."

She watched him go slowly down the steps, one at a time. Then she closed the door and skipped back into the bedroom. She unfastened her dress and stepped out of it, the worn grey fabric suddenly distasteful to her. For a brief second she gazed at her full, rounded body, her hands on her hips.

She laughed with excitement, turning a little, her eyes bright. What a wonderful body, bursting with life. A swelling breast—she touched herself. The flesh was firm. There was so much, so many things to do! She gazed about her, breathing quickly. So many things! She started the water running in the bathtub and then went to tie her hair up.

The wind blew around him as he trudged home. It was late, the sun had set and the sky overhead was dark and cloudy. The wind that blew and nudged against him was cold, and it penetrated through his clothing, chilling him. The boy felt tired, his head ached, and he stopped every few minutes, rubbing his forehead and resting, his heart laboring. He left Elm Street and went up Pine Street. The wind screeched around him, pushing him from side to side. He shook his head, trying to clear it. How weary he was, how tired his arms and legs were. He felt the wind hammering at him, pushing and plucking at him.

He took a breath and went on, his head down. At the corner he stopped, holding on to a lamppost. The sky was quite dark, the street lights were beginning to come on. At last he went on, walking as best he could.

"Where is that boy?" May Surle said, going out on the porch for the tenth time. Ralf flicked on the light and they stood together. "What an awful wind."

The wind whistled and lashed at the porch. The two of them looked up and down the dark street, but they could see nothing but a few newspapers and trash being blown along.

"Let's go inside," Ralf said. "He sure is going to get a licking when he gets home."

They sat down at the dinner table. Presently May put down her fork. "Listen! Do you hear something?"

Ralf listened.

Outside, against the front door, there was a faint sound, a tapping sound. He stood up. The wind howled outside, blowing the shades in the room upstairs. "I'll go see what it is," he said.

He went to the door and opened it. Something grey, something grey and dry was blowing up against the porch, carried by the wind. He stared at it, but he could not make it out. A bundle of weeds, weeds and rags blown by the wind, perhaps.

The bundle bounced against his legs. He watched it drift past him, against the wall of the house. Then he closed the door again slowly.

"What was it?" May called.

"Just the wind," Ralf Surle said.

The Wager

Robert L. Fish

I suppose if I were watching television coverage of the return of a lunar mission and Kek Huuygens climbed out of the command module after splashdown, I shouldn't be greatly surprised. I'd be even less surprised to see Kek hustled aboard the aircraft carrier and given a thorough search by a suspicious Customs official. Kek, you see, is one of those men who turn up at very odd times in unexpected places. Also, he is rated by the customs services of nearly every nation in the world as the most talented smuggler alive. Polish by birth, Dutch by adopted name, the holder of a valid U.S. passport, multilingual, a born sleight-of-hand artist, Kek is an elusive target for the stolid bureaucrat who thinks in terms of hollow shoe heels and suitcases with false bottoms. Now and then over the years, Kek has allowed me to publish a little of his lore in my column. When I came across him last, however, he was doing something very ordinary in a commonplace setting. Under the critical eye of a waiter, he was nursing a beer at a table in that little sunken-garden affair in Rockefeller Center.

Before I got to his table, I tried to read the clues. Kek had a good tan and he looked healthy. But his suit had a shine that came from wear rather than from silk thread. A neat scissors trim didn't quite conceal the fact that his cuffs were frayed. He was not wearing his usual boutonniere.

"I owe you three cognacs from last time—Vaduz, wasn't it?—and I'm buying," I said as I sat down.

"You are a man of honor," he said and called to the waiter, naming a most expensive cognac. Then he gave me his wide, friendly smile. "Yes, you have read the signs and they are true—but not for any reasons you might imagine. Sitting before you, you can observe the impoverishment that comes from total success. Failure can be managed, but success can be a most difficult thing to control. . . ."

Hidden inside every Kek Huuygens aphorism there is a story somewhere. But if you want it produced, you must pretend complete indifference. "Ah, yes," I said, "failure is something you know in your heart. Success is something that lies in the eye of the beholder. I think—"

"Do you want to hear the story or don't you?" Kek said. "You can't use it in your column, though, I warn you."

"Perhaps in time?"

"Perhaps in time, all barbarous Customs regulations will be repealed," he said. "Perhaps the angels will come down to rule the earth. Until then, you and I alone will share this story." That was Kek's way of saying "Wait until things have cooled off."

It all began in Las Vegas (Huuygens said) and was primarily caused by two unfortunate factors: one, that I spoke the word banco aloud and, two, that it was heard. I am still not convinced that the player against me wasn't the world's best card manipulator, but at any rate, I found myself looking at a jack and a nine, while the best I could manage for myself was a six. So I watched my money disappear, got up politely to allow the next standee to take my place and started for the exit. I had enough money in the hotel safe to pay my bill and buy me a ticket back to New York—a simple precaution I recommend to all who never learn to keep quiet in a baccarat game—and a few dollars in my pocket, but my financial position was not one any sensible banker would have lent money against. I was sure something would turn up, as it usually did, and in this case it turned up even faster than usual, because I hadn't even reached the door before I was stopped.

The man who put his hand on my arm did so in a completely friendly manner, and I recalled him as being one of the group standing around the table during the play. There was something faintly familiar about him, but even quite famous faces are disregarded at a baccarat table; one is not there to collect autographs. The man holding my arm was short, heavy, swarthy and of a type to cause instant distaste on the part of any discerning observer. What caught and held my attention was that he addressed me by name—and in French. "M'sieu Huuygens?" he said. To my absolute amazement, he pronounced it correctly. I acknowledged that I was, indeed, M'sieu Kek Huuygens. "I should like to talk with you a moment and to buy you a drink," he said.

"I could use one," I admitted, and I allowed him to lead me into the bar. As we went, I noticed two men who had been standing to one side studying their fingernails; they now moved with us and took up new positions to each side, still studying their nails. One would think that fingernails were a subject that could quickly bore, but apparently not to those two. As I sat down beside my chubby host, I looked at him once more, and suddenly recognition came.

He saw the light come on in the little circle over my head and smiled, showing a dazzling collection of white teeth, a tribute to the art of the dental laboratory.

"Yes," he said, "I am Antoine Duvivier," and waved over a waiter. We ordered and I returned my attention to him. Duvivier, as you must know—even newspapermen listen to the radio, I assume—was the president of the island of St. Michel in the Caribbean, or had been until his loyal subjects decided that presidents should be elected, after which he departed in the middle of the night, taking with him most of his country's treasury. He could see the wheels turning in my head as I tried to see how I could use this information to my advantage, and I must say he waited politely enough while I was forced to give up on the problem. Then he said, "I have watched you play at baccarat."

We received our drinks and I sipped, waiting for him to go on.

"You are quite a gambler, M'sieu Huuygens," he said, "but, of course, you would have to be, in your line of work." He saw my eyebrows go up and added quite coolly, "Yes, M'sieu Huuygens, I have had you investigated, and thoroughly. But please permit me to explain that it was not done from idle curiosity. I am interested in making you a proposition."

I find, in situations like this, the less said the better, so I said nothing.

"Yes," he went on, "I should like to offer you—" He paused, as if reconsidering his words, actually looking embarrassed, as if he were guilty of a *gaffe*. "Let me rephrase that," he said and searched for a better approach. At last he found it. "What I meant was, I should like to make a *wager* with you, a wager I am sure should be most interesting to a gambler such as yourself."

This time, of course, I had to answer, so I said, "Oh?"

"Yes," he said, pleased at my instant understanding. "I should like to wager twenty thousand dollars of my money, against two dollars of yours, that you will *not* bring a certain object from the Caribbean through United States Customs and deliver it to me in New York City."

I must admit I admire bluntness, even though the approach was not particularly unique. "The odds are reasonable," I admitted. "One might even say generous. What type of object are we speaking of?"

He lowered his voice. "It is a carving," he said. "A Tien Tse Huwai, dating back to eight centuries before Christ. It is of ivory and is not particularly large; I imagine it could fit into your coat pocket, although, admittedly, it would be bulky. It depicts a village scene—but you, I understand, are an art connoisseur; you may have heard of it. In translation, its name is *The Village Dance*." Normally, I can control my features, but my surprise must have shown, for Duvivier went on in the same soft voice. "Yes, I have it. The carving behind that glass case in the St. Michel National Gallery is a copy—a plastic casting, excellently done, but a copy. The original is at the home of a friend in Barbados. I could get it that far, but I was afraid to attempt bringing it the rest of the way; to have lost it would have been tragic. Since then, I have been looking for a man clever enough to get it into the States without being stopped by Customs." He suddenly grinned, those white blocks of teeth almost blinding me. "I am offering ten-thousand-to-one odds that that clever man is *not* you."

It was a cute ploy, but that was not what interested me at the moment.

"M'sieu," I said simply, "permit me a question: I am familiar with the Tien *Village Dance*. I have never seen it, but it received quite a bit of publicity when your National Gallery purchased it, since it was felt—if you will pardon me—that the money could have been used better elsewhere. However, my surprise a moment ago was not that you have the carving; it was at your offer. The Tien, many years in the future, may, indeed, command a large price, but the figure your museum paid when you bought it was, as I recall, not much more than the twenty thousand dollars you are willing to —ah—wager to get it into this country. And that value could only be realized at a legitimate sale, which would be difficult, it seems to me, under the circumstances."

Duvivier's smile had been slowly disappearing as I spoke. Now he was looking at me in disappointment.

"You do not understand, M'sieu," he said, and there was a genuine touch of sadness in his voice at my incogitancy. "To you, especially after your losses tonight, I am sure the sum of twenty thousand dollars seems a fortune, but, in all honesty, to me it is not. I am not interested in the monetary value of the carving; I have no intention of selling it. I simply wish to own it." He looked at me with an expression I have seen many times before—the look of a fanatic, a zealot. A Collector, with a capital C. "You cannot possibly comprehend," he repeated, shaking his head. "It is such an incredibly lovely thing . . ."

Well, of course, he was quite wrong about my understanding, or lack of it; I understood perfectly. For a moment, I almost found myself liking the man; but only for a moment. And a wager is a wager, and I had to admit I had never been offered such attractive odds before in my life. As for the means of getting the carving into the United States, especially from Barbados, I had a thought on that, too. I was examining my idea in greater detail when his voice broke in on me.

"Well?" he asked, a bit impatiently.

"You have just made yourself a bet," I said. "But it will require a little time."

"How much time?" Now that I was committed, the false friendliness was gone from both voice and visage; for all practical purposes, I was now merely an employee.

I thought a moment. "It's hard to say. It depends," I said at last. "Less than two months but probably more than one."

He frowned. "Why so long?" I merely shrugged and reached for my glass. "All right," he said grudgingly. "And how do you plan on getting it through Customs?" My response to this was to smile at him gently, so he gave up. "I shall give you a card to my friend in Barbados, which will release the carving into your care. After that" —he smiled again, but this time it was a bit wolfish for my liking—

"our wager will be in effect. We will meet at my apartment in New York."

He gave me his address, together with his telephone number, and then handed me a second card with a scrawl on it to a name in Barbados, and that was that. We drank up, shook hands and I left the bar, pleased to be working again and equally pleased to be quitted of Duvivier, if only for a while.

Huuygens paused and looked at me with his satanic eyebrows tilted sharply. I recognized the expression and made a circular gesture over our glasses, which was instantly interpreted by our waiter. Kek waited until we were served, thanked me gravely and drank. I settled back to listen, sipping. When next Huuygens spoke, however, I thought at first he was changing the subject, but I soon learned this was not the case.

Anyone who says the day of travel by ship has passed (Huuygens went on) has never made an examination of the brochures for Caribbean cruises that fill and overflow the racks of travel agencies. It appears that between sailings from New York and sailings from Port Everglades—not to mention, Miami, Baltimore, Norfolk and others—almost everything afloat must be pressed into service to transport those Americans with credit cards and a little free time to the balmy breezes and shimmering sands of the islands. They have trips for all seasons, as well as for every taste and pocketbook. There are bridge cruises to St. Lucia, canasta cruises to Trinidad, golf cruises to St. Croix. There are seven-day cruises to the Bahamas, eight-day cruises to Jamaica, 13-day cruises to Martinique; there are even—I was not surprised to see—three-day cruises to nowhere. And it struck me that even though it was approaching summer, a cruise would be an ideal way to travel; it had been one of my principal reasons for requiring so much time to consummate the deal.

So I went to the travel agency in the hotel lobby and was instantly inundated with schedules and pamphlets. I managed to get the reams of propaganda to my room without a bellboy, sat down on the bed and carefully made my selection. When I had my trip laid out to my satisfaction, I descended once again to the hotel lobby and presented my program to the travel agent there. He must have thought I was insane, but I explained I suffered from Widget

Syndrome and required a lot of salt air, after which he shrugged and picked up the phone to confirm my reservations through New York. They readily accepted my credit card for the bill—which I sincerely hoped to be able to honor by the time it was presented—and two days later, I found myself in Miami, boarding the M. V. Andropolis for a joyous 16-day cruise. It was longer than I might have chosen, but it was the only one that fit my schedule and I felt that I had—or would, shortly—earn the rest.

I might as well tell you right now that it was a delightful trip. I should have preferred to have taken along my own feminine companionship, but my finances would not permit it; there are, after all, such hard-cash outlays as bar bills and tips. However, there was no lack of unattached women aboard, some even presentable, and the days—as they say—fairly flew. We had the required rum punch in Ocho Rios, fought off the beggars in Port-au-Prince, visited Bluebeard's Castle in Charlotte Amalie and eventually made it to Barbados.

Barbados is a lovely island, with narrow winding roads that skirt the ocean and cross between the Caribbean and Atlantic shores through high stands of sugar cane that quite efficiently hide any view of approaching traffic; but my rented car and I managed to get to the address I had been given without brushing death more than three or four times. The man to whom I presented the ex-president's card was not in the least perturbed to be giving up the carving; if anything, he seemed relieved to be rid of its responsibility. It was neatly packaged in straw, wrapped in brown paper and tied with twine, and I left it exactly that way as I drove back to the dock through the friendly islanders, all of whom demonstrated their happy, carefree insouciance by walking in the middle of the road.

There was no problem about carrying the package aboard. Other passengers from the M. V. Andropolis were forming a constant line, like ants, to and from the ship, leaving empty-handed to return burdened with Wedgwood, Hummel figures, camera lenses and weirdly woven straw hats that did not fit. I gave up my boarding pass at the gangplank, climbed to my proper deck and locked myself in my stateroom, interested in seeing this carving upon which M'sieu Antoine Duvivier was willing to wager the princely sum of 20,000 United States dollars.

The paper came away easily enough. I eased the delicate carving from its bed of straw and took it to the light of my desk lamp. At first I was so interested in studying the piece for its authenticity that the true beauty of the carving didn't strike me; but when I finally came to concede that I was, indeed, holding a genuine Tien Tse Huwai in my hands and got down to looking at the piece itself, I had to admit that M'sieu Duvivier, whatever his other failings, was a man of excellent taste. I relished the delicate nuances with which Tien had managed his intricate subject, the warmth he had been able to impart to his cold medium, the humor he had been genius enough to instill in the ivory scene. Each figure in the relaxed yet ritualistic village dance had his own posture, and although there were easily 40 or 50 men and women involved, carved with infinite detail on a plaque no larger than six by eight inches and possibly three inches in thickness, there was no sense of crowding. One could allow himself to be drawn into the carving, to almost imagine movement or hear the flutes. I enjoyed the study of the masterpiece for another few minutes and then carefully rewrapped it and tucked it into the air-conditioning duct of my stateroom, pleased that the first portion of my assignment had been completed with such ease. I replaced the grillwork and went upstairs to the bar, prepared to enjoy the remaining three or four days of balmy breezes—if not shimmering sands, since Barbados had been our final port.

The trip back to Miami was enjoyable but uneventful. I lost in the shuffleboard tournament, largely due to a nearsighted partner, but in compensation I picked up a record number of spoons from the bottom of the swimming pool and received in reward, at the captain's party, a crystal ashtray engraved with a design of Triton either coming up or going down for the third time. What I am trying to say is that, all in all, I enjoyed myself completely and the trip was almost compensation for the thorough—and humiliating—search I had to suffer when I finally went through Customs in Miami. As usual, they did everything but disintegrate my luggage, and they handled my person in a manner I normally accept only from young ladies. But at last I was free of Customs—to their obvious chagrin—and I found myself in the street in one piece. So I took myself and my luggage to a hotel for the night.

And the next morning I reboarded the M. V. Andropolis for its next trip—in the same cabin—a restful three-day cruise to nowhere. . . .

Huuygens smiled at me gently. My expression must have caused the waiter concern—he probably thought I had left my wallet at home—for he hurried over. To save myself embarrassment, I ordered another round and then went back to staring at Huuygens.

I see (Kek went on, his eyes twinkling) that intelligence has finally forced its presence upon you. I should have thought it was rather obvious. These Caribbean cruise ships vary their schedules, mixing trips to the islands with these short cruises to nowhere, where they merely wander aimlessly upon the sea and eventually find their way back—some say with considerable luck—to their home port. Since they touch no foreign shore, and since even the ships' shops are closed during these cruises, one is not faced with the delay or embarrassment of facing a Customs agent upon one's return. Therefore, if one were to take a cruise *preceding* a cruise to nowhere and were to be so careless as to inadvertently leave a small object—in the air-conditioning duct of his stateroom, for example—during the turnaround, he could easily retrieve it on the second cruise and walk off the ship with it in his pocket, with no fear of discovery.

Which, of course, is what I did . . .

The flight to New York was slightly anticlimactic, and I called M'sieu Duvivier as soon as I landed at Kennedy. He was most pleasantly surprised, since less than a month had actually elapsed, and said he would expect me as fast as I could get there by cab.

The ex-president of St. Michel lived in a lovely apartment on Central Park South, and as I rode up in the elevator, I thought of how pleasant it must be to have endless amounts of money at one's disposal; but before I had a chance to dwell on that thought too much, we had arrived and I found myself pushing what I still think was a lapis-lazuli doorbell set in a solid-gold frame. It made one want to weep. At any rate, Duvivier himself answered the door, as anxious as any man I have ever seen. He didn't even wait to ask me in or inquire as to my taste in aperitifs.

"You have it?" he asked, staring at my coat pocket.

"Before we go any further," I said, "I should like you to repeat the exact terms of our wager. The *exact* terms, if you please."

He looked at me in irritation, as if I were being needlessly obstructive.

"All right," he said shortly. "I wagered you twenty thousand dollars of my money against two dollars of yours that you would *not* bring me a small carving from Barbados through United States Customs and deliver it to me in New York. Is that correct?"

I sighed. "Perfectly correct," I said and reached into my pocket. "You are a lucky man. You won." And I handed him his two dollars . . .

I stared across the table at Huuygens. I'm afraid my jaw had gone slack. He shook his head at me, a bit sad at my lack of comprehension.

"You can't possibly understand," he said, almost petulantly. "It is so incredibly lovely . . ."

Scream in a Soundproof Room

Michael Gilbert

It was second nature in Orloff to watch people without appearing to do so.

So, as Ladislas Petrov walked slowly up and down the handsome, paneled room that was partly his old drawing room and partly his new library, Orloff took out a lighter, lit a cigarette, and put away his lighter, and polished his nails and examined the toes of his own boots. Though his eyes rested rarely on his host his attention was on him the whole time.

The precaution was unconsciousness, the fruits of the life that Orloff had lived: nearly forty years of it since, as a boy of ten, he had started by carrying messages for the anarchist underground.

How old had he been when he had first been flogged? Fourteen was it? Or fifteen? How old when first condemned to death, and saved by some quirk of the absolute monarchy? Saved to see that monarchy go down in blood and dust and bitter humiliation; saved to see himself, as Party Secretary, the effective ruler of the country that had once hung him to a steel ring and beaten him.

It was purely unconscious, because Orloff had no reason now to distrust or to fear Ladislas Petrov. Petrov was that rarity, a Communist leader who had succeeded in reaching retirement. Rich, no longer ambitious, politically secure, dangerous to no one, he lived on in his handsome villa at Provst, a living exception to the rule that no revolutionary man dies in his bed.

"It is the joinery which is so clever," he said. "You see? Each edge dovetailed to the other, but the dovetails hide each other successively, so that in the end, no joint appears."

He stroked with his finger the clean poplar wood which, fashioned into book shelves and pediment, ran the length of the wall.

The man who had fashioned it was in the room with them. He had completed his work on the bookcases and the presses and was finishing now the woodwork of the new door. Orloff had noticed the door as he came in. It was solid and very heavy, but so beautifully balanced and hung that it moved to a finger's touch. You would imagine almost that a breath would open or shut it. When it closed, it slid into the jamb with that soft kiss that meant fitting to a hundredth of an inch on every side.

"We have fine carpenters still in our country," he agreed.

"You must not say 'carpenter.' I made that mistake myself at first. A carpenter is a man who builds houses. He has a big saw, to cut beams, and a heavy hammer, to drive nails." Petrov made a pantomime of sawing and hammering and laughed at his own clowning. "This man is a cabinet maker. He is a craftsman, a precision worker."

Although the workman was within hearing and took in every word they said, both men spoke about him as if he were not there, or had no proper understanding.

Orloff turned his searchlight attention on him for a moment. He was a big, brown-faced, white-haired man with a smile. An unusually good advertisement for the regime.

"You pay him?"

"Nothing, but for each day's work I give him a month's privilege ticket. If he works here twelve days he will be able to live well for a year—is that right?"

Finding himself addressed, the man smiled and bobbed his head. A privilege ticket enabled him to buy, at low cost, the extra fats and meat and milk that, in the normal way, only senior party members could enjoy.

"It is good work. It makes a handsome room."

His eye was still on the man. On his face, his hands, his canvas sack of tools. Orloff's intelligence picked up one fact—two facts—but failed, for the moment, to translate them.

"I gave some thought to it," agreed Petrov complacently. "First, we designed the shutters." The shutters flanked the long, single window which looked straight across Lake Plerny. They were cleverly designed but did not entirely conceal the fact that the windows themselves were barred, like the windows of a cell, by steel bars. Even in retirement a revolutionary leader could not neglect certain safeguards.

It would be a difficult room to attack, thought Orloff. One narrow, barred window. One heavy door. He had no doubt that under the fine paneling was steel plate. The walls were so thick that they were almost soundproof. An easy room to defend. But why think of that now? There was no fighting nowadays. No opposition. They were getting fat. Fat and soft.

Petrov suddenly laughed. "We are all three cabinet makers," he said. "You realize that? All three in this room."

It was true, thought Orloff. Difficult to realize now, as you looked at old Papa Petrov. Difficult to see in him the fighter, the man who had held the post office for nearly a week in the first May rising, held it with a handful of men and boys, little ammunition and no food.

Even more difficult to see the ruthless prosecutor of the purges. The man who had placed his own brother on trial for treason and countersigned the order for his execution without emotion. The man who, when everyone else had cried, "Halt," had gone one step further—and then another.

Who had shot, with the guilty Rabotkin, the innocent Kometsy. Who had said, as Kometsy was prosecuted and handed to the Security Police, "He is innocent now, perhaps. But he has the look of a man who may be guilty some day."

Orloff found himself thinking of things he had not remembered for many years, things he had thought buried under the heap of the intervening time. Those had been days when every man carried his head loose on his shoulders.

Why did his mind come back to Kometsy? Perhaps because he had been the greatest, and the last, of the victims. And as an oak, when felled in a thicket, brings down a host of lesser trees, so had tumbled all Kometsy's friends.

His secretaries. His family. His department. His friends. His wife had taken poison. There was a brother, Andreas. Something about Andreas? He had escaped. By great good fortune Andreas had been in Washington at the time of the trials, and by better fortune had had his family with him.

So rapidly had these thoughts passed through Orloff's mind that he found Petrov was still laughing at his own stupid joke.

"I have made and unmade many cabinets in my time," he repeated.

But Orloff was still looking at the workman, who had just finished his work on the door jamb with a few strokes of a spokeshave. A first-class workman, indeed, thought Orloff, who knew something of most things. Not one to massacre his material and then hide the scars behind sandpapering and putty. His finished product was clean wood, cleanly worked.

"Was your father a carpenter?" he asked suddenly.

"Indeed, greatness," said the man, speaking for the first time, "and his father before him."

"I thought it might be so," said Orloff. "You do not often see tools like this now."

It was a gauger plane that had caught his eye. A lovely instrument of bright steel and brass. He picked it up and twirled the gauge screw which regulated with micrometer precision the depth and set of the blade.

"It would take you—what—a year—to buy such a tool?"

"More, greatness," said the man. "I work little for money. Many of these my father left me. Others came to me before—before the Liberation."

Orloff nearly smiled. He guessed that if the man had been alone he would have said something very different.

He was packing away his tools now, with careful hands, as a surgeon might lay aside his instruments. Each chisel with its edge hidden in a wad of oakum, the graded drills, the curious gouges, the small, thin, heavy, brass-backed saw.

When he had done he bobbed to the two men asking leave to withdraw himself from their presence.

Petrov smiled, and made a gesture of dismissal with his hand. The man opened the door and ambled through, then he turned, smiled again, and closed the door behind him.

The little sigh which it made hung on the air.

Petrov moved again to the window. Below the terrace wall the waters winked in the setting sun.

"When I die," he said, "I will leave instructions in my will for my coffin to be taken out and sunk in the middle of the lake. They say it is bottomless—an old volcano—"

"I think," said Orloff, in his hard, incisive voice, "that you should check up on that man. The sooner the better."

"That man?"

"The man who's just left. Who does he call himself?"

"I never asked him his name," said Petrov. "The local co-operative sent him."

"Even local co-operatives have been known to make mistakes," said Orloff, drily.

"Are you sure you're not—"

"—letting my suspicious mind run away with me? No. I'm not sure. But my suspicious mind has just told me two things which my eyes saw five minutes ago. Do you remember the gauger plane? It would cost you—in this country today—oh, thirty dollars. Would a man like that earn thirty dollars in a year? In three years?"

"But he told you," said Petrov. "It came down to him from his father."

"That sort of plane did not exist five years ago."

"I see," said Petrov. He walked across to the fireplace and touched the bell. "Are you sure?"

"I know about these things," said Orloff. "It is a precision instrument, first invented for the aircraft industry, in America. But it was not only the plane. Did you not see his hands?"

"I saw them," said Petrov. "But they said nothing to me. What did they show to you?"

"Fresh blisters. Blisters from this job he has been doing here in the past twelve days. In the palm, from the butt of his chisel. On the side of the index finger from the handle of his saw."

"Why not?" said Petrov. "He has used both chisel and saw. I have seen myself."

"A carpenter," said Orloff, contemptuously. "And the son of a carpenter. A man who had handled tools since he was in knee breeches. Those parts of his hands would be like leather. And a third thing—"

His voice was so sharp that Petrov stopped pacing and stood still, looking at him.

"*Why has no one answered your bell?*"

"It is that old fool, Sebastian," said Petrov. "He is getting deaf. If he is not in his pantry he does not hear the bell—"

"Perhaps," said Orloff.

He walked across the room, his feet noiseless on the heavy carpet, and turned the handle of the new door. It turned quite freely. But the door remained shut.

He threw his weight back, once, twice. So little impression did he make that he might have been pulling against a tree.

"He has locked us in?"

"From the feel of it," said Orloff, "I should surmise that the door has been screwed to the jamb with half a dozen very long screws. You'd best try the telephone, though I should guess it is little use."

Petrov seized the instrument, listened a moment, jiggling it, and then put it back. "Dead," he said.

"Does your window open?" Orloff asked.

"The bars—"

"I had no intention of getting out of it. I wished to shout for help."

He had crossed the room as he spoke. Petrov came with him. Something seemed to have happened to the window. The catch could be opened, but their combined strength could not move the sash by a fraction up or down.

Quite suddenly the air in the room seemed stifling. Orloff ran to the mantelpiece, picked up a heavy iron candlestick, ran back, and swung it hard at the glass.

The next moment the candlestick had clattered to the floor. The glass was scarcely scratched.

"Bullet proof," said Petrov. For some reason he had dropped his voice to a whisper. "That man—could he have been Andreas?"

"It might have been," said Orloff. "It cannot be coincidence that his name was in my mind, too. I hardly knew him, but there was something in the look. Sit down, man, and stop sweating."

"What—how—what does he hope to do?"

Good God, thought Orloff, with a spasm of disgust, I was right. The old man's gone soft. There's no fight left in him.

"Sit down," he said again. "If he aims to suffocate us, the less air we use the better. It's a big room. Someone will come soon."

"Not before morning," said Petrov. "Not unless we can attract attention."

"A lot can happen in twelve hours," said Orloff. "If I am not back by nightfall, my own office will start to panic." For the first time that afternoon a very faint smile appeared round his lips. "They'll probably think I've crossed the Curtain."

"Stop talking," said Petrov. His voice was high. Like a woman about to plunge into the emotional depths of a tantrum.

Orloff looked sharply at him. Then he heard it, too.

Somewhere behind the bookshelves, behind the beautiful paneling, and the clever joinery: a deep, purposeful, purring, clicking, pendulum note.

"Maybe we haven't got twelve hours after all," said Orloff, resignedly. "Maybe not even one."

It was not too bad until Petrov started to scream.

Return of Verge Likens

Davis Grubb

And the funny part was that not even Riley McGrath's own friends blamed Verge Likens for killing him. Some even found a kind of wry, burlesque justice in the ponderous, infallible way that Verge went about bringing Riley's death to pass. Because whatever fear or awe or envy the people of Tygarts County felt for Riley McGrath, self-elected emperor of our state, they knew that he'd had no right to shoot down Verge's father, old Stoney Likens, that night at the Airport Inn. The two boys, Verge and Wilford, came when Sheriff Reynolds sent for them, and they viewed the body of the old man with bleak, hill-born muteness.

"It was Mister McGrath that done it," explained Fred Starcher, who ran the roadhouse. "But Stoney taken and swung at him with a beer bottle. So it was self-defense."

Verge looked at Fred and Sheriff Reynolds with flat, dead eyes. "Daddy didn't have no gun on him," he said patiently, "so I can't see no fair reason for Mister McGrath shooting him."

And the brother Wilford stood by, dumbly heeding the exchange. He was slack-mouthed with fascination, his eyes darting from one man to the other in turn, his moonface bland with an idiot and almost blasphemous innocence.

"If Daddy had had a gun," Verge went on, "it would have been different. But it isn't self-defense when a man with a gun shoots down a man that don't have none."

Fred Starcher opened his mouth to explain again how it all had been and then he saw the eyes, cold and flat as creek stones.

"Well," he said, looking away, "it seemed to me like it was self-defense."

Although it wouldn't have mattered much one way or the other whether it had been self-defense or premeditated murder or just plain target practice. Because there wasn't a man in the state of West Virginia who could stand up against Riley McGrath for very long without losing his job, his bank account or some of his blood. But there was no more argument. For suddenly, like wraiths, Verge and Wilford were gone out of the place into the March dark, roaring up the highway for home in Stoney's old fruit truck.

"Bud, don't take it so hard," Wilford said. "Like as not Mister McGrath was drunk."

The flat eyes, turning from the highway to Wilford, shone with loathing in the dark. "He was your daddy, too," Verge said. "Your blood kin. You gutless rat."

"Don't talk like that, Bud!" Wilford whined. "If there was something to be done I'd be all for it. But there ain't!"

"Yes there is," said Verge, his eyes fixed on the traffic stripe. "There is something to be done and I am fixing to do it."

"What?"

"Kill Mister McGrath," Verge said.

"Kill Mi—! Bud, you must be crazy!" Wilford cried out. "Mister McGrath's the biggest man in the whole state of West Virginia! Why, don't Senator Marcheson hisself sit and drink seven-dollar whiskey with Mister McGrath in the Stonewall Jackson lobby every time he comes to town? Don't every policeman in town tip his cap when Mister McGrath walks by?"

"That don't matter a bit," said Verge. "I'll find a way. It may take me a little time, but I'll find a way to do it."

And that was all Verge Likens ate or drank or breathed or dreamed about from that night on. . . .

One night after supper, months later when the brothers were alone and neither had spoken for nearly an hour, Wilford felt suddenly as if the impalpable violence of Verge's obsession had secretly turned on him.

"Then dammit!" he shrilled to the pale, quiet profile of his brother, who sat in the shadow of the trumpet vines along the porch, "why don't you get it over with? Why don't you hide out along the fence by the Airport Inn some night and shoot him in the back? He comes there all the time with that black-haired Mary from Baltimore Street! Why don't you—"

"No, Wilford," Verge said quietly, with neither surprise nor anger at his brother's outburst. "I want Mister McGrath to see my face when I kill him. If I taken and shot him in the dark, that way he wouldn't never know it was me that done. When I do it, I want Mister McGrath to look at my face a good long while and know who it is. And I want to be sure the killing takes a slow, long while."

Rush Sigafoose was shaving Riley McGrath in his number one chair when Wilford found him next morning. Wilford was shaking so badly that he was afraid he would not be able to make the speech he had lain awake all night considering.

He sat down in one of the straight-backed chairs under the shelf of lettered shaving mugs to wait until the morning ritual was finished. At last Riley McGrath labored down from the chair and stripped a greenback from his expensive billfold. Wilford stood up, quaking.

"Mister McGrath," he said, wringing his cotton cap.

"Yes, son?"

"Mister McGrath," Wilford said, feeling a little courage coming back, "I sure would be glad if I could talk to you for a little while."

"Certainly, my boy," said the great man. "Come along across the street to my office. I have an appointment in half an hour with Judge Beam but I can give you a moment of my time. A man should never grow too important to keep in touch with the people of his home town."

The office, musty, small, cluttered as a pack rat's nest, was deathly still as the two seated themselves: Wilford in the stiff split-bottom chair by the window and Riley McGrath in the creaking swivel chair behind the old, scratched desk upon which he had parlayed the fortunes of a state. Wilford watched while Riley licked the tip of an expensive Havana and clipped it thoughtfully.

"It's about my brother Verge," said Wilford, wetting his lips and staring at Riley McGrath's sober blue tie. "Our daddy was Stoney Likens."

Riley McGrath cracked a kitchen match into flame with his

thumbnail. He puffed silently for a moment and though Wilford could not see them, he could feel the grey eyes appraising him, weighing the situation, seeing it simultaneously from every possible angle.

"That matter was settled during the last term of Judge Beam's court," Riley McGrath said presently. "Your father attacked me, son. I shot him in self-defense that night. Nobody regretted the incident more than I did."

"It's my brother Verge," Wilford reiterated, as if he had not been listening at all. "I just don't want nothing to happen to my brother, Mister McGrath. He's all I got left now."

"Nothing need happen to your brother, son," grunted Riley McGrath. He leafed through some papers on his desk, already finished with the interview.

"Something might," Wilford said. He cleared his throat and listened for a moment to the coaxing, pointless shrilling of a wren outside.

"Verge claims he is fixing to kill you, Mister McGrath," Wilford said.

Riley McGrath leaned back in his chair and blew a cloud of smoke toward the dusty, yellow window. "That's a very foolish idea for your brother to entertain," he said. "Very foolish, son."

"I thought—" gasped Wilford, and then swallowed. "If maybe you was to send for him, Mister McGrath. Talk to him. If maybe you was to explain to Verge how it was self-defense after all. It might help, Mister McGrath. 'Deed to God, I don't want nothing happening to Verge."

"Nothing will happen to your brother," Riley McGrath said, "so long as he behaves himself in this town."

Wilford sighed despairingly and stared at his hands, twisting the cap on his knees.

Riley McGrath's eyes were as cold as gun metal now.

"I understand, however," he continued, "that the death of your father may have brought about certain—expenses. I've thought about it often. And now I'm going to do something—though I don't feel I'm actually obliged to do it—that may spread oil on troubled waters."

Wilford watched as Riley McGrath opened the alligator billfold and counted out five one-hundred-dollar bills; he watched him slip them into an envelope and toss it across the desk.

Verge didn't say anything right away when Wilford finally got around to confessing what he had done that day in town. It was after supper and Verge was squatting on the porch steps, cleaning his rifle and listening silently as Wilford babbled on apologetically.

"That sure was a fool trick, Wilford," Verge said after a bit. "But it don't change nothing. There's nothing you can do about Mister McGrath getting killed and there is nothing he can do about it either. There's nothing any mortal in Tygarts County or in the whole state of West Virginia can do about it."

Then Wilford was still for a while before he pulled out the manila envelope and told his brother about the five one-hundred-dollar bills. Verge laid down the rifle and came up on the porch to the rocker where Wilford sat and took the envelope out of his hand. He looked at it and then at Wilford, not laughing, not angry, not glad, not seeming to think or feel anything at all.

"This will make things a sight easier," Verge said. "It will save a lot of time and fuss, I reckon. It will bring the day that much closer. I hope you thanked Mister McGrath, Wilford."

"Bud," Wilford stammered. "I—I don't recollect if I—I—"

"I hope you did," Verge said again, folding the envelope carefully and slipping it into his shirt pocket. "That certainly was real nice of Mister McGrath to do that, Wilford."

All that night Wilford listened to Verge moving restlessly about the house and when dawn stood suddenly white against the windows he started from a brief, troubled slumber and saw his brother by the bed, dressed in the single cheap mail-order suit he possessed, his good white shirt a vivid wedge in the shadow, his square, small face as mute and baffling as ever.

"Why, where you going to, Bud?" gasped Wilford, struggling up under the old Army blanket.

"I'm catching the morning bus to Charleston," Verge said. "I'll be gone a good long while, I reckon. Good-by, Wilford."

"*Where?*"

"To Charleston," said Verge. "I told you that once. I'm going to school with that money."

"School!" whispered Wilford. "Why, that's real fine, Bud! A body can't do with too much learning and that's for certain. What kind of a school?"

"The kind of school," said Verge (and even in the dim light Wilford could feel that the flat eyes were not looking at him nor at anything) "where I can learn to kill Mister McGrath the right way. Slow. So he'll have to look at my face a good long while and know it's coming and there'll not be any way for him to get at that big blue pistol of his. I don't know when I'll be back. Be sure and take good care of the place, Wilford."

And that was all there was to it. Wilford had crept naked and shivering to the dusty window and watched his brother's thin, unforgiving shape fade into the mist, moving as inexorably as the piston of some machine.

Wilford worked on alone at his job at the box factory in town during the next lonely months, moving about uneasily, needing the companionship of his brother and yet dreading the day when Verge should return. Often at night he would start up in the dark, sweating and a-crawl with panic, feeling suddenly that he should run to Riley McGrath and try again to warn him somehow of the awful, unremitting purpose of which Riley McGrath could not be aware inasmuch as he had never laid eyes on Verge Likens' person. Until at last it seemed to Wilford that neither Verge nor the murder nor Riley McGrath himself had ever even existed.

In all the sixteen months Verge was away, Wilford had received only a penny post card from him, two weeks after the morning he had left. There was no message on it at all. A penny post card from a drugstore with a picture of the Kanawha County Courthouse, colored with the cheap, naïve innocence of flowers at a country funeral and yet somehow in itself as obsessed and malevolent as Verge himself. No message at all. This would be Verge's way of saying that he had arrived.

Of course, Riley McGrath himself had dismissed the whole business from his mind months before. Because, naturally enough, he had never really been frightened in the beginning. Yet, for some reason, the whole affair came into his mind that last morning in Rush Sigafoose's barbershop as he watched Wilford drive down Beech Street in the old fruit truck on his way to the box factory. Riley McGrath lay back, smothered and wallowing in Roman comfort beneath the steaming towels. He was chuckling at the memory of the whole absurd encounter as Rush Sigafoose's new barber stropped the razor and whistled softly to himself.

"Rush," Riley had murmured from beneath the steaming cloths, "how's Nevada and the kids?"

Rush Sigafoose remembered that part of it well because those were the last words Riley ever said to him. Yet it was a long time before Rush knew anything was wrong. He had gone back into the storeroom for some fresh linen and a bottle of bay rum and even then, after he had been puttering around the marble shelves for nearly five minutes, he wasn't on to what was going on in the chair. And then he saw them in the mirror like figures in some monstrous waxworks pantomime: Riley McGrath, his head strained back in the head rest as far as it would go, his face purple and livid by turns and his mouth shaping idiot sounds that Rush could not hear and didn't much want to. Rush dropped the comb he had been cleaning and started quickly toward them.

"Don't come a foot closer, Mister Sigafoose," Verge Likens said softly, the bright, hollow-ground razor light as a hair on Riley McGrath's pulsing throat. "For if you do—I'll cut Mister McGrath clean to the neckbone."

So Rush sat down, shaking and sick to his stomach, and watched them there for maybe half an hour, listening and trying to make out what it was that Verge Likens was saying to Riley McGrath. Because that was the worst part of all: Verge taking the pains to shave Riley and then telling him who he was and talking to him all that terrible time with the cold, honed Sheffield blade pressed taut against the fat folds of Riley's throat; taking all that time to kill a man and all the while talking to him in that flat, crooning whisper.

Rush Sigafoose used to tell that part of the story next to last and then he would always wind up the telling in the same way. He'd tell about Verge going to barber college down in the capital city for a year and a half on that five hundred dollars just to learn how to kill a man slow. And how he came back to Tygarts County at last and took a cheap room in the hotel by the depot and dropped by to pester Rush Sigafoose about a job every morning for nearly a month.

Rush had finally hired him the morning before—not knowing him from Adam himself—and that was the holy irony of it. Rush always said that Verge Likens was the darnedest natural-born barber he'd ever seen. He swore to that. Because when Doc Brake came down from the courthouse that morning and looked at Riley McGrath's body he said there wasn't so much as a mark on his throat. Not so much as a single scratch.

The Fair Chance

James Hay, Jr.

She opened the door of her flat, and at once stood face to face with the ruin of her world. It had come as she had pictured it a thousand times. Unexpectedly. Suddenly. Without a chance to save herself.

The man whose ring had brought her to the door stood, without taking off his hat, staring at her out of quick eyes, an inoffensive smile drawing up the corners of his mouth. His round, slightly fat face conveyed an impression of habitual watchfulness. In the seven years that had passed since she had seen him he had not changed. The long, stubborn line of his jaw was the same; so was the suggestion of lionlike strength in his thick, stooped shoulders.

"Hello, Mayme," he said in a rumbling baritone, the motion of his lips scarcely perceptible.

For a moment she could not speak. She leaned with her right shoulder against the door casing, her left hand still on the knob. Her face had gone instantly cold and gray, like a winter's twilight. She looked at him drearily.

"Leavit," she said at last, slowly, "Leavit, the detective."

"Yes, Steve Leavit," he said. "Guess I'll have to come in, Mayme."

Unsmiling now, he was a man intent on his business, making no attempt to exult over her. He acted as if the offense for which she was wanted had been committed that day instead of seven years ago.

Resistance was out of the question. She stepped back and threw the door farther open. Prematurely gray hair and the lines that come from courageous fighting against hardship made her look older than her twenty-five years. But even with the pallor of fright she was almost handsome. Her face had strength in it.

When the detective had crossed the threshold he waited for her to close the door and precede him down the narrow hall. She went with flying feet. On her way to answer his ring she had seen that the clock on the bookcase in the living room pointed to six minutes to six. And her husband was invariably home by six! The thought drummed through her brain: "George will be here any minute—in five minutes at the outside! I've got to make it easy for him, be worthy of him!"

As she traversed the short distance of the hall her mind worked with incredible swiftness. Her whole beloved past flashed into view; her wedding day four years ago; George's saying he would never believe bad, not even a little bad, of her, no matter what anybody might tell him; the happiness of being trusted and honored always! She locked her teeth against the moaning cry, "My dear happiness!"

In the well kept but cheaply furnished little living room she turned and faced Leavit. She noticed with surprise that she was weak, like a woman suffering heat prostration. Her tongue was rough, as if it had sand on it. Irregular, jagged patches of white fire flashed past her eyes. She put her hand on his arm.

"Mr. Leavit, give me a fair chance, will you?" she implored him, the words coming in a rush. "I'm married now, and my husband will be here any minute, and I don't want him to see me arrested. The shock, the grief of it, would kill him! Don't take me before eight-thirty! Give me till eight-thirty! That's only two hours and a half, Mr. Leavit. I'll make him go out by then, and then I'll leave a note for him and go with you!"

Leavit took off his black derby hat and put it down beside the clock on the bookcase. The living room was so small that, when he did that, he could sit down in a chair beside the center table without taking another step. He did so, moving with a slowness that tortured her.

"What do you mean by a fair chance, Mayme?" he asked, looking up to her standing on the other side of the table. "Ain't seven years a fair—"

"I mean a fair chance to make it as easy for him as I can, to get away so it will hurt him as little as possible!" she interrupted, through her clenched teeth. "He'll be here in three minutes now. In three minutes or sooner! He—"

Leavit put up his hand. "Not so fast, Mayme! Not—"

"I'm not Mayme any more!" she corrected him. "I was Loula Bentley when he met me, out in Chicago, making my own living. His name's George Paxton. He's a bookkeeper. And we've been married four years. And he loves me. Loves me so! And I— Oh, my God, Mr. Leavit, I love him so it's going to kill me having to leave him this way and tell him I—I was on the books at headquarters for stealing! And I never stole a thing in my life! Not a thing! You, you who've hunted me for seven years, Mr. Leavit, you know I'm innocent! I—"

"But," Leavit objected, with a lift of his shoulders, "you were indicted for stealing, and you jumped your bond. You—"

She interrupted him again, coming around the table and taking hold of him, grasping his arm with both of her hands.

"I didn't do it!" she said, fiercely, her utterance so hurried that she spoke in a hoarse whisper. "I didn't! I was living among crooks because I couldn't help it then, but I never did a crooked thing in all my life. I stayed straight. You know it! And you've got to give me a chance."

He shook himself free of her grasp, showing his impatience.

"Why?" he demanded. "Why have I got?"

The question infuriated her. She fought down an impulse to laugh in his face, to revile him.

She went back to her chair opposite his and looked over his shoulder at the clock on the bookcase. Two minutes to six! Two minutes more! In a second she prayed her whole heart wordlessly: "Oh, to be worthy of George! To make this thing easy for him!" Her chest hurt her. Her tongue was sanded again, and thick. But she answered him without hesitation, pleading.

"Because you're a human being!" she said, leaning toward him, her weight on her clenched fists resting on the table. "And you've got a wife! And you've hunted me for seven years, and a few hours won't matter to you, but they'll mean a little less of hell for me—and for my husband!"

She went back to him and, sinking to her knees, clasped his right shoulder. Her fingers dug into his muscles until they bruised him.

"I saved your life once, Mr. Leavit!" she said. "You remember that, don't you? I was sixteen years old then. 'Hump' Browning had it all framed to get you; and I got on to it, and I went to you and told you about it. Yes, you do remember it! You know you do! So I'm asking you now to pay me back for that—such a little pay! He'll be here in a few seconds! Just a chance to write him a note and explain and keep him from seeing a policeman lead me away! It isn't much. Just two hours and a half, so I can ease this blow to the man who's built and furnished and kept up heaven for me. Do that for me, Mr. Leavit! Do—"

They heard footsteps in the corridor outside the flat. She clung to him, her fingers kneading his shoulder.

"He's coming!" she said, in a whisper. "Just the two hours and a half! I'll tell him you're an old friend of mine, just dropped in, just found out where I was!" She shook him, staring with hot eyes into his.

"All right, Mayme," he growled quickly. "But no tricks; remember!" He caught her hand and made her feel, through his coat below the left arm, the outline of the automatic pistol slung there.

She got to her feet, and as she rose put up a shaking hand to smooth back her disheveled hair. Her husband, who got away from work later than she, always left the latchkey to her. He was ringing the doorbell now.

She went to the door into the little hall and gave him her usual welcoming hail. "Coming, Georgie, pronto!"

Her wish to succeed in this desperate play was so intense that it hurt her like a burn. She thought, "I've had to do some good acting before; I can do it now." And at once her mind seized a greater measure of command over her body. She felt the tide of her blood thrust the pallor from her cheeks. The thickness went out of her tongue. By the time she got to the front door and opened it her hands were steady, her voice nearly normal. Only her breathing betrayed her; it was still fast from the pounding of her heart. He noticed it as she stood on her tiptoes and put up her face for his kiss.

"Why, you're—" he began, with a look of worry.

"Excitement!" she answered his unvoiced inquiry gaily, and stood aside, drawing his attention to the other end of the hall, where, she knew, the plain-clothes man was standing watching her every move, listening for even a hint of treachery to her bargain with him. "Here's a surprise for you, George!"

She went forward with him a step or two and introduced him. "This is the great and only husband, Steve!" she said, a proud playfulness in her tone. "And, George, this is Steve Leavit, an old friend of mine, an old playfellow even when we were kids in Phila-delphia."

Paxton put out his hand, with a warm smile. He was a pleasant-faced fellow in his early thirties, slender and a little taller than the average. His paleness, from constant indoor work, was in striking contrast to his black hair and eyes.

"I hadn't seen him for nearly eight years," she rattled on, preced-ing them into the living room. "He hadn't an idea I was in New York! Just happened to run plump into me on Thirty-third street!"

She found herself possessed of two intelligences. Her laughing chatter to the two men was a curtain behind which she flayed her-self with the scourge of bitterness. Why, she asked herself contemp-tuously, had she been fool enough to believe that the effrontery of living under the New York authorities' noses would be her greatest protection? Why had she trusted to her white hair and a retired life to save her? In view of this catastrophe now, her folly made her frantic.

Leavit played his part naturally. The gameness of the woman compelled his admiration. He caught himself wondering whether she would last it out or give him the job of carrying her off in screaming hysterics.

But he watched both her and Paxton with incessant keenness; and once his alertness was rewarded. Before she went back to the kitchen to finish her interrupted task of getting the dinner he caught sight of their reflection in a mirror above the piano when they evidently believed themselves unobserved. Paxton, with uplifted eyebrows, flashed her a look of inquiry and mock jealousy, a move of his head indicating the visitor. Her reply to that was a *moue*, a mouth puckered as for a kiss, and widened, laughing eyes, all of which said as plainly as words could have done, "He's all right; and don't you dare to pretend even that you're jealous!" The intimate understanding in this byplay, the unqualified loyalty and devotion of each to the other expressed in their interchange of glance and smile, gave the detective a clear idea of how great their happiness must be. He was glad he had given her the chance.

His vigilance, however, did not relax. For seven years this woman, who had successfully defied his skill and the resources of the whole country's thief-hunting machine, had never been entirely out of his mind. Her escape had been a blot on his record. Now that she was under his hand at last, he proposed to give her no opportunity to get away a second time.

His surveillance, he knew, was flawless. During his entire stay in the flat, save for that one brief scene reflected in the mirror, she made no attempt to speak a word or make a sign unknown to Leavit; and Paxton, reassured by her *moue*, devoted himself to making his wife's friend feel at home.

While she was in the kitchen putting the chops and the two vegetables into dishes she worked automatically, her mind busy with the unceasing resolve, "To be worthy of him in this! To make it easy for him!"

The men went together to the bathroom to wash up.

When she called them into the little box of a dining room the meal was on the table. Throughout the dinner she led the talk, making it almost entirely a series of reminiscences of her early girlhood in Philadelphia, with frequent descriptions of persons and places that kept Paxton interested.

Leavit, saying little and maintaining his hawklike scrutiny of them, noted their good comradeship. He saw, too, that her hand never once trembled. Her voice had a fresh and girlish note in it, an overtone faintly suggestive of bubbling laughter. Experienced as he was in the fears that come into human eyes, he could detect no shadow of anxiety, even in hers. The longer the thing lasted the more he admired her.

Under her surface show of happy remembrance she was calculating desperately, "I've got to keep it up only till eight-thirty! Only till eight-thirty! If I can hold out that long! Oh, if I only can!" At intervals which seemed to her ages long she allowed herself the painful luxury of a turn of her head and a glance into the living room to tell, by the clock on the bookcase, what time it was, how many minutes more of this heartbreaking pretense she had to endure. Now and then she flexed the muscles of her arms and legs to throw off the clutch of a lethargy heavy as paralysis. The forced smiling made her lips stiff; they felt like cardboard. She was alternately flaming hot and freezing cold.

"Seven-thirty!" she thought as they finished the pie which she had brought from the delicatessen on her way home. "Seven-thirty, and I've got to make the next play!"

She looked across the table at Paxton and spoke in a tone of banter.

"George," she said, with a slant of her eye and a low laugh that made Leavit partner in the teasing, "here's where you get a pleasant surprise! I'm going to send you out to the movies now all by yourself! My meeting with Steve has brought up something I want to talk over with him."

Paxton gave Leavit a swift, keen glance before he looked at her, a flush stealing into his cheeks. He laughed like a man embarrassed.

"Talk over what?" he asked her.

"Oh, be a good sport!" she said, urgency sounding through her levity. "Be a sport, and get out for the evening. All joking aside, this may bring us some profit. And," she concluded, with a slight catch in her throat which she could not prevent, "you'll know all about it soon, anyway."

Leavit was moved by that to come to her help. "Really, Mr. Paxton," he said, seriously, "it ought to do you good and me, too. You'll see later why I wanted to talk about it first with only your wife."

Paxton hesitated, undecided. She had an agonizing longing to catch him by the throat, to shake him into speech, to shout, "Yes! Yes! Yes!" to throw off all this terrible burden of fear and caution.

"Oh, George," she said, sharply, "don't be silly! Have you forgotten I know as much about business as you do?"

To Leavit's surprise, Paxton did not answer that at once, but sat looking down at the table cloth, the line of a frown deepening between his eyebrows. The detective saw that, in this pause, Mrs. Paxton's lower lip hung a little away from her teeth, that her eyelids lifted and fell rapidly.

She was thinking: "Why doesn't he say yes and go out of here? I can't stand it! I've got to stand it! Nearly an hour more! One hour!" She prayed with an intensity which, she thought, should lift her husband out of his chair.

Paxton recovered himself handsomely. "I beg your pardon, both of you," he said with a start from his abstraction. "I had made another appointment for this evening, for both of us—but I can arrange it." He turned to Leavit with a smile. "It's a meeting with a fellow and his wife that might mean a little money for me. But, before I go, have a cigarette."

Leavit heard the long, quivering sigh with which the woman welcomed her husband's decision. She thought, "The worst is over now!" But with even that small degree of relaxation the white patches danced before her eyes again; the faintness, as from extreme heat, was upon her in waves. She had to brace herself, like a man setting himself to resist a rush of superior numbers.

"Yes, thanks," Leavit said, accepting the cigarette.

Mrs. Paxton led the way into the living room. She made no move to follow her husband into the hall, where, on coming in, he had hung up his coat and hat. Without the strength to carry on a conversation during these, the crucial moments of her loving deception, she heard him shuffle his feet while getting into his heavy coat and then, with quick, even stride, go down the hall to the corridor door. Leavit, in his chair by the center table, was watching her, the everlasting wariness in his face.

When the door slammed she sprang out of her chair as if propelled by an outside and irresistible force. Her movement was so unexpected and violent that Leavit started half from his seat to put a hand on her shoulder.

She smiled at him pitifully, drooping against the table. Her face was crimson, her eyeballs suffused with blood, her lips abnormally red and full.

"Nervous!" she explained, her voice thin and weak. "It's been terrible, Mr. Leavit!"

"I guess it was," he said, "but—"

"I'm burning up!" she complained, moistening her thickened lips with the end of her tongue. "Burning up! But I did get away with it, didn't I?" she asked him, a pathetic pride in her voice. "Didn't I do all right?"

"Yes; you've got nerve, all right," he said. "But your time's up now. Let's go."

He made a move to push his chair back.

She went with slow, tottering steps from the table to the little desk in the corner on his left.

"No," she begged; "not yet! You said you'd give me a fair chance, a chance to make it as easy for him as I could! Don't spoil it, Mr. Leavit. Let me write him the note explaining. Just a short note! You wouldn't be so rude to—"

"All right," he stopped her, his impatience growing. "But don't be long! There ain't much etiquette in arresting people."

She sat down at the desk and picked up a pen. Tears were in her eyes at last. They went over, falling down her cheeks. She made him uneasy. Going on like that, she might lose her self-control any minute!

"Oh!" she wailed, and, dropping her voice, appealed to Leavit. "What can I say to him? How is a woman to tell her husband that she's gone, gone forever, for years, to jail, to the penitentiary on framed up evidence? How can I—"

She was halted by a stentorian command, sharp as the crack of a whip.

"Put your hands up, Leavit!" ordered her husband, at whom she was gazing now over Leavit's head, her bloodshot eyes big with bewilderment.

Leavit, wheeling in his chair to face the hall door, in which Paxton stood, reached at the same moment toward the pistol under his coat.

"Stop it, or I'll shoot!" Paxton said, in a clipped, tense voice. "And put your hands up! And you, Loula, don't you move!"

Leavit, having seen Paxton's revolver, obeyed and sat motionless. Paxton came into the room and stood beside his wife.

Leavit, watching her now with an acuteness surpassing his previous shrewd intentness, noted that she, absorbed in her husband's movements, was in reality utterly surprised. Employing to the utmost all his genius for observation, he saw, in the next moment, suspicion born in her eyes, and on top of that came her fear. Not the same sort of fear with which she had recognized him at the door two hours and a half ago. This was a bitterer fear, a more devastating thing. He saw that it crushed her; her chest sank in; her shoulders came closer together; and an artery in her neck, as she held her head back to watch her husband's face, throbbed as if to beat down its walls.

Thought travels fast in a moment like that. The detective, clearly realizing his own helplessness, was able also to follow the woman's feelings. They were, he perceived, a troop of torture. She realized, he saw, that she had endangered her husband's trust in her by mercifully trying to hide her past from him; she was horribly afraid that he was convinced of her guilt.

But what guilt? Leavit saw her eyelids flutter wider to the shock of that speculation, saw even that she asked herself, in her light-

ning-like analysis of this new thunderbolt fallen upon her, whether
Paxton, groping in the dark of suspicion and ignorance, had not
tried her unheard and doomed her to punishment for a crime worse
than that for which she had been indicted.

After Paxton's command, she was the first to speak.

"No!" she said in a half choked voice. "Not that, George! You've
got it wrong! I'll tell you exactly—Mr. Leavit will say I'm telling the
truth."

"Be quiet," Paxton interrupted her, keeping his glance always on
Leavit. "Keep quiet, Loula," he repeated, without harshness.

"Now, sir!" he said to Leavit. "There won't be much etiquette to
this, either!" He addressed his wife again. "Loula, take that pistol
away from him and give it to me."

She did so with trembling fingers, putting the gun into Paxton's
left hand. She sank slowly into the chair nearest him, her eyes
never leaving his face. Leavit could see that he himself meant little
to her now; that bewilderment and fear of her husband were
equally lively in her expression. It was as if she wept aloud, "How
will this man whom I have deceived punish me?"

Paxton spoke to Leavit. His voice, pitched low and tense, carried
a deadly and unqualified menace.

"I could have killed you just now and got away with it," he said,
"the moment I heard you identify yourself as a copper about to arrest my wife. You see, this gun's got a silencer on it. But I heard her
say just now that you'd promised her a fair chance. That stopped
me long enough to find out what it meant. Loula, what was it?"

"It was this way," she explained breathlessly, without a glance at
Leavit. "He was going to take me to the station house before you
came in, but I knew it would break your heart to see me arrested,
and I asked him to give me a chance to write you a note explaining,
to make it as easy as possible for you, darlin'. We would have met
you on the stairs if we had gone out then. And he did just what I
asked. He was fine, George; just fine! And I've never stolen a cent
in all my life!"

"I see," Paxton resumed, ignoring her disclaimer. "Now, then,
Mr. Leavit, I'm going to give you a fair chance in return for that. If
you take it, all right. If you don't, I'll kill you where you sit, as sure
as the sun rises."

His manner displayed an inevitability that was unmistakable.

There was no bluff in him. Leavit, looking up into his eyes, knew that he would do what he said.

"Put your hands down if you want to," Paxton suggested. "Now, to let you understand what this fair chance means, I'm going to explain things to you. Unknown to my wife, I've known for five years that she was a fugitive from justice and indicted for theft."

Leavit, with a swift side glance at her, saw her lips fall open and her left hand go to her heart as if to crush down its leaping pulse. A great wonder was upon her. She might as well have cried out, "How much more splendid is this man than I have ever suspected!"

"But that," Paxton was saying, "didn't mean anything to me, because I knew her. She is a good woman. I know she wouldn't steal and has never stolen. She's my woman. She's my whole world and all my life, because, without her, the world wouldn't be worth fooling with. Do you get that? Understand what this woman, my woman, means to me and what I think of her?"

"Yes," Leavit replied curtly.

"Good," said Paxton. "Then you understand that I will do anything to save her. She's worth saving. She loves me. I am not low lived enough to hand her over to the law to make a disgraced, sorrowing, and broken thing of her when she's got every right under the blue sky to live out her life, happy, loved, and useful. It's my duty to save her. It's your duty," he said, contempt in his pronunciation of the word, "your duty to hand her over to ruin and wreckage.

"But before I'll stand for that," he added, through his set teeth, "I'll kill you. I will, so help me God! Now, here's your fair chance. If my wife will say that you can be trusted to keep your promise, I'll let you walk out of here the moment you say you will never arrest her or tell anybody else who or where she is."

Keeping both gun and eye on Leavit, he asked his wife, "What do you say, Loula?"

Leavit did not look at her. For all the two men saw of her, she was alone in the world, unprompted, unguided. She tried to think and could not. Her one vague feeling was thankfulness that her husband had the upper hand. She found herself saying mentally again and again, "Thank God! My dear happiness! Thank God!" The ticking of the clock was the only sound in the room. The men were motionless, waiting.

After a long pause she managed to say aloud, "Yes," and then, with greater strength, "Yes, oh yes! He'll be on the level."

Leavit gave no sign of relief.

"All right, then," Paxton brought the thing to its climax. "What do you say, Leavit?"

His wife, seeing that his mind was made up to shoot if necessary, framed in her consciousness one sentence of prayer, "Make him promise!" But the task of influencing Leavit's decision was more than she, drained now of all vitality, could undertake. Her thoughts, wild on the treadmill of confusion, arrived at nothing. The idea of murder was awful to her. Suspense closed down upon her like the walls of a room coming together. A pressure banded her forehead. Her breath moved her lower lip with a "plup" sound. She thought, by keeping her mind full of her husband, by shutting Leavit away from her thought, to make her agony more supportable.

Leavit at last reached his decision. It was a choice between surrender and certain death. He did not have a fighting chance even.

"You've got me," he said, with a steady look at Paxton. "I can't see any good in getting killed because I'd like to arrest a woman who's innocent, maybe." He shrugged his shoulders and added: "I promise you she'll always be safe from me."

When the door of the flat clicked shut behind him they listened until his footsteps died away down the corridor. Paxton was standing at the living room door into the hall, his wife near the table in the living room. They faced each other.

He was trembling violently. The gun dropped unnoticed from his hand. His face was like a limp white rag with two holes in it through which little fires burned. He tried to laugh, making an unpleasant sound of it.

A cold sweat came out suddenly on her forehead and, in little torrents, ran down the sides of her face. Her lower lip was curiously twisted. She put up her arms a little way weakly, holding them out to him.

"Well," he said, going to her and putting an arm around her, "we did it! Did it exactly the way we've always said we would—if we had to! And you were fine!"

"It came so unexpectedly! It scared me to death!" she said, shuddering. "And, oh, George, I hate so for us to have to do it because of me!"

"Don't say we didn't have a right to!" he commanded her lovingly. "You are innocent. And a little acting like ours here tonight suits me a whole lot better than letting a bunch of thick-headed cops ruin a good woman's life!"

Paste a Smile on a Wall

John Keefauver

He let his eyes soar now, let them climb high and proud up to a window of the house he was walking to. For there, behind that window, in that room, was something better than sleep—and much better than smiles pasted on a wall.

He had almost run up the hill toward the house, at dusk, his back to Monterey Bay and his daytime dishwashing job in a restaurant on Cannery Row. Washing the last pan, scouring the last pot, he'd pulled his head out of steam and, with a wave or two, had hurried, face up and even trying to smile, out of the kitchen, leaving cooks and waitresses wondering what it was all about. Dobby never used to wave, you know; Dobby never used to lift his face up off the floor. Never had before, until the last week or so. And everybody knew he couldn't smile.

But they didn't know about the new secret something in his room, something that could easily change a man. He called her Peggy Ann—but he knew she wasn't real.

They all knew him along the Row, skinny, bent-over, blue-jeaned Dobby, always looking at the ground, plodding to and from his dishwashing job. Dobby, face down, face always in dishwashing steam or on the ground; only dirty dishes and pots and pans and his feet ever really got to see his face, they said. Without a hunchback, he was the Hunchback of Cannery Row. That's what they all said.

Dobby was ugly, his face grotesque. A bucket of boiling water on a stove, his reaching hand, his boy face tilted up then; a pull, and down over his head and face the water had come. The screams. Only the memory had faded; the scar remained; it had grabbed all his face, like cement, or glass, and long ago, long before his now late-twenty years, he had given up trying to smile: when he'd tried, something else had come out, something that made people turn and look away and hurry off. They thought, "Poor Dobby," but they kept on walking by. No wonder he likes a bent-over job, they said; lets him hide his face in steam.

Only thing better about Dobby was that he didn't have to shave. That's what they said along Cannery Row.

Yet worse—for him and for the people who looked away and kept on walking by—was that *they* couldn't smile at him, except for the quick kind, the kind that really didn't count. Dobby couldn't give a smile, and he couldn't receive one. He had even given up trying to smile for only himself.

He'd learned to find his smiles in magazines, in pictures there; many nights, at first, he just sat in his room and looked and looked at all the painted smiles, looking so much he wore the pages down. But he never tried to smile back; it didn't seem right.

Then, later, he'd got a pair of scissors and begun to cut the best smiles out of his magazines. He put them—his smiles—in little boxes he'd covered with pink paper, like Christmas. Cutting them out and putting them away made smiles seem more like his own, something to have, like other people. But he didn't tell a soul about what he did; it just didn't seem right to tell it. He was ugly, but he didn't want to be thought crazy, too.

And then, not too many months ago now, he'd gotten a better idea. He thought of something he could do with his boxfuls of smiles, something that would make it much easier for him to look at them all the time whenever he was in his room. Without even asking his landlady, he'd pasted his smiles all over the walls of his room—all kinds, big and little ones, ones in between, men and women's; he even had a horse's smile. All over the old wallpaper he pasted them until he had a roomful of smiles.

But still he didn't smile back; it didn't seem right.

When the landlady finally came into his room and saw what he had done, she puffed up until her face turned an angry pink. She was a big woman, bigger than Dobby, chunky, nearly square, twice the age of him, worn, widowed, toughened by it all, seemed like to Dobby. He was scared of her. He would have moved out a long time ago—but the room was cheap, she kept it clean, and when he had first moved in, she had tried to smile at him, tried more than once—then gave it up. Now she was like everybody else: she looked the other way and kept on walking by.

"Dobby," she had said, "you'll have to tear that paper off those walls." Paper, she had said. Paper, she called his smiles.

So he had torn them off, very carefully so that they wouldn't be hurt. And he had put them back into the boxes, those that weren't ruined. It was a sad thing, a bad thing, and he would have definitely moved away that time except that . . . well . . . that room was his home. Other people had homes; oughtn't he to have one, too?

Even with his smiles now off the wall and back into his pink boxes, Dobby still stopped every once in a while to hunt through trash cans for magazines with smiles. He'd stop at cans on his way from work to his room in the old, paint-faded Victorian house and rummage through the trash.

Which was what he was doing at dusk one day when he found behind a Lighthouse Avenue department store a mannequin with a smile.

He saw her smile first. She was sticking out of a trash can smiling at him. And as he came closer and looked and kept on looking, she *kept on* smiling, she didn't pinch her smile off and look away like everybody else.

"Hi," Dobby said; he was playing a little game.

And even better, Dobby found out that he could smile back at her and smile his smile that never came out looking like a smile, and she *still* didn't look away, she *still* didn't go away. *She kept on smiling.* Smiling and smiling and smiling. A big happy baby doll, that's what she was.

But most important was that with her he could smile back and it seemed all right.

"Hi," he said again, still playing his little game. He knew she wasn't real.

Oh, he had seen other baby dolls—mannequins—in windows of stores, and he had seen that they were smiling. He had stopped and looked at them many times, glad they were able to smile, jealous, too, and they had been nice to look at. But they were different, the ones in store windows, all dressed up fancy and proud and glittery and new, impersonal, for the public. The smiling doll he'd found, now, it was cold and naked and one leg was broken off, all by herself in a dirty trash can with night coming on, discarded.

And she was smiling at *him;* nobody else was around. At *him!*

So Dobby took her home with him, he smuggled her inside his plain-furnished room. He went out and bought a dress for her, a red dress, like Christmas, too, and a hat; he got a brand new mop head, dyed it black, used it for a wig. Then he propped her up behind a bureau in a corner; this way her broken leg wouldn't show. When he'd leave his room in the morning to go to work, he'd hide her in his closet; the landlady mustn't ever know. And as soon as he got home at night he'd bring her out where he could smile at her and she'd smile back. He called her Peggy Ann; there was no doubt at all that she ought to have a name.

Along Cannery Row they could see the change in Dobby, although they didn't know why it had come about, all in a few days, too. And Dobby wasn't about to tell them, tell about smiling Peggy Ann. Everybody would have laughed at him—not smiled—and thought that he was crazy. Dobby seemed to have more grit in him, everybody agreed; he didn't go slinking around all the time, looking the other way; he didn't bend over so much when he walked, he looked up sometimes from the ground. His hat brim wasn't pulled down so low over his face, you know, and he even waved at you sometimes. And Dobby himself was considering quitting his dishwashing job and getting a better kind.

It was a good feeling, it was—damn good—hurrying home to a Peggy Ann like everybody else, nearing home and looking up at his window with eyes high and proud.

Then one evening, like all the others during the last week or so, he'd rushed home from work and climbed the stairs so fast that by the time he reached the door of his room he was panting bad. He opened the door smiling—it seemed all right to smile now—and hurried to his closet and looked, then reached, then looked and reached again, and then—letting what was left of his smile go— *again, again,* calling, "Peggy Ann?" and louder, "Peggy Ann!"

Peggy Ann was gone.

He heard the heavy steps of the landlady coming up the stairs, but he kept on calling for Peggy Ann, looking under the bed, looking behind the bureau, looking in the closet, calling, "Peggy Ann!"

"I took your Peggy Ann, if that's what you call her," the landlady said as she came lumbering into the room. "I took her, I threw her out. And you're getting out next. Pack up and leave."

Her words like an icicle jammed into his brain.

"Keeping a . . . a half-woman, half-doll in my room. Why, it's immoral, it's wicked. It's perverse!"

Turning the icicle in his brain.

"Where is she! Where is she!"

"She's out back in the trash can, where do you think? You'll never bring her in here again. A slut she is, the way you dressed her up, keeping her in your room. A slut! I fixed her good. Peggy Ann, indeed!"

But Dobby was past her now and going down the stairs, running, tearing out the front door and around to the back, eyes not even looking once at the ground.

He saw her before he reached the can. Her face was smashed, she was sticking out of the can. Smile, smashed, sticking out of the can. He stopped in front of her, icicle still working in his brain.

He felt her broken lips and murmured, "Peggy Ann." He felt again; he tried to make them smile. They crumbled. "Peggy Ann." Plaster from her lips stuck to his hand.

He did not know the landlady was behind him until she said, "Into the trash can with her, good riddance. I hit her with a hammer just to make sure."

And Dobby screamed and swung with all his might, and felt the knot of his fist thud into the live woman's face. And screamed and swung again, again; he beat her to the ground, unconscious, or dead.

And then, before he gathered up what was left of Peggy Ann and plodded off across the backyard looking at the ground, he tried— and failed—to set the landlady's lips into a smile for him and Peggy Ann. It seemed the right thing to do.

But now the landlady couldn't smile either. And on second thought, this seemed the right thing, too.

The Alarming Letters from Scottsdale

Warner Law

C. BENNINTON & SON
PUBLISHERS
551 FIFTH AVE.
NEW YORK 10071

May 27, 1972

Henry Hesketh, Esq.
"Hesketh Hill"
Rural Route #1
Scottsdale
Arizona 85256

Dear Godfather Henry:

Hello, there! How are you? Long time no hear. How comes the newest Homer McGrew mystery novel? It's been over three months since Dad and I responded enthusiastically to your outline, and not even a note from you.

As you well know, if we don't get the manuscript soon, it will be too late for our Fall list, which would mean that for the first time in nineteen years there won't be a new Homer McGrew for Christmas.

Since you live all alone up in that hilltop showplace without a phone, we worry when you don't keep in touch.

Dad is away on his annual European business trek, so I'll be minding the store until he gets back.

Do drop me a line, soon.

Your loving Godson,
Bill Benninton

HESKETH HILL

SCOTTSDALE

ARIZONA

June 1, 1972

Dear Godson Bill:

I am just fine, but thanks for wondering. I hadn't realized so much time had gone by.

I was halfway through the new Homer McGrew when I was captured by a dog.

That is, I was cooking beef stew à la Erle Stanley Gardner—I wheedled his recipe from him, years back—when a large dog walked in my kitchen. He looked to be a cross between a German shepherd and something, and he was painfully thin and obviously starving. So of course I gave him some stew, and he hasn't left my side to this day. I've never had a dog before, ever.

He wore no collar. I tried to find his owner, but failed. He's far from a cute or even handsome dog; he looks to be a dignified ten or so years old.

But he has remarkable eyes. They are clear and direct and intelligent, and they remind me strongly of the eyes of Dashiell Hammett, whom I first met in the '30's, when he was pioneering the tough detective novel, and had just become famous for *The Maltese Falcon*. Hammett was not only my close friend but my teacher; much of what I know about the mystery novel came from him. He also spent a long weekend here with me a few years before his death in 1961. Anyways, in his honor I've named the dog Dashiell—Dash, for short. He seldom leaves my side, and even insists on sleeping on the foot of my bed, which is sometimes not too comfortable for me because he's gained considerable weight.

Dash sits now at my feet as I type, and whenever I pause he slaps a foot with a paw as if to say, "Get back to work, you lazy lout!" I imagine he merely likes the clatter of the electric type-writer.

But I swear to you that Dash is close to being human; he seems to understand every word I say. And—don't laugh, now—he even helps me with my story problems. That is, whenever my plot could go one way or another, I explain the alternatives to him—trying to use the same tone of voice—and Dash listens attentively. When he doesn't fancy my suggestions, he lays his head on the floor and sighs wearily; when he does like an idea, his eyes light up—just as Dashiell Hammett's used to when he encouraged me—and he slaps his tail vigorously on the carpet. Dash has saved me from going up many blind alleys.

Anyway, I've decided to put Homer McGrew aside and write instead a book titled: *Dash—My Exciting True Life Experiences As a Dog Detective*. It will be written by Dash himself in the first person, "As Told To Henry Hesketh." Naturally, I will have to do considerable inventing.

Please give my love to father Cyrus when next you write him.

Love,
Henry

June 8, 1972

Dear Henry:

I was relieved to hear that you're well, and pleased that you've found such a good friend in Dash. A book about a dog detective might well be a fine idea. After all, Lassie herself often plays a detective role.

However, might it not be better to finish the Homer McGrew first? You will disappoint many, many of your eager fans if there's not a new mystery novel from you this year.

By the way, I've just learned that Homer is nudging Perry Mason in total paperback sales. This is no small achievement, and I don't think you'll ever have to worry about money, for as long as you live.

I feel I should warn you that Dad has always had an aversion to what he calls "literary anthropomorphism," by which he means the ascription of human qualities to things not human. He will not read —let alone publish—books written in the first person by dogs, cats, parrots, automobiles or frying pans. He was once sent into such a

rage by a four-pound manuscript titled: *I WAS AN UNSLOTH-
FUL THREE-TOED SLOTH* that he broke his office window with
it and it fell six stories down to the street and narrowly missed Ben-
nett Cerf, who happened to be walking by.

Dad is fully aware that many good writers have written successfully in this manner, but it's simply not his cup of tea.

Had you considered writing about Dash in the third person?

Dad writes from London that his trip is going well. Next stop,
Edinburgh.

Love,
Bill

June 12, 1972

Dear Bill:

I'm sorry, but I have grown goddamn weary of Homer McGrew
over the years, and I'd like to write something else for a change.

But apart from this, your letter upset me and made me unhappy,
and when I read the letter aloud to Dash, he listened with hurt
eyes and then went into a corner and whimpered.

But I will let Dash speak for himself: Dear Mr. Benninton:

I was considerably disappointed to hear that your father would
not be interested in the book I am writing about my life as a Dog
Detective, in the first person.

The reason that Henry wants *me* to write the book is because he
wants the reader to know how I really think about things, rather
than what Henry *thinks* I think.

Would you believe that I'm learning to TYPE!? Yes, I AM! One
night when Henry went to bed, he left his electric typewriter running by mistake, and I wandered into his office and got into his
chair and began to strike the letters with my paws. I like the
sound it makes. I like best the automatic repeating keys that go
XXXXXXX AND. . . . . .

Henry heard me typing and came in and was amazed, but was a
little disappointed because what I typed made no sense at all. But
then my paws are so big I can't strike one key at a time.

Then Henry got a wonderful idea, and he took two unsharpened
pencils and fastened them to my front paws with adhesive tape, so
that the eraser ends stuck out three or so inches past my paws, and
with these pencils I can touch one key at a time.

Henry sits me in his typing chair with a strap around me so I won't fall forwards or sideways.

Then he holds my paws and touches the keys with the pencils, and black marks appear on the paper, like magic!

Here is an example of my typing:

HII XXXXXXXXXXTH ERE!! THID ID DADH T Y X X X X X X X X X X-PINGGGG!!!. . . .

Of course I make mistakes. But I am learning about the space bar and the automatic carriage return, which I like to hit because they make nice noises.

Now, Henry is trying to teach me to type *without* holding my paws. He thinks I might learn to type my own name—by rote, as it were. He is using what he calls the "conditioned reflex and reward system." He points to the letter "D," and if I strike it I get one of the tidbits I like, such as foie gras on a cracker, or a chocolate-covered cherry. Then if I next hit an "A" I get another tidbit.

The story of my life is coming along fine! Yesterday I wrote a chapter about my very first case as a Detective. In it, I tracked some hijackers to their hideout and was held prisoner by them. But I found an electric light wall switch and I turned it off and on and off and on and the police finally saw it and came and captured the crooks.

Now I am going to try to type all by myself!

Your pal,
DASXX DAS . . . H

P.S. I think that is pretty good for a dog!!

June 15, 1972

Cyrus Benninton, Esq.
The George Hotel
Edinburgh
Scotland

Dear Dad:

I'm enclosing some recent letters between Henry Hesketh and myself. I'm more than a little worried; I feel he's on the verge of flipping.

Were he another kind of writer, I wouldn't be too concerned. But Henry has always been as tough-minded and as cynical and as hardheaded as his own Homer McGrew.

It's not that I'm greatly concerned about getting a new mystery out of him; it's his state of mind that worries me.

Do you have any suggestions as to what I might do to help ease him through and then out of his present mental condition?

Your loving son,
Bill

June 18, 1972

Dear Son:

I'm gravely concerned by what Henry's letters reveal. The fact that he is still a good writer makes me have continually to remind myself that poor Dash can't be held responsible for what Henry keeps putting into his mind. The poor dog is just sitting in his dignity in his corner minding his own business—or sitting under duress at Henry's typewriter and being bribed by tidbits—while Henry imagines what is going on in the dog's non-existent conscious mind.

This damn dog fixation and this rather sickening cuteness run directly counter to Henry's nature—as I've come to know it over twenty-seven years.

It must be remembered that Henry is pushing seventy-five, and that he boozes it up quite a bit, and has been through five marriages, but has lived all alone on his hill for the last eleven years.

Don't forget also that Henry began as a serious novelist, but failed, and then turned to writing Homer McGrews. These made him rich, but he's always thought of himself as a failure.

Although literary anthropomorphism may not be my cup of tea, I do find some charm in it, in moderation, for it's after all a conscious effort of the mind to project itself into the minds of animals, thus making us feel less alone in our trip through Space-Time.

But there is a big difference between this conscious projection and an unconscious removal of part of the mind into the imagined minds of animals. It's similar to retreating into a dream world to escape the real world.

This is what Henry's doing, and it could well mean that he is hiding that part of himself which he dislikes in the "mind" of his dog. This is close to being a kind of death wish; it could presage suicide.

I of course feel sorry for Dash, who is slowly being murdered. Not so much by Henry. After all, Dash could refuse all those fattening tidbits, or he could run away. But, lacking any consciousness of self, the dog is being killed by his incapacity to deny his own appetites.

To be practical: I have two suggestions. The first is that you get from your Uncle Fred the name of a good Scottsdale psychiatrist, and have him standing by.

The second is that you put your tongue in your cheek and write a letter of encouragement about Dash's autobiography. Lie about me, if it helps. It's possible that Henry could purge himself of this nonsense by finishing the book.

Surely there cannot be more than *one* book in this dog. Unless, of course, Henry should teach the dog to play the piano. A second volume, titled: *How I Played Chopin in Carnegie Hall* is a fearful prospect.

I joke because I am really quite worried about Henry. Edinburgh I find a lonely city. That I love you goes without saying. That I miss you I will say.

Dad

June 23, 1972

Dear Friend Dash:

Thanks so much for the letter. I think it's wonderful that you're learning to type! Maybe you will get so good that you can type your whole book all by yourself! The more I read what you write, the more I like the idea of your own book in your own words about your own exciting life as a Dog Detective.

Dad has changed his mind and would love to publish your book. So hurry and finish it, fella! My best to Henry.

Your pal,
Bill Benninton

C. BENNINTON & SON
PUBLISHERS
551 FIFTH AVE.
NEW YORK 10071

June 23, 1972

Harold F. Seller, MD
Medical-Dental Bldg.
Scottsdale, Arizona

Dear Dr. Seller:

Dr. Frederick Carter of this city has given me your name. He is my uncle, and he remembers you well from Menninger Clinic days. He thinks you might be willing to help my father and myself with a problem.

As you may know, the novelist Henry Hesketh lives outside Scottsdale. We've published his Homer McGrew mysteries for many years, and he's my father's close friend, and also my godfather.

Recently, my father and myself have become increasingly disturbed by his letters to me. Put bluntly and unscientifically, they seem to indicate a growing mental disturbance in relation to his pet dog. More than that I don't think I should say, lest you prejudge him.

We are hoping that this condition will pass. But if it worsens, would it be possible for you to visit Henry Hesketh on some pretext, and give us your impression of his behavior? It goes without saying that we would expect to pay you a fee for this.

Cordially,
William Benninton

June 27, 1972

Dear Bill:

Henry says I can call you by your first name. I am so thrilled that you and your father like the idea of my book after all!

I am now writing a chapter about my last master who was so

angry with me because I could not learn the MORSE CODE and he was mean and beat me with a stick and let me get all skinny and hungry all the time. So I jumped out of a truck near Scottsdale and looked around, hoping I'd find some nice person. I am so happy it was Henry, because he has given me such a nice warm home and lots of affection and he feeds me so GOOD!

My typing is coming along just fine! Henry doesn't have to point at the letters any more. I have made a connection in my mind between the SOUND of the letters and the various keys, and so Henry stands by me and TELLS me the letters and I try to hit the right ones, and if I do I get a tidbit. Henry has found that next to chocolate cherries I like caviar on a cracker the best. The real caviar, all the way from Iran! I eat a whole big jar every day.

Henry found me a big pair of glasses without any lenses in them and he puts them on my head with a rubber band. He's also bought me a baseball cap which he puts on my head backwards. I didn't like these at first because they are scarcely dignified, but Henry says I look distinguished and he has taken photos of me at the typewriter, to illustrate my book.

Henry and I have so many good times together. Except I was a BAD DOG the other night. Henry never sleeps very well, and this night he had a few boozies and some sleeping pills, and he always sleeps with his head under his pillow, and anyway during the night I got so lonely I came up the bed and went to sleep on Henry's pillow and almost smothered him! So now I have to sleep on his feet and not on his head.

Henry says I should type something all by myself to end this letter. Here it is. Henry is going to leave the room.

XXXXXXXXXX. . . .HI T HER . . .E THID IDDASHTY XXXXXXXXXXXXPINGGG BYEB. . . . . . .YE

P.S. Henry came back and said that was so good that I am going to get a chocolate eclair full of real whipped cream!

HAROLD F. SELLER, MD
MEDICAL-DENTAL BLDG.
SCOTTSDALE
ARIZONA

June 28, 1972

Dear Mr. Benninton:

On a professional basis I would be extremely reluctant to intrude upon the privacy of Henry Hesketh.

However, as it happens I know him, casually. I met him first in a local bookstore, some months ago. I told him I was a Homer McGrew fan, and that I was lucky enough to own some rare first editions of the earliest books. He said that if I ever wished them autographed, I should stop by his house.

Time passed, and I never got around to it. A month ago I met him in the street. He reminded me I hadn't been by with my books.

I still haven't paid him the visit. But should you tell me you feel the need has arisen, I will make a point of dropping by, since I have a valid reason.

I won't do this as a doctor. Forget any fee. I will do it because I admire Hesketh, and because Fred Carter is an old friend, and because you and your father are so obviously concerned, and also, because we are all members of the human race together.

Sincerely,
Harold F. Seller

July 5, 1972

HIII THEREXXXXX THIDID DAS HTYXXXX PING. . . .
Dear Bill:

Do you know that I typed that all by myself, when Henry was asleep? Yes, I did!

Henry leaves the pencils on my paws all night, and his electric typewriter humming and his light on in his office, because sometimes in the night I come in and jump into his chair and support myself with my left paw on the lid of the typewriter and strike the keys with the pencil on my right paw. Henry comes in and finds my typing in the morning, and if it makes any sense at all he gives me a big dish of LOBSTER NEWBURG for my breakfast.

I've just written a wonderful chapter about how I went after and tracked down a mean old porcupine who had been girdling and killing Henry's big pine trees, except that when I caught the animal I got a lot of his NASTY quills in my face and nose. Henry had to pull them all out one by one and it HURT! OoooooooooH! But Henry kissed it well and the pain has gone ALL AWAY.

Henry has ordered an electric organ for me. He is going to teach me to play BACH on it! Whatever that is. He says if I get good enough maybe I can give a little recital in a church he knows, near here. He says I can also make some recordings, and sell them to lots of people! Bye, bye, now. I am going to type again just for you.

HI THER ETHID IS DAS HT XXXXYPING. . . . BYE-BYEEEEEXXXXXX

NEW YORK NY SRX TC 559
JUL 7 72 HAROLD SELLER
MD MEDICAL DENTAL
BLDG SCOTTSDALE ARIZ
2:22 PM

I FEEL IT WOULD BE WISE IF YOU WOULD VISIT HESKETH AT YOUR EARLY CONVENIENCE

BENNINTON

SCOTTSDALE ARIZ PFG 732
JULY 8 72 BENNINTON 551
FIFTH AVE NYC 11:23 AM

I AM GRIEVED TO REPORT THAT WHEN I VISITED HESKETH THIS MORNING I FOUND THAT HE HAD DIED IN HIS SLEEP. AUTHORITIES NOTIFIED. WRITING DETAILS. MY SYMPATHY TO YOU.

SELLER

HAROLD F. SELLER, MD
MEDICAL-DENTAL BLDG.
SCOTTSDALE
ARIZONA

July 8, 1972

Dear Mr. Benninton:

Again let me extend my sympathy to you and your father. I realize you have lost a dear friend. I drove to Hesketh's house around nine this morning. There was no answer to my several rings, but a dog barked inside. When no one came to the door, I decided to leave.

But as I was walking back to my car, a huge dog came around the corner of the house and up to me. He is the most monstrously obese dog I've ever seen. He is so outrageously fat he can scarcely walk. Also, and this puzzled me at first, there were pencils taped to his paws—eraser ends protruding. I finally guessed that their purpose was to keep him from scratching himself.

The dog indicated I should come with him, and he led me around the house to an open glass door. It was through this that I found Hesketh in his bed, his head under his pillow. He had been dead for some hours.

The blueness of his skin clearly indicated asphyxia. But how? There was no sign of any struggle.

Three clues gave me a probable answer. There were a few remaining drops of whiskey in a glass on the bedside table. There was also a bottle of sleeping pills. In addition, the top side of his pillow was covered with dog hairs.

So I can only conclude that Hesketh had ingested both alcohol and barbiturates, and went to sleep with his head under his pillow. Suicide is not indicated, for the sleeping pill bottle was very nearly full. I feel sure he would have awakened in the morning.

But I fear that during the night this huge dog came and lay upon his master's pillow and suffocated Hesketh while he remained in an intensely deep sleep.

It is tragic and ironic and somewhat incredible, but it is certainly physically possible, considering the great weight of the dog.

I then walked around the house to find a phone, but there is none. Nothing was amiss, but Hesketh's electric typewriter had been left running in his office, and his desk lamp was on. While switching off the typewriter, I noticed some typing in the machine. I tried to read it, but couldn't. It is gibberish—typed, I fear, by a man who has had quite a few drinks and pills and is falling asleep at the typewriter. Or, possibly, it could be some kind of code, but I greatly doubt it. I pulled this typing out of the machine because I didn't want to have anyone find it and try to make something out of it. The circumstances of Hesketh's death will make enough newspaper copy as it is.

When I left the house the dog was anxious to come with me, and so I took him.

After reporting the news to the sheriff's office in person, I stopped off with the dog at the office of a veterinary surgeon friend.

When he examined the dog he was gravely shocked—even horrified. He said he had never seen a dog who had been so grossly overfed. He surmised that the dog had been deprived of proper food and had been fed large quantities of sugars and fats. He told me that if this diet had continued much longer the poor dog was doomed to die.

I have decided to keep the dog, until and unless someone lays claim to him. I would like to restore him to good condition, with a proper diet and exercise.

Also, I find the dog tremendously appealing. He is affectionate, and in his ability to understand my every word he seems close to being human.

I've lived alone since my wife died two years ago, and I'll be happy to have the dog for company. He will have a good home with me.

Sincerely,
Harold F. Seller

P.S. I enclose the sheet of paper I found in Hesketh's typewriter. It's possible that this random typing might make some sense to you, although I very much doubt it.

H.F.S.

TH ISISD ASHTYPING. . . . . . . IW XXXXASBE I INGMUR
DERE DBY MYINABI LI T YTOCONQ UERM YO WNGREE

D. . . . . ITWA SEI THERHE N R Y O R M E XXXXX
X X IAMDOUBL YSOR RYFO RMYC RIME BEC AUS ENO
WINM. . . . . . YN EX TREINCARNA TIONOI WILHAV E
TOCOMEBACKASANEV. . . . . . . ENLOW ERCREA TUR
ESUCHASARA T XXXXXXXXXX THI SIS DAS HIELLHAM-
METTT YP I N G. . . . .

My Last Book

Clayre and Michel Lipman

The room was unnaturally quiet. Even at this hour of the night, there should have been some slight noise. A creak, a whisper, a crack from the fire on the hearth, a taxi horn.

My fingers were busy with the knot, my eyes on the girl who stood quiet and tense against the book-lined wall. I could see no feeling in her pale, lovely face. No horror; no pity. Not even hate. I settled the rope around my neck and pulled it tight with hands that trembled only slightly. Too tight. I tugged to loosen the strangling loop. One idea elbowed the others in my mind. "It's only a matter of seconds, Naida," I said, careful not to stumble too soon from the stacks of books on which I stood. "Remember now."

"Don't do it, Eric." Her voice was as flat and expressionless as her face. I had never been able to guess what thoughts coursed through her devious mind. Naida did not think like other women.

"I've *got* to do this."

"You've always said you had to—I don't believe it. You just do it to torture me."

"You're being childish, Naida."

A smile seemed to soften her features. Shyly? Tenderly? Mona Lisa. The smile vanished as she said, "*Wait!*"

"What is it?" My lips were dry.

"Someone coming." Steel flashed as she hid the knife behind her.

Steps sounded in the corridor outside the darkened apartment; hesitated, then went on. I watched her implacably waiting. Had she really smiled?

"They've gone by," I said unnecessarily.

She ignored that. "Is it worth it, Eric?" Expressionless words. No clue to her thoughts.

I would not answer. I would wait just one more moment. One moment! What good was a moment spent standing on a pile of books with a rope around my neck? I swallowed. It was difficult, the rope had tightened somehow. I rubbed damp palms against my thighs. I'd loosened the rope a minute ago and now it was tight again. The edge of my brain that was hardly part of me reached out for words and molded them into phrases. *His mind was like a caged and frantic wild bird* . . . No, that wasn't any good. *His mind, on wild bird's wings* . . . Better. I'd work on that; polish it up tomorrow. Tomorrow? *Even in his last moment a man still plans for tomorrow; there is never an end to dreaming.* I must remember that phrase. It was good.

The rope. Perhaps I'd sweated and the hemp had absorbed the moisture and shrunk. No, it wouldn't do that. Well, there was no use waiting any longer—I had to get on with it. I had a novel to finish.

"I'm about ready," I said. The words had a dry, woody sound; I visualized a glass of water. There would be more time if I asked for water. I imagined the water in my thirsty mouth. *The swallowing, the rope's thousand needles stabbing his throat; the shock of cold down his hot, queasy gullet.* . . . No, I didn't want a glass of water.

I stared at the girl, waiting. As though she would wait through eternity with only the hint of a smile—a secret, cold smile—on her blood-red lips.

My mind raced, definitions sharp. My perceptions were intense and detailed. Everything about Naida, and about the room was etched fiercely into the sensitive lobes of my brain. *Firelight tinting old copper. The ugly gap on the bookshelves shadowed like a purpling wound.* My desk littered with papers, the detritus of the novel I was working on. *And the window,* said the other part of my mind, *open from the top as though inviting his soul to escape. Escape, to where there was no future and no past.* Too self-conscious. Discard. Reject. There was something else behind the words pressing forward to be born. *Queer, malevolent foetuses.* Heavy, amorphous thoughts that stirred and cried of matters unintelligible, pregnant with the suggestion of sly, indecent laughter. Always about Naida.

I had slammed shut the ports of my mind, but now the bolts were sheared and memory came pouring in to choke my senses. I looked at her, lithe body pressed to the wall. Even in repose there'd always been a suggestion of movement in her; a *grey quiescent sea swelling with unseen currents* . . .

Yes, there had always been that quality about her. I'd recognized it at our first meeting when I felt the first slow drumbeat of desire. In her final acceptance there was neither candor nor reticence, giving nor denying. Often I'd told myself that I should have been satisfied with that, and yet I was not. I'd been conscious, even in our most intimate moments, of secret reserves at odds with her warm and ready caresses. Questions had tumbled through my mind and there had been no answers. Not once, in our months together, had there been a revelation of Naida's deeper, innermost thoughts. Not once had she given herself to the luxury of anger, rage, hatred or passion.

Not even when the baby died.

I suppose she had grieved. Her eyes, that had been luminous, were for a time then shadowed with shock. But I couldn't be sure, because of the strange way she'd withdrawn from me. I'd thought at first she was blaming me for Sunny's death. I'd been deep in the opening chapter of my last book the day Naida went out, warning me to look into the nursery every so often. I did look in once while Naida was gone. But later, when I was deep in that scene between Dora and Andrew—the scene two critics called a masterpiece of scalding realism—it happened. I felt horrible, but . . . A real artist cannot be blamed for something that happens while he is in the throes of creation. She understood that.

After a period of brooding withdrawal, she came back to me. She seemed to draw even closer. She was quicker to please me, to antic-ipate my needs, to comfort and reassure me when the flow of inspi-ration ran dry. Creative genius isn't given to everyone. Those who have it need a woman who can understand it and consecrate her own life to it. A woman like Naida. After all she had what other women might envy, a comfortable living, and a man who was growing to real literary stature. I hadn't treated her badly. Even during my dry spells I'd been reasonably monogamous. That affair with Annette had only been because I was completely disoriented by the shock of Sunny's death. I'd explained that to Naida and she hadn't fussed a bit. "It's the pattern," she'd said, and I thought that was a fair example of her tolerance, her understanding.

After that, my work had flowed along swiftly. Until the present dry spell, the worst I'd ever had. Drained, empty, exhausted. A hole in my brain—like a doughnut—whenever I tried to think. I knew I'd been hard to live with this time. But she'd taken it all with quiet patience while I'd typed and retyped the scored and raddled pages. Her only protest came when I told her I must hang myself this time. "No, I couldn't go through with it," she'd said, knowing what her part must be. "Don't make me, Eric."

But I'd insisted, and she stacked the books while I penned the note "To Whom It May Concern." She got the rope and sharpened the knife to a thin, keen edge. She steadied me with her shoulder as I balanced myself on the stack of books and tied the knot . . .

I swallowed, choking a little.

She repeated, "Is it worth it, Eric?" Now the phrase sounded like a line in a well-rehearsed play, packed with meanings quite apart from itself. "Another second might be too late."

At last I sensed genuine emotion beneath her careful indifference. Tumescent emotion, rising at last to the surface, and there was an answering stir in me—a new, powerful surge of feeling. What was she hiding? I had a right to know. My hands ached to grip those slim, brown shoulders and shake her hidden thoughts until they rolled, like bright marbles, across the floor. Then I might know what curled so cunningly in her brain, what caused the squirming and twisting of my doubts; those queer, intuitive doubts which kept returning to torment me.

Could it be . . . ? In agony I strained my neck to glance at the neatly stacked pages of finished typescript in their accustomed place on top of the filing cabinet.

No. It couldn't be that. From the beginning Naida had always refused to read a word I wrote. In typescript or book form. "How could I read your work with critical detachment?" she would say. "I know too much about the sources . . ." So she could not have read this particular scene in the middle of my last book, the finest thing, I know, that I have ever done. Torn hot and bleeding from the very body of life itself . . . Why think of that at all? Only *now* is important, I told myself, *now* while she stands there waiting—for what?

For me to die?

I wet my lips and tasted warm salt. No reason for panic, I told myself. This should be no worse than the other half dozen times I'd pushed her and myself to the very edge of life. The tarantula bite. The sleeping tablets. The wrist-slashing. The underground-cave scene of my fourth book, with a man—myself—drowning in icy water, and his only possible chance of rescue a slender line in the hand of a woman half mad with love and hate . . . No wonder critics spoke respectfully of my violent realism. Those compelling scenes in my books had been actual records of my own intimacies with death. *Death as a woman, beautiful and mysterious!*

During each of those experiments I'd trusted Naida completely; gave no thought to being entirely in her power. Why should I this time?

"Naida!" Panic squeezed the sound. "Naida!" My convulsive movement cost me my balance. I was caught unprepared when the books slid. My eyes bulged almost to bursting, my legs jerked and my arms strove upward, tearing at the rope. Through the distorted sight of my tortured eyes, I could see her watching me. She was smiling—smiling—as I gasped away my life, the knife motionless in her hand. This time she was letting me die. And she would get away with it. Light danced in a mottled pattern and dimmed away as darkness fogged my senses.

My eyes opened sullenly. Naida was kneeling beside me rubbing life into my numb wrists. My aching body drank greedily of good, sweet air. The rope was gone. The books were back on their shelf. How long had I been unconscious? Five minutes? Ten?

"You wanted to kill me." Frog-words leapt clumsily from my clogged throat.

"Yes, I wanted to kill you." Words without passion.

My thoughts would not sort themselves. I knew she was speaking the truth, yet truth evaded me. How could she remain so calm, so expressionless? "Why, Naida?"

She took a glass from the coffee table and lifted my head as I gulped stinging whisky. Warmth grew in me. I was still alive. Life had never tasted so good.

"I hoped some day you would come to understand what you are

doing to me, Eric. I hoped because I loved you. But your work and yourself are all you really care about. It took me a long while to realize that. Your selfishness took poor Annette and those other women you laughed about afterward, and wrote into your novels. And the shoving of your life into my hands . . . Easy for you, Eric, but what about me? What if the antidote didn't take effect? Or I couldn't get the tourniquet on your arm in time? Did you ever think how *I* felt about that? Watching you almost die over and over and trying to remember every detail to tell you afterward!"

She was angry, I thought pleasurably. *Anger flushed through her cheeks and sparkled her eyes; her wilful breasts fell and rose as if to leave their gentle confinement.* Good. A little polish and it might go . . . Sudden, new pain dragged at my stomach, then eased. I took a deep breath, "You did cut me down, didn't you, Naida? So you can't deny you still love me, can you?"

"Can't I?" Coldness in her dark eyes; coldness in her voice. I knew if I touched her that her flesh, too, would be cold. "Love. Do you know how many kinds there are? Or hate? Or both together? All mixed up until your brain is filled with a million tiny explosions? Until your heart weeps and the tears fall into the emptiness inside?"

Another wave of pain caught me; cold sweat needled through my pores. There was a strange taste in my mouth . . . Alarm clanged through my nerves. "That whisky . . ."

"Yes, Eric. That whisky. Aconite."

"*Aconite!*" I struggled to get at her but pain-born weakness pushed me back. I knew the poison; I had used it two novels back. Hours dying, conscious to the last.

I stared at her as she remained on her knees, slim hands folded, anger gone, watching me, her lovely oval face still grave and empty. *Death as a woman, beautiful and mysterious* . . . Tears stung my eyes. Fright, rising, red pain, and the knowledge that I would never write that line across white paper. Why had she chosen this monstrous end for me? Why hadn't she let me go mercifully with the rope around my neck?

Naida rose and turned to the filing cabinet, stood on tiptoe to reach for the pages of completed typescript I was so sure she had not read.

Almost absent-mindedly she turned to the middle section. In a flat, colorless voice, without looking at me, she began to read aloud those words torn hot and bleeding from the body of life itself.

"*So simple, Howard thought, with a tremor of awe, as he stood silent and alone in the shadowed nursery. So swift. No struggles now. The baby's tiny body lay still with a stillness that was not sleep. His own baby, his son—dead because he had not lifted a hand to help when he saw what was happening. Dead because of his great curiosity—his lust to experience every sensation that life could offer, however hideous—the ancient sin of lust for knowledge at any cost. . . . Now he was a man set apart from his fellow-men. He would walk alone through the rest of his life with fearful knowledge hidden in his breast that no one could ever suspect. The knowledge that he might have stopped this and didn't . . .*"

Naida looked up from the script of my last book. Her voice was low, detached, almost tolerant. She said, "Hanging was too good for you."

Homicidal Hiccup

John D. MacDonald

You say you've been reading the series of articles in the Baker City *Journal* about how Mayor Willison cleaned up the city?

Brother, those articles are written for the sucker trade—meaning no offense, you understand.

Oh, I'll admit that the city is clean now—but not because of Willison. Willison is a cloth-head. He doesn't even know how Baker City got cleaned up. Being a politician, he's glad to jump in and take credit, naturally.

That's right. I know exactly how it happened, and it isn't going to be printed in any newspapers, even if I am a reporter. You spring for a few rounds of bourbon and I'll give it to you—just the way it happened.

You know about Johnny Howard. I don't pretend to understand him, or the guys like him. Maybe something happens when they're little kids, and by the time they get grown up, they have to run everything.

Nice-looking guy, in a way. Lean and dark and tall. But those gray eyes of his could look right through you and come out the other side. He came into town five, six years ago. Just discharged after three months in the Army. Heart or something. Twenty-six, he was then. Nice dresser. Sam Jorio and Buddy Winski were running the town between them. Anyway, Johnny Howard went to work for

Sam Jorio. Two months later I hear talk that they're having some kind of trouble and that is ten days before Sam Jorio, all alone in his car, goes off that cliff just south of town. Burned to nothing. Nobody can prove it isn't an accident, but there's lots of guessing.

With the boss gone, Buddy Winski tried to move in and take over Sam's boys. But he didn't figure on Johnny. He met Johnny at the bar of the Kit Club on Greentree Road and Johnny busted his beer bottle on the edge of the bar and turned Buddy Winski's face into hamburg. When Buddy got out of the hospital, he left town. There wasn't anything else to do. All his boys had teamed up with Johnny Howard.

Inside of a year Johnny not only had everything working smooth as glass in town, but he had things organized that Sam Jorio and Buddy Winski hadn't even thought of. Take a little thing like treasury pools. Syndicates are always trying to move in on a town this size. Buddy and Sam used to each have their own. Not Johnny. He folded up Sam's pool and Buddy's pool and let the syndicate come in. He gave them protection in return for two cents on every two-bit ticket. He made more out of it than Winski and Jorio ever thought of.

Another thing. No flashy cars for Johnny. No, sir. A little old black sedan with special plates in the body and special glass in the windows. That was Johnny. No going into the clubs, even the two that belonged to him, with a big gang and a batch of fancy women. Johnny had all his parties in the suite on the top floor of the Baker Hotel. All kinds of wine. Good musicians.

And, of course, Bonny was always with him. Always the same girl. Bonny Gerlacher is the right name. Bonny Powers, she called herself.

Five-foot-two on tiptoe with ocean-color eyes, dark red hair, and a build you wanted to tack on the wall over your bed.

Twenty-three or so, and looked sixteen.

Nobody messed with Bonny. And kept on living. Not with Johnny Howard around.

Well, things went along for a few years, and I guess Johnny was filling up safe-deposit boxes all over this part of the country with that green stuff. Johnny and Bonny. He was smart. Nobody could touch him. Estimates on his personal take went as high as a million and a half a year. He paid taxes on the net from the two clubs.

Nothing else. The Feds smelled around for a long time, but they couldn't find anything.

The way he kept on top was by cracking down on anybody who stepped out of line so hard and so fast that it gave you the shivers.

Then Satch Connel got sick and the doc told him to retire and go to Florida if he wanted to live more than another half-hour.

Satch Connel ran a store next to the big high school. And he gave his regular payoff to Johnny Howard. Howard's boys kept Satch supplied with slot machines for the back room, reefers for the kids, dirty pictures and books. Stuff like that. I don't think Johnny Howard's end of the high school trade ran to more than three hundred a week. Peanuts to a guy like Johnny Howard.

So Satch sold out and a fellow named Walter Maybree bought it. This Maybree is from out of town and he has the cash in his pants and he buys it.

The same week he takes over, he tosses out the pinball machines and the punch boards and the other special items for the high school kids. You see, this Maybree has two kids in the high school. It gave him a different point of view from what Satch had. With Satch, nothing counted.

This Maybree paints the place inside and out and puts in a juke box and a lot of special sticky items at the soda bar and pretty soon it is like a recreation room you can maybe find run by a church.

Johnny Howard sends a few boys over to this Maybree, but Walt Maybree, being fairly husky, tosses them out onto the sidewalk. If that was all he did, maybe Johnny would have let the whole thing drop. But, no. Maybree writes a letter to the paper, and the stupid paper lets it get printed, and it says some pretty harsh things about a certain racketeer who wants him to cheat the school kids and sell them dope and filth.

Some of the wise boys around town talk to Johnny Howard and Johnny says, in that easy way of his, "Maybree'll either play along or stop breathing."

You got to understand about a statement like that. Once Johnny makes it, he has to follow through. If he doesn't, every small fry in town will figure Johnny is losing his grip and they'll try to wriggle out from under and maybe the organization will go to hell.

So, being in the line of business he's in, once Johnny Howard makes a statement like that, he has to do exactly like he says.

It would have been like pie, a shot from a car or even a ride into the country, except that a number of citizens are tired of Johnny Howard, and they get to Maybree and convince him that he is in trouble. The next thing, Maybree's wife and kids leave town with no forwarding address and the talk is that when the heat's off they'll come back and not before.

Walter Maybree moves a bunk into the back of the store, so there is no chance of catching him on the street. A whole bunch of square citizens get gun licenses before Johnny can get to the cops to stop the issuing of them, and they all do guard duty with Walt Maybree.

Business goes on as usual, and Maybree has a tight look around his mouth and eyes, and without it being in the paper all of Baker City knows what's going on and are pulling for Maybree. That's the trouble with ordinary citizens. They sit on the sidelines and cheer, but only once in a blue moon is one of them, like Maybree, out there in front with his guard up.

The bomb that was tossed out of a moving car didn't go over so good. The boys in the car were in a hurry, so the bomb bounced off the door frame instead of going through the plateglass window. It busted the windows when it went off, but it didn't do any other damage. At the corner, the sedan took a slug in the tire and slewed into a lamppost and killed the driver. The other guy tried to fight his way clear and took a slug between the eyes.

The next day Johnny Howard was really in trouble. His organization began to fall apart right in front of his face, and everybody in the know was laughing at him because a punk running a soda shop was bluffing him to a standstill.

I can't tell you how I found out about this next part, but Johnny spends two days thinking, and then he gets hold of Madge Spain, who keeps the houses in line, and gives her some orders, and she shows up at the Baker Hotel with three of her youngest gals.

Johnny looks them over carefully, but they won't do because they look too hard and no amount of frosting on the cake is going to make any one of them look like a high school kid. Their high school days are too far behind them.

But he knows the idea is good and he is doing a lot of brooding about it and he has the dope he wants from Doc Harrington, one of his boys, who is sort of an amateur physician. He has the method all worked out, but nobody who can do it.

Bonny is worried about him, and finally she gets him talking and he tells her all about his plan, and she says that the whole thing is simple. *She'll* do it.

You've got to understand that in their own funny way they love each other. It just about makes Johnny sick to think of his Bonny killing anybody, because that is not woman's work. And maybe Bonny wouldn't normally knock anybody off, but because it is her Johnny who is in this mess, she will wiggle naked over hot coals to get him out of it.

The plan isn't bad. As soon as Maybree dies, all this trouble Johnny is having dies with him. It doesn't much matter how Maybree gets it, as long as he does.

This Doc Harrington has got hold of some curare. It is a South American poison and they use it in this country in small doses to make convulsions ease up when they give people shock therapy. It paralyzes muscles. Jam a little bit in the bloodstream and it will paralyze the heart action. *Poof!* Like that. Quick as a bullet.

The bodyguards that are protecting Walt Maybree during business hours are on the lookout for hard characters who look like they might rub Maybree out in a direct way. Johnny Howard figures they will not be on the lookout for high school gals.

For the next two days he has Bonny practicing with a soda straw and these little wooden darts he has fixed up. They just fit in a soda straw. A needle on one end and paper things on the other to make them fly right.

Walt Maybree works behind his own soda fountain.

The idea is that Bonny goes in there as a high school girl and she has the little dart with the curare on in the end of her hand. She sits at the fountain and tucks the dart in the end of the soda straw, puts it up to her lips, and puffs, sticking the little dart into the back of Maybree's hand, or, better yet, his throat.

When he keels over, she goes out with the crowd.

Probably Bonny laughed and kidded a lot when she was up in the suite practicing on the cork target with the little darts. Probably Johnny Howard kidded back, but neither of them must have thought it was very funny. To Johnny Howard it was okay to rub out the competition with hot lead, but sending your gal out to kill somebody with a blowgun is something else indeed.

Anyway, the pressure on Johnny was getting worse every day, and his boys were mumbling and it was only a question of time until somebody turned hero and blasted Johnny.

On the day that was set, Bonny went in her black dress and her high heels and her dark red hair piled high on her head and unlocked the door to the room she had rented near the high school. The little dart with the sticky stuff on the needle end was wrapped in tissue paper and was in a little box in her purse. She had a suitcase with her.

The black dress fitted snugly on Bonny's curves. She took off the dress and the nylons and the high-heeled shoes and put on scuffed, flat moccasins and a shortish tweed skirt and a sloppy sweater. She let that wonderful dark red hair fall around her shoulders, and she tied a scarf thing around her shining head.

She had schoolbooks with her. She took them out of the suitcase, held them in her arm, and looked in the chipped mirror over the oak bureau. Carefully she smiled. Bonny the high school lass. But with too much makeup. She swabbed all the makeup off and put back just a little. It looked better.

Her knees were shaking and her lips felt numb. Her heart was fluttering. No woman can go out to commit murder without something taking place inside her.

One little thing had to be added. She took the big purse she was leaving behind, took out the half-pint flask that Johnny Howard had given her two years before, and tilted it up to her lips. The raw liquor burned like fire, but it steadied her down. That was what she wanted.

It had all been timed just right. She left the room, carrying the books, and walked to the high school. She went in the door, and, when she got halfway down the hall, the noon whistle went off and the doors opened and the hall filled with kids.

Bonny felt funny until she saw that she wasn't being noticed. She went right through the building and out the other door and became part of the crew that stormed the gates of Walt Maybree's Drugstore.

Between the thumb and first finger of her right hand she tightly held the little messenger of death.

The liquor was warm in her stomach, and she made an effort not to breathe in anybody's face. She was a little late to get a seat at the counter, and so she waited, quietly and patiently, and while she waited she thought of Johnny Howard. It was only by thinking of Johnny that she could go through with the whole thing.

When there was a vacant stool she edged in, piled her books on the counter, made her voice higher, her eyes wider, and ordered what she had heard one of the other kids order—"A special milk-shake."

She selected a straw out of the metal container near her, peeled the paper off it, and waited. Maybree was down at the other end of the counter, and a boy with a pimply face made her milkshake and put it in front of her. It was "special." It contained two kinds of ice cream, a handful of malt, and an egg.

Bonny dipped her straw into it and sucked up the sweet, heavy mixture. She kept her eye on Maybree. He began to move up toward her. She pinched her straw so that it was useless, selected a fresh one, and stripped the paper off it. With a deft, practiced gesture, she slipped the little dart, point first, into the end of it.

She lifted it to her lips.

Maybree strolled down near her and stood still, his hand braced on the inside edge of the counter.

It was thus that he glanced at the very good-looking high school girl with the sea-colored eyes. He heard an odd sound, saw those sea-colored eyes glaze, and he gasped as she went over backward, her pretty head striking the asphalt tile of the floor with a heavy thud, her dark red hair spilling out of the bandanna when the knot loosened. She was dead even as she hit the floor.

That's why I get a bang out of the mayor claiming to have cleaned up this town. Hell, he couldn't have cleaned it up if Johnny Howard had been running things. When the mayor started his cleanup, Johnny Howard was gone, and weak sisters were trying to climb into the vacated saddle.

Yeah, Johnny Howard disappeared that same day that Bonny died. They didn't locate him for five days. They found him in that furnished room that still held Bonny's usual clothes. The landlady had been hearing a funny noise. They found Johnny Howard on his hands and knees, going around and around the room, butting his head into the wall now and then. He told them he was looking for Bonny. They've got him out in the state sanitarium now, giving him shock treatments, but they say it'll never work with him.

That's right. Bonny made a mistake. Just one mistake. You see, she didn't realize that by taking that huge slug of bourbon and then drinking half of that sticky milkshake she'd signed her own death warrant. They found the little dart embedded in the inside of her lower lip.

You can't mix bourbon and milkshake without getting a terrible case of hiccups.

Gone Girl

Ross Macdonald

It was a Friday night. I was tooling home from the Mexican border in a light blue convertible and a dark blue mood. I had followed a man from Fresno to San Diego and lost him in the maze of streets in Old Town. When I picked up his trail again, it was cold. He had crossed the border, and my instructions went no further than the United States.

Halfway home, just above Emerald Bay, I overtook the worst driver in the world. He was driving a black fishtail Cadillac as if he were tacking a sailboat. The heavy car wove back and forth across the freeway, using two of its four lanes, and sometimes three. It was late, and I was in a hurry to get some sleep. I started to pass it on the right, at a time when it was riding the double line. The Cadillac drifted towards me like an unguided missile, and forced me off the road in a screeching skid.

I speeded up to pass on the left. Simultaneously, the driver of the Cadillac accelerated. My acceleration couldn't match his. We raced neck and neck down the middle of the road. I wondered if he was drunk or crazy or afraid of me. Then the freeway ended. I was doing eighty on the wrong side of a two-lane highway, and a truck came over a rise ahead like a blazing double comet. I floorboarded the gas pedal and cut over sharply to the right, threatening the Cadillac's fenders and its driver's life. In the approaching headlights, his face was as blank and white as a piece of paper, with charred black holes for eyes. His shoulders were naked.

At the last possible second he slowed enough to let me get by. The truck went off onto the shoulder, honking angrily. I braked gradually, hoping to force the Cadillac to stop. It looped past me in an insane arc, tires skittering, and was sucked away into darkness.

When I finally came to a full stop, I had to pry my fingers off the wheel. My knees were remote and watery. After smoking part of a cigarette, I U-turned and drove very cautiously back to Emerald Bay. I was long past the hot-rod age, and I needed rest.

The first motel I came to, the Siesta, was decorated with a vacancy sign and a neon Mexican sleeping luminously under a sombrero. Envying him, I parked on the gravel apron in front of the motel office. There was a light inside. The glass-paned door was standing open, and I went in. The little room was pleasantly furnished with rattan and chintz. I jangled the bell on the desk a few times. No one appeared, so I sat down to wait and lit a cigarette. An electric clock on the wall said a quarter to one.

I must have dozed for a few minutes. A dream rushed by the threshold of my consciousness, making a gentle noise. Death was in the dream. He drove a black Cadillac loaded with flowers. When I woke up, the cigarette was starting to burn my fingers. A thin man in a gray flannel shirt was standing over me with a doubtful look on his face.

He was big-nosed and small-chinned, and he wasn't as young as he gave the impression of being. His teeth were bad, the sandy hair was thinning and receding. He was the typical old youth who scrounged and wheedled his living around motor courts and restaurants and hotels, and hung on desperately to the frayed edge of other people's lives.

"What do you want?" he said. "Who are you? What do you want?" His voice was reedy and changeable like an adolescent's.

"A room."

"Is that all you want?"

From where I sat, it sounded like an accusation. I let it pass. "What else is there? Circassian dancing girls? Free popcorn?"

He tried to smile without showing his bad teeth. The smile was a dismal failure, like my joke. "I'm sorry, sir," he said. "You woke me up. I never make much sense right after I just wake up."

"Have a nightmare?"

His vague eyes expanded like blue bubblegum bubbles. "Why did you ask me that?"

"Because I just had one. But skip it. Do you have a vacancy or don't you?"

"Yessir. Sorry, sir." He swallowed whatever bitter taste he had in his mouth, and assumed an impersonal obsequious manner. "You got any luggage, sir?"

"No luggage."

Moving silently in tennis sneakers like a frail ghost of the boy he once had been, he went behind the counter, and took my name, address, license number, and five dollars. In return, he gave me a key numbered fourteen and told me where to use it. Apparently he despaired of a tip.

Room fourteen was like any other middle-class motel room touched with the California-Spanish mania. Artificially roughened plaster painted adobe color, poinsettia-red curtains, imitation parchment lampshade on a twisted black iron stand. A Rivera reproduction of a sleeping Mexican hung on the wall over the bed. I succumbed to its suggestion right away, and dreamed about Circassian dancing girls.

Along towards morning one of them got frightened, through no fault of mine, and began to scream her little Circassian lungs out. I sat up in bed, making soothing noises, and woke up. It was nearly nine by my wristwatch. The screaming ceased and began again, spoiling the morning like a fire siren outside the window. I pulled on my trousers over the underwear I'd been sleeping in, and went outside.

A young woman was standing on the walk outside the next room. She had a key in one hand and a handful of blood in the other. She wore a wide multi-colored skirt and a low-cut gypsy sort of blouse. The blouse was distended and her mouth was open, and she was yelling her head off. It was a fine dark head, but I hated her for spoiling my morning sleep.

I took her by the shoulders and said, "Stop it."

The screaming stopped. She looked down sleepily at the blood on her hand. It was as thick as axle grease, and almost as dark in color.

"Where did you get that?"

"I slipped and fell in it. I didn't see it."

Dropping the key on the walk, she pulled her skirt to one side with her clean hand. Her legs were bare and brown. Her skirt was stained at the back with the same thick fluid.

"Where? In this room?"

She faltered, "Yes."

Doors were opening up and down the drive. Half a dozen people began to converge on us. A dark-faced man about four and a half feet high came scampering from the direction of the office, his little pointed shoes dancing in the gravel.

"Come inside and show me," I said to the girl.

"I can't. I won't." Her eyes were very heavy, and surrounded by the bluish pallor of shock.

The little man slid to a stop between us, reached up and gripped the upper part of her arm. "What is the matter, Ella? Are you crazy, disturbing the guests?"

She said, "Blood," and leaned against me with her eyes closed.

His sharp glance probed the situation. He turned to the other guests, who had formed a murmuring semicircle around us.

"It is perfectly hokay. Do not be concerned, ladies and gentlemen. My daughter cut herself a little bit. It is perfectly all right."

Circling her waist with one long arm, he hustled her through the open door and slammed it behind him. I caught it on my foot and followed them in.

The room was a duplicate of mine, including the reproduction over the unmade bed, but everything was reversed as in a mirror image. The girl took a few weak steps by herself and sat on the edge of the bed. Then she noticed the blood spots on the sheets. She stood up quickly. Her mouth opened, rimmed with white teeth.

"Don't do it," I said. "We know you have a very fine pair of lungs."

The little man turned on me. "Who do you think you are?"

"The name is Archer. I have the next room."

"Get out of this one, please."

"I don't think I will."

He lowered his greased black head as if he were going to butt me. Under his sharkskin jacket, a hunch protruded from his back like a displaced elbow. He seemed to reconsider the butting gambit, and decided in favor of diplomacy.

"You are jumping to conclusions, mister. It is not so serious as it looks. We had a little accident here last night."

"Sure, your daughter cut herself. She heals remarkably fast."

"Nothing like that." He fluttered one long hand. "I said to the people outside the first thing that came to my mind. Actually, it was a little scuffle. One of the guests suffered a nosebleed."

The girl moved like a sleepwalker to the bathroom door and switched on the light. There was a pool of blood coagulating on the black and white checkerboard linoleum, streaked where she had slipped and fallen in it.

"Some nosebleed," I said to the little man. "Do you run this joint?"

"I am the proprietor of the Siesta Motor Hotel, yes. My name is Salanda. The gentleman is susceptible to nosebleed. He told me so himself."

"Where is he now?"

"He checked out early this morning."

"In good health?"

"Certainly in good health."

I looked around the room. Apart from the unmade bed with the brown spots on the sheets, it contained no signs of occupancy. Someone had spilled a pint of blood and vanished.

The little man opened the door wide and invited me with a sweep of his arm to leave. "If you will excuse me, sir, I wish to have this cleaned up as quickly as possible. Ella, will you tell Lorraine to get to work on it right away pronto? Then maybe you better lie down for a little while, eh?"

"I'm all right now, Father. Don't worry about me."

When I checked out a few minutes later, she was sitting behind the desk in the front office, looking pale but composed. I dropped my key on the desk in front of her.

"Feeling better, Ella?"

"Oh. I didn't recognize you with all your clothes on."

"That's a good line. May I use it?"

She lowered her eyes and blushed. "You're making fun of me. I know I acted foolishly this morning."

"I'm not so sure. What do *you* think happened in thirteen last night?"

"My father told you, didn't he?"

"He gave me a version, two of them in fact. I doubt that they're the final shooting script."

Her hand went to the central hollow in her blouse. Her arms and shoulders were slender and brown, the tips of her fingers carmine. "Shooting?"

"A cinema term," I said. "But there might have been a real shooting at that. Don't you think so?"

Her front teeth pinched her lower lip. She looked like somebody's pet rabbit. I restrained an impulse to pat her sleek brown head.

"That's ridiculous. This is a respectable motel. Anyway, Father asked me not to discuss it with anybody."

"Why would he do that?"

"He loves this place, that's why. He doesn't want any scandal made out of nothing. If we lost our good reputation here, it would break my father's heart."

"He doesn't strike me as the sentimental type."

She stood up, smoothing her skirt. I saw that she'd changed it. "You leave him alone. He's a dear little man. I don't know what you think you're doing, trying to stir up trouble where there isn't any."

I backed away from her righteous indignation—female indignation is always righteous—and went out to my car. The early spring sun was dazzling. Beyond the freeway and the drifted sugary dunes, the bay was Prussian blue. The road cut inland across the base of the peninsula and returned to the sea a few miles north of the town. Here a wide blacktop parking space shelved off to the left of the highway, overlooking the white beach and whiter breakers. Signs at each end of the turnout stated that this was a County Park, No Beach Fires.

The beach and the blacktop expanse above it were deserted except for a single car, which looked very lonely. It was a long black Cadillac nosed into the cable fence at the edge of the beach. I braked and turned off the highway and got out. The man in the driver's seat of the Cadillac didn't turn his head as I approached him. His chin was propped on the steering wheel, and he was gazing out across the endless blue sea.

I opened the door and looked into his face. It was paper white. The dark brown eyes were sightless. The body was unclothed except for the thick hair matted on the chest, and a clumsy bandage tied around the waist. The bandage was composed of several blood-stained towels, held in place by a knotted piece of nylon fabric whose nature I didn't recognize immediately. Examining it more closely, I saw that it was a woman's slip. The left breast of the garment was embroidered in purple with a heart, containing the name, "Fern," in slanting script. I wondered who Fern was.

The man who was wearing her purple heart had dark curly hair, heavy black eyebrows, a heavy chin sprouting black beard. He was rough-looking in spite of his anemia and the lipstick smudged on his mouth.

There was no registration on the steeringpost, and nothing in the glove compartment but a half-empty box of shells for a .38 automatic. The ignition was still turned on. So were the dash and headlights, but they were dim. The gas gauge registered empty. Curlyhead must have pulled off the highway soon after he passed me, and driven all the rest of the night in one place.

I untied the slip, which didn't look as if it would take fingerprints, and went over it for a label. It had one: Gretchen, Palm Springs. It occurred to me that it was Saturday morning and that I'd gone all winter without a weekend in the desert. I retied the slip the way I'd found it, and drove back to the Siesta Motel.

Ella's welcome was a few degress colder than absolute zero. "Well!" She glared down her pretty rabbit nose at me. "I thought we were rid of you."

"So did I. But I just couldn't tear myself away."

She gave me a peculiar look, neither hard nor soft, but mixed. Her hand went to her hair, then reached for a registration card. "I suppose if you want to rent a room, I can't stop you. Only please don't imagine you're making an impression on me. You're not. You leave me cold, mister."

"Archer," I said. "Lew Archer. Don't bother with the card. I came back to use your phone."

"Aren't there any other phones?" She pushed the telephone across the desk. "I guess it's all right, long as it isn't a toll call."

"I'm calling the Highway Patrol. Do you know their local number?"

"I don't remember." She handed me the telephone directory.

"There's been an accident," I said as I dialed.

"A highway accident? Where did it happen?"

"Right here, sister. Right here in room thirteen."

But I didn't tell that to the Highway Patrol. I told them I had found a dead man in a car on the parking lot above the county beach. The girl listened with widening eyes and nostrils. Before I finished she rose in a flurry and left the office by the rear door.

She came back with the proprietor. His eyes were black and bright like nailheads in leather, and the scampering dance of his feet was almost frenzied. "What is this?"

"I came across a dead man up the road a piece."

"So why do you come back here to telephone?" His head was in butting position, his hands outspread and gripping the corners of the desk. "Has it got anything to do with us?"

"He's wearing a couple of your towels."

"What?"

"And he was bleeding heavily before he died. I think somebody shot him in the stomach. Maybe you did."

"You're loco," he said, but not very emphatically. "Crazy accusations like that, they will get you into trouble. What is your business?"

"I'm a private detective."

"You followed him here, is that it? You were going to arrest him, so he shot himself?"

"Wrong on both accounts," I said. "I came here to sleep. And they don't shoot themselves in the stomach. It's too uncertain, and slow. No suicide wants to die of peritonitis."

"So what are you doing now, trying to make scandal for my business?"

"If your business includes trying to cover for murder."

"He shot himself," the little man insisted.

"How do you know?"

"Donny. I spoke to him just now."

"And how does Donny know?"

"The man told him."

"Is Donny your night keyboy?"

"He was. I think I will fire him, for stupidity. He didn't even tell me about this mess. I had to find it out for myself. The hard way."

"Donny means well," the girl said at his shoulder. "I'm sure he didn't realize what happened."

"Who does?" I said. "I want to talk to Donny. But first let's have a look at the register."

He took a pile of cards from a drawer and riffled through them. His large hands, hairy-backed, were calm and expert, like animals that lived a serene life of their own, independent of their emotional owner. They dealt me one of the cards across the desk. It was inscribed in block capitals: Richard Rowe, Detroit, Mich.

I said: "There was a woman with him."

"Impossible."

"Or he was a transvestite."

He surveyed me blankly, thinking of something else. "The HP, did you tell them to come here? They know it happened here?"

"Not yet. But they'll find your towels. He used them for bandage."

"I see. Yes. Of course." He struck himself with a clenched fist on the temple. It made a noise like someone maltreating a pumpkin. "You are a private detective, you say. Now if you informed the police that you were on the trail of a fugitive, a fugitive from justice. . . . He shot himself rather than face arrest. . . . For five hundred dollars?"

"I'm not that private," I said. "I have some public responsibility. Besides, the cops would do a little checking and catch me out."

"Not necessarily. He *was* a fugitive from justice, you know."

"I hear you telling me."

"Give me a little time, and I can even present you with his record."

The girl was leaning back away from her father, her eyes starred with broken illusions. "Daddy," she said weakly.

He didn't hear her. All of his bright black attention was fixed on me. "Seven hundred dollars?"

"No sale. The higher you raise it, the guiltier you look. Were you here last night?"

"You are being absurd," he said. "I spent the entire evening with my wife. We drove up to Los Angeles to attend the ballet." By way of supporting evidence, he hummed a couple of bars from Tchaikovsky. "We didn't arrive back here in Emerald Bay until nearly two o'clock."

"Alibis can be fixed."

"By criminals, yes," he said. "I am not a criminal."

The girl put a hand on his shoulder. He cringed away, his face creased by monkey fury, but his face was hidden from her.

"Daddy," she said. "Was he murdered, do you think?"

"How do I know?" His voice was wild and high, as if she had touched the spring of his emotion. "I wasn't here. I only know what Donny told me."

The girl was examining me with narrowed eyes, as if I were a new kind of animal she had discovered and was trying to think of a use for.

"This gentleman is a detective," she said, "or claims to be."

I pulled out my photostat and slapped it down on the desk. The little man picked it up and looked from it to my face. "Will you go to work for me?"

"Doing what, telling little white lies?"

The girl answered for him: "See what you can find out about this —this death. On my word of honor, Father had nothing to do with it."

I made a snap decision, the kind you live to regret. "All right. I'll take a fifty-dollar advance. Which is a good deal less than five hundred. My first advice to you is to tell the police everything you know. Provided that you're innocent."

"You insult me," he said.

But he flicked a fifty-dollar bill from the cash drawer and pressed it into my hand fervently, like a love token. I had a queasy feeling that I had been conned into taking his money, not much of it but enough. The feeling deepened when he still refused to talk. I had to use all the arts of persuasion even to get Donny's address out of him.

The keyboy lived in a shack on the edge of a desolate stretch of dunes. I guessed that it had once been somebody's beach house, before sand had drifted like unthawing snow in the angles of the walls and winter storms had broken the tiles and cracked the concrete foundations. Huge chunks of concrete were piled haphazardly on what had been a terrace overlooking the sea.

On one of the tilted slabs, Donny was stretched like a long albino lizard in the sun. The onshore wind carried the sound of my motor to his ears. He sat up blinking, recognized me when I stopped the car, and ran in to the house.

I descended flagstone steps and knocked on the warped door. "Open up, Donny."

"Go away," he answered huskily. His eye gleamed like a snail through a crack in the wood.

"I'm working for Mr. Salanda. He wants us to have a talk."

"You can go and take a running jump at yourself, you and Mr. Salanda both."

"Open it or I'll break it down."

I waited for a while. He shot back the bolt. The door creaked re-
luctantly open. He leaned against the doorpost, searching my face
with his eyes, his hairless body shivering from an internal chill. I
pushed past him, through a kitchenette that was indescribably
filthy, littered with the remnants of old meals, and gaseous with
their odors. He followed me silently on bare soles into a larger
room whose sprung floorboards undulated under my feet. The picture window had been broken and patched with cardboard. The
stone fireplace was choked with garbage. The only furniture was an
army cot in one corner where Donny apparently slept.

"Nice homey place you have here. It has that lived-in quality."

He seemed to take it as a compliment, and I wondered if I was
dealing with a moron. "It suits me. I never was much of a one for
fancy quarters. I like it here, where I can hear the ocean at night."

"What else do you hear at night, Donny?"

He missed the point of the question, or pretended to. "All
different things. Big trucks going past on the highway. I like to hear
those night sounds. Now I guess I can't go on living here. Mr.
Salanda owns it, he lets me live here for nothing. Now he'll be kicking me out of here, I guess."

"On account of what happened last night?"

"Uh-huh." He subsided onto the cot, his doleful head supported
by his hands.

I stood over him. "Just what did happen last night, Donny?"

"A bad thing," he said. "This fella checked in about ten o'clock—"

"The man with the dark curly hair?"

"That's the one. He checked in about ten, and I gave him room
thirteen. Around about midnight I thought I heard a gun go off
from there. It took me a little while to get my nerve up, then I went
back to see what was going on. This fella came out of the room,
without no clothes on. Just some kind of a bandage around his
waist. He looked like some kind of a crazy Indian or something. He
had a gun in his hand, and he was staggering, and I could see that
he was bleeding some. He come right up to me and pushed the gun
in my gut and told me to keep my trap shut. He said I wasn't to tell
anybody I saw him, now or later. He said if I opened my mouth
about it to anybody, that he would come back and kill me. But now
he's dead, isn't he?"

"He's dead."

I could smell the fear on Donny: there's an unexplained trace of canine in my chromosomes. The hairs were prickling on the back of my neck, and I wondered if Donny's fear was of the past or for the future. The pimples stood out in bas-relief against his pale lugubrious face.

"I think he was murdered, Donny. You're lying, aren't you?"

"Me lying?" But his reaction was slow and feeble.

"The dead man didn't check in alone. He had a woman with him."

"What woman?" he said in elaborate surprise.

"You tell me. Her name was Fern. I think she did the shooting, and you caught her red-handed. The wounded man got out of the room and into his car and away. The woman stayed behind to talk to you. She probably paid you to dispose of his clothes and fake a new registration card for the room. But you both overlooked the blood on the floor of the bathroom. Am I right?"

"You couldn't be wronger, mister. Are you a cop?"

"A private detective. You're in deep trouble, Donny. You'd better talk yourself out of it if you can, before the cops start on you."

"I didn't do anything." His voice broke like a boy's. It went strangely with the glints of gray in his hair.

"Faking the register is a serious rap, even if they don't hang accessory to murder on you."

He began to expostulate in formless sentences that ran together. At the same time his hand was moving across the dirty gray blanket. It burrowed under the pillow and came out holding a crumpled card. He tried to stuff it into his mouth and chew it. I tore it away from between his discolored teeth.

It was a registration card from the motel, signed in a boyish scrawl: Mr. and Mrs. Richard Rowe, Detroit, Mich.

Donny was trembling violently. Below his cheap cotton shorts, his bony knees vibrated like tuning forks. "It wasn't my fault," he cried. "She held a gun on me."

"What did you do with the man's clothes?"

"Nothing. She didn't even let me into the room. She bundled them up and took them away herself."

"Where did she go?"

"Down the highway towards town. She walked away on the shoulder of the road and that was the last I saw of her."

"How much did she pay you, Donny?"

"Nothing, not a cent. I already told you, she held a gun on me."

"And you were so scared you kept quiet until this morning?"

"That's right. I was scared. Who wouldn't be scared?"

"She's gone now," I said. "You can give me a description of her."

"Yeah." He made a visible effort to pull his vague thoughts together. One of his eyes was a little off center, lending his face a
stunned, amorphous appearance. "She was a big tall dame with
blondey hair."

"Dyed?"

"I guess so, I dunno. She wore it in a braid like, on top of her
head. She was kind of fat, built like a lady wrestler, great big wa-
termelons on her. Big legs."

"How was she dressed?"

"I didn't hardly notice, I was so scared. I think she had some
kind of a purple coat on, with black fur around the neck. Plenty of
rings on her fingers and stuff."

"How old?"

"Pretty old, I'd say. Older than me, and I'm going on thirty-
nine."

"And she did the shooting?"

"I guess so. She told me to say if anybody asked me, I was to say
that Mr. Rowe shot himself."

"You're very suggestible, aren't you, Donny? It's a dangerous
way to be, with people pushing each other around the way they
do."

"I didn't get that, mister. Come again." He batted his pale blue
eyes at me, smiling expectantly.

"Skip it," I said and left him.

A few hundred yards up the highway I passed an HP car with
two uniformed men in the front seat looking grim. Donny was in
for it now. I pushed him out of my mind and drove across country
to Palm Springs.

Palm Springs is still a one-horse town, but the horse is a Palomino with silver trappings. Most of the girls were Palomino, too.
The main street was a cross-section of Hollywood and Vine trans-
ported across the desert by some unnatural force and disguised in
western costumes which fooled nobody. Not even me.

I found Gretchen's lingerie shop in an expensive-looking arcade
built around an imitation flagstone patio. In the patio's center a little fountain gurgled pleasantly, flinging small lariats of spray
against the heat. It was late in March, and the season was ending.

Most of the shops, including the one I entered, were deserted except for the hired help.

It was a small shop, faintly perfumed by a legion of vanished dolls. Stockings and robes and other garments were coiled on the glass counters or hung like brilliant treesnakes on display stands along the narrow walls. A henna-headed woman emerged from rustling recesses at the rear and came tripping towards me on her toes.

"You are looking for a gift, sir?" she cried with a wilted kind of gaiety. Behind her painted mask, she was tired and aging and it was Saturday afternoon and the lucky ones were dunking themselves in kidney-shaped swimming pools behind walls she couldn't climb.

"Not exactly. In fact, not at all. A peculiar thing happened to me last night. I'd like to tell you about it, but it's kind of a complicated story."

She looked me over quizzically and decided that I worked for a living, too. The phony smile faded away. Another smile took its place, which I liked better. "You look as if you'd had a fairly rough night. And you could do with a shave."

"I met a girl," I said. "Actually she was a mature woman, a statuesque blonde to be exact. I picked her up on the beach at Laguna, if you want me to be brutally frank."

"I couldn't bear it if you weren't. What kind of a pitch is this, brother?"

"Wait. You're spoiling my story. Something clicked when we met, in that sunset light, on the edge of the warm summer sea."

"It's always bloody cold when I go in."

"It wasn't last night. We swam in the moonlight and had a gay time and all. Then she went away. I didn't realize until she was gone that I didn't know her telephone number, or even her last name."

"Married woman, eh? What do you think I am, a lonely hearts club?" Still, she was interested, though she probably didn't believe me. "She mentioned me, is that it? What was her first name?"

"Fern."

"Unusual name. You say she was a big blonde?"

"Magnificently proportioned," I said. "If I had a classical education I'd call her Junoesque."

"You're kidding me, aren't you?"

"A little."

"I thought so. Personally I don't mind a little kidding. What did she say about me?"

"Nothing but good. As a matter of fact, I was complimenting her on her—er—garments."

"I see." She was long past blushing. "We had a customer last fall some time, by the name of Fern. Fern Dee. She had some kind of a job at the Joshua Club, I think. But she doesn't fit the description at all. This one was a brunette, a middle-sized brunette, quite young. I remember the name Fern because she wanted it embroidered on all the things she bought. A corny idea if you ask me, but that was her girlish desire and who am I to argue with girlish desires."

"Is she still in town?"

"I haven't seen her lately, not for months. But it couldn't be the woman you're looking for. Or could it?"

"How long ago was she in here?"

She pondered. "Early last fall, around the start of the season. She only came in that once, and made a big purchase, stockings and nightwear and underthings. The works. I remember thinking at the time, here was a girlie who suddenly hit the chips but heavily."

"She might have put on weight since then, and dyed her hair. Strange things can happen to the female form."

"You're telling me," she said. "How old was—your friend?"

"About forty, I'd say, give or take a little."

"It couldn't be the same one then. The girl I'm talking about was twenty-five at the outside, and I don't make mistakes about women's ages. I've seen too many of them in all stages, from Quentin quail to hags, and I certainly do mean hags."

"I bet you have."

She studied me with eyes shadowed by mascara and experience. "You a policeman?"

"I have been."

"You want to tell mother what it's all about?"

"Another time. Where's the Joshua Club?"

"It won't be open yet."

"I'll try it anyway."

She shrugged her thin shoulders and gave me directions. I thanked her.

It occupied a plain-faced one-story building half a block off the main street. The padded leather door swung inward when I pushed it. I passed through a lobby with a retractable roof, which contained a jungle growth of banana trees. The big main room was decorated with tinted desert photomurals. Behind a rattan bar with a fishnet canopy, a white-coated Caribbean type was drying shot-glasses with a dirty towel. His face looked uncommunicative.

On the orchestra dais beyond the piled chairs in the dining area, a young man in shirt sleeves was playing bop piano. His fingers shadowed the tune, ran circles around it, played leapfrog with it, and managed never to hit it on the nose. I stood beside him for a while and listened to him work. He looked up finally, still strum-ming with his left hand in the bass. He had soft-centered eyes and frozen-looking nostrils and a whistling mouth.

"Nice piano," I said.

"I think so."

"Fifty-second Street?"

"It's the street with the beat and I'm not effete." His left hand struck the same chord three times and dropped away from the keys. "Looking for somebody, friend?"

"Fern Dee. She asked me to drop by some time."

"Too bad. Another wasted trip. She left here end of last year, the dear. She wasn't a bad little nightingale but she was no pro, Joe, you know? She had it but she couldn't project it. When she warbled the evening died, no matter how hard she tried, I don't wanna be snide."

"Where did she lam, Sam, or don't you give a damn?"

He smiled like a corpse in a deft mortician's hands. "I heard the boss retired her to private life. Took her home to live with him. That is what I heard. But I don't mix with the big boy socially, so I couldn't say for sure that she's impure. Is it anything to you?"

"Something, but she's over twenty-one."

"Not more than a couple of years over twenty-one." His eyes darkened, and his thin mouth twisted sideways angrily. "I hate to see it happen to a pretty little twist like Fern. Not that I yearn—"

I broke in on his nonsense rhymes: "Who's the big boss you mentioned, the one Fern went to live with?"

"Angel. Who else?"

"What heaven does he inhabit?"

"You must be new in these parts—" His eyes swiveled and fo-cused on something over my shoulder. His mouth opened and closed.

A grating tenor said behind me: "Got a question you want answered, bud?"

The pianist went back to the piano as if the ugly tenor had wiped me out, annulled my very existence. I turned to its source. He was standing in a narrow doorway behind the drums, a man in his thirties with thick black curly hair and a heavy jaw blue-shadowed by closely shaven beard. He was almost the living image of the dead man in the Cadillac. The likeness gave me a jolt. The heavy black gun in his hand gave me another.

He came around the drums and approached me, bull-shouldered in a fuzzy tweed jacket, holding the gun in front of him like a dangerous gift. The pianist was doing wry things in quickened tempo with the dead march from *Saul*. A wit.

The dead man's almost-double waved his cruel chin and the crueler gun in unison. "Come inside, unless you're a government man. If you are, I'll have a look at your credentials."

"I'm a freelance."

"Inside then."

The muzzle of the automatic came into my solar plexus like a pointing iron finger. Obeying its injunction, I made my way between empty music stands and through the narrow door behind the drums. The iron finger, probing my back, directed me down a lightless corridor to a small square office containing a metal desk, a safe, a filing cabinet. It was windowless, lit by fluorescent tubes in the ceiling. Under their pitiless glare, the face above the gun looked more than ever like the dead man's face. I wondered if I had been mistaken about his deadness, or if the desert heat had addled my brain.

"I'm the manager here," he said, standing so close that I could smell the piney stuff he used on his crisp dark hair. "You got anything to ask about the members of the staff, you ask me."

"Will I get an answer?"

"Try me, bud."

"The name is Archer," I said. "I'm a private detective."

"Working for who?"

"You wouldn't be interested."

"I am, though, very much interested." The gun hopped forward like a toad into my stomach again, with the weight of his shoulder behind it. "Working for who did you say?"

I swallowed anger and nausea, estimating my chances of knocking the gun to one side and taking him bare-handed. The chances seemed pretty slim. He was heavier than I was, and he held the automatic as if it had grown out of the end of his arm. You've seen too many movies, I told myself. I told him: "A motel owner on the coast. A man was shot in one of his rooms last night. I happened to check in there a few minutes later. The old boy hired me to look into the shooting."

"Who was it got himself ventilated?"

"He could be your brother," I said. "Do you have a brother?"

He lost his color. The center of his attention shifted from the gun to my face. The gun nodded. I knocked it up and sideways with a hard left uppercut. Its discharge burned the side of my face and drilled a hole in the wall. My right sank into his neck. The gun thumped the cork floor.

He went down but not out, his spread hand scrabbling for the gun, then closing on it. I kicked his wrist. He grunted but wouldn't let go of it. I threw a punch at the short hairs on the back of his neck. He took it and came up under it with the gun, shaking his head from side to side.

"Up with the hands now," he murmured. He was one of those men whose voices go soft and mild when they are in a killing mood. He had the glassy impervious eyes of a killer. "Is Bart dead? My brother?"

"Very dead. He was shot in the belly."

"Who shot him?"

"That's the question."

"Who shot him?" he said in a quite white-faced rage. The single eye of the gun stared emptily at my midriff. "It could happen to you, bud, here and now."

"A woman was with him. She took a quick powder after it happened."

"I heard you say a name to Alfie, the piano-player. Was it Fern?"

"It could have been."

"What do you mean, it could have been?"

"She was there in the room, apparently. If you can give me a description of her?"

His hard brown eyes looked past me. "I can do better than that. There's a picture of her on the wall behind you. Take a look at it. Keep those hands up high."

I shifted my feet and turned uneasily. The wall was blank. I heard him draw a breath and move, and tried to evade his blow. No use. It caught the back of my head. I pitched forward against the blank wall and slid down it into three dimensions of blankness.

The blankness coagulated into colored shapes. The shapes were half human and half beast and they dissolved and reformed. A dead man with a hairy breast climbed out of a hole and doubled and quadrupled. I ran away from them through a twisting tunnel which led to an echo chamber. Under the roaring surge of the nightmare music, a rasping tenor was saying:

"I figure it like this. Vario's tip was good. Bart found her in Acapulco, and he was bringing her back from there. She conned him into stopping off at this motel for the night. Bart always went for her."

"I didn't know that," a dry old voice put in. "This is very interesting news about Bart and Fern. You should have told me before about this. Then I would not have sent him for her and this would not have happened. Would it, Gino?"

My mind was still partly absent, wandering underground in the echoing caves. I couldn't recall the voices, or who they were talking about. I had barely sense enough to keep my eyes closed and go on listening. I was lying on my back on a hard surface. The voices were above me.

The tenor said: "You can't blame Bartolomeo. She's the one, the dirty treacherous lying little bitch."

"Calm yourself, Gino. I blame nobody. But more than ever now, we want her back, isn't that right?"

"I'll kill her," he said softly, almost wistfully.

"Perhaps. It may not be necessary now. I dislike promiscuous killing—"

"Since when, Angel?"

"Don't interrupt, it's not polite. I learned to put first things first. Now what is the most important thing? Why did we want her back in the first place? I will tell you: to shut her mouth. The government heard she left me, they wanted her to testify about my income. We wanted to find her first and shut her mouth, isn't that right?"

"I know how to shut her mouth," the younger man said very quietly.

"First we try a better way, my way. You learn when you're as old as I am there is a use for everything, and not to be wasteful. Not even wasteful with somebody else's blood. She shot your brother, right? So now we have something on her, strong enough to keep her mouth shut for good. She'd get off with second degree, with what she's got, but even that is five to ten in Tehachapi. I think all I need to do is tell her that. First we have to find her, eh?"

"I'll find her. Bart didn't have any trouble finding her."

"With Vario's tip to help him, no. But I think I'll keep you here with me, Gino. You're too hot-blooded, you and your brother both. I want her alive. Then I can talk to her, and then we'll see."

"You're going soft in your old age, Angel."

"Am I?" There was a light slapping sound, of a blow on flesh. "I have killed many men, for good reasons. So I think you will take that back."

"I take it back."

"And call me Mr. Funk. If I am so old, you will treat my gray hairs with respect. Call me Mr. Funk."

"Mr. Funk."

"All right, your friend here, does he know where Fern is?"

"I don't think so."

"Mr. Funk."

"Mr. Funk." Gino's voice was a whining snarl.

"I think he's coming to. His eyelids fluttered."

The toe of a shoe prodded my side. Somebody slapped my face a number of times. I opened my eyes and sat up. The back of my head was throbbing like an engine fueled by pain. Gino rose from a squatting position and stood over me.

"Stand up."

I rose shakily to my feet. I was in a stone-walled room with a high beamed ceiling, sparsely furnished with stiff old black oak chairs and tables. The room and the furniture seemed to have been built for a race of giants.

The man behind Gino was small and old and weary. He might have been an unsuccessful grocer or a superannuated barkeep who had come to California for his health. Clearly his health was poor. Even in the stifling heat he looked pale and chilly, as if he had caught chronic death from one of his victims. He moved closer to me, his legs shuffling feebly in wrinkled blue trousers that bagged at the knees. His shrunken torso was swathed in a heavy blue turtleneck sweater. He had two days' beard on his chin like moth-eaten gray plush.

"Gino informs me that you are investigating a shooting." His accent was Middle-European and very faint, as if he had forgotten his origins. "Where did this happen, exactly?"

"I don't think I'll tell you that. You can read it in the papers tomorrow night if you are interested."

"I am not prepared to wait. I am impatient. Do you know where Fern is?"

"I wouldn't be here if I did."

"But you know where she was last night."

"I couldn't be sure."

"Tell me anyway to the best of your knowledge."

"I don't think I will."

"He doesn't think he will," the old man said to Gino.

"I think you better let me out of here. Kidnaping is a tough rap. You don't want to die in the pen."

He smiled at me, with a tolerance more terrible than anger. His eyes were like thin stab-wounds filled with watery blood. Shuffling unhurriedly to the head of the mahogany table behind him, he pressed a spot in the rug with the toe of one felt slipper. Two men in blue serge suits entered the room and stepped towards me briskly. They belonged to the race of giants it had been built for.

Gino moved behind me and reached to pin my arms. I pivoted, landed one short punch, and took a very hard counter below the belt. Something behind me slammed my kidneys with the heft of a trailer truck bumper. I turned on weakening legs and caught a chin with my elbow. Gino's fist, or one of the beams from the ceiling, landed on my neck. My head rang like a gong. Under its clangor, Angel was saying pleasantly:

"Where was Fern last night?"

I didn't say.

The men in blue serge held me upright by the arms while Gino used my head as a punching bag. I rolled with his lefts and rights as well as I could, but his timing improved and mine deteriorated. His face wavered and receded. At intervals Angel inquired politely if I was willing to assist him now. I asked myself confusedly in the hail of fists what I was holding out for or who I was protecting. Probably I was holding out for myself. It seemed important to me not to give in to violence. But my identity was dissolving and receding like the face in front of me.

I concentrated on hating Gino's face. That kept it clear and steady for a while: a stupid square-jawed face barred by a single black brow, two close-set brown eyes staring glassily. His fists continued to rock me like an air-hammer.

Finally Angel placed a clawed hand on his shoulder, and nodded to my handlers. They deposited me in a chair. It swung on an invisible wire from the ceiling in great circles. It swung out over the desert, across a bleak horizon, into darkness.

I came to, cursing. Gino was standing over me again. There was an empty water-glass in his hand, and my face was dripping. Angel spoke up beside him, with a trace of irritation in his voice:

"You stand up good under punishment. Why go to all the trouble, though? I want a little information, that is all. My friend, my little girl-friend, ran away. I'm impatient to get her back."

"You're going about it the wrong way."

Gino leaned close, and laughed harshly. He shattered the glass on the arm of my chair, held the jagged base up to my eyes. Fear ran through me, cold and light in my veins. My eyes were my connection with everything. Blindness would be the end of me. I closed my eyes, shutting out the cruel edges of the broken thing in his hand.

"Nix, Gino," the old man said. "I have a better idea, as usual. There is heat on, remember."

They retreated to the far side of the table and conferred there in low voices. The young man left the room. The old man came back to me. His storm troopers stood one on each side of me, looking down at him in ignorant awe.

"What is your name, young fellow?"

I told him. My mouth was puffed and lisping, tongue tangled in ropes of blood.

"I like a young fellow who can take it, Mr. Archer. You say that you're a detective. You find people for a living, is that right?"

"I have a client," I said.

"Now you have another. Whoever he is, I can buy and sell him, believe me. Fifty times over." His thin blue hands scoured each other. They made a sound like two dry sticks rubbing together on a dead tree.

"Narcotics?" I said. "Are you the wheel in the heroin racket? I've heard of you."

His watery eyes veiled themselves like a bird's. "Now don't ask foolish questions, or I will lose my respect for you entirely."

"That would break my heart."

"Then comfort yourself with this." He brought an old-fashioned purse out of his hip pocket, abstracted a crumpled bill and smoothed it out on my knee. It was a five-hundred-dollar bill.

"This girl of mine you are going to find for me, she is young and foolish. I am old and foolish, to have trusted her. No matter. Find her for me and bring her back and I will give you another bill like this one. Take it."

"Take it," one of my guards repeated. "Mr. Funk said for you to take it."

I took it. "You're wasting your money. I don't even know what she looks like. I don't know anything about her."

"Gino is bringing a picture. He came across her last fall at a recording studio in Hollywood where Alfie had a date. He gave her an audition and took her on at the club, more for her looks than for the talent she had. As a singer she flopped. But she is a pretty little thing, about five foot four, nice figure, dark brown hair, big hazel eyes. I found a use for her." Lechery flickered briefly in his eyes and went out.

"You find a use for everything."

"That is good economics. I often think if I wasn't what I am, I would make a good economist. Nothing would go to waste." He paused and dragged his dying old mind back to the subject: "She was here for a couple of months, then she ran out on me, silly girl. I heard last week that she was in Acapulco, and the federal grand jury was going to subpoena her. I have tax troubles, Mr. Archer, all my life I have tax troubles. Unfortunately I let Fern help with my books a little bit. She could do me great harm. So I sent Bart to Mexico to bring her back. But I meant no harm to her. I still intend her no harm, even now. A little talk, a little realistic discussion with Fern, that is all that will be necessary. So even the shooting of my good friend Bart serves its purpose. Where did it happen, by the way?"

The question flicked out like a hook on the end of a long line.

"In San Diego," I said, "at a place near the airport: the Mission Motel."

He smiled paternally. "Now you are showing good sense."

Gino came back with a silver-framed photograph in his hand. He handed it to Angel, who passed it on to me. It was a studio portrait, of the kind intended for publicity cheesecake. On a black velvet divan, against an artificial night sky, a young woman reclined in a gossamer robe that was split to show one bent leg. Shadows accentuated the lines of her body and the fine bones in her face. Under the heavy makeup which widened the mouth and darkened the half-closed eyes, I recognized Ella Salanda. The picture was signed in white, in the lower righthand corner: "To my Angel, with all my love, Fern."

A sickness assailed me, worse than the sickness induced by Gino's fists. Angel breathed into my face: "Fern Dee is a stage name. Her real name I never learned. She told me one time that if her family knew where she was they would die of shame." He chuckled drily. "She will not want them to know that she killed a man."

I drew away from his charnel-house breath. My guards escorted me out. Gino started to follow, but Angel called him back.

"Don't wait to hear from me," the old man said after me. "I expect to hear from you."

The building stood on a rise in the open desert. It was huge and turreted, like somebody's idea of a castle in Spain. The last rays of the sun washed its walls in purple light and cast long shadows across its barren acreage. It was surrounded by a ten-foot hurricane fence topped with three strands of barbed wire.

Palm Springs was a clutter of white stones in the distance, diamonded by an occasional light. The dull red sun was balanced like a glowing cigar-butt on the rim of the hills above the town. A man with a bulky shoulder harness under his brown suede windbreaker drove me towards it. The sun fell out of sight, and darkness gathered like an impalpable ash on the desert, like a column of blue-gray smoke towering into the sky.

The sky was blue-black and swarming with stars when I got back to Emerald Bay. A black Cadillac followed me out of Palm Springs. I lost it in the winding streets of Pasadena. So far as I could see, I had lost it for good.

The neon Mexican lay peaceful under the stars. A smaller sign at his feet asserted that there was No Vacancy. The lights in the long low stucco buildings behind him shone brightly. The office door was open behind a screen, throwing a barred rectangle of light on the gravel. I stepped into it, and froze.

Behind the registration desk in the office, a woman was avidly reading a magazine. Her shoulders and bosom were massive. Her hair was blond, piled on her head in coroneted braids. There were rings on her fingers, a triple strand of cultured pearls around her thick white throat. She was the woman Donny had described to me.

I pulled the screen door open and said rudely: "Who are you?"

She glanced up, twisting her mouth in a sour grimace. "Well! I'll thank you to keep a civil tongue in your head."

"Sorry. I thought I'd seen you before somewhere."

"Well, you haven't." She looked me over coldly. "What happened to your face, anyway?"

"I had a little plastic surgery done. By an amateur surgeon."

She clucked disapprovingly. "If you're looking for a room, we're full up for the night. I don't believe I'd rent you a room even if we weren't. Look at your clothes."

"Uh-huh. Where's Mr. Salanda?"

"Is it any business of yours?"

"He wants to see me. I'm doing a job for him."

"What kind of a job?"

I mimicked her: "Is it any business of yours?" I was irritated. Under her mounds of flesh she had a personality as thin and hard and abrasive as a rasp.

"Watch who you're getting flip with, sonny boy." She rose, and her shadow loomed immense across the back door of the room. The magazine fell closed on the desk: it was *Teen-age Confessions*. "I am Mrs. Salanda. Are you a handyman?"

"A sort of one," I said. "I'm a garbage collector in the moral field. You look as if you could use me."

The crack went over her head. "Well, you're wrong. And I don't think my husband hired you, either. This is a respectable motel."

"Uh-huh. Are you Ella's mother?"

"I should say not. That little snip is no daughter of mine."

"Her stepmother?"

"Mind your own business. You better get out of here. The police are keeping a close watch on this place tonight, if you're planning any tricks."

"Where's Ella now?"

"I don't know and I don't care. She's probably gallivanting off around the countryside. It's all she's good for. One day at home in the last six months, that's a fine record for a young unmarried girl." Her face was thick and bloated with anger against her stepdaughter. She went on talking blindly, as if she had forgotten me entirely: "I told her father he was an old fool to take her back. How does he know what she's been up to? I say let the ungrateful filly go and fend for herself."

"Is that what you say, Mabel?" Salanda had softly opened the door behind her. He came forward into the room, doubly dwarfed by her blond magnitude. "I say if it wasn't for you, my dear, Ella wouldn't have been driven away from home in the first place."

She turned on him in a blubbering rage. He drew himself up tall and reached to snap his fingers under her nose. "Go back into the house. You are a disgrace to women, a disgrace to motherhood."

"I'm not *her* mother, thank God."

"Thank God," he echoed, shaking his fist at her. She retreated like a schooner under full sail, menaced by a gunboat. The door closed on her. Salanda turned to me:

"I'm sorry, Mr. Archer. I have difficulties with my wife, I am ashamed to say it. I was an imbecile to marry again. I gained a senseless hulk of flesh, and lost my daughter. Old imbecile!" he denounced himself, wagging his great head sadly. "I married in hot blood. Sexual passion has always been my downfall. It runs in my family, this insane hunger for blondeness and stupidity and size." He spread his arms in a wide and futile embrace on emptiness.

"Forget it."

"If I could." He came closer to examine my face. "You are injured, Mr. Archer. Your mouth is damaged. There is blood on your chin."

"I was in a slight brawl."

"On my account?"

"On my own. But I think it's time you leveled with me."

"Leveled with you?"

"Told me the truth. You knew who was shot last night, and who shot him, and why."

He touched my arm, with a quick, tentative grace. "I have only one daughter, Mr. Archer, only the one child. It was my duty to defend her, as best as I could."

"Defend her from what?"

"From shame, from the police, from prison." He flung one arm out, indicating the whole range of human disaster. "I am a man of honor, Mr. Archer. But private honor stands higher with me than public honor. The man was abducting my daughter. She brought him here in the hope of being rescued. Her last hope."

"I think that's true. You should have told me this before."

"I was alarmed, upset. I feared your intentions. Any minute the police were due to arrive."

"But you had a right to shoot him. It wasn't even a crime. The crime was his."

"I didn't know that then. The truth came out to me gradually. I feared that Ella was involved with him." His flat black gaze sought my face and rested on it. "However, I did not shoot him, Mr. Archer. I was not even here at the time. I told you that this morning, and you may take my word for it."

"Was Mrs. Salanda here?"

"No sir, she was not. Why should you ask me that?"

"Donny described the woman who checked in with the dead man. The description fits your wife."

"Donny was lying. I told him to give a false description of the woman. Apparently he was unequal to the task of inventing one."

"Can you prove that she was with you?"

"Certainly I can. We had reserved seats at the theatre. Those who sat around us can testify that the seats were not empty. Mrs. Salanda and I, we are not an inconspicuous couple." He smiled wryly.

"Ella killed him then."

He neither assented, nor denied it. "I was hoping that you were on my side, my side and Ella's. Am I wrong?"

"I'll have to talk to her, before I know myself. Where is she?"

"I do not know, Mr. Archer, sincerely I do not know. She went away this afternoon, after the policemen questioned her. They were suspicious, but we managed to soothe their suspicions. They did not know that she had just come home, from another life, and I did not tell them. Mabel wanted to tell them. I silenced her." His white teeth clicked together.

"What about Donny?"

"They took him down to the station for questioning. He told them nothing damaging. Donny can appear very stupid when he wishes. He has the reputation of an idiot, but he is not so dumb. Donny has been with me for many years. He has a deep devotion for my daughter. I got him released tonight."

"You should have taken my advice," I said, "taken the police into your confidence. Nothing would have happened to you. The dead man was a mobster, and what he was doing amounts to kidnaping. Your daughter was a witness against his boss."

"She told me that. I am glad that it is true. Ella has not always told me the truth. She has been a hard girl to bring up, without a good mother to set her an example. Where has she been these last six months, Mr. Archer?"

"Singing in a night club in Palm Springs. Her boss was a racketeer."

"A racketeer?" His mouth and nose screwed up, as if he sniffed the odor of corruption.

"Where she was isn't important, compared with where she is now. The boss is still after her. He hired me to look for her."

Salanda regarded me with fear and dislike, as if the odor originated in me. "You let him hire you?"

"It was my best chance of getting out of his place alive. I'm not his boy, if that's what you mean."

"You ask me to believe you?"

"I'm telling you. Ella is in danger. As a matter of fact, we all are." I didn't tell him about the second black Cadillac. Gino would be driving it, wandering the night roads with a ready gun in his armpit and revenge corroding his heart.

"My daughter is aware of the danger," he said. "She warned me of it."

"She must have told you where she was going."

"No. But she may be at the beach house. The house where Donny lives. I will come with you."

"You stay here. Keep your doors locked. If any strangers show and start prowling the place, call the police."

He bolted the door behind me as I went out. Yellow traffic lights cast wan reflections on the asphalt. Streams of cars went by to the north, to the south. To the west, where the sea lay, a great black emptiness opened under the stars. The beach house sat on its white margin, a little over a mile from the motel.

For the second time that day, I knocked on the warped kitchen door. There was light behind it, shining through the cracks. A shadow obscured the light.

"Who is it?" Donny said. Fear or some other emotion had filled his mouth with pebbles.

"You know me, Donny."

The door groaned on its hinges. He gestured dumbly to me to

come in, his face a white blur. When he turned his head, and the light from the living room caught his face, I saw that grief was the emotion that marked it. His eyes were swollen as if he had been crying. More than ever he resembled a dilapidated boy whose growing pains had never paid off in manhood.

"Anybody with you?"

Sounds of movement in the living room answered my question. I brushed him aside and went in. Ella Salanda was bent over an open suitcase on the camp cot. She straightened, her mouth thin, eyes wide and dark. The .38 automatic in her hand gleamed dully under the naked bulb suspended from the ceiling.

"I'm getting out of here," she said, "and you're not going to stop me."

"I'm not sure I want to try. Where are you going, Fern?"

Donny spoke behind me, in his grief-thickened voice: "She's going away from me. She promised to stay here if I did what she told me. She promised to be my girl—"

"Shut up, stupid." Her voice cut like a lash, and Donny gasped as if the lash had been laid across his back.

"What did she tell you to do, Donny? Tell me just what you did."

"When she checked in last night with the fella from Detroit, she made a sign I wasn't to let on I knew her. Later on she left me a note. She wrote it with a lipstick on a piece of paper towel. I still got it, hidden in the kitchen."

"What did she write in the note?"

He lingered behind me, fearful of the gun in the girl's hand, more fearful of her anger.

She said: "Don't be crazy, Donny. He doesn't know a thing, not a thing. He can't do anything to either of us."

"I don't care what happens, to me or anybody else," the anguished voice said behind me. "You're running out on me, breaking your promise to me. I always knew it was too good to be true. Now I just don't care any more."

"I care," she said. "I care what happens to me." Her eyes shifted to me, above the unwavering gun. "I won't stay here. I'll shoot you if I have to."

"It shouldn't be necessary. Put it down, Fern. It's Bartolomeo's gun, isn't it? I found the shells to fit it in his glove compartment."

"How do you know so much?"

"I talked to Angel."

"Is he here?" Panic whined in her voice.

"No. I came alone."

"You better leave the same way then, while you can go under your own power."

"I'm staying. You need protection, whether you know it or not. And I need information. Donny, go in the kitchen and bring me that note."

"Don't do it, Donny. I'm warning you."

His sneakered feet made soft indecisive sounds. I advanced on the girl, talking quietly and steadily: "You conspired to kill a man, but you don't have to be afraid. He had it coming. Tell the whole story to the cops, and my guess is they won't even book you. Hell, you can even become famous. The government wants you as a witness in a tax case."

"What kind of a case?"

"A tax case against Angel. It's probably the only kind of rap they can pin on him. You can send him up for the rest of his life like Capone. You'll be a heroine, Fern."

"Don't call me Fern. I hate that name." There were sudden tears in her eyes. "I hate everything connected with that name. I hate myself."

"You'll hate yourself more if you don't put down that gun. Shoot me and it all starts over again. The cops will be on your trail, Angel's troopers will be gunning for you."

Now only the cot was between us, the cot and the unsteady gun facing me above it.

"This is the turning point," I said. "You've made a lot of bum decisions and almost ruined yourself, playing footsie with the evilest men there are. You can go on the way you have been, getting in deeper until you end up in a refrigerated drawer, or you can come back out of it now, into a decent life."

"A decent life? Here? With my father married to Mabel?"

"I don't think Mabel will last much longer. Anyway, I'm not Mabel. I'm on your side."

I waited. She dropped the gun on the blanket. I scooped it up and turned to Donny:

"Let me see that note."

He disappeared through the kitchen door, head and shoulders drooping on the long stalk of his body.

"What could I do?" the girl said. "I was caught. It was Bart or me. All the way up from Acapulco I planned how I could get away. He held a gun in my side when we crossed the border; the same way when we stopped for gas or to eat at the drive-ins. I realized he had to be killed. My father's motel looked like my only chance. So I talked Bart into staying there with me overnight. He had no idea who the place belonged to. I didn't know what I was going to do. I only knew it had to be something drastic. Once I was back with Angel in the desert, that was the end of me. Even if he didn't kill me, it meant I'd have to go on living with him. Anything was better than that. So I wrote a note to Donny in the bathroom, and dropped it out the window. He was always crazy about me."

Her mouth had grown softer. She looked remarkably young and virginal. The faint blue hollows under her eyes were dewy. "Donny shot Bart with Bart's own gun. He had more nerve than I had. I lost my nerve when I went back into the room this morning. I didn't know about the blood in the bathroom. It was the last straw."

She was wrong. Something crashed in the kitchen. A cool draft swept the living room. A gun spoke twice, out of sight. Donny fell backwards through the doorway, a piece of brownish paper clutched in his hand. Blood gleamed on his shoulder like a red badge.

I stepped behind the cot and pulled the girl down to the floor with me. Gino came through the door, his two-colored sports shoe stepping on Donny's laboring chest. I shot the gun out of his hand. He floundered back against the wall, clutching at his wrist.

I sighted carefully for my second shot, until the black bar of his eyebrows was steady in the sights of the .38. The hole it made was invisible. Gino fell loosely forward, prone on the floor beside the man he had killed.

Ella Salanda ran across the room. She knelt, and cradled Donny's head in her lap. Incredibly, he spoke, in a loud sighing voice:

"You won't go away again, Ella? I did what you told me. You promised."

"Sure I promised. I won't leave you, Donny. Crazy man. Crazy fool."

"You like me better than you used to? Now?"

"I like you, Donny. You're the most man there is."

She held the poor insignificant head in her hands. He sighed, and his life came out bright-colored at the mouth. It was Donny who went away.

His hand relaxed, and I read the lipstick note she had written him on a piece of porous tissue:

"Donny: This man will kill me unless you kill him first. His gun will be in his clothes on the chair beside the bed. Come in and get it at midnight and shoot to kill. Good luck. I'll stay and be your girl if you do this, just like you always wished. Love. Ella."

I looked at the pair on the floor. She was rocking his lifeless head against her breast. Beside them, Gino looked very small and lonely, a dummy leaking darkness from his brow.

Donny had his wish and I had mine. I wondered what Ella's was.

The Interceptor

Barry N. Malzberg

He has been in the hotel room for a long time. No pleasure that, but he thinks he has the crime figured out at last. It must have been his wife.

Everything, *everything* points to her. She must have killed Robinson in temper; then, when the placement of the securities next to the corpse would have tied the murder to her, turned the thing around and implicated him with that phone call which brought him to the scene just three minutes ahead of the police.

"Come over," she said. "Something really terrible has happened; I appeal to you," and linked to her in the end, unable to understand what was going on, he had come and had nearly been apprehended.

If he had not run immediately—but no sense in thinking about that now. He had gotten away from the police, just barely, and now at last he had solved the mystery. No time for speculation. No need for it either.

The motives were clear. Robinson and his wife must have been having an affair, had carried it on unknown to him for a long time, his business partner and wife, and Robinson, bored, had been looking for a way out. Wryly he thinks that he could have warned Robinson about entrapment if only the man had been frank with him. In fact, regardless of consequences, Robinson might well have broken off the relationship if only given a little more time. And she could not bear to see it end that way, being that kind of a woman.

Yes, that must be it. He has nailed it to the ground. He lights another cigarette, looks around the room, paces to the window and looks at 72nd Street three floors below him, addicts milling in front of the hotel. He had been smart to have selected a location like this to be hidden, although the circumstances were not of the best. If nothing else, living in this hotel for some weeks had made him socially conscious.

Perhaps it was not merely a crime of passion, though. His wife must have known that sooner or later Robinson would let slip news of the affair and the divorce would have been shattering. At all costs the woman believed in appearances. She would not even have a bedroom fight unless she was made up for it.

He sighs, walks away from the window. Relief overtakes him. It is good to know that he has the matter straightened out for himself at last and not a moment too soon. The police are closing in; even with the help of the inspector he could not remain in flight from the authorities forever. And to be apprehended in a hotel like this—

He picks up the phone to call the inspector and give him the explanation that will, at last, set him free. As he inhales deeply to brace himself, a fragment of dust in the foul hotel room penetrates his lungs in the wrong way and he coughs. He coughs repeatedly, wheezing, feeling the first stab of an asthma attack. Enough. Enough of cigarettes. In his new life he will definitely give up the habit. He stubs out his forty-third cigarette of the day and dials the inspector's home number.

He thinks at last that he has got the thing clear in his mind. Not soon enough to have saved the agony of flight but not too late. Not by a damned sight too late. He lights a cigarette to celebrate this. When everything is over he will give up the habit but now he will indulge himself. The murderer was Robinson.

Robinson! It all ties together. His business parner and his wife must have been having an affair for many years until his wife had lost interest and had told the man that she had reached the end, that the worn-out affair was not worth the risk of a lost marriage.

In a fit of jealous rage Robinson must have killed her in the offices, then planted the incriminating securities next to her and fled.

The securities had led the police inevitably to him and with his wife dead and Robinson out of the country he did not have a chance. It had been clever of Robinson to arrange that illness of his father in Italy, diabolically so, and no details had ever been checked. Did Robinson even have a father?

And so he had no choice but to become a fugitive while he tried to piece the crime together himself. He had to find the explanation that would free him of the authorities and restore him to the life that for so long he had taken for granted. But it had been difficult. Now the police had infiltrated into the hotel itself. The dope traffic in the halls and outside might distract them for a while; still, it could be only a matter of time until they traced down his room number, poured into his door holding guns, and arrested him.

Fortunately, he had at last worked out the true explanation of the crime. He would be saved. If he could only reach the inspector quickly enough to start the process in motion—

He coughs. The air in this old and vicious hotel, once elegant, now destroyed, located in an undesirable area of the city he has always hated even in the good years when he and his young wife lived here, this air has become increasingly foul, and in the bargain, due to the terrible impact of the murder and then the building pressures on him, he has been smoking too much, even beyond his normal excess.

He has always had a morbid fear of getting lung cancer and dying slowly, although his own doctor had assured him just two months ago, shortly before the nightmare began, that for a man of forty-seven he was in perfect health. Slight elevation of the blood pressure; suspicious fullness around the area of the spleen, yes, but these were not serious problems and could be controlled. Lung cancer was contradicted under all circumstances.

He thinks now of his doctor, a thin, nervous internist who had also treated his wife, been taciturn about her condition, had insisted on the sanctity of that relationship and of his files.

Funny that the doctor had never known anything about the man's personal life, although he had been treating the two of them for seven years. No pictures on his desk that might be indicative, no wife or children squinting or smiling imbecilically at the degrees framed on the wall opposite.

Perhaps she was having an affair with the doctor then as well. This was not impossible. She was a passionate woman for whom he had had little time for many years. Pressures of business. Building the firm. Acquiring securities. There might have been quite a few.

Robinson's problem, in fact, might not have been the end of the affair but the discovery that he was merely another in a procession. Robinson had vanity over his insecurity. This would have been unbearable to him. Looked at in that way, the situation creates sympathy for Robinson as well. Tragic, he thinks. All of it was tragic: missed circumstances, lapsed opportunities, an exercise in misdirection. No time to take the long view, however, or to want to go back. It is too late for this.

Procedures. Stick to the *modus operandi* as he had seen it established. First, the call to the inspector to clear himself. Then the meeting with the inspector to give the details, the abandonment of charges, the hunt for the true murderer, Robinson.

He thinks he knows how the man can be found. In Italy or New York Robinson's habits are still as naked to him as only those of a lifelong business partner can be. It is not for nothing that they have worked together, shared his wife.

At last, soon or late, in the presence of the police or alone, he will come face to face with the man, possibly in some dismal hotel room just like this one. Staggering against the walls, sweating, coughing, mumbling, choking. Robinson may look very much as he has over these weeks. He will feel sympathy for the man as only one who has shared these circumstances could.

"I forgive you," he will say, reaching forward to touch Robinson. "I'm sorry, it was not merely your fault but mine too. I relieve you of your guilt. All right, it is all right," and will connect then, a springing clasp, wrist to wrist, and Robinson will disintegrate before him, weeping.

"I didn't mean to do it," he will say, "I had no choice. It was just that I was so frightened," and will cast him a look so full of pleading and mercy that it will contain all the vengeance he ever needed. As for the rest of it, the arrest, arraignment, trial, incarceration, he will play no role. He will let the authorities do as they will for the urge for vengeance will be out of him. Will anyone understand this?

Passion and loss. That was what it was. He can surely make this clear to the inspector, who is himself an understanding man who in his business must have seen many interesting cases like this. He and the inspector someday will share those reminiscences in a cocktail lounge or at a good restaurant on the East Side. He and the inspector. His salvation and his friend.

He picks up the phone, knowing the number so well that he could, if a blind man, find it expertly. He dials the number.

FINALLY, as a suddenness, all of it falls into place for him. The doctor. *All the time it would have to have been the doctor.*

Yes, yes! The man must have known his wife well. It had been seven years after all. He had treated her, understood from the confidences she would have given that she was lonely and abandoned, resentful of the way his original interest in her had fragmented into a hundred other meaningless concerns.

The doctor, hearing all of this on late afternoons in the gray of the empty office, must have taken all of these for signals instead of desperate secrets and tried to interest her in having an affair with him—when suddenly, stunningly, she turned on him in revulsion and then laughed at his desires. How well he knew this; she was exactly that kind of a woman.

"Where did you ever get that idea?" his wife must have said. "Just because I told you a few things did you think it meant that I would go to bed with you? I wouldn't touch you, you foul little man. Hire a good-looking nurse and try it on her."

"No," the doctor would have said, "you can't say this to me. You cannot. There must be some reason—"

"I'll say anything I want," his wife would have answered, "I'm paying the bills. You don't even exist in my life if I don't want you to. Where could you have gotten the idea I would touch you?" She had that streak; it would have been what she said. And the doctor, a simple man enthralled by his desires, would have been unable to deal with it.

So, he had killed her. After saying what she did, his wife must have turned to leave the office, but before she could even reach the door the doctor had, in a fit of passion, ended her life. With a scalpel or hypodermic injection or whatever else doctors kept in their examining rooms.

They weren't regulated, that was the trouble. An M.D. could get away with anything, once you had that degree on the wall. But it did not guarantee that you could have sex with your patients.

That was the point at which he had gone wrong. It would have been a clean wound—he knew his business, after all—with very little bleeding and after that with crazed skill the doctor would have disposed of the weapon and erased all signs of his own implication in the crime.

Had she died immediately? Or had she hung on, gasping on the floor for a few moments, her eyes slowly glazing as she stared at the fluorescence? Well, no need to be too graphic; he will think of that some other time. He wants to think that it was a clean, quick death; even for her cruelty she should not have suffered.

The securities then. With the woman lying at last dead before him, the doctor's passion would have turned to panic and then at last to mad cunning as the thought came to him that without witnesses and with the fact of a sterile marriage there would be an available suspect.

If he could plant the securities near the body, then the investigation would inevitably turn away from him, despite the fact that it was his office, and toward the husband with whose fate those securities were inextricably linked.

The doctor would not even have to worry about getting the corpse from the office; it would be credible that the husband would want to kill her in surroundings where someone else would be implicated.

Double reverse. Sitting in the hotel room he nods slowly, being able to appreciate, as he thinks the thing through, the doctor's cunning all the way down the line.

So the doctor had done it then. There was plenty of information from the wife over seven years and he knew exactly where to look. He had seized the securities, placed them on top of the corpse and then closed up his office, knowing that all of this would shortly be found by the authorities, who would make the connections.

The trap had sprung well. If he had not finally had the alertness and good sense to consider the issue of the doctor, the man without whom, damningly, the crime could not have worked, he would never have gotten out. But finally, through his own thought and effort, the crime had been solved.

If he can get the facts to the right people in time.

Robinson first. He must call Robinson and give him the explanation slowly, carefully, just the way he has worked it out.

His business partner is a ponderous man; he must take time to explain and not confuse him by hurrying. Still, he knows that he can be counted on: if it were not for Robinson smuggling him away from home at the critical moment and into this dismal but safe hotel room, he would at this moment be in a cell, awaiting trial and conviction.

Still, he thinks, Robinson could have shown better taste in hotels; even at this level there must be a better place, and the drug traffic is incessant.

But his partner and friend of almost a quarter-century, the only man he could ever trust, had stood by him as none of the others would, not even the inspector. Robinson insisted steadfastly that he was innocent, that he never could have done it. And had bought just enough time from the inspector to put him, for the moment, out of their grasp.

But only for the moment. He must remember that. Like his poor wife, he had run out of time.

He will tell Robinson and his partner will go to the inspector on his behalf with the story. Once the police know which trail to investigate, the crime will open up before them, just as for himself it has opened in this grim hotel room.

The doctor's hasty disappearance, his failure to contact the answering service, the peculiar aspect of the corpse, the way in which the office was left—all of these will assume a different cast in the inspector's mind. He is too tough and shrewd to deny the obvious once it is presented to him and will direct the police to close down on the evidence which must surely lurk in the doctor's file. And surely the doctor had had friends to whom he might have, before his flight, intimated the truth.

While he stays hidden, Robinson his one connection to the authorities, the crime will unravel about them and he will be able to come out of this with his life intact, his reputation restored.

The loss of his wife and the pitiful way in which his marriage has ended are dreadful, of course, but he realizes that in some corridor of the heart he must have abandoned her long ago.

There had almost never been a marriage. For this and the murder itself he will have to make atonement in some intricate way, pay some measure of penance beyond what he has already by living these dreadful weeks.

But enough of that for now. The thing to do is to call Robinson and begin the springing of the levers which, as they are released one by one, will send him back to the world.

He returns from the window at which he has been pacing, casting idle looks downward at 72nd Street. Three teenage boys are assaulting someone's convertible and as scars appear on the old car's body he has been thinking about the less visible assassins who have been working on him all this time. He coughs at some rancid odor that whisks in and out of the window.

Then, swallowing determinedly, he picks up the phone. He knows where Robinson will be. The number is engraved into him. He sighs and shakes his head. He dials.

At last he sees the answer and hopes that it is not too late. It must have been at the corner of his mind for a while. Again and again he had pushed it off because it had been too insane, too unreasonable, but now he can no longer turn back. The truth is agony, but the truth will set him free.

It is the inspector.

The inspector from the beginning had been too casual about his involvement in the case, too insidious in wanting to know personal facts, not willing himself to yield hard facts or opinions which would establish his own thoughts on the case, the position which a legitimate police official would have to take.

And the matter of identity as well. Never once had the inspector offered identification. And, accepting unthinkingly as he would have to the presence of an inspector on a major murder case, he had never asked for identification. If he had, the whole case might have broken in front of him then, but it was a risk the man identifying himself as the "inspector" had been willing to take. He was clever, he was a brilliant actor, and it had turned out not to be a risk at all.

The inspector. The inspector! Oh, this man must have loved his wife for a long time, loved and hated her as well, watched her from a distance, then slowly infiltrated himself into her life.

Who knew what manner of man he might be? Who could even touch the mask? How could his wife, that gentle, diffuse woman distracted by her own sorrow, have doubted whatever nonsensical stories he gave her to explain his original appearance? The inspector had fooled him—a hard, sophisticated businessman with half a million dollars in hidden, accumulated, tax-free securities—for a long time; his wife would never have questioned any part of him.

So, it must have been with Robinson that the plan, in all its diabolicism, had been conceived. The "inspector" and Robinson bending their heads against one another, sharing dreadful confidences from the beginning. Murder his wife to begin and then plant the securities, which Robinson somehow had remembered seeing that day when inadvertently he had left them on his desk and gone out for lunch, near the corpse in order to tie the crime inextricably to the husband. He was already in trouble with the securities once discovered; what more logical, after tax evasion, than murder? Authorities, particularly police, thought in this way.

Robinson would have been the only possible means of divining the location of the securities in the office, and the "inspector" must have worked with him carefully to set up the plan. How they must have laughed! and then their faces lapsing into purpose as they had gathered more tightly to roll up the net.

The "inspector's" motives would always be shrouded—he can accept this, there are things in life which he will never know—but Robinson's would not. He would have needed the securities for himself, control of the business, immunity from detection. An embezzlement of twenty-five long years' duration would have shortly been discovered anyway, and everything would have collapsed. The annual audit, he thinks excitedly, was just about due under the new accounts for the first time.

Robinson would have known that he had very little time to act. This was part of the motive, but will also make the solution easier. As it was, Robinson stood to benefit in two ways. He would hide the embezzlement forever and he would assume full control of the firm.

Until now, then, the plan in its malevolence and cunning had worked well. If it had not been for this last-minute deduction on which Robinson and the "inspector" could not have counted, it would have succeeded. But now, given only a little more time he could clear himself and bring it down around them.

The police. He will call the police and tell them everything patiently, carefully. Already they have traced him to this miserable, dangerous hotel. Patrolmen have parked cars outside. They are prowling through the gray corridors pounding at doors, ignoring the drug traffic in their eagerness to get at him. It will not be long until they trace his room number through the little clerk downstairs and find him.

But the same drives, he hopes, that enabled them to trace his whereabouts so skillfully will underline their willingness to listen.

Surely the authorities want this crime solved as much as he does.

And once the pieces begin to fall into place—the "inspector" who is not an inspector, the strange behavior of Robinson, the circumstances of the firm's accounting—the end will come quickly. The "inspector" at least must, as part of the plan, remain in sight, continuing his normal activities, being accessible. The police will find him quickly, and quickly the confirming story will emerge.

For many years Robinson himself has been under great strain; these last few weeks must have been a nightmare for him as well—a dread tight-roping between necessity to continue and the urge to confess.

Robinson will be found. He will tell them everything quickly.

So. The police. He will call them now and set in motion that series of events which will free him. The authorities will not be able to bring back his wife and he realizes that to a certain extent that does make the crime his because he allowed their marriage to die. But this is something for which he will have to atone carefully, in a private way, in whatever years remain.

For an instant he thinks of phoning his doctor instead and having him make the call to the police to negotiate a meeting, but he realizes that it is too late for this kind of caution and so he picks up the phone with determination, choking slightly. Fetid air pours from the walls. Decrepit. The hotel is impossible. You cannot blame tenants for the quality of lives they must lead living here.

But he, he at least will live in better circumstances soon. In possession of himself for the first time in many weeks, he leans forward intensely.

But it occurs to him in the midst of dialing that he has, so far, murdered his wife, his doctor, his business partner and the police inspector sent out for routine questioning on these murders and that he is very tired of hiding in a hotel room, becoming bored with the reduction he had made of his life. Figures. He needs more figures in his speculations, that is all. He cannot manipulate just the four of them forever.

"Pardon me," he says to the desk clerk, who has come politely on the line after the long hold. "Pardon me, but would you bring me another cup of coffee and maybe a bottle of scotch up here?" He has a relationship with the desk clerk. It is a familiar errand.

"And I'll have something extra for you," he adds cunningly to speed the little clerk on his errand and puts down the phone.

"Yes, sir, here it is," the clerk says, entering a few moments later . . . and then falls dead with a .32 caliber bullet in his heart, falls dead on the sheets beside him, and as he does so the doctor, the inspector, his wife, and Robinson all turn to congratulate the clerk with relief on their faces and to welcome at last a new member into the club.

Doctor's Dilemma

Harold Q. Masur

As soon as we reached the courthouse corridor Papa's face convulsed like a baby's in torment. "I'm dying," he moaned. "I'm bleeding to death."

"You're fine, Papa," I said. "You'll outlive us all."

"Ten grand." A sob caught in his throat. "I posted bail for that lunatic client on your say-so, Counselor. 'Don't worry,' you told me. 'There's no risk.' So where is he? Why didn't he show up in court?"

Papa was Nick Papadopolous, bald, swarthy, barrel-shaped, with capillaries tracing a ruby pattern across his ample nose. "You're a bail bondsman," I said. "There are risks in every business. You win some, you lose some."

It wrung a groan of anguish from his throat. "You have to find him, Counselor. You owe it to me. I trusted you. You heard what the judge said. Have him in court by ten o'clock tomorrow morning or forfeit bail. If he took off, so help me, Jordan, I'll finish you with every bondsman in town. You'll never be able to raise another nickel."

"He'll be here, Papa. I'll have him in court tomorrow morning if I have to carry him. Jaffee is not a bail jumper. He has too much at stake."

I believed it. Would a trained physician, a hospital intern, risk his career and his future by jumping bail and holing up somewhere because he's charged with felonious assault? Not likely. Dr. Allan Jaffee, a splendid physical specimen, young, handsome, studious, ambitious, seemed to have everything—except willpower. He was an obsessive gambler; poker, craps, roulette, sporting events, anything. He had already run through a sizable inheritance and now, with no liquid assets, he was in the hole to his bookie for four thousand dollars. So he stalled. So the bookie had dispatched some muscle to pressure the doctor, which turned out to be a mistake. Young Jaffee, a former collegiate welterweight champ, had inflicted upon the collector a bent nose, the need for extensive dental work, and various multiple abrasions, contusions, and traumas.

Because it was a noisy affair, someone had called the law. The cops shipped the collector off in an ambulance and promptly processed Jaffee into the slammer.

At the preliminary hearing, despite my plea of self-defense, the judge agreed with the assistant D.A. that high bail was appropriate under the circumstances. He sternly labeled the fists of a trained boxer as dangerous weapons, and set the trial date.

So at 10:00 this morning, the clerk had bawled: "The People of the State of New York versus Allan Jaffee." The judge was on the bench, the jury was in the box, the prosecutor was ready, defense counsel was ready, everybody on tap—except the defendant. He hadn't shown.

"Your Honor," I said, "the accused is a medical doctor training at Manhattan General. It is possible that he was detained by an emergency. So it seems we have a problem—"

"No, Counselor. *We* have no problem. *You* have a problem. And you have twenty minutes to solve it." He called a recess.

So I had sprinted out of the courtroom, down the corridor to a booth, and got on the horn to the hospital, but they had no knowledge of Jaffee's whereabouts. I tried his apartment. The line was busy. Apparently he hadn't even left yet.

When the twenty minutes were gone, I approached the bench and I said to the glaring judge, "If it please your Honor, I would beg the Court's indulgence for—"

He cut me off. "The Court's indulgence is exhausted, Mr. Jordan. This is intolerable, a blatant disregard of the State's time and money. A warrant will be issued forthwith for immediate execution by the marshal. If the accused has left the jurisdiction of this Court, bail will be forfeit. Your deadline is tomorrow morning, sir. Ten o'clock." He rapped his gavel and called the next case.

Papa's agitation was understandable. With a worldwide liquidity crisis, ten grand was important money. I disengaged his fingers from my sleeve and went back to the telephone. Still a busy signal; I tried twice more—no change. So I said the hell with it and went out and flagged a cab and rode up to East 79th Street.

Jaffee lived on the second floor of an aging brownstone. He did not answer the bell. The door was open and I walked into utter chaos. The place had been ransacked and pillaged. I headed for the bedroom, expecting the worst.

He was on the floor, propped up against the bed. This time he had been hopelessly overmatched. Somebody, more likely several somebodies, had worked him over good. His face was hamburger. He tried to talk, but it was an incoherent guttural croak. The doctor needed a doctor, but soon.

I looked for the telephone and saw the handset hanging off the hook, which explained the busy signal. I hung up, jiggled, finally got a dial tone, and put a call through to Manhattan General. I told them that one of their interns had been injured, that he was in critical condition, and I gave them his name and address, adding, "This is an emergency. Better step on it if you don't want to lose him."

I turned back and found him out cold, unconscious—probably a blessing.

When the ambulance arrived, I was allowed to ride along, and sat beside the driver while first aid was being administered in the back. We careened through traffic with the siren wailing, running a few signals and frightening a lot of pedestrians.

"Who clobbered him?" the driver asked.

"I don't know. I found him like that."

"You a friend of Doc Jaffee's?"

"I'm his lawyer."

"Hey, now! He was supposed to be in court this morning, wasn't he?"

"You know about that?"

"Sure. He was on ambulance duty this week and he told me about it. Said he owed a bundle to his bookie but couldn't raise a dime. Said he banged up a guy who came to collect, strictly self-defense, but his lawyer told him you never know what a jury might do. So he was pretty jumpy yesterday morning. Man, Jaffee was one sorry character, and that's why I couldn't understand the change."

"What change?"

"The change in his mood. All morning he's got a long jaw, his face at half past six, and then suddenly he's walking on air, laughing and full of jokes."

"When did it happen?"

"Right after we got that stewardess."

"What stewardess?"

"The one from Global Airlines." He made a face. "Poor kid. She had taken one of those airport limousines from Kennedy and it dropped her off at Grand Central. She was crossing Lexington when the taxi clipped her. Boy, he must've been moving. She was a mess. Jaffee didn't think she'd make it. I don't know what he did back there, but he was working on her, oxygen, needles, everything, until we got her to Emergency. It was after he came out and hopped aboard for another call that I noticed the change. It was weird. Nothing chewing at him anymore. Smiling from ear to ear."

"Do you remember the girl's name?"

"Korth, Alison Korth. I remember because Doc Jaffee was so busy helping the Emergency team that I had to fill out the forms."

He swung the ambulance east one block, cut the siren, turned up a ramp, and ran back to help wheel the patient through a pair of swinging doors, where people were waiting to take over. A formidable-looking nurse blocked my path and ordered me to wait in the reception lounge.

I sat among gloomy-faced people, thinking about young Jaffee. The obvious assumption was that his bookie, a man named Big Sam Tarloff, could not sit back idly and do nothing after one of his collectors had been so injudiciously handled by a deadbeat. People would laugh. Under the circumstances, how could he keep potential welshers in line? So he would have to make an example of Jaffee.

I was restless and fidgety. Curiosity precluded inactivity. So I got up and wandered over to the reception desk and asked the girl for Miss Alison Korth. She consulted her chart.

"Room 625."

I took the elevator up and marched past the nurse's station, found the number and poked my head through a partially open door. The girl on the bed was swathed in bandages, eyes closed, heavily sedated, left arm and right leg in traction, her face pitifully dwindled and gray.

A voice startled me. "Are you one of the doctors?"

I blinked and then saw the speaker, seated primly on a chair against the wall. She looked drawn and woebegone.

"No, ma'am," I said.

"Well, if you're another insurance man from the taxi company, go away. We're going to retain a lawyer and you can talk to him."

"That's the way to handle it," I said. "Are you a friend of Alison's?"

"I'm her sister."

"Stick to your guns. Don't let any of those clowns try to pressure you into a hasty settlement."

She stood up and came close, her eyes dark and intense. "Did you know Alison?"

"No, ma'am."

"Who *are* you?" I gave her one of my cards and she looked at it, frowning. "Scott Jordan. The name sounds vaguely familiar. But we haven't asked anyone for a lawyer. Are you an ambulance chaser?"

"Hardly, Miss Korth. I don't handle automobile liability cases."

"Then who do you represent?"

"Dr. Allan Jaffee."

"The intern who treated Alison in the ambulance?"

"Yes."

"He's very nice. He looked in on Alison several times yesterday while I was here." Her frown deepened. "I don't understand. Why does Dr. Jaffee need a lawyer?"

"It's a long story, Miss Korth. I'd like to tell you about it over a cup of coffee. There's a rather decent cafeteria in the building." She looked dubious and I added, "There's nothing you can do for your sister at the moment, and the hall nurse can page you if anything develops."

She thought for a moment, then nodded and accompanied me along the corridor to the elevator, stopping briefly to confer at the nurse's station. The elevator door opened and a man stepped out. He stopped short.

"Hello, Vicky."

"Hello, Ben," she said, without warmth.

"How is Alison?"

"About the same," she replied.

"Has she regained consciousness?"

"Just for a moment, but they gave her some shots and she's sleeping now. She shouldn't be disturbed."

He lifted an eyebrow in my direction, a tall, blunt-featured man with dark curly hair, wearing sports clothes. Vicky introduced us.

"This is Captain Ben Cowan, the copilot on Alison's last flight. Scott Jordan."

He nodded fractionally. "Were you just leaving?"

"We're on our way to the cafeteria," I said.

"May I join you?"

"I think not," Vicky said. "Mr. Jordan and I have some business to discuss."

He registered no reaction to the rebuff. "I see. Well, would you tell Alison that I was here and that I'll look in again?"

"Of course."

Going down in the elevator there was no further dialogue between them. Captain Cowan left us on the lobby floor and we descended to the lower level. I brought coffee to a small corner table.

"You don't seem overly fond of the captain," I said.

"I detest him."

"Is he a close friend of Alison's?" I pursued the thought.

She made a face. "Alison's infatuated, crazy about him. And I don't like it one tiny bit. I think Ben Cowan is bad medicine."

"In what way?"

"Call it instinct, feminine intuition. Alison and I have always been very close. She shares my apartment whenever her flight lays over in New York. She started going with Cowan about a year ago and she's been moonstruck ever since, sort of in a daze. She used to confide in me. But now, since Ben, she's become withdrawn, even secretive. Alison's not very practical. She was always naive and trusting and I worry about her. And now this—this—" Her chin began to quiver, but she got it under control and blinked back tears.

I sipped coffee and gave her time to recover. After a while, in a small rusty voice, she asked me about Allan Jaffee. So I told her about the gambling debt, the fight and the assault charge, and his failure to appear in court. I told her about going to his apartment and finding him half dead from a merciless beating. Vicky was shocked, but it took her mind off Alison only briefly. She grew fidgety, so I took her back to the sixth floor and then went down to find someone who could brief me on Jaffee's condition.

I spoke to a resident who looked stumbling tired and furiously angry; tired because he'd been working a ten-hour tour and angry because they kept him repairing damages inflicted by people on people. "I'm sorry, sir," he told me. "Dr. Jaffee can talk to no one."

"Not even his lawyer?"

"Not even his Maker. For one thing, his jaw is wired. For another, we've got him under enough sedation to keep him fuzzy for twenty-four hours."

"Will he be able to write?"

"Yes. After a couple of fractured fingers knit properly. Try again in a couple of days."

A couple of days might be too late and I was in no mood to wait. So I went out and was waving for a cab when a hand fell on my shoulder. It was Captain Ben Cowan of Global Airlines.

"I'm sorry if I seem persistent, Mr. Jordan," he said. "But I'm terribly worried about Alison and I can't seem to get any information at the hospital. Everything is one big fat secret with those people. I thought, since you're a friend of Vicky's, you might know something."

"Why don't you ask her yourself?"

He looked rueful. "Vicky and I are not on the same wavelength. I don't think she likes me."

"Well, the fact is, Captain, I don't have any information myself."

"Haven't the doctors told Vicky anything?"

"We didn't discuss it. I don't know either of the girls very well, Captain. I met Vicky only today."

"Oh?" A deep frown scored his forehead. "Vicky gave me an entirely different impression. I thought you'd gone to the hospital to see her."

"Not her. A client of mine."

"A client?" he said, puzzled.

"I'm an attorney. I represent the intern who treated Alison at the accident."

"Jaffee?"

"Right. Dr. Allan Jaffee."

"Well, then, I guess you can't be much help."

"Afraid not," I agreed as a cab pulled up in answer to my signal.

Tarloff's was a secondhand bookstore on lower Fourth Avenue, a large and profitable establishment stocking a few splendid first editions and managed by the owner's brother-in-law. On the second floor Sam Tarloff operated a frenetically busy horse parlor with half a dozen constantly ringing telephones manned by larcenous-eyed employees. Big Sam, a heavy, bear-shaped man with an incongruously seraphic smile, sat on a platform watching everything and everybody.

He recognized me and said cordially, "Well, Counselor, good to see you. Let's use my private office." I followed him into a small room. He beamed at me. "And what is your pleasure, Mr. Jordan?"

"Nubile young cheerleaders," I told him. "Right now, however, I would like to see your hands."

"What for?"

"Come off it, Samuel. You know as well as I do that Dr. Jaffee is in the hospital."

"Where else should he be? He works there."

"Not as an employee at the moment. As a patient."

"What happened to him?"

"Somebody clubbed him half to death. I want to see if you have any bruised knuckles."

"Me? You think I did it?"

"You, or one of your men. It's a logical conclusion."

"Because he hurt one of my employees?"

"That, yes, and because he still owes you money."

"You're wrong, Counselor. He does not owe me money. He paid off last night, every cent, in cash, including interest."

"Samuel, I'm an old hand. Where would Jaffee get that kind of money on an intern's salary?"

"Not my business, Counselor. I gave him a receipt. Ask him."

"He can't talk. His jaw is wired."

"So look in his pockets. He's got it somewhere."

After countless hours of grilling people on the witness stand, you develop an instinct for the perjurer. Tarloff was not lying. I believed him. "You have lines out, Sam. Tell me, who do you think worked him over?"

He turned up a palm. "I don't know. But it was in the cards, Counselor, it had to happen sooner or later. Jaffee is a very reckless young man. He gambles without capital. Who knows, maybe he was into the Shylocks for a bundle too. I'll ask around if you want."

"I'd appreciate that."

"How about a little tip, Counselor, a filly in the third at Belmont? Only please take your business to an off-track betting window."

"Not today, Samuel. May I use one of your phones?"

"Be my guest."

I rang Manhattan General and got through to Vicky Korth in her sister's room, still keeping the vigil. I asked her if Alison was close to anyone else at Global. She gave me a name, Ann Leslie, another stewardess, who generally stayed at the Barbizon, a hostelry for single females. Vicky offered to phone and tell her to expect me.

I found Ann Leslie waiting in the lobby, a slender girl, radiating concern, wanting to know when she could visit Alison.

"In a couple of days," I said.

"Darn!" She made a tragic face. "We're flying out again on Wednesday."

"Where to?"

"Same destination. Amsterdam. Same crew too, except for Alison. I'll miss her."

"I imagine Captain Ben Cowan will miss her too."

She squinted appraisingly. "You know about him?"

"Vicky told me. And she's not happy about it."

Ann Leslie tightened her mouth. "Neither am I. That Cowan—he's a chaser, a womanizer. He uses people. He made passes at me too, before Alison joined the crew, but I wouldn't have any part of him. I just don't trust him. Have you met Ben?"

"Yes. He seems genuinely fond of Alison."

"It's an act, believe me."

"Is he openly attentive to her?"

"They're not keeping it a secret, if that's what you mean."

"Would you know why he didn't accompany her into Manhattan yesterday when you put down at Kennedy?"

"Yes. Because he was held up at Customs. They wanted to talk to him in one of those private rooms. I was there and I heard him tell Alison to go ahead without him and that he'd meet her later."

"Are members of the crew usually held up at Customs?"

"Not as a rule. They never bothered me. But it couldn't have been much because I know he's flying out with us again on Wednesday, on our next flight."

We talked for a while longer and I thanked her and promised to tell Alison that Ann would be in to see her as soon as the doctors permitted it. I left and cabbed over to Jaffee's apartment. The super recognized me and let me in.

I stood and surveyed the chaos. Nothing had been left untouched. Even the upholstery had been razored open and kapok strewed over the floor. Desk drawers were pulled out and overturned. I hunkered down, sifting through papers. I did not find any receipt from Sam Tarloff, but after about an hour I did find something even more interesting: a duplicate deposit slip from the Gotham Trust, bearing yesterday's date, and showing a deposit of $34,000.

I straightened and took it to a chair and stared at it, wondering how Jaffee, persumably broke, without credit, could manage a deposit of that magnitude. I saw that it was not a cash deposit. The $34,000 was entered in the column allotted to checks.

But a check from whom? And for what? As I studied it, I felt a sudden surge of excitement, of anticipation, because the Gotham Trust was my own bank, an institution in which I had certain connections. Bank records are not quite as inviolate as most people believe.

Twenty minutes later, I marched through the bank's revolving doors and approached the desk of Mr. Henry Wharton, an assistant vice-president for whom I had performed a ticklish chore only four months before. He rose to shake my hand. Then he sat back and listened to my request. He frowned at Jaffee's deposit slip and rubbed his forehead and looked up at me with a pained expression.

"Well, now, Mr. Jordan, this is highly irregular."

"I know."

"It is not the policy of this bank to make disclosures about our depositors."

"I know."

"You're making it very difficult for me."

"I know."

He sighed and levered himself erect and disappeared into some hidden recess of the bank. I waited patiently. He was perspiring slightly when he returned. He cleared an obstruction from his throat. "You understand this is strictly confidential."

"Absolutely."

He lowered his voice. "Well, then, according to our microfilm records the deposit was made by a check drawn to the order of Dr. Allan Jaffee by the firm of Jacques Sutro, Ltd. I assume you recognize the name."

"I do, indeed. And I'm deeply indebted, Harry."

"For what? I haven't told you a thing."

"That's right. Now, would it be possible for me to get a blowup of that microfilm?" He turned pale and a convulsive shudder almost lifted him out of the chair, and I added quickly, "All right, Harry, forget it. I'm leaving."

He was not sorry to see me go.

Mr. Jacques Sutro is a dealer in precious gems, operating out of the elegant second floor of a Fifth Avenue town house. Sutro, a portly specimen with silver hair and a manner as smooth as polished opal, folded his beautifully-manicured hands and listened to me with a beautiful smile that displayed some of the finest porcelain dentures in captivity.

"And so," I concluded, "as Dr. Jaffee's attorney, I would appreciate a few details about any transaction you had with him."

"Why not discuss it with your client?"

"I would if I could, Mr. Sutro. Unfortunately, Dr. Jaffee had an accident and he's a patient at Manhattan General under very heavy sedation. It may be days before he can talk. In the meantime I'm handling his legal affairs and it's imperative for me to fill out the picture."

Sutro pushed his lips thoughtfully. "Would you mind if I called the hospital?"

"Not at all. Please do."

He got the number, spoke into the mouthpiece, listened intently, then nodded and hung up. He spread his fingers. "You must understand that I knew young Jaffee's father before the old man died."

"So did I, Mr. Sutro. As a matter of fact, he took me into his office when I first got out of law school. That's why I'm interested in the son's welfare."

"I see. Well, the old gentleman was a valued customer of mine. He purchased some very fine pieces for his wife when she was alive. And later he even acquired some unset stones as a hedge against inflation. Young Allan liquidated them through my firm after his father died. Then yesterday afternoon, he came here and offered to sell some additional stones he had inherited."

"Merchandise you recognized?"

"No. But young Jaffee assured me that his father had bought gems from various other dealers too. I examined the pieces and offered him a very fair price."

"How much did you offer?"

"Forty thousand dollars. He said he needed some cash right away, an emergency in fact, and that he couldn't wait for my check to clear the bank. He said if I let him have four thousand in cash, he would knock two thousand off the total price. So I gave him the cash and a check for the balance, thirty-four thousand." Sutro looked mildly anxious. "Nothing wrong in that, is there, Counselor?"

I shrugged noncommittally. Within a very short time, Mr. Sutro, I suspected, was due for a severe shock, but I was going to let someone else give it to him. He was chewing the inside of his cheek when I left.

What I needed now was Vicky Korth's cooperation. I went looking for her at the hospital but she was not in Alison's room and neither was Alison. The room had been cleaned out, the bed freshly made; there was no sign of any occupancy. I felt a cold, sinking sensation and headed for the nurses' station.

Two girls in white were on duty. My inquiry seemed to upset them both. Their response was neither typical nor brisk. Alison Korth had suddenly developed serious respiratory problems and despite all efforts they had lost her.

I had no way of knowing whether Vicky wanted to be alone or would welcome company. My own experience led me to believe that most mourners crave the solace of visitors. I checked her address in the telephone directory and rode uptown.

Vicky answered my ring and opened the door. The shock of Alison's death had not yet fully registered. She looked dazed and numb and she needed a sympathetic ear.

"Oh, Scott," she said in a small trembly voice, "it didn't really have to happen. They were careless . . ."

"Who?" I asked.

"The nurses, the doctors, somebody . . ."

We sat down and I held her hand. "Tell me about it."

"She—she was having trouble breathing and they put her in oxygen. It's my fault. I left her alone. I went down for a sandwich and when I came back I saw that something was wrong. Her face was dark and I saw that the equipment had come loose, the tube from the oxygen tank, and Alison was—was . . ." Her eyes filled and she hid her face against my chest.

I said quietly, "You couldn't have anticipated anything like that, Vicky. You must not condemn yourself for lack of omniscience."

After a while, she sat back and wanted to reminisce, to talk about their childhood. She was touched by nostalgia and bittersweet memories. It was good therapy. She even smiled once or twice.

When she finally ran out of words, I began to talk. I put her completely into the picture. I told her about my interviews, about my deductions and my conclusions. I told her that Alison had been used, and that I needed her help, and told her what I wanted her to do.

She sat quietly and brooded at me for a long moment, then she got up and went to the telephone. She dialed a number and said in a wooden voice, "This is Vicky. I thought you ought to know, Alison died this afternoon. I'm calling you because she'd want me to. The funeral is Thursday. Services at Lambert's Mortuary . . . Oh, I see. Well, if you wish, you can see her in the reposing room this evening. I made arrangements at the hospital when they gave me a package with Alison's things. I'll be there myself at six. Please let her friends know."

It was almost seven o'clock. I sat alone in Vicky's apartment and waited. My pupils had expanded to the growing darkness. A large brown parcel lay on the coffee table. Behind me, a closet door was open and waiting. Traffic sounds were muted. I kept my head cocked, concentrating, an ear bent in the direction of the hall door.

I was not quite sure how I would play it if he came. I was not even sure that he would come, but then, without warning, the doorbell rang. It seemed abnormally loud. I did not move. There was a pause and it rang again. Standard operating procedure: ring first to make sure no one is at home. I held my breath. Then it came, a metallic fumbling at the lock. I glided quickly into the closet, leaving the door slightly ajar, giving me an adequate angle of vision.

Hinges creaked and a pencil beam probed the darkness. A voice called softly, "Vicky, are you home?" Silence. Overhead lights clicked on. He came into view and I saw his eyes encompass the room in a quick circular sweep. He walked to the coffee table, picked up the parcel, and tore open the wrapping. He spread out the contents, staring at Alison's clothes.

"It's no use, Cowan," I said, showing myself. "You won't find them here."

His head pitched sideways and he stood impaled, jaws rigid.

I said, "You are one miserable, gold-plated, card-carrying, full-time rat. Conning a naive and trusting little cupcake like Alison Korth into doing your dirty work."

"What the hell are you talking about?"

"That's a dry hole, Cowan. Step out of it. You know what I'm talking about. Diamonds. Unset stones from Amsterdam. Your moonlighting sideline as a copilot on Global. You suspected you were under surveillance and you got Alison to smuggle a shipment off the plane and into the country for you. Concealed on her person. That's why you were clean when they fanned you at Kennedy yesterday."

His mouth was pinched. "You've got bats loose, Mr. Lawyer."

"Save it, Cowan. The deal was blown when Alison had an accident and was taken to the hospital. You thought the stones were discovered when she was undressed and you sweated that one out. But when nothing happened you began to wonder and reached a conclusion. The ambulance intern would have to loosen her uniform to use his stethoscope, so he must have found the stuff taped to her body. You checked him out and that's why you knew his name when I told you that the intern who'd treated Alison at the accident was a client of mine.

"You asked me what happened to him. Why did anything have to have happened to him? I'd go to the hospital if I wanted to see him because he worked there, wouldn't I? But you already knew what happened because you made it happen. You broke into his apartment to search for the loot and you heard him come back and you ambushed him. You hit him from behind, but Jaffee is not an easy man to cool, and even wounded he fought back. I don't know, maybe you even had help. Maybe you tried to make him talk."

Cowan stood like a statue carved out of stone.

"You got nothing from Jaffee," I said, "and nothing from his apartment. So maybe you were wrong about him. Maybe Alison had concealed the stones somewhere in her clothes and nobody had found them. That's why you came here tonight after Vicky told you she'd brought Alison's belongings back here to the apartment. You had to find out, and you knew Vicky would be at the mortuary."

He took a step toward me.

"Careful," I said. "You don't think I'd tackle a murderer by my-self."

"Murderer?"

"Yes, Cowan. I'd make book on it. You're a shrewd specimen. You had to cover all contingencies. Suppose the hospital *had* found the diamonds and *had* notified the cops and they were keeping a lid on it until they could question Alison. A girl like her, she'd melt under heat. They could turn her inside out. She'd make a clean breast of it, and you'd be blown. So she had to go. She had to be eliminated. So you loitered and waited until you saw Vicky leave, and then you managed to slip into Alison's room and tamper with the equipment. You cut off her oxygen and watched her die. The cops know what to look for now and they're checking the hospital equipment thoroughly for your prints."

That tore it. He thought he could cut his losses by splitting, so he whirled and slammed through the door, but I hadn't been kidding. The cops were all set for him outside in the corridor.

It seldom comes up roses for all.

Vicky lost her sister, but gained a suitor—me. U.S. Customs de-scended on Jacques Sutro and seized the smuggled diamonds. Su-tro's lawyers attached Jaffee's bank account and recovered the $34,000 check he had deposited. Mr. Sutro still wanted his four grand cash and I referred him to Big Sam Tarloff. Fat chance.

Allan Jaffee healed nicely. The episode may even have cured his gambling addiction. He copped a plea on the gem charge and turned state's evidence against Ben Cowan. Cowan was going to be out of circulation until he was a rickety old man. For me, represent-ing Jaffee was an act of charity. I never got paid.

Only Nick Papadopolous emerged unscathed. The judge can-celed forfeiture of Jaffee's bail bond and Papa got his money back. He was delirious. He invited Vicky and me out to dinner. That was two weeks ago. We're still trying to digest the stuff.

Mother by Protest

Richard Matheson

In the hall he put down his suitcase. "How have you been?" he asked.

"Fine," she said, with a smile.

She helped him off with his coat and hat and put them in the hall closet.

"This Indiana January sure feels cold after six months in South America."

They walked into the living room, arms around each other.

"What have you been doing with yourself?" he asked.

"Oh . . . not too much," she said. "Thinking about you."

He smiled and hugged her.

"That's a lot," he said.

Her smile flickered a moment, then returned. She held his hand tightly. And, suddenly, although he didn't realize it at first, she was wordless. He'd gone over this moment in his mind so often that the sharpness of its anti-climax later struck him. She smiled and looked into his eyes while he spoke but the smile kept fading and her eyes kept evading his at the very moments he wanted their attention most.

Later in the kitchen she sat across from him as he drank the third cup of her hot, rich coffee.

"I won't sleep tonight," he said grinning, "but I don't want to."

Her smile was only obliging. The coffee burned his throat and he noticed she wasn't drinking any of the first cup she'd poured for herself.

"No coffee for you?" he asked.

"No, I . . . I don't drink it anymore."

"On a diet or something?"

He saw her throat move.

"Sort of," she said.

"That's silly," he said. "Your figure is perfect."

She seemed about to say something. Then she hesitated. He put down his cup.

"Ann, is . . ."

"Something wrong?" she finished.

He nodded.

She lowered her eyes. She bit her lower lip and clasped her hands before her on the table. Then her eyes closed and he got the feeling that she was shutting herself away from something hopelessly terrible.

"Honey, what *is* it?"

"I guess . . . the best way is to just . . . just up and *tell* you."

"Well, of course, sweetheart," he said anxiously. "What is it? Did something happen while I was gone?"

"Yes. And no."

"I don't understand."

She was looking at him suddenly. The look was haunted and it made him shudder.

"I'm going to have a baby," she said.

He was about to cry out—but that's wonderful! He was about to jump up and embrace her and dance her around the room.

Then it hit him, driving the color from his face.

"What?" he said.

She didn't answer because she knew he'd heard.

"How . . . long have you known?" he asked, watching her eyes hold motionless on his face.

She drew in a shaking breath and he knew her answer would be the wrong one. It was.

"Three weeks," she said.

He sat there looking blankly at her and stirring the coffee without realizing. Then he noticed and, slowly, he drew out the spoon and put it down beside the cup.

He tried to say the word but he couldn't. It trembled in his vocal cords. He tensed himself.

"Who?" he asked her, his voice toneless and weak.

Her eyes were black on him, her face ashen. Her lips trembled when she told him.

She said, "No one."

"*What?*"

"David," she said carefully, "I . . ."

Then her shoulders slumped.

"No one, David. No one."

It took a moment for the reaction to hit him. She saw it on his face before he turned it away from her. Then she stood up and looked down at him, her voice shaking.

"David, I swear to God I never had anything to do with any man while you were gone!"

He sank back numbly against the chair back. God, oh God, what could he say? A man comes back from six months in the jungle and his wife tells him she's pregnant and asks him to believe that . . .

His teeth set on edge. He felt as if he were involved in the beginning of some hideously smutty joke. He swallowed and looked down at his trembling hands. Ann, Ann! He wanted to pick up his cup and hurl it against the wall.

"David, you've got to bel—"

He stumbled up and out of the room. She was behind him quickly, clutching for his hand.

"David, you've *got* to believe me. I'll go insane if you don't. It's the only strength that's kept me going—the hope that you'd believe me. If you don't . . ."

Her words broke off and they stared bleakly at each other. He felt her hand holding his. Cold.

"Ann, what do you want me to believe? That my child was conceived five months after I left you?"

"David, if I were guilty would I . . . be so *open* in telling you? You know how I feel about our marriage. About you."

Her voice lowered.

"If I'd done what you think I've done, I wouldn't tell you," she said, "I'd kill myself."

He kept looking helplessly at her as if the answer lay in her anxious face. Finally he spoke.

"We'll . . . go to Doctor Kleinman," he said. "We'll . . ."

Her hand dropped away from his.

"You don't believe me, do you?"

His voice was tortured.

"You know what you're asking of me, don't you?" he said. "Don't you, Ann? I'm a scientist. I can't accept the incredible . . . just like that. Don't you think I *want* to believe you? But . . ."

She stood before him a long time. Then she turned away a little and her voice was well controlled.

"All right," she said quietly, "do what you think is best."

Then she walked out of the room. He watched her go. Then he turned and walked slowly to the mantel. He stood looking at the kewpie doll sitting there with its legs hanging down over the edge. *Coney Island* read the words on her dress. They'd won it on their honeymoon trip eight years before.

Homecoming.

The word was a dead word now.

"Now that the welcomes are done for," said Doctor Kleinman," "what are you doing here? Catch a bug in the jungle?"

Collier sat slumped in the chair. For a few seconds he glanced out the window. Then he turned back to Kleinman and told him quickly.

When he'd finished they looked at each other for a silent moment.

"It's *not* possible, is it?" Collier said then.

Kleinman pressed his lips together. A grim smile flickered briefly on his face.

"What can I say?" he said. "No, it's impossible? No, not as far as observation goes? I do not know, David. We assume that the sperms survive in the cervix canal no more than three to five days, maybe a little longer. But even if they do . . ."

"They can't fertilize," Collier finished.

Kleinman didn't nod or answer but Collier knew the answer. Knew it in simple words that were pronouncing doom on his life.

"There's no hope then," he said quietly.

Kleinman pressed his lips together again and ran a reflective finger along the edge of his letter opener.

"Unless," he said, "it is to speak to Ann and make her understand you will not desert her. It is probably fear which makes her speak as she does."

". . . will not desert her," Collier echoed in an inaudible whisper and shook his head.

"I suggest nothing, mind you," Kleinman went on. "Only that it is possible Ann is too hysterically frightened to tell you the truth."

Collier rose, drained of vitality.

"All right," he said indecisively, "I'll speak to her again. Maybe we can . . . work it out."

But when he told her what Kleinman had said she just sat in the chair and looked at him without expression on her face.

"And that's it," she said. "You've decided."

He swallowed.

"I don't think you know what you're asking of me," he said.

"Yes, I know what I'm asking," she answered. "Just that you believe in me."

He started to speak in rising anger, then checked himself.

"Ann," he said, "just *tell* me. I'll do my best to understand."

Now she was losing temper too. He watched her hands tighten, then tremble on her lap.

"I hate to spoil your noble scene," she said. "But I'm not pregnant by another man. Do you understand me—believe me?"

She wasn't hysterical now or frightened or on the defensive. He stood there looking down at her, feeling numb and confused. She never had lied to him before and yet . . . what was he to think?

She went back to her reading then and he kept standing and watching her. These are the facts, his mind insisted. He turned away from her. Did he really know Ann? Was it possible she was something entirely strange to him now? Those six months.

What had happened during those six months.

He stood making up the living-room couch with sheets and the old comforter they had used when they were first married. As he looked down at the thick quilting and the gaudy patterns now faded from innumerable washings, a grim smile touched his lips.

Homecoming.

He straightened up with a tired sigh and walked over to where the record player scratched gently. He lifted the arm up and put on the next record. He looked at the inside cover of the album as Tschaikowsky's *Swan Lake* started.

To my very own darling. Ann.

They hadn't spoken all afternoon or evening. After supper she'd gotten a book from the case and gone upstairs. He'd sat in the living room trying to read *The Fort Tribune,* trying even harder to relax. Yet how could he? Could a man relax in his home with his wife who carried a child that wasn't his? The newspaper had finally slipped from his lax fingers and fallen to the floor.

Now he sat staring endlessly at the rug, trying to figure it out.

Was it possible the doctors were wrong? Could the life cell exist and maintain its fertilizing capacity for, not days, but months? Maybe, he thought, he'd rather believe that than believe Ann could commit adultery. Theirs had always been an ideal relationship as close an approximation of The Perfect Marriage as one could allow possible. Now this.

He ran a shaking hand through his hair. Breath shuddered through him and there was a tightness in his chest he could not relieve. A man comes home from six months in the . . .

Put it out of your mind!—he ordered himself, then forced himself to pick up the paper and read every word in it including comics and the astrology column. *You will receive a big surprise today,* the syndicated seer told him.

He flung down the paper and looked at the mantel clock. After ten. He'd been sitting there over an hour while Ann sat up in bed reading. He wondered what book was taking the place of affection and understanding.

He rose wearily. The record player was scratching again.

After brushing his teeth he went out into the hall and started for the stairs. At the bedroom door he hesitated, glanced in. The light was out. He stopped and listened to her breathing and knew she wasn't asleep.

He almost started in as a rushing sense of need for her covered him. But then he remembered that she was going to have a baby and it couldn't possibly be his baby. The thought made him stiffen. It turned him around, thin-lipped, and took him down the stairs and he slapped down the wall switch to plunge the living room into darkness.

He felt for the couch and sank down on it. He sat for a while in the dark smoking a cigarette. Then he pressed the stub into an ashtray and lay back. The room was cold. He climbed under the sheets and comforter and lay there shivering. *Homecoming.* The word oppressed him again.

He must have slept a little while, he thought, staring up at the black ceiling. He held up his watch and looked at the luminous hands. Three twenty. He grunted and rolled onto his side. Then he raised up and shook the pillow to puff it up.

He lay there thinking of her. Six months away and here, on the first night home, he was on the living room couch while she lay upstairs in bed. He wondered if she was frightened. She still had a little fear of the darkness left over from her childhood. She used to hug against him and press her cheek against his shoulder and go to sleep with a happy sigh.

He tortured himself thinking about it. More than anything else he wanted to rush up the stairs and crawl in beside her, feel her warm body against him. Why don't you? asked his sleepy mind. Because she's carrying someone else's child, came the obedient answer. Because she's sinned.

He twisted his head impatiently on the pillow. Sinned. The word sounded ridiculous. He rolled onto his back again and reached for a cigarette. He lay there smoking slowly, watching the glowing tip move in the blackness.

It was no use. He sat up swiftly and fumbled for the ashtray. He had to have it out with her, that was all. If he reasoned with her, she'd tell him what had happened. Then they'd have something to go on. It was better that way.

Rationalization, said his mind. He ignored it as he trudged up the icy steps and hesitated outside the bedroom.

He went in slowly, trying to remember how the furniture was placed. He found the small nightlamp on the bureau and turned the knob. The tiny glow pushed away darkness from itself.

He shivered under his heavy robe. The room was freezing, all the windows open wide. But, as he turned, he saw Ann lying there clad only in a thin silk nightgown. He moved quickly to the bed and pulled the bedclothes up over her, trying not to look at her body. Not now, he thought, not at a time like this. It would distort everything.

He stood over the bed and watched her sleep. Her hair was spead darkly over the pillow. He looked at her white skin, her soft red lips. She's a beautiful woman, he almost spoke the words aloud.

He turned his head away. All right, the word was ridiculous but it was true. What else would you call the betrayal of marriage? Was there a better word than sinned?

His lips tightened. He was remembering how she'd always wanted a baby. Well, she had one now.

He noticed the book next to her on the bed and picked it up. *Basic Physics.* What on earth was she reading that for? She'd never shown the remotest interest in the sciences except for perhaps a little sociology, a smattering of anthropology. He looked down curiously at her.

He wanted to wake her up but he couldn't. He knew he'd be struck dumb as soon as her eyes opened. I've been thinking, I want to discuss this sensibly, his mind prompted. It sounded like a soap opera line.

That was the crux of it, the fact that he was incapable of discussing it with her sensibly or not. He couldn't leave her, neither could he thrash it out as he'd planned. He felt a tightening of anger at his vacillation. Well, he defended angrily, how can a man adjust to such a circumstance? A man comes home from six months in . . .

He moved back from the bed and sank down on the small chair that stood beside the bureau. He sat there shivering a little and watching her face. It was such a childlike face, so innocent.

As he watched she stirred in her sleep, writhing uncomfortably under the blankets. A whimper moved her lips, then, suddenly, her right hand reached up and heaved the blankets aside so that they slid off the edge of the bed. Her feet kicked them away completely. Then a great sigh trembled her body and she rolled onto her side and slept, despite the shivering that began almost immediately.

Again he stood, dismayed at her actions. She'd never been a restless sleeper. Was it a habit she'd acquired while he was gone? It's guilt—his mind said, disconcertingly. He twitched at the infuriating idea and, walking over to the bed, he tossed the blankets over her roughly.

When he straightened up he saw that her eyes were on him. He started to smile, then wrenched it from his lips.

"You're going to get pneumonia if you keep throwing off the bedclothes," he said irritably.

She blinked. "What?" she said.

"I *said* . . ." he started, then stopped. There was too much anger piling up in him. He fought it off.

"You're kicking off the blankets," he said, in a flat voice.

"Oh," she said, "I . . . I've been doing it for about a week now."

He looked at her. What now?—the thought came back.

"Would you get me a drink of water?" she asked.

He nodded, glad for the excuse to take his eyes from her. He padded into the hall and bathroom and ran the water until it got cold, then filled up the glass.

"Thank you," she said softly as he handed it to her.

"Welcome."

She drank all of it in one swallow, then looked up guiltily.

"Would you . . . mind getting me another one?"

He looked at her for a moment, then took the glass and brought her another drink. She drank it just as quickly.

"What have you been eating?" he asked, feeling a strange tightness at finally talking to her but about such an irrelevant topic.

"Salt . . . I guess," she said.

"You must have had an awful lot."

"I have, David."

"That's not good."

"I know." She looked at him imploringly.

"What do you want—*another* glass?" he asked.

She lowered her eyes. He shrugged. He didn't think it was right but he didn't care to argue about it. He went to the bathroom and got her the third drink. When he got back her eyes were closed. He said, "Here's your water," but she was asleep. He put down the glass.

As he watched her he almost felt an uncontrollable desire to lie beside her, hold her close and kiss her lips and face. He thought of all the nights he'd lain awake in the sweltering tent thinking about Ann. Rolling his head on the pillow almost in agony because she was so far away. He had the same feeling now. And yet, although he stood beside her, he couldn't touch her.

Turning abruptly, he snapped off the nightlamp and left the bedroom. He went downstairs and threw himself down on the couch and dared his brain not to fall asleep. His brain conceded and he fell into a blank, uneasy slumber.

When she came into the kitchen the next morning she was coughing and sneezing.

"What did you do, throw off the blankets again?" he said.

"Again?" she asked.

"Don't you remember me coming up there?"

She looked at him blankly.

"No," she said.

They looked at each other for a moment. Then he went to the cupboard and took out two cups.

"Can you drink coffee?" he asked.

She hesitated a moment. Then she said, "Yes."

He put the cups down on the table, then sat down and waited. When the coffee started spurting up into the glass dome of the pot, Ann stood and picked up a pot-holder. Collier watched her pour the black, steaming fluid into the cups. Her hand shook a little as she poured his cup and he shrank back to avoid getting splashed.

He waited until she was sitting down, then asked grumpily, "What are you reading *Basic Physics* for?"

Again the blank, uncertain look.

"I don't know," she said. "It just . . . caught my interest for some reason."

He spooned sugar into his coffee and stirred, hearing her pour cream into hers.

"I . . . thought you . . ." He took a breath. "I thought you had to drink skimmed milk. Or something," he said.

"I felt like a cup of coffee."

"I see."

He sat there looking morosely at the table, drinking the burning coffee in slow sips. He forced himself to sink into a dull, edgeless cloud. He almost forgot she was there. The room disappeared, all its sights and sounds falling away.

Then her cup banged down. He started.

"If you're not going to talk to me, we might as well end it right now!" she said angrily. "If you think I'm going to stick around until you feel like talking to me, you're wrong!"

"What would you like to do!" he flared back. "If you found out I'd fathered some other woman's child, how would *you* feel?"

She closed her eyes and a look of strained patience held her face tautly.

"Listen, David," she said, "for the last time, *I have not committed adultery*. I know it spoils your role of the injured spouse but I can't help that. You can make me swear on a hundred Bibles and I'll still tell you the same thing. You can put truth serum in me and I'll tell you the same thing. You can strap me to a lie detector and my story will still be the same. David, I'm . . . !"

She couldn't finish. A spasm of coughing began shaking her body.

Her face darkened and tears ran down her cheeks as she gripped the side of the table with whitened fingers, gasping for breath.

For a moment he forgot everything except that she was in pain. He jumped up and ran to the sink for water. Then he patted her back gently while she drank. She thanked him in a choking voice. He patted her back once more, almost longingly.

"You'd better stay in bed today," he said, "that's a bad cough you have. And I'd . . . you'd better pin down the blankets so you don't . . ."

"David, what are you going to do?" she asked unhappily.

"Do?"

She didn't explain.

"I'm . . . not sure, Ann," he said. "I want with all my heart to believe you. But . . ."

"But you can't. Well, that's that."

"Oh, *stop* jumping to conclusions! Can't you give me some time to work it out? For God's sake, I've only been home one day."

For a brief moment he thought he saw something of the old warmth in her eyes. Maybe she could see, behind his anger, how much he wanted to stay. She picked up her coffee.

"Work it out then," she said. "I *know* what the truth is. If you don't believe me . . . then work it out your own clever way."

"Thank you," he said.

When he left the house she was back in bed, bundled up warmly, coughing and reading avidly, *An Introduction To Chemistry*.

"Dave!"

Professor Mead's studious face broke into a grin. He put down the tweezers he'd been moving the microsope slide with and shoved out his right hand. Johnny Mead, former All-American quarterback, was twenty-seven, tall and broad, sporting a perpetual crewcut. He held Collier's hand in a firm grip.

"How's it been, boy?" he asked. "Had enough of those Matto Grosso vermin?"

"More than enough," Collier said, smiling.

"You're looking good, Dave," Mead said. "Nice and tan. You must make quite a sight around this campus of leprous-skinned faculty."

They moved across the wide laboratory toward Mead's office, passing students bent over their microscopes and working the testing instruments. Collier got a momentary feeling of return, then lost it in the irony that he should get the feeling here and not at home.

Mead closed the door and waved Collier to a chair.

"Well, tell me all about it, Dave," he said. "Your daring exploits in the tropics."

Collier cleared his throat.

"Well, if you don't mind, Johnny," he said, "there's something else I want to talk to you about now."

"Fire away, boy."

Collier hesitated.

"Understand now," he said, "I'm telling you this under strictest confidence and only because I consider you my best friend."

Mead leaned forward in his chair, the look of youthful exuberance fading as he saw that Collier was worried.

Collier told him.

"No, Dave," Johnny said when he was finished.

"Listen, Johnny," Collier went on, "I know it sounds crazy. But she's insisted so forcibly that she's innocent that . . . well, frankly, I'm at a loss. Either she's had such an emotional breakdown that her mind has rejected the memory of . . . of . . ."

His hands stirred helplessly in his lap.

"Or?" Johnny said.

Collier took a deep breath.

"Or else she's telling the truth," he said.

"But . . ."

"I know, I know," Collier said. "I've been to our doctor. Kleinman, you know him."

Johnny nodded.

"Well, I've been to him and he said the same thing you don't have to say. That it's impossible for a woman to become pregnant five months after intercourse. I know that but . . ."

"What?"

"Isn't there some other way?"

Johnny looked at him without speaking. Collier's head dropped forward and his eyes closed. After a moment he made a sound of bitter amusement.

"Isn't there some other way," he mocked himself. "What a stupid question."

"She insists she's had no . . ."

Collier nodded wearily.

"Yes," he said. "She . . . Yes."

"I don't know," Johnny said, running the tip of a forefinger over his lower lip. "Maybe she's hysterical. Maybe . . . David, *maybe she isn't pregnant at all.*"

"What!"

Collier's head snapped up, his eyes looking eagerly into Johnny's.

"Don't jump the gun, Dave. I don't want that on my conscience. But, well . . . hasn't Ann always wanted a baby? I think she has—wanted it bad. Well . . . it may be just a crazy theory but I think it's possible that the emotional . . . *drain* of being separated from you for six months could cause a false pregnancy."

A wild hope began to surge in Collier, irrational he knew but one he clutched at, desperately.

"I think you should talk to her again," Johnny said. "Try to get more information from her. Maybe even do what she suggests and try hypnosis, truth serum, anything. But . . . *boy*, don't give up! I *know* Ann. And I trust her."

As he half ran down the street he kept thinking how little credit was due him for finding the trust he needed. But, at least, thank God, he had it for now. It filled him with hope, it made him want to cry out—it has to be true, it *has* to be!

Then, as he turned into the path of the house, he stopped so quickly that he almost fell forward and his breath drew in with a gasp.

Ann was standing on the porch in her nightgown, an icy January wind whipping the fragile silk around the full contours of her body. She stood on the frost-covered boards in her bare feet, one hand on the railing.

"*Oh, my God,*" muttered Collier in a strangled voice as he raced up the path to grab her.

Her flesh was bluish and like ice when he caught her and when he looked into her wide, staring eyes, a bolt of panic drove through him.

He half led, half dragged her into the warm living room and set her down in the easy chair before the fireplace. Her teeth were chattering and breath passed her lips in wheezing gasps. His hands shook as he ran around frantically getting blankets, plugging in the heating pad and placing it under her icy feet, breaking up wood with frenzied motions and starting a fire, making hot coffee.

Finally, when he'd done everything he could, he knelt before her and held her frigid hands in his. And, as he listened to the shivering of her body reflected in her breath, a sense of utter anguish wrenched at his insides.

"Ann, Ann, what's the *matter* with you?" he almost sobbed. "Are you out of your mind?"

She tried to answer but couldn't. She huddled beneath the blankets, her eyes pleading with him.

"You don't have to talk, sweetheart," he said. "It's all right."

"I . . . I . . . I . . . h-*had to go out*," she said.

And that was all. He stayed there before her, his eyes never leaving her face. And, even though she was shaking and gripped by painful seizures of coughing, she seemed to realize his faith in her because she smiled at him and, in her eyes, he saw that she was happy.

By supper time she had a raging fever. He put her in bed and gave her nothing to eat but all the water she wanted. Her temperature fluctuated, her flushed, burning skin becoming cold and clammy in almost seconds.

Collier called Kleinman about six and the doctor arrived fifteen minutes later. He went directly to the bedroom and checked Ann. His face became grave and he motioned Collier into the hall.

"We must get her to the hospital," he said quietly.

Then he went downstairs and phoned for an ambulance. Collier went back in to the bedside and stood there holding her limp hand, looking down at her closed eyes, her feverish skin. Hospital, he thought, oh my God, the hospital.

Then a strange thing happened.

Kleinman returned and beckoned once more for Collier to come out in the hall. They stood there talking until the downstairs bell rang. Then Collier went down to let them in and the two orderlies and the intern followed him up the stairs carrying their stretcher.

They found Kleinman standing by the bed staring down at Ann in speechless amazement.

Collier ran to him.

Kleinman lifted his head slowly.

"She is cured," he said in awed tones.

"What?"

The intern moved quickly to the bed. Kleinman spoke to him and to Collier.

"The fever is gone," he said. "Her temperature, her respiration, her pulse beat—all are normal. She has been completely cured of pneumonia in . . ."

He checked his pocket watch.

"In seventeen minutes," he said.

Collier sat in Kleinman's waiting room staring sightlessly at the magazine in his lap. Inside, Ann was being x-rayed.

There was no doubt anymore, Ann was pregnant. X-rays at six weeks had shown the fetus inside her. Once more their relationship suffered from doubt. He was still concerned for her health but, once more, was unable to speak to her and tell that he believed in her. And, though he'd never actually told her of his renewed doubt, Ann had felt it. She avoided him at home, sleeping half the time, the other half reading omnivorously. He still couldn't understand that. She'd gone through all his books on the physical sciences, then his texts on sociology, anthropology, philosophy, semantics, history and now she was reading geography books. There seemed no sense to it.

And, all during this period, while the form in her body changed from a small lump to a pear shape, to a globe, then an ovoid—she'd been eating an excess of salt. Doctor Kleinman kept warning her about it. Collier had tried to stop her but she wouldn't stop. Eating salt seemed a compulsion.

As a result she drank too much water. Now her weight had come to the point where the over-size fetus was pressing against her diaphragm causing breathing difficulty.

Just yesterday Ann's face had gone blue and Collier had rushed her to Kleinman's office. The doctor had done something to ease the condition, Collier didn't know what. Then Ann had been x-rayed and Kleinman told Collier to bring her back the next day.

The door opened and Kleinman led Ann out of his office.

"Sit, my dear," he told her. "I want to talk to David."

Ann walked past Collier without looking at him and sat down on the leather couch. As he stood, he noticed her reaching for a magazine. *Scientific American.* He sighed and shook his head as he walked into Kleinman's office.

As he moved for the chair, he thought, for what seemed the hundredth time, of the night she'd cried and told him she had to stay because there was no place else to go. Because she had no money of her own and her family was dead. She'd told him that if it wasn't for the fact that she was innocent she'd probably kill herself for the way he was treating her. He had stood beside the bed, silent and tense, while she cried, unable to argue, to console, even to reply. He'd just stood there until he could bear it no longer and then walked out of the room.

"What?" he said.

"I say look at these," Kleinman said grimly.

Kleinman's behavior had changed too in the past months, declining from confidence to a sort of confused anger.

Collier looked down at the two x-ray plates, glanced at the dates on them. One was from the day before, the other was the plate Kleinman had just taken.

"I don't . . ." Collier started.

Kleinman told him, "Look at the size of the child."

Collier compared the plates more carefully. At first he didn't see. Then his startled eyes flicked up suddenly.

"Is it possible?" he said, feeling a crushing sense of the unreal on him.

"It has happened," was all Kleinman said.

"But . . . *how?*"

Kleinman shook his head and Collier saw the doctor's left hand on the desk grip into a fist as if he were angered by this new enigma.

"I have never seen the like of it," Kleinman said. "Complete bone structure by the seventh week. Facial form by the eighth week. Organs complete and functioning by the end of the second month. The mother's insane desire for salt. And now this . . ."

He picked up the plates and looked at them almost in belligerence.

"How can a child *decrease* its size?" he said.

Collier felt a pang of fear at the mystified tone in Kleinman's voice.

"It is clear, it is clear," Kleinman shook his head irritably. "The child had grown to excess proportions because of the mother drinking too much water. To such proportions that it was pressing dangerously against her diaphragm. And now, in *one* day, the pressure is gone, the size of the child markedly decreased."

Kleinman's hands snapped into hard fists.

"It is almost," he said nervously, "as if the child knows what is going on."

"No more salt!"

His voice rose in pitch as he jerked the salt shaker from her hand and stamped over to the cupboard. Then he took her glass of water and emptied most of it into the sink. He sat down again.

She sat with her eyes shut, her body trembling. He watched as tears ran slowly from her eyes and down her cheeks. Her teeth bit into her lower lip. Then her eyes opened; they were big, frightened eyes. She caught a sob in the middle and hastily brushed her tears aside. She sat there quietly.

"Sorry," she murmured and, for some reason, Collier got the impression that she wasn't talking to him.

She finished the remaining water in a gulp.

"You're drinking too much water again," he said. "You know what Doctor Kleinman said."

"I . . . try," she said, "but I can't help it. I feel such a need for salt and it makes me so thirsty."

"You'll have to stop drinking so much water," he said coldly. "You'll endanger the child."

She looked startled as her body twitched suddenly. Her hands slipped from the table to press against her swollen stomach. Her look implored him to help her.

"What is it?" he asked hurriedly.

"I don't know," she said. "The baby kicked."

He leaned back, muscles unknotted.

"That's to be expected," he said.

They sat quietly awhile. Ann toyed with her food. Once he saw her reach out automatically for the salt, then raise her eyes in slight alarm when her fingers didn't find the shaker.

"David," she said, after a few minutes.

He swallowed his food. "What?"

"Why have you stayed with me?"

He couldn't answer.

"I don't know, Ann. I don't know."

The look of slight hope on her face left and she lowered her head.

"I thought," she said, "maybe . . . because you were staying . . ."

The crying again. She sat there not even bothering to brush aside the tears that moved slowly down her cheeks and over her lips.

"Oh, *Ann*," he said, half irritably, half in sorrow.

He got up to go to her. As he did her body twitched again, this time more violently, and her face went blank. Again she cut off her sobs and rubbed at her cheeks with almost angry fingers.

"I can't *help* it," she said slowly and loudly.

Not to him. Collier was sure it was not to him.

"What are you talking about?" he said nervously.

He stood there looking down at his wife. She looked so helpless, so afraid. He wanted to pull her against himself and comfort her. He wanted to . . .

Still sitting, she leaned against his chest while he stroked her soft brown hair.

"Poor little girl," he said. "My poor little girl."

"Oh David, *David,* if only you'd believe me. I'd do anything to make you believe me, anything. I can't stand to have you so cold to me. Not when I know I haven't done anything wrong."

He stood there silently and his mind spoke to him. There is a chance, it said, a chance.

She seemed to guess what he was thinking. Because she looked up at him and there was absolute trust in her eyes.

"Anything, David, *anything.*"

"Can you hear me, Ann?" he said.

"Yes," she said.

They were in Professor Mead's office. Ann lay on the couch, her eyes closed. Mead took the needle from Collier's fingers and put it on the desk. He sat on the corner of the desk and watched in grim silence.

"Who am I, Ann?"

"David."

"How do you feel, Ann?"

"Heavy. I feel heavy."

"Why?"

"The baby is so heavy."

Collier licked his lips. Why was he putting it off, asking these extraneous questions? He knew he wanted to ask. Was he too afraid? What if, despite her insistence on this, she gave the wrong answers?

He gripped his hands together tightly and his throat seemed to become a column of rock.

"Dave, not too long," Johnny cautioned.

Collier drew in a rasping breath.

"Is it . . ." he started, then swallowed with difficulty, "is it . . . *my* child, Ann?"

She hesitated. She frowned. Her eyes flickered open for a second, then shut. Her entire body writhed. She seemed to be fighting the question. Then the color drained from her face.

"*No,*" she said through clenched teeth.

Collier felt himself stiffening as if all his muscles and tendons were dough expanding and pushing out his flesh.

"Who's the father?" he asked, not realizing how loud and unnatural his voice was.

At that, Ann's body shuddered violently. There was a clicking sound in her throat and her head rolled limply on the pillow. At her sides, the white fists opened slowly.

Mead jumped over and put his fingers to her wrist. His face was taut as he felt for the pulsebeat. Satisfied, he lifted her right eyelid and peered at the eye.

"She's really out," he said, "I told you it wasn't a good idea to give serum to such a heavily pregnant woman. You should have done it months ago. Kleinman won't like this."

Collier sat there not hearing a word, his face a mask of hopeless distress.

But the words hardly came out. He felt something shake in his chest. He didn't realize what it was until it was too late. Then he ran shaking hands over his cheeks and stared at the wet fingers with incredulous eyes. His mouth opened, closed. He tried to cut off the sobs but he couldn't.

He felt Johnny's arm around his shoulders.

Collier jammed his eyes shut, wishing that his whole body could be swallowed up in the swimming darkness before his gaze. His chest heaved with trembling breaths and he couldn't swallow the lump in his throat. His head kept shaking slowly. My life is ended, he thought, I loved and trusted her and she has betrayed me.

"Dave?" he heard Johnny say.

Collier grunted.

"I don't want to make things worse. But . . . well, there's still a hope, I think."

"Huh?"

"Ann didn't answer your question. She didn't say the father was . . . another man," he finished weakly.

Collier pushed angrily to his feet.

"Oh *shut up*, will you?" he said.

Later they carried her to the car and Collier drove her home.

Slowly he took off his coat and hat and let them drop on the hall chest. Then he shuffled into the living room and sank down on his chair. He lifted his feet to the ottoman with a weary grunt. He sat there, slumped over, staring at the wall.

Where was she?—he wondered. Upstairs reading probably, just as he'd left her this morning. She had a pile of library books by the bed. Rousseau, Locke, Hegel, Marx, Descartes, Darwin, Bergson, Freud, Whitehead, Jeans, Eddington, Einstein, Emerson, Dewey, Confucius, Plato, Aristotle, Spinoza, Kant, Schopenhauer, James—an endless assortment of books.

And the way she read them. As if she were sitting there and rapidly turning the pages without even looking at what was written on them. Yet he knew she was getting it all. Once in a while she'd let a phrase drop, a concept, an idea. She was getting every word.

But why?

Once he had gotten the wild idea that Ann had read something about acquired characteristics and was trying to pass along this knowledge to her unborn child. But he had quickly put aside the idea. Ann was intelligent enough to know that such a thing was patently impossible.

He sat there shaking his head slowly, a habit he'd acquired in the past few months. Why was he still with her? He kept asking himself the question. Somehow the months had slipped by and still he was living in this house. A hundred times he'd started to leave and changed his mind. Finally he'd given up and moved into the back bedroom. They lived now like landlord and tenant.

His nerves were starting to go. He found himself obsessed with an overwhelming impatience. If he was walking from one place to another he would suddenly feel a great rush of anger that he had not already completed the trip. He resented all transport, he wanted things done immediately. He snapped at his pupils whether they rated it or not. His classes were being so poorly conducted that he'd been called before Doctor Peden, the head of the Geology Department. Peden hadn't been too hard on him because he knew about Ann, but Collier knew he couldn't go on like this.

His eyes moved over the room. The rug was thick with dust. He'd tried going over it with the vacuum whenever he thought of it, but it piled up too fast to keep pace with. The whole house was going to pot. He had to take care of his laundry. The machine in the basement hadn't been used for months. He didn't know how to operate it and Ann never touched it now. He took the clothes to the laundromat downtown.

When he'd commented once on the slovenliness of the house, Ann had looked hurt and started to cry. She cried all the time now and always the same way. First, as if she was going to continue for an hour straight. Then, suddenly, with lurching abruptness, she would stop crying and wipe away the tears. He got the impression sometimes that it had something to do with the child, that she stopped for fear the crying would affect the baby. Or else it was the other way around, he thought, that the baby didn't like . . .

He closed his eyes as if to shut out the thought. His right hand tapped nervously and impatiently on the arm of the chair. He got up restlessly and walked around the room running a forefinger over flat surfaces, wiping the dust off on his handkerchief.

He stood staring malignantly at the heap of dishes in the sink, the unkempt condition of the curtains, the smeared linoleum. He felt like rushing upstairs and letting her know that, pregnancy or no pregnancy, she was going to snap out of this doldrum and act like a wife again or he was leaving.

He started through the dining room, then halfway to the stairs he hesitated, halted completely. He went back to the stove slowly and put the flame on underneath the coffee pot. The coffee would be stale but he'd rather drink it that way than make more.

What was the use? She'd try to talk to him and tell him she understood but then, as if she were under a spell, she'd start to cry. And, after a few moments, she'd get that startled look and stop crying. As a matter of fact she was even beginning to control her tears from the outset. As if she knew that the crying wasn't going to work so she might as well not start at all.

It was eerie.

The word brought him up short. That was it—*eerie*. The pneumonia. The decrease in fetal size. The reading. The desire for salt. The crying and the stopping of it.

He found himself staring at the white wall over the stove. He found himself shuddering.

Ann didn't tell us the father was another man.

When he came in she was in the kitchen drinking coffee. Without a word he took the cup from her and poured the remainder of it into the sink.

"You're not supposed to drink coffee," he said.

He looked into the coffee pot. He'd left it almost full that morning.

"Did you drink *all* of it?" he asked angrily.

She lowered her head.

"For God's sake, don't cry!"

"I . . . I won't," she said.

"Why do you drink coffee when you know you're not supposed to?"

"I just couldn't stand it anymore."

"*Oh-h,*" he said, clenching his teeth. He started out of the room.

"David, I can't help it," she called after him, "I can't drink water. I have to drink *something*. David, can't—can't you! . . ."

He went upstairs and took a shower. He couldn't concentrate on anything. He put down the soap and then forgot where. He stopped shaving before he was done and wiped off the lather. Then, later, while he was combing his hair, he noticed half his face still bearded and, with a muffled curse, he lathered again and finished.

The night was like all the others except for one thing. When he went into the bedroom for clean pajamas he saw that she was having difficulty focusing her eyes. And, while he lay in the back bedroom correcting test papers, he heard her giggling. Later he tossed around for several hours before he slept and all that time she kept giggling at something. He wanted to slam the door shut and drown out the sound but he couldn't. He had to leave the door open in case she needed him during the night.

At last he slept. For how long he didn't know. It seemed only a moment before he lay there blinking up at the dark ceiling.

"*Now am I alien and forgotten, O lost of traveled night.*"

First he thought he was dreaming.

"*Murk and strangeness, here am I in ever night, hot, hot.*"

He sat up suddenly then, his heart jolting.

It was Ann's voice.

He threw his legs over the side of the bed and found his slippers. He pushed up quickly and padded to the door, shivering as the cold air chilled the rayon thinness of his pajamas. He moved into the hall and heard her speaking again.

"Dream of goodbyes, forsaken, plunged in swelling liquors, cry I for light, release me from torment and trial."

All spoken in a singsong rhythm, in a voice that was Ann's and not Ann's, more high-pitched, more tense.

She was lying there on her back, her hands pressed to her stomach. It was moving. He watched the flesh ripple under the thinness of her nightgown. She should have been chilled without any blankets but she seemed warm. The bedside lamp was still on, the book —*Science and Sanity*, Korzybski—fallen from her fingers and lying half open on the mattress.

It was her face. Sweat drops dotted it like hundreds of tiny crystals. Her lips were drawn back from her teeth.

Her eyes wide open.

"Kin of the night, sickened of this pit, O send me not to make the way!"

He felt a horrible fascination in standing there listening to her. But she was in pain. It was obvious from her whitened skin, the way her hands, like claws, raked the sheet at her sides into mounds of wadded, sweat-streaked cotton.

"I cry, I cry," she said, *"Rhyuio Gklemmo Fglwo!"*

He slapped her face and her body lurched on the bed.

"He again, the hurting one!"

Her lips spread wide in a scream. He slapped her again and focus came to her eyes. She lay there staring up at him in complete horror. Her hands jumped to her cheeks, pressing against them. She seemed to recoil into the bed. Her pupils shrank to pinpoints in the milkwhite of her eyes.

"No," she said, *"no."*

"Ann, it's me, David! You're all right!"

She looked uncomprehendingly at him for a long moment, her breasts heaving with tortured breaths.

Then, suddenly, she was relaxed and recognized him. Her lower jaw went slack and a moan of relief filled her throat.

He sat down beside her and took her in his arms. She clung to him, crying, her face into his chest.

"All right, baby, let it out, let it out."

Again. The choking off of sobs, the suddenly dried eyes, the pulling away from him, the blank look.

"What is it?" he asked.

No answer. She stared at him.

"Baby, what *is* it? Why can't you cry?"

Something crossed her face, then slipped away.

"Baby, you should cry."

"I don't want to cry."

"Why not?"

"He won't let me," she blurted out.

Suddenly, they were both silent, staring at each other and, he knew, in an instant, that they were very close to the answer.

"*He?*" he asked.

"No," she said suddenly. "I don't mean it. I don't mean that. I don't mean *he*, I mean something else."

For a long time they sat there looking at each other. Then, speaking no more, he made her lie down and covered her up. He got a blanket and stayed the rest of the night in the chair by the bureau. When he woke up in the morning, cramped and cold, he saw that she'd thrown off the blankets again.

Kleinman told him that Ann had adjusted to cold. There seemed to be something added to her system which was sending out heat to her when she needed it.

"And all this salt she takes." Kleinman threw up his hands. "It is beyond sense. You would think the child thrives on a saline diet. Yet she no longer gains excess weight. She does not drink water to combat the thirst. What does she do to ease the thirst?"

"Nothing," Collier said. "She's always thirsty."

"And the reading, it goes on?"

"Yes," said Collier.

"And the talking in her sleep?"

"Yes."

Kleinman shook his head.

"Never in my life," he said, "have I seen a pregnancy like this."

She finished up the last of the huge pile she'd been constantly augmenting. She took all the books back to the library.

A new development began.

She was seven months pregnant. It was May and Collier noticed that the oil was filthy, the tires were unnaturally worn and there was a dent in the left rear fender.

"Have you been using the car?" he asked her one Saturday morning. It was in the living room, the phonograph was playing Brahms.

"Why?" she asked.

He told her and she said irritably, "If you already know, why do you ask me?"

"Have you?"

"Yes, I've been using the car. Is that permissible?"

"You needn't be sarcastic."

"Oh, no," she said angrily, "I needn't get sarcastic. I've been pregnant seven months and not once have you believed that some other man isn't the father. No matter how many times I've told you that I'm innocent, you still won't say—I believe you. And *I'm* sarcastic. Oh, honest, David, you're a panic, a real panic."

She stamped over to the phonograph and turned it off.

"I'm *listening* to it," he said.

"That's too bad. I don't like it."

"Since when?"

"Oh, leave me alone."

He caught her by the wrist as she turned away.

"Listen," he said, "maybe you think the whole thing has been a vacation for me. I come home from six months research and find you pregnant. Not by me! I don't care what you say, I'm *not* the father and neither I nor anyone else knows any way but one for a woman to get pregnant. Still I haven't left. I've watched you turn into a book-reading machine. I've had to clean the house when I could, cook most of the meals, take care of our clothes—as well as teach every day at the college. I've had to look over you as I would a child, keeping you from kicking off the blankets, keeping you from eating too much salt, from drinking too much water, too much coffee, from smoking too much . . ."

"I've stopped smoking myself," she said, pulling away.

"Why?" he threw at her suddenly.

She looked blank.

"Go ahead," he said, "say it. Because *he* doesn't like it."

"I stopped smoking myself," she repeated. "I can't stand them."

"And now you don't like music."

"It . . . hurts my stomach," she said, vaguely.

"Nonsense," he said.

Before he could stop her, she'd gone out the front door into the blazing sunlight. He went to the door and watched her get into the car clumsily. He started to call to her but she'd started the motor and couldn't hear him. He watched the car disappear up the block doing fifty in second gear.

"How long has she been gone now?" Johnny asked.

Collier glanced nervously at his watch.

"I don't know exactly," he said. "Since around nine-thirty I guess. We'd argued, as I said . . ."

He broke off nervously and checked his watch again. It was past midnight.

"How long has she been driving like this?" Johnny asked.

"I don't know, Johnny. I told you I just found out."

"Doesn't her size . . . ?" started Johnny.

"No, the baby isn't big anymore." Collier spoke the astounding now in a matter-of-fact voice. He ran a shaky hand through his hair.

"You think we should call the police?" he asked.

"Wait a little."

"What if she's had an accident?" Collier said. "She's not the best driver in the world. Why in God's name did I let her go? Seven months pregnant and I let her go driving. Oh, I ought to be . . ."

He felt himself getting ready to crack. All this tension in his house, this strange and endlessly distressing pregnancy—it was getting to him. A man couldn't hold onto tension for seven months and not feel it. He couldn't keep his hands from shaking anymore. He'd developed a habit of presistent blinking to use up some of the nervous energy.

He paced across the rug to the fireplace and stood there tapping his nails nervously on the shelf.

"I think we should call the police," he said.

"Take it easy," Johnny warned.

"What would you advise?" Collier snapped.

"Sit down. Right there. That's it. Now relax. She's all right, believe me. I'm not worried about Ann. She's probably had a flat or an engine failure somewhere in the middle of nowhere. How many times have I heard you go on about needing a new battery? It probably died, that's all."

"Well . . . wouldn't the police be able to find her a lot quicker?"

"All right, boy, if it'll make you happier. I'll call them."

Collier nodded, then started up as a car passed in the street. He rushed to the window and drew back the blinds. Then he bit his lips and turned back. He went back to the fireplace while Johnny moved for the hall phone. He listened to Johnny dialing, then twitched as the receiver was put down hurriedly.

"Here she is," Johnny said.

They led her into the front room, dizzy and confused. She didn't answer Collier's frantic questions. She headed straight for the kitchen as if she didn't notice them.

"Coffee," she said in a guttural voice.

At first Collier tried to stop her, then he felt Johnny's hand on his arm.

"Let her go," Johnny said. "It's time we got to the bottom of this."

She stood in front of the stove and turned the flame up high under the coffee pot. She ladled in careless spoonfuls, then slammed on the lid, and stood looking down at it studiedly.

Collier started to say something but, once more, Johnny restrained him. Collier stood restively in the kitchen doorway, watching his wife.

When the brown liquid started popping up into the dome, Ann grabbed the pot off the stove without using a potholder. Collier drew in his breath and gritted his teeth.

She poured out the steaming liquid and it sloshed up the sides of the used cup on the table. Then she slammed down the pot and reached hungrily for the cup.

She finished the whole pot in ten minutes.

She drank without cream or sugar, as if she didn't care what it tasted like. As if she didn't taste it at all.

Only when she'd finished did her face relax. She slumped back in the chair and sat there a long time. They watched her in silence.

Then she looked up at them and giggled.

She pushed up and fell against the table. Collier heard Johnny draw in sudden breath.

"My God," he said, "she's *drunk!*"

She was a heavy, unwieldy form to get up the stairs, especially since she gave them no assistance. She kept humming to herself—a strange, discordant melody that seemed to move in indefinable tone steps, repeated and repeated like the sound of low wind. There was a beatific smile on her face.

"A lot of good that did," Collier muttered.

"Be patient, be patient," Johnny whispered back.

"Easy enough for you to . . ."

"Shhh," Johnny quieted him but Ann didn't hear a word they said.

She stopped humming as soon as they put her down on the bed and had fallen into a deep sleep before they straightened up. Collier drew a thin blanket over her and put a pillow under her head. She didn't stir as he lifted her head.

Then the two men stood in silence beside the bed. Collier looked down at the wife he no longer understood. His mind swam with painful discordances and, through them all, burned the horrible strain of doubt that had never left him. Who was the father of her child? Even though he couldn't leave her, even though he felt a great loving pity for her—they could never be close again until he knew.

"I wonder where she goes?" Johnny asked. "When she drives, I mean."

"I don't know." Sullenly.

"She must have gone pretty far to wear down the tires so much. I wonder if . . ."

That was when she started again.

"*Send me not,*" she said.

Johnny gripped Collier's arm.

"Is that it?" he asked.

"I don't know yet."

"*Black, black drive me out, horror in these shores, heavy heavy.*" Collier shuddered.

"That's it," he said.

Johnny knelt hurriedly beside the bed and listened carefully.

"*Breathe me, implore my fathers, seek me out in washing pain, send me not to make the way.*"

Johnny stared at Ann's taut features. She looked as if she was in pain again. And yet it was not her face, Collier suddenly realized. The expression wasn't hers.

Ann threw off the blanket and thrashed on the bed, sweat breaking out on her face.

"*To walk on shores of orange sea, cool, to tread the crimson fields, cool, the raft on silent waters, cool, to ride upon the desert- land, cool, return me fathers of my fathers, Rhyuio Gklemmo Fglwo.*"

Then she was silent except for tiny groans. At her sides, her hands clutched the sheets and her breaths were labored and uneven.

Johnny straightened up and looked at Collier. Neither of them spoke a word.

They sat with Kleinman.

"What you suggest is fantastic," the doctor said.

"Listen," Johnny said, "let's run it down. One—the excess saline requirements, not the requirements of a normal pregnancy. Two—the cold, the way Ann's body adjusted to it, the way she was cured of pneumonia in minutes."

Collier sat staring numbly at his friend.

"All right," Johnny said, "first the salt. In the beginning it made Ann drink too much water. She gained weight and then her weight endangered the child. What happened? She no longer was allowed to drink water."

"Allowed?" Collier asked.

"Let me finish," Johnny said. "About the cold; it was as if the child needed cold and forced Ann to stay cold—until it realized that by acquiring itself some comfort it was endangering the very vessel it lived in. So it cured the vessel of pneumonia. It adjusted the vessel to cold."

"You talk as if . . ." Kleinman started.

"The effects of cigarettes," Johnny said. "Excuse me, Doctor, Ann could have smoked in moderation without endangering herself or the child. Yet she stopped altogether. It might have been an ethical point, true. Again, it might be that the child reacted violently to nicotine, and, in a sense, forbade her to . . ."

Kleinman interrupted irritably, "You talk as if the child were directing its mother rather than being helpless, subject to its mother's actions."

"Helpless?" was all Johnny said.

Kleinman didn't go on. He pressed his lips together in annoyed surrender and tapped nervously on his desk. Johnny waited a moment and then, seeing that Kleinman wasn't going to continue, he went on.

"Three—the aversion to music which she once loved. Why? Because it was music? I don't think so. *Because of the vibrations.* Vibrations which a normal child wouldn't even notice, being so insulated from sound not only by the layers of its mother's epidermis but by the very structure of its own hearing apparatus. Apparently, this . . . child . . . has much keener hearing.

"The coffee," he said. "It made her drunk. Or—it made *it drunk.*"

"Now wait," Collier started, then broke off.

"And now," Johnny said, "as to her reading. It fits in too. All those books—more or less the basic works in every field of knowledge, a seemingly calculated study of mankind and his every thought."

"What are you driving at?" Collier spoke nervously.

"Think, Dave! All these things. The reading, the trips in the car. As if she were trying to get as much information as she could about life in our civilization. As if the child were . . ."

"You are not implying that the child was . . ." Kleinman began.

"Child?" Johnny said grimly. "I think we can stop referring to it as a child. Perhaps the body is childlike. But the mind—*never.*"

They were deadly silent. Collier felt his heart pulsing strangely in his chest.

"Listen," Johnny said. "Last night Ann—or the . . . *it*—was drunk. Why? Maybe because of what it's learned, what it's seen. I hope so. Maybe it was sick and wanted to forget."

He leaned forward.

"Those visions Ann had; I think they tell the story—as crazy as it is. The deserts, the marshes, the crimson fields. Add the cold. Only one thing wasn't mentioned and I think that's probably because they don't exist."

"What?" Collier asked, reality scaling away from him.

"The canals," Johnny said. "*Ann has a Martian in her womb.*"

For a long time they looked at him in incredulous silence. Then both started talking at once, protesting with nervous horror in their voices. Johnny waited until the first spasm of their words had passed.

"Is there a better answer?" he asked.

"But . . . *how?*" Kleinman asked heatedly. "How could such a pregnancy be effected?"

"I don't know," Johnny said. "But why? I think I know."

Collier was afraid to ask.

"All through the years," Johnny said, "there's been no end of talk and writing about the Martians, about flying saucers. Books, stories, movies, articles—always with the same theme."

"I don't . . ." Collier began.

"I think the invasion has finally come," Johnny said. "At least a tryout. I think this is their first attempt—invasion by flesh. To place an adult life cell from their own planet into the body of an Earth woman. Then, when this fully matured Martian mind is coupled to the form of an Earth child—the process of conquest begins. This is their experiment, I think, their test. If it works . . ."

He didn't finish.

"But . . . oh, that's *insane*," Collier said, trying to push away the fear that was crowding him in.

"So is her reading," said Johnny. "So are the trips in the car. So is her coffee drinking and her dislike of music and her pneumonia healing and her standing out in the cold and the reduction of body size and the visions and that crazy toneless song she sang. What do you want, Dave—a blueprint?"

Kleinman stood up and went to his filing cabinets. He pulled out a drawer and came back to the desk with a folder in his hand.

"I have had this in my files for three weeks now," he said. "I have not told you. I did not know how. But this information, this *theory*," he quickly amended, "compels me to . . ."

He pushed the x-ray slide across the desk to them.

They looked at it and Collier gasped. Johnny's voice was awed. "*A double heart*," he said.

Then his left hand bunched into a fist.

"That clinches it!" he said. "Mars has two-fifths the gravity of Earth. They'd need a double heart to drive their blood or whatever it is they have in their veins."

"But . . . it does not need this here," Kleinman said.

"Then there's some hope," Johnny said. "There are rough spots in this invasion. The Martian cell would, of genetic necessity, cause certain Martian characteristics in the child—the double heart, the acute hearing, the need for salt, I don't know why, the need for cold. In time—and if this experiment works—they may iron out these difficulties and be able to create a child with only the Martian mind and every physical characteristic Earthlike. I don't know but I suspect the Martian is also telepathic. Otherwise how would it have known it was in danger when Ann had pneumonia?"

The scene flitted suddenly across Collier's mind—him standing beside the bed, the thought—*the hospital, oh God, the hospital.* And, under Ann's flesh, a tiny alien brain, well versed by then in the terms of Earth, plucking at his thought. Hospital, investigation, discovery . . . He shuddered convulsively.

". . . we to do?" he caught the tail end of Kleinman's question. "Kill the . . . the *Martian* after it is born?"

"I don't know," Johnny said. "But if this . . . ," he shrugged, "this *child* is born alive and born normal—I don't think killing would help. I'm sure they must be watching. If the birth is normal—they might assume their experiment is a success whether we killed the child or not."

"A Caesarian?" Kleinman said.

"Maybe," Johnny said. "But . . . would they be sure they've failed if we had to use artificial means to destroy . . . their first invader? No, I don't think it's good enough. They'd try again, this time somewhere where no one could check on it—in an African village, in some unavailable town, in . . ."

"We can't leave that . . . that *thing* in her!" Collier said in horror.

"How do we know we can remove it," Johnny said grimly, "and not kill Ann?"

"What?" Collier asked, feeling as if he were some brainless straight man for horror. Johnny exhaled raggedly.

"I think we have to wait," he said. "I don't think we have any choice."

Then, seeing the look on Collier's face he hurriedly added, "It's not hopeless, boy. There are things in our favor. The double heart which might drive the blood too fast. The difficulties of combining alien cells. The fact that it's July and the heat might destroy the Martian. The fact that we can cut off all its salt supply. It can all help. But, most of all, because the Martian isn't happy. It drank to forget and—what were its words? *O, send me not to make the way.*"

"Let's hope it dies of despair," he said.

"Or?" Collier asked hollowly.

"Or else this . . . miscegenation from space succeeds."

Collier dashed up the stairs, his heart pounding with a strange ambivalent beat. Knowing at last that she was innocent was horribly balanced by knowledge of the danger she was in.

At the top of the stairs he stopped. The house was silent and hot in the late afternoon.

They were right, he suddenly realized, right in advising him not to tell her. It hadn't actually struck him until then, he'd thought it wrong not to let her know. He'd thought she wouldn't mind as long as she knew what it was, as long as she had his faith again.

But now he wondered. It was a terrifying thing, the import of it made him tremble. Might not the knowledge of this horror drive her into hysterics; she'd been bordering on breakdown for the past three months.

His mouth tightened and he walked into the room.

She lay on her back, her hands resting limply on her swollen stomach, her lifeless eyes staring up at the ceiling. He sat down on the edge of the bed. She didn't look at him.

"Ann."

No answer. He felt himself shiver. I can't blame you, he thought, I've been harsh and thoughtless.

"Sweetheart," he said.

Her eyes moved slowly over and their gaze on him was cold and alien. It was the creature in her, he thought, she didn't realize how it controlled her. She must never realize. He knew that then, clearly.

He leaned over and pressed his cheek against hers.

"Darling," he said.

A dull, tired voice, hardly audible. "What?"

"Can you hear me?" he said.

She didn't reply.

"Ann about the baby."

There was a slight sign of life in her eyes.

"What about the baby?"

He swallowed.

"I . . . I know that . . . that it isn't the baby of . . . another man."

For a moment she stared at him. Then she muttered, "Bravo," and turned her head away.

He sat there, hands gripped into tight fists, thinking—well, that's that, I've killed her love completely.

But then her head turned back. There was something in her eyes, a tremulous questioning.

"What?" she said.

"I believe you," he said. "I know you've told me the truth. I'm apologizing with all my heart . . . if you'll let me."

For a long moment nothing seemed to register. Then she took her hands from her stomach and pressed them against her cheeks. Her wide brown eyes began to glisten as they looked at him.

"You're not . . . fooling me?" she asked him.

For a moment he hung suspended, then he threw himself against her.

"Oh, Ann, Ann," he said. "I'm sorry. I'm so sorry, Ann."

Her arms slid around his neck and held him. He felt her breasts shake with inner sobs. Her right hand caressed his hair.

"David, David . . ." She said it like that, over and over.

For a long time they remained there, silent and at peace. Then she asked, "What made you change your mind?"

His throat moved.

"I just did," he said.

"But why?"

"No reason, honey. I mean, of course, there was a reason. I just realized that . . ."

"You've doubted me for seven months, David. Why did you change your mind now?"

He felt a burst of rage at himself. Was there nothing he could tell her that would satisfy her?

"I think I've misjudged you," he said.

"Why?"

He sat up and looked at her without the answer. The look of soft happiness was leaving her face. Her expression was taut and unyielding.

"*Why*, David?"

"I told you, sweet . . ."

"You didn't tell me."

"Yes, I did. I said I think I've misjudged you."

"That's no reason."

"Ann, don't let's argue now. Does it matter if . . ."

"Yes, it matters a lot!" she said, her voice breaking, as her breath caught.

"And what about your biological assurances?" she said. "No woman can have a baby without being impregnated by a man. You always made that very clear. What about that? Have you given up your faith in biology and transferred it to me?"

"No, darling," he said. "I simply know things I didn't know before."

"What things?"

"I can't tell you."

"More secrets! Is this Kleinman's advice, just a trick to make my last month cozy? Don't lie to me, I know when you're lying to me."

"Ann, don't get so excited."

"I'm not excited!"

"You're shouting. Now stop it."

"I will not stop it! You toy with my feelings for more than half a year and now you want me to be calmly rational! Well, I won't be! I'm sick of you and your pompous attitude! I'm tired of . . . *Uhhh!*"

She lurched on the bed, her head snapping as she jerked her head from the pillow, all the color drained from her face in an instant. Her eyes on him were the eyes of a wounded child, dazed and shocked.

"*My insides!*" she gasped.

"Ann!"

She was half sitting now, her body shaking, a wild, despairing groan starting up in her throat. He grabbed her shoulders and tried to steady her. The Martian!—the thought clutched at his mind—it doesn't like her angry!

"It's all right, baby, all r—"

"He's hurting me!" she cried. "He's hurting me, David! *Oh God!*"

"He can't hurt you," he heard himself say.

"No, no, no, I can't stand it," she said between clenched teeth. "*I can't stand it.*"

Then, as abruptly as the attack had come, her face relaxed utterly. Not so much with actual relaxation as with a complete absence of all feeling. She looked dizzily at David.

"I'm numb," she said quietly, "I . . . can't . . . feel . . . a . . ."

Slowly she sank back on the pillow and lay there a second with her eyes open. Then she smiled drowsily at Collier.

"Good night, David," she said.

And closed her eyes.

Kleinman stood beside the bed.

"She is in perfect coma," he said, quietly. "More accurately I should say under hypnotic trance. Her body functions normally but her brain has been . . . frozen."

Johnny looked at him.

"Suspended animation?"

"No, her body functions. She is just asleep. I cannot wake her."

They went downstairs to the living room.

"In a sense," Kleinman said, "she is better off. There will be no upsets now. Her body will function painlessly, effortlessly."

"The Martian must have done it," Johnny said, "to safeguard its . . . home."

Collier shuddered.

"I'm sorry, Dave," Johnny said.

They sat silent a moment.

"It must realize we know about it," Johnny said.

"Why?" asked Collier.

"It wouldn't be tipping off its hand completely if it thought there was still a chance of secrecy."

"Maybe it could not stand the pain," said Kleinman.

Johnny nodded. "Yes, maybe."

Collier sat there, his heart beating strainedly. Suddenly he clenched his fists and drove them down on his legs.

"Meanwhile, what are we supposed to do!" he said. "Are we helpless before this . . . this *trespasser?*"

"We can't take risks with Ann," was all Johnny said and Kleinman nodded once.

Collier sank in the chair. He sat staring at the kewpie doll on the mantel. *Coney Island* read the doll's dress and on the belt—*Happy Days.*

"*Rhyuio Gklemmo Fglwo!*"

Ann writhed in unconscious labor on the hospital bed. Collier stood rigidly beside her, his eyes fastened to her sweat-streaked face. He wanted to run for Kleinman but he knew he shouldn't. She'd been like this twenty hours now—twenty hours of twisting, teeth-clenching agony. When it had started he'd cut his classes completely to stay with her.

He reached down with trembling fingers to hold her damp hand. Her fingers clamped on his until the grip almost hurt. And, as he watched in numbed horror, he saw passing across his wife's features—the slitted eyes, the thin, drawn-back lips, the white skin pulled rigidly over facial bones.

"*Pain! Pain! Spare me, fathers of my fathers, send me not to . . .* !"

There was a clicking in her throat, then silence. Her face suddenly relaxed and she lay there shivering weakly. He began to pat her face with a towel.

"In the yard, David," she muttered, still unconscious.

He bent over suddenly, his heart jolting.

"In the yard, David," she said, "I heard a sound and I went out. The stars were bright and there was a crescent moon. While I stood there I saw a white light come over the yard. I started to run back to the house but something hit me. Like a needle going into my back and my stomach. I cried out but then it was blank and I couldn't remember. Anything. I tried to tell you David, but I couldn't remember, I couldn't remember. I couldn't . . ."

A hospital. In the corridor the father paces, his eyes feverish and haunted. The hall is hot and silent in the early August morning. He walks back and forth restlessly and his hands are white fists at his sides.

A door opens. The father whirls as a doctor comes out. The doctor draws down the cloth which has covered his mouth and nose. He looks at the man.

"*Your wife is well,*" *says the doctor.*

The father grabs the doctor's arm.

"*And the baby?*" *he asks.*

"*The baby is dead.*"

"*Thank God,*" *the father says.*

Still wondering if in Africa, in Asia . . .

Coincidence

William F. Nolan

When Harry Dobson's wife suggested they spend their last night together (before Harry's trip) in a New York hotel he agreed. It was to be a kind of instant second honeymoon, and Harry savored the drive down from Westport with his wife cuddled close to him. It reminded Harry of the early days, before the house and kids had aged them both. The kids were grown and gone, but the house in Westport, with its high upkeep and higher taxes, dragged at Harry like a weight. He enjoyed the overnight stay in a New York hotel, enjoyed the sexual passion he was still able to inspire in Margaret.

What Harry Dobson *didn't* enjoy was having his wife bump him awake with a naked hip at 6 A.M. in the morning.

"What's wrong?" he wanted to know.

"It's the man in the next room," whispered Margaret, pressing close to him in the double bed. "He's been moaning. He woke me up."

"So he's probably sick, maybe drunk. Who cares?"

"It's what he's moaning that spooks me," said Margaret. "I want you to hear him. I think he's some kind of maniac."

"Okay, okay," Harry grunted. And he listened to the agonized words which filtered through the thin walls of the hotel room.

"I've killed," moaned the man. "I've killed. I've killed."

"He keeps repeating that over and over," Margaret whispered. "I think you'd better do something."

"Do what?" asked Harry, propping himself against the pillow to light a cigarette. "Maybe he's just having a bad dream."

"But he keeps saying it over and over. It really spooks me. We could be next door to a murderer."

"So what do you suggest?"

She blinked at him, absently stroking her left breast. "Call the manager. Have someone investigate."

Harry sighed, kicked off the blankets and padded barefoot to the house phone on the dresser. He picked up the receiver, waited for the switchboard to acknowledge.

"This is Harry Dobson in room 203. There's a character next door who's moaning about having killed somebody. He's been keeping us awake. Yeah . . . he's in 202. Right next door."

Harry listened, holding the phone, slowly stubbing out his cigarette on the glass top of the dresser.

"What's happening?" asked Harry's wife.

"They're checking to see who's in 202."

"He's stopped moaning," she said.

"No, no," said Harry into the receiver. "*I'm* in 203. Okay, forget it, just forget it."

He slammed down the phone.

"What's wrong?"

"The stupid idiot on the desk has my name down for *both* rooms!"

"Couldn't it be a coincidence?" Margaret asked. "I mean, your name isn't *that* unusual. There must be several Harry Dobsons in New York."

"Not door-to-door in the same damn hotel," he said. "Anyhow, they claim they can't do anything about the guy and unless he gets violent in there to just ignore him." He shook his head. "That's New York for you."

"I think we'd better leave," said Margaret. She got up and walked to the bathroom.

Harry blew out his breath in disgust, got his pants off the chair and began dressing. He was scheduled to fly back to L.A. this morning anyhow, so he'd get to the airport a little early. He could have breakfast there.

He and his wife left the hotel room.

In the elevator she told him she'd write him at least once a week while he was gone. He was sweet, she told him, and if it hadn't been for the maniac in 202 their night together would have been beautiful.

"Sure," said Harry Dobson.

They said goodbye in the lobby. Then Harry checked out, giving the desk clerk hell for mixing up the room numbers. "I represent a major firm," he told the clerk. "I'm an important man, damnit! What if someone wanted to reach me? My messages might have gone to a nut in 202. Do you understand me?"

The desk clerk said he was very sorry.

Harry walked out to a cab. Gray rain drizzled down from a soot-colored sky and a chill November wind blew the rain against Harry's face.

"Kennedy Airport," he said to the driver. But before he climbed into the taxi he paused. *He's watching you. That bastard in 202 is watching you.* Harry shaded his eyes against the rain and peered upward at the second-floor street window of room 202.

A tall man was at the open window, ignoring the blowing rain, glaring down at him. The man's face was dark with anger.

Harry stared, unblinking. *Good grief, he even looks like me. Like an older version of me. No wonder the clerk mixed us up. Well, to hell with him!*

By the time his jet soared away from New York Harry Dobson had put the man from 202 firmly out of his thoughts. Harry was concerned with the report he'd be making to the sales manager back in California. He was working out some statistics on a board in his lap when he happened to notice the passenger in the window seat directly across the aisle.

What—it's him! Can't be. Left him back in New York.

The passenger had been reading a magazine; now he raised his head and swung his eyes slowly toward Harry Dobson. Cold hatred flowed from those eyes.

The tourist section was only half filled and Harry had no trouble getting another seat several rows back. Damned if he'd sit there and let this creep give him the evil eye. Maybe Margaret was right; maybe the guy *was* some kind of maniac.

At Los Angeles International Harry was the first passenger to disembark. Inside the airport building he arranged for a porter to collect his flight baggage. Then he waited for it in a cab near the door. Harry didn't want to risk running into the weirdo at the baggage pickup.

So far so good. The guy was nowhere in sight.

His baggage arrived and Harry tipped the porter and gave the taxi driver an address in West Los Angeles. As the car rolled onto the freeway Harry relaxed. Apparently the man had made no attempt to follow him. It was over.

Harry paid the driver, carried his bags into the rented apartment, took some Scotch from his briefcase and poured himself a drink. He felt fine now. He checked the window just to be certain the guy hadn't followed him. The street below was empty.

Harry unpacked, took his suits to the closet, opened the sliding door—and fell back, gasping.

The man was there, inside the closet. He stood in the darkness, smiling like a fiend. Then he dived at Harry's throat, hands closing on his windpipe. Harry kicked free, tumbled over a chair, twisting away from his attacker.

That's when the man pulled the knife from his belt.

Harry scrambled around the bed, putting space between himself and his attacker. No good trying for the door; the man would have him if he tried that.

"Who—are you?" gasped Harry. "What—what do you want from me?"

"I want to kill you," said the man, smiling. "That's all you need to know."

Keeping himself between Harry and the door he began slashing with the knife—ripping the blade into mattress, chairs, curtains, clothing—as Harry watched in numb terror.

But when the man pulled Margaret's photo from Harry's briefcase, and drove the knife through it a red rage replaced the fear in Harry Dobson; the bastard was human, after all. Harry was ten years younger, stronger.

The man was half turned toward the bed when Harry struck him with a heavy table lamp. The other fell backward, stunned, dropping the knife.

"You crazy sonuvabitch," Harry shouted, snapping up the knife and driving it into the man's back. Once. Twice. Three times. The man grunted, then did not move. Harry stood over him for a long, long moment—but he did not move again.

Who is he? Who the hell is he? Harry could find no identification on the body. He thought of calling the police but decided that was too risky. There were no witnesses. The apartment had not been burglarized nor were there signs of a forced entry. *Bastard must have had a key.* To the police, it would appear that Harry Dobson had coldly murdered this man.

Insane! I don't even know him. Which is exactly why you must get rid of the body. Once he's gone there'll be no way to link you to his death.

That night Harry cleaned up the apartment, placed the blanket-wrapped corpse in the trunk of his car and drove out along the ocean, past Malibu, to a deserted stretch of beach—where he dumped the weighted body into the water.

He was a madman. Simply because you complained about him at the hotel he followed you to the West Coast and tried to kill you. You have no reason to feel guilt. Forget all this. Live your life and forget him.

Harry Dobson tried to do that. When his wife called him he didn't mention what had happened. And when his business trip ended he returned to New York, and resumed his life.

A decade passed. Each time the face of the dead man from 202 loomed in his mind Harry Dobson shut down the vision. Finally he could look back upon the entire incident as a kind of bizarre dream. He felt neither guilt nor fear.

Then, almost ten years to the month, Harry found himself at the same hotel in New York. He was in town on his annual business trip and, this particular visit, had decided to stay at this hotel to prove that the ghost of the man he'd killed was truly exorcised.

In fact, to close the circle, he asked the clerk for the old room, 203.

"Sorry, sir, but that room is occupied. However, I can give you the one right next to it, room 202. Will that be satisfactory?"

Irony. The dead man's room. All right, Harry said, that would be satisfactory.

Room 202 contained a double bed, white glass-topped dresser, circular table and chair, a standing brass lamp in the corner . . . *He remembered the furniture!* But that was because it was the same, exactly the same, as 203. The rooms on this floor were no doubt identically furnished. The odd thing was that the decor hadn't been changed in ten years.

Harry took a fresh bottle of Scotch from his suitcase and poured a solid drink for himself. The Scotch eased him, reduced his tension. It was late, near midnight, and after several more belts of Scotch he was ready for sleep, amused at the drama of the situation, no longer tense at the prospect of sleeping in a room once occupied by a man he had stabbed to death.

Near morning, Harry began to mumble in his sleep. He was having a bad dream, a nightmare about being tried and convicted of murder. The attorney was hammering at him on the witness stand and Harry had broken under the verbal assault. "I've killed," he admitted. "I've killed. I've killed." Over and over. "Killed . . . killed . . . killed . . ."

He finally awoke, sweating, wide-eyed. *Wow, what a hellish dream! It's this room. That's what triggered it, allowed it to take control of my subconscious. But I'm all right now. I'm fine. The dream's over.*

He became aware of voices in 203 filtering through the thin wall of the room. A woman's voice, whispery but sharp, and upset. "I think you'd better do something."

"Do what?" asked a man's voice, muffled but distinct. "Maybe he's just having a bad dream."

"But he keeps saying it over and over. It really spooks me. We could be next door to a murderer."

"So what do you suggest?"

"Call the manager. Have someone investigate."

Harry heard the springs squeak as the man climbed out of bed. He heard him pick up the phone and say, "This is Harry Dobson in room 203. There's a character next door who's moaning about having killed somebody . . ."

Harry didn't want to hear any more. He walked into the bathroom and vomited into the bowl, remaining on his knees until he heard the door finally slam in 203.

Then, shaking, he walked back into his room and called the desk. "Who—who's registered in 203?"

"Uh . . . that's Mr. Dobson, sir. But he's checking out."

"All right," said Harry evenly. And he put down the phone.

He walked over to the street window, threw it open. Gray rain, whipped by a chill wind, blew in upon him, stinging his face.

A man came out of the hotel, hailed a cab. Just before he got into the taxi he turned to look up at Harry, shading his eyes against the wet. Younger. A face like his, but ten years younger. *The murder-ing bastard!* Harry glared down at him.

And when the man was gone, and he had called the airport to confirm his flight back to Los Angeles, Harry Dobson took the knife out of his suitcase and held it in his hand for a long, long moment.

Knowing, beyond any doubt, that he would eventually die by it.

The Same Old Grind

Bill Pronzini

There were no customers in the Vienna Delicatessen when Mitchell came in at two on a Thursday afternoon. But that wasn't anything unusual. He'd been going there a couple of times a week since he'd discovered the place two months ago, and he hadn't seen more than a dozen people shopping there in all that time.

It wasn't much of a place. Just a little hole-in-the-wall deli tucked down at the end of a side street, in an old neighborhood that was sliding downhill. Which was exactly the opposite of what he himself was doing, Mitchell thought. He was heading *uphill*—out of the slums he'd been raised in and into this section of the city for a few months, until he had enough money and enough connections, and then uptown where the living was easy and you drank champagne instead of cheap bourbon and ate in fancy restaurants instead of dusty old delis.

But he had to admit that he got a boot out of coming to the Vienna Delicatessen. For one thing, the food was good and didn't cost much. And for another the owner, Giftholz, amused him. Giftholz was a frail old bird who talked with an accent and said a lot of humorous things because he didn't understand half of what you rapped to him about. He was from Austria or someplace like that, been in this country for thirty years, but damned if he didn't talk like he'd just come off the boat.

What Giftholz was doing right now was standing behind the deli counter and staring off into space. Daydreaming about Austria, maybe. Or about the customers he wished he had. He didn't hear Mitchell open the door, but as soon as the little bell overhead started tinkling, he swung around and smiled in a sad hopeful way that always made Mitchell think of an old mutt waiting for some-body to throw him a bone.

"Mr. Mitchell, good afternoon."

Mitchell shut the door and went over to the counter. "How's it going, Giftholz?"

"It goes," Giftholz said sadly. "But not so well."

"The same old grind, huh?"

"Same old grind?"

"Sure. Day in, day out. Rutsville, you dig?"

"Dig?" Giftholz said. He blinked like he was confused and smoothed his hands over the front of his clean white apron. "What will you have today, Mr. Mitchell?"

"The usual. Sausage hero and an order of cole slaw. Might as well lay a brew on me too."

"Lay a brew?"

Mitchell grinned. "Beer, Giftholz. I want a beer."

"Ah. One beer, one sausage hero, one cole slaw. Yes."

Giftholz got busy. He didn't move too fast—hell, he was so frail he'd probably keel over if he *tried* to move fast—but that was all right. He knew what he was doing and he did it right: lots of meat on the sandwich, lots of slaw. You had to give him that.

Mitchell watched him for a time. Then he said, "Tell me something, Giftholz. How do you hang in like this?"

"Please?"

"Hang in," Mitchell said. "Stay in business. You don't have many customers and your prices are already dirt cheap."

"I charge what is fair."

"Yeah, right. But you can't make any bread that way."

"Bread?" Giftholz said. "No, my bread is purchased from the bakery on Union Avenue."

Mitchell got a laugh out of that. "I mean money, Giftholz. You can't make any *money*."

"Ah. Yes, it is sometimes difficult."

"So how do you pay the bills? You got a little something going on the side?"

"Something going?"

"A sideline. A little numbers action, maybe?"

"No, I have no sideline."

"Come on, everybody's got some kind of scam. I mean, it's a dog-eat-dog world, right? Everybody's got to make ends meet any way he can."

"That is true," Giftholz said. "But I have no scam. I do not even know the word."

Mitchell shook his head. Giftholz probably *didn't* have a scam; it figured that way. One of these old-fashioned merchant types who were dead honest. And poor as hell because they didn't believe in screwing their customers and grabbing a little gravy where they could. But still, the way things were these days, how did he stand up to the grind? Even with his cheap prices, he couldn't compete with the big chain outfits in the neighborhood that had specials and drawings and gave away stamps; and he had to pay higher and higher wholesale prices himself for the stuff he sold. Yet here he was, still in business. Mitchell just couldn't figure out how guys like him did it.

Giftholz finished making the sandwich, put it on a paper plate, laid a big cup of slaw beside it, opened a beer from his small refrigerator, and put everything down on the counter. He was smiling as he did it—a kind of proud smile, like he'd done something fine.

"It is two dollars, please, Mr. Mitchell."

Two dollars. Man. The same meal would have cost him four or five at one of the places uptown. Mitchell shook his head again, reached into his pocket, and flipped his wallet out.

When he opened it and fingered through the thick roll of bills inside, Giftholz's eyes got round. Probably because he'd never seen more than fifty bucks at one time in his life. Hell, Mitchell thought, give him a thrill. He opened the wallet wider and waved it under Giftholz's nose.

"That's what real money looks like, Giftholz," he said. "Five bills here, five hundred aces. And plenty more where that came from."

"Where did you earn so much money, Mr. Mitchell?"

Mitchell laughed. "I got a few connections, that's how. I do little jobs for people and they pay me big money."

"Little jobs?"

"You don't want me to tell you what they are. They're private jobs, if you get my drift."

"Ah," Giftholz said, and nodded slowly. "Yes, I see."

Mitchell peeled out the smallest of the bills, a fiver, and laid it on the counter. "Keep the change, Giftholz. I feel generous today."

"Thank you," Giftholz said. "Thank you so much."

Mitchell laughed again and took a bite of his hero. Damned good. Giftholz made the best sandwiches in the city, all right. How could you *figure* a guy like him?

He ate standing up at the counter; there was one little table against the back wall, but from here he could watch Giftholz putter around in slow motion. Nobody else came into the deli; he would have been surprised if somebody had. When he finished the last of the hero and the last of the beer, he belched in satisfaction and wiped his hands on a napkin. Giftholz came over to take the paper plate away; then he reached under the counter and came up with a bowl of mints and a small tray of toothpicks.

"Please," he said.

"Free mints? Since when, Giftholz?"

"It is because you are a good customer."

It is because I gave you a three-buck tip, Mitchell thought. He grinned at Giftholz, helped himself to a handful of mints, and dropped them into his coat pocket. Then he took a toothpick and worked at a piece of sausage that was stuck between two of his teeth.

Giftholz said, "You would do me a small favor, Mr. Mitchell?"

"Favor? Depends on what it is."

"Come with me into the kitchen for a moment."

"What for?"

"There is something I would show you."

"Like what?"

"It is something of interest. Please, it will only take a short time."

Mitchell finished excavating his teeth, tucked the toothpick into a corner of his mouth, and shrugged. What the hell, he might as well humor the old guy. He had time; he didn't have any more little jobs to do today. And there wouldn't be any gambling or lady action until tonight.

"Sure," he said. "Why not."

"Good," Giftholz said. "*Wunderbar.*"

He gestured for Mitchell to come around behind the counter and then doddered through a door into the kitchen. When Mitchell went through after him he didn't see anything particularly interesting.

Just a lot of kitchen equipment, a butcher's block table, a couple of cases of beer, and some kind of large contraption in the far corner.

"So what do you want to show me?" he asked.

"Nothing," Giftholz said.

"Huh?"

"Really I would ask you a question."

"What question?"

"If you speak German."

"German? You putting me on?"

"Putting you on?"

For some reason Mitchell was beginning to feel short of breath. "Listen," he said, "what do you want to know a thing like that for?"

"It is because of my name. If you were to speak German, you see, you would understand what it means in English translation."

Short of breath and a little dizzy, too. He blinked a couple of times and ran a hand over his face. "What do I care what your damned name means."

"You should care, Mr. Mitchell," Giftholz said. "It means 'poison wood.'"

"Poison—?" Mitchell's mouth dropped open, and the toothpick fell out of it and fluttered to the floor. He stared at it stupidly for a second.

Poison wood.

Then he stopped feeling dizzy and short of breath; he stopped feeling anything. He didn't even feel the floor when he fell over and hit it with his face.

Giftholz stood looking down at the body. Too bad, he thought sadly. Ah, but then, Mr. Mitchell had been a *Strolch*, a hoodlum; such men were not to be mourned. And as he had said himself in his curious idiom, it was a dog-eat-dog world today. Everything cost so much; everything was so difficult for a man of honesty. One truly did have to make ends meet any way one could.

He bent and felt for a pulse. But of course there was none. The poison paralyzed the muscles of the heart and brought certain death within minutes. It also, as he well knew, became neutralized in the body after a short period of time, leaving no toxic traces.

Giftholz picked up the special toothpick from the floor, carried it over to the garbage pail. After which he returned and took Mr. Mitchell's wallet and put it away inside his apron.

One had to make ends meet any way one could. Such a perfect phrase that was. But there was another of Mr. Mitchell's many phrases which still puzzled him. The same old grind. It was *not* the same old grind; it had not been the same old grind for some time.

No doubt Mr. Mitchell meant something else, Giftholz decided.

And began to laboriously drag the body toward the large gleaming sausage grinder in the far corner.

Twenty-two Cents a Day

Jack Ritchie

"Are you bitter?" the reporter asked.

I raised an eyebrow. "Bitter? Heavens to Betsy, no."

"But you spent four years in prison for a crime you didn't commit."

I smiled gently. "For which the state amply reimbursed me six thousand beautiful U.S. dollars."

He had evidently done some figuring before the interview. "That comes to about seventeen cents for every hour you spent behind bars."

I shrugged. "You must remember that in addition I earned the regular twenty-two cents per day. Possibly all this qualifies me for the Poverty Program, but on the other hand I had very few expenses while in residence."

"What are you going to do with the rest of your life?"

He was a very young reporter, so I forgave him. "Young man, four years has not entirely ruined me. The best is yet to be."

Warden Denning handed me a manila envelope. "Would you check the contents, George, and sign a receipt? These are the personal things you had with you when you arrived."

"What's the first thing you're going to do when you get out of here?" the reporter asked.

"Buy a gun," I said.

Warden Denning glanced at me sharply. "Now, George, you know perfectly well that a man on parole . . ."

I smiled. "But I am *not* on parole, Warden. I am free without strings, eligible to vote and other things."

The reporter chewed on his pencil. "Why do you want to buy the gun before everything else?"

"I like guns," I said. "As a matter of fact I had a small collection before I went to prison."

He continued to probe. "What's the *second* thing you're going to do when you get out of here?"

"See my lawyer."

"Henry McIntyre?"

"No, not that one. I mean Matt Nelson. I've always felt that his incompetence was at least fifty percent responsible for the loss of four years of my life."

"He was your lawyer at the trial?"

"Yes."

The reporter was thoughtful. "Will you get around to seeing the two men who testified against you?"

I took the wallet out of the manila envelope, checked it, and put it into my pocket. "It's a small world. Coincidental meetings do occur."

The warden sent me on to the Personnel Office where some last minute red tape was unraveled, and when I returned he was talking to Henry McIntyre. They broke off their conversation as I re-entered the room.

Henry McIntyre had been responsible for my release. He is a member of a lawyers' organization which specializes in pursuing cases in which it was felt that injustice had been done. He is one of those intense, singleminded individuals who cannot be swerved from his course once he is convinced he is right—and that is fairly often. He is, in short, the kind of a man I ordinarily detest. However, this was no time to be ungrateful.

"You may send me your bill," I said. "I honor all my debts."

He shook his head. "No. We do these things only in the interests of justice. Money—or personal publicity—has nothing to do with it. And besides, you averaged only seventeen cents an hour and if I charged you, and the papers got hold of the story . . ." He sighed and moved on to another subject. "Now, we wouldn't want you to do anything rash."

"Rash?"

"I mean justice has now been served—even if it has been a bit tardy."

"Really? Justice has been served? You mean to say that the two miserable wretches who committed perjury have now taken my place in prison?"

"Well, no. We really couldn't expect that much."

"But I should still smile and carry on cheerfully?"

"Well, yes, in a way. I mean that revenge will get you no place. And besides that, it would look bad for our organization. After all, we are responsible for releasing you into society, and it would be a blot on our record if you should suddenly take it into your head to . . ." He waved a hand and let the preposition dangle in mid-air.

I picked up my zipper bag and prepared to leave. "I assure you, McIntyre, that I do nothing suddenly. I always think things over carefully before I decide to act."

It was a two-hour bus ride to the city and I arrived there at approximately four that afternoon.

I walked down the avenue to Witco's Sport Shop and spent some time browsing before I purchased a new Ruger automatic. I had it cased and wrapped and went on to Fourth Street. At the Saxton Building I hesitated, then changed my mind. No, Matt Nelson was not a man I cared to see on an empty stomach. I would have a good meal and a night's rest before I would face him.

I had dinner and registered at the Medwin Hotel. In my room, I had whiskey and soda sent up and had barely settled myself for my first civilized drink in four years when my door buzzer sounded.

Two men stood in the hall and both displayed wallets upon which were fastened the shields of city detectives.

The spokesman, gray-haired and evidently a veteran of the force, introduced himself. "I'm Sergeant Davis. Could we have a few words with you?"

"Of course," and I let them in.

Davis turned down the drinks I offered and got to the point. "We always like to prevent things. We feel that an ounce of prevention is worth a pound of cure."

I wondered idly how one would translate something like that into metric weights.

Davis took a chair. "You bought a gun, didn't you, Mr. Whitcomb?"

I frowned. "Have you been following me?"

He nodded. "We were tipped off by a few people, including your lawyer. They filled us in on the situation, and we've had our eye on you ever since you stepped off the bus. What do you intend to do with the gun?"

"Shoot it some time," I said. "And cherish it and keep it free from grime and rust." Evidently I had not answered his question.

"You know it isn't worth it," he said. "You couldn't get away with it."

"Get away with what?"

He studied me for a moment. "Now look, you're an intelligent man. During your time in prison you became the warden's secretary, and he says that he's never had a more competent man on the job. Why do you have to do something so foolish?"

I smiled. "Please don't worry, Sergeant. I never do anything foolish. Never, except by accident."

He stared at me unblinkingly and then sighed. "All right. I can see I'm getting no place. But remember, we're still keeping an eye on you."

When they left I returned to my whiskey and soda and refilled whenever necessary. The next morning I woke up promptly at six-fifteen—a habit which I had acquired in the past few years—and I might even have gotten out of bed, except for the hangover. Perhaps there is something to be said for clean, regular living after all.

I remained in bed throughout the morning, gradually recuperating. In the afternoon, after lunch, I went to the First National Bank and deposited my six-thousand-dollar check. Then I went on to the Saxton Building.

When I entered Matt Nelson's suite of offices, it was almost three. Sergeant Davis, his partner, and a rather frightened-appearing secretary, were waiting in the anteroom.

Davis eyed the package I carried under my left arm. "What's that?"

"A pistol," I said.

He shook his head sadly. "Look, have you got a permit to carry one?"

"I don't need a permit to carry it cased; only if I have it concealed on my person."

"Why didn't you leave the pistol in your room? Why bring it here?"

"I checked out of my hotel this morning. They're really too expensive, you know. You wouldn't happen to know where I could find a small efficiency apartment?"

"Why don't you pack that gun in your zipper bag?"

"It's quite full. I simply can't squeeze it in."

Over my protests, Davis proceeded to search me and my possessions. When he finished, he turned toward the door leading to Matt Nelson's private office and raised his bass voice. "He's clean."

The door to Matt Nelson's office opened slightly and he peeked out. "What do you mean 'clean'? He has a gun, hasn't he?"

"But no ammunition," Davis said.

The door opened wider and Nelson seemed more confident. "Well, well, Mr. Whitcomb, nice to see you again after all these years. I'm happy things turned out all right."

"No thanks to you," I said dryly. "I'd like to have a few words with you."

"Of course," Nelson said. "Come right in." He stopped Davis from following me. "I'd like to talk to Mr. Whitcomb alone, please."

Nelson was a rather sharp-featured, low-browed creature. When I had retained him, I'd had doubts about him, but had laid them aside in the face of a recommendation from an acquaintance. That had been a mistake.

When Nelson sat down at his desk, he opened the top drawer slightly.

I noticed the butt of a revolver. Evidently he was protecting himself against the possibility that I had throttling in mind.

He smiled again. "Mr. Whitcomb, I know you are an intelligent man."

"Thank you," I said. "I have heard that a number of times recently, but I did not come here for compliments." I regarded him with the accumulated distaste of four years. "Not only did you completely and absolutely bungle my defense at the trial, but you had the incredible gall to render a bill for $876.14."

He shrugged. "What difference does that make now? You didn't pay a cent."

"I didn't happen to have the money. But what really infuriates me was your attempt to garnishee my wages in prison. There I was sweating in the prison laundry for a miserable twenty-two cents a day and yet . . ."

He waved a hand deprecatingly. "I just thought there was the possibility that you might have something put away and I could scare it out of you." He shrugged. "Besides, the judge threw it out of court."

"Nevertheless, I find it utterly unforgivable."

Nelson leaned forward. "Look, I'm not a stupe and neither are you. I know you weren't just going to walk in here and shoot me."

"You're certain of that?"

"Well . . . not *absolutely* certain. What I really think is that for a long time you've been planning, and since you have brains you've cooked up something real clever, isn't that right? Something real sneaky? Maybe not even a gun? Or a knife? Or—well—anything obvious? And you can wait? You've got time? You can play this war of nerves?"

I looked out of the window.

"Look," Nelson said, "you don't scare me, but I'm a busy man and I can't take this cat and mouse stuff. I mean I just don't have the time. So I'll tell you what I'll do. You don't owe me $876.14 anymore." He took a piece of paper from the half-opened desk drawer and shoved it in front of me. "A receipt. Marked paid in full and signed by me."

I glanced at the sheet of paper.

"I know, I know," Nelson said quickly. "A receipt is just a piece of paper and it doesn't buy you anything. The State gave you six thousand dollars and maybe you figure you have more than that coming? I don't blame you. It was a bum rap. You may not believe me, but I did my best."

He was right. I didn't believe him.

He reached into the desk again and this time brought out a thick envelope. He fanned the bills. "Count them. Six thousand dollars in hundreds. I'll match the State, dollar for dollar. But that doesn't mean I admit a thing. I've just got charity in my heart."

I examined the money. "This isn't exactly why I came here. And what am I supposed to do for this six thousand?"

"Just leave me alone." His voice rose slightly. "I don't care what you do to anybody else. That's none of my business. But leave me alone."

I pocketed the bills and smiled slowly. "Very well. You have convinced me of your sincerity. I shall leave and never return."

Downstairs I walked for approximately two blocks before I

verified the fact that I was being followed. I proceeded to enter buildings, ride elevators, ascend and descend stairs. Finally I exited into an alley, confident that I had eluded my shadow.

I turned into the avenue and almost into the arms of a rather tall, eager man. He seemed to welcome me. "You lost him," he said.

"Lost who?" I asked warily.

"The cop."

"And just who are you?"

"James Hogan, confidential investigations, et cetera. They were going to hire a lawyer, but then they realized that he might consider what they wanted done to be unethical. But a private detective is geared to do almost anything nowadays, so they hired me."

"Who did?"

"Clark and Tilford."

"Ah, yes, the contemptible liars who cost me four years of my life."

He waggled a finger. "You won't be able to get at them, you know. The authorities have been forewarned and Clark and Tilford have a police guard. Twenty-four hours a day."

"Good for them."

He smiled slyly. "But you can wait, can't you? Weeks, months, years, and eventually you will get revenge? You will bide your time and watch and wait. A hundred years, if necessary?"

"Frankly, I consider a hundred years out of the question."

"Ah, then you must have something immediate in mind? Something fiendishly clever?"

"Why shouldn't I? I've had plenty of time to think about it, and I'd still be languishing in jail if my lawyer hadn't discovered that Clark was nearsighted."

"Well, Clark didn't exactly *know* he was nearsighted. He thought that's the way things looked to everybody, until his wife got tired of having him stumble over things and sent him to an optometrist. But actually it didn't really make any difference if he *was* or was *not* nearsighted, he would have lied anyway."

I sighed. "Why?"

"It was a spur of the moment thing," Hogan said. "Here was Clark, leading a completely drab, humdrum sort of life, with one day pretty much like the other. He was really a quite *unimportant* man, to his wife, his family, his neighbors—the world. Then here came this opportunity, this chance to be . . . well, *noticed*."

I was incredulous. "You mean that just because Clark wanted to be noticed he was ready to bear false witness and railroad another man to—"

Hogan interrupted. "He didn't exactly *know* that he was railroading you. He thought he was just backing up Tilford."

I took a deep breath. "And what about Tilford? Why did *he* lie?"

"He didn't want his car searched."

"I suppose he had a dead body in the trunk?"

"No. One hundred pounds of oleomargarine."

I closed my eyes.

"Now, here's the picture," Hogan said. "It was two o'clock in the morning. Tilford had just come from visiting his brother in Illinois and he'd loaded up with the oleomargarine because it's a lot cheaper than the more expensive spread. So he's driving through the empty city streets when he hears this burglar alarm ringing and it seems to be coming from Karnecki's Supermarket. Being curious, he stops his car, gets out, and goes to the plate glass windows and looks in. He sees nothing, but then he hears the squad cars coming. He decides he doesn't want to get involved, so he starts back for his car. But just then the first squad car pulls up and the cops jump out with their guns drawn. They come toward him and he sees immediately what they've got in mind. They think he's the one who set off the alarm, so he panics."

"Why the devil should he panic? In this day and age surely an innocent man has nothing to fear from the law." I thought about that and cleared my throat. "Go on."

"He wasn't really worried about being accused of trying to rob the supermarket. But while the police were clearing him, wouldn't they go about searching his car? For burglar tools or something like that? And then they'd find the oleomargarine, and suppose that got into the newspapers?"

I shook my head. "I am aware that Wisconsin remains the only state in the Union with a restrictive tax on oleo. But it is common practice for Wisconsinites to load up with oleo whenever they have the opportunity to cross the borders of the state, and I have yet to hear of anyone arrested by the police just because he was found in possession of—"

"True," Hogan said. "But don't you remember? At the trial? Tilford worked for the Lakeside Dairies—in the *Butter* Division. If it ever got out that he used oleo in his own household, well . . ."

I understood. "His public image would be destroyed? Also he'd get fired?"

"Precisely," Hogan said, "so he pointed in a general westerly direction and shouted, *'There he goes! He ran out the back way!'*"

"I can understand his desire to divert attention from himself," I said, "but when I and half a dozen others were plucked from the neighborhood streets and brought to him, why couldn't he simply have said that he had never seen any of us before?"

"He was going to, but the police had been questioning him in the meantime and he felt they were getting a little suspicious because he was so nervous. He thought they might decide to search his car anyway. So he just pointed once again and said, *'That's him! That's the man!'*"

The very remembrance of his accusing finger still rankled me. "So in order to maintain his Dr. Jekyll–Mr. Hyde existence, he was willing to send me to prison?"

"Not exactly. What he was going to do was go home, put the oleo in his walk-in cooler and then go back to the police and say he was sorry, but he had made a mistake."

"But obviously he didn't."

"No. Because just as Tilford finished his identification, Clark, seeing his own opportunity for recognition, stepped forward from the small crowd that had gathered, and pounded in another nail, so to speak. So later, Tilford, figuring that Clark's identification was legitimate, came to the conclusion that there was really no point in him changing his own story. The police might become suspicious again and he could still get into a lot of trouble."

I sighed. "And I suppose that Clark—for his part—felt perfectly safe in grabbing a little of the publicity because he thought that *Tilford* was telling the truth?"

Hogan nodded. "That's the way it went until McIntyre discovered that Clark was nearsighted but hadn't been fitted for glasses until two months after your conviction. Clark couldn't bear to come out bald-faced and confess that he had lied, but he did admit that he wasn't *really* certain that he had seen you at all. Then, of course, when Tilford heard *that,* his conscience began bothering him and he finally had to admit that he *too* wasn't really positive anymore. And—well, here you are, free as a bird."

"Obviously Clark and Tilford are not going to tell the authorities the whole truth, but why have you told *me?*"

"Because I am appealing to your compassion and mercy. These are not evil men. They meant you no harm."

"But they did manage to deprive me of four years of feeedom."

He held up a hand. "Clark and Tilford have talked things over. They agree that perhaps there has been a slight miscarriage of justice, so they have decided that just to make things right, they're each going to send you fifteen dollars a week. Forever."

I rubbed my jaw. "*Ad infinitum?*"

"Well," Hogan said, "whichever is longer."

I mulled over the offer for half a minute. "Why don't they just present me with some lump sum? Like six thousand dollars?"

He smiled wisely. "And after you got the six thousand dollars, what would there be to prevent you from wreaking your revenge upon Clark and Tilford anyway?" He chuckled. "No. I advised them to arrange this payment system. Then you will not be tempted to kill the geese that lay the golden eggs."

I gave that some thought too. "Well, it *would* pay the rent," I said finally.

Hogan and I parted amicably and I went into the nearest bar.

How strange fate turns, I thought. Here I had gone to Matt Nelson with a personal check for $876.14 in my wallet. In my book, a debt is a debt, even if it is to an incompetent like Nelson, but instead. . . .

I sipped my whiskey.

As for Clark and Tilford, I had not exactly wished them a long life, but I'd had no intention of interfering with the natural course of their longevity . . . and now I had twelve thousand dollars and a weekly annuity of thirty dollars.

That tended to make one cautious—to avoid taking chances.

But no, I had to go through with it. It was a matter of professional pride. I had never failed before.

So at two o'clock that morning I was once again before the safe in Karnecki's Supermarket, and this time I did not commit the error of accidentally tripping the burglar alarm.

Evil Star

Ray Russell

Dear Mr. Bernstein:

At the request of your publisher and our client, my colleagues and I have now read and discussed the typescript of your book. We are pleased to report that, with the exception of some isolated sections which we will specify, the book is not, in our opinion, actionable and should not expose you to litigation when published. It is a work of scholarly analysis, thoroughly documented, and even though much of it is pungently expressed, it lies well within the area of fair comment. You have obviously "done your homework," amassed considerable research, and consistently cited "chapter and verse," so to speak, in tracing the sources of Avery Bream's work. Your extensive parallel excerpts from his writings and the writings of others, from which you demonstrate his were derived, put you on firm legal, as well as literary, ground.

These parallels of style and subject matter are most impressive. Your own cleverness is rivalled only by that of Mr. Bream himself. I refer to his technique of borrowing a plot from one writer and re-telling it in the style of another, thus achieving an artful act of camouflage undetected until now. I was astonished to learn, for instance, that his most famous bestseller, *Evil Star*, is practically a carbon copy of Dreiser's *An American Tragedy*, done in the style (or, as you put it, "filtered through the prism") of James Branch

Cabell. It was likewise illuminating to discover that his acclaimed *Midnight Mushrooms* is little more than *Othello* with the races switched, told in the manner of early Saroyan, and with no acknowledgement to Shakespeare (unless we count the title, a quotation from *The Tempest*); and that his *Pristine Christine* is none other than the Agatha Christie classic, *The Murder of Roger Ackroyd*, as it might have been written by Burroughs (you should clarify as to whether you have reference to William or to Edgar Rice) and with the Christine of the title (a play on Christie?) taking the place of the original victim. We suggest a title change, however, for Chapter III, in which the bulk of these and other parallels are cited. Even though *The Thieving Magpie* is the title of a famous opera, words like "thief" should be avoided.

On p. 97, after you quote Bream's statement, "I am the equal, in my fashion, of Tolstoy, Proust and Joyce" (from an interview in *Newsweek*), you make your point elegantly when you say: "The painter Ingres told those who likened him to Raphael, 'I am very small, just *so high,* next to him.' The composer Rossini made a pilgrimage to kneel before the manuscript score of Mozart's *Don Giovanni,* declaring it a sacred relic." Why not leave it at that? To add, as you do, that Bream is "a conceited pig" not fit to "empty the bedpans" of Tolstoy, et al., is painting the lily, as well as flirting with litigation.

A similar example of gilding refined gold occurs on p. 118, following your sentence, "For over a decade, he has been promising to astound us with a vast confessional tome of Rousseau-like candor in which he will beat his breast and cry *mea culpa* to a host of sins, literary and otherwise; but the years come and go, and the guilt-heavy volume never appears." That is fine, but the short burst that follows ("What's the matter, Bream—*chicken?*") is, from the legal point of view, touchy.

Our Mr. Vieck asks me to say that, speaking now not as attorneys but as impartial readers, we hope we may be forgiven for commenting on the language you employ in Chapter VIII to describe the first Mrs. Bream. It seems inordinately biased in her favor. This is not, I reiterate, a legal point, but for you to call her "an angel whose delicate foot scarce touched the sordid earth when she walked" (p. 130), "too good by far, too radiant for this world" (p. 131), "an anthology of all the virtues" (p. 132), "a fount of undemanding, uncomplaining love" (p. 133), "a golden spirit the like of which no mortal eye will ever see again" (p. 134), etc., strikes us as somewhat excessive. When such phrases are read alongside your less than complimentary remarks about her husband, the contrast tends to cast doubt upon your academic detachment.

In Chapter IX, *Champion of the Overdog*, you walk a tightrope in showing Bream as being a far cry from the fearless anti-Establishment crusader and spokesman for writers' rights he pretends to be. The change or deletion of a few passages should make the chapter safe from litigation. Second paragraph, p. 155, the word "coward" is ill-advised, as is the phrase in the next paragraph, "soul of a weasel." Pp. 157–158 make vivid reading, but in them you are guilty of that with which you charge Bream: lack of substantiation. "His oft-repeated claim to have broken the writing arm of a magazine editor who had 'emasculated' his prose," you say, "is less piquant than it might be if he would, just once, name the offending butcher." Good point, but you spoil it (and skate on thin legal ice) when you add: "In fact, that editor has privately recounted the truth about the famous fray. Bream, it seems, had offered a timorous, whining protest to the emendations, thus provoking the overworked editor to gruffly respond. 'Damn it. I sweated blood to make that unreadable swill fit for human consumption. And this is the thanks I get? You're lucky I publish your shit at all!' On the stressed word, the angered editor brought his fist down forcibly on his desk, breaking the little finger of his right hand." *You* do not name the editor, either, you see, so the authenticity of both versions is suspect.

The same chapter (p. 159) contains a passage that could be considered defamatory not only to Bream but also to Siegfried Rheinfahrt, the book publisher. I refer to the quoted letter, from and to unidentified sources, which describes an incident at a booksellers' convention: "You should have seen our dearly beloved Aviary buttering up that Nazi goniff, Rheinfahrt. I mean, it's one thing for Aviary to change his name and try to pass for goy, and it's another for him to fawn upon and flatter that lizard who's not only a crook but an anti-Semite. Most of us snubbed Siggie cold, but not ol' Aviary. Oh, no. It was nauseating. He did everything but kiss the s.o.b.'s ass, and maybe in the *privvissy*, as he'd say in that phony accent he's begun to affect, of his hotel suite, he even did that." The passage should be excised.

Are you sure of your facts (p. 201) when you describe Bream

"running from bookstore to bookstore, spending his entire advance check buying up copies of his novel to get it on the [bestseller] list . . ."? What proof of this could you provide, if challenged? On the same page, how can you possibly know that he "not only wined and dined" but also "tickled more than the fancy" of the "aging female critic" who, according to you, "bears a startling resemblance to Samuel Johnson"? Moreover, if we understand what you are suggesting in the "tickled" line, does this not contradict the allegation in your p. 492 footnote (see below)? Please think about these points carefully.

I'm afraid we cannot recommend the retention of your allusions to Bream's income in the form they are now presented (p. 299). Nor do we quite understand the precise nature of your charges. Do you mean to imply that he failed to declare a substantial portion of his earnings for that year? That is a serious allegation. Or do you merely mean that he lied to the press, inflating the true figures in order to appear more affluent and successful than he actually was? Do you really plan to reproduce photocopies of his IRS returns? (I refer to such phrases as "See Plate 1," "See Plate 2," and so on.) How were these documents obtained?

Your comments about his mother (p. 307) present no legal problem because she is deceased, although in some quarters these passages may be criticized on grounds of taste.

The telephone conversation between Bream and his psychoanalyst (pp. 349–350) poses a quadruple problem, however. First: it could only have been obtained by wiretap, which is illegal. Second: it puts both patient and doctor in a most unfavorable light. Third: as our forensic medicine expert, Dr. Kenney, reminds us, you are not a licensed psychiatrist, so you are not legally qualified to diagnose Bream's mental condition as displaying evidence of "self-destructive tendencies . . . irreversible paranoia . . . dangerously sociopathic hostilities . . . desire for humiliation and punishment . . . schizoid hallucinations and delusions," etc. Fourth: as you point out by the long parallel quotations in the righthand columns of these pages, the phone coversation is identical, word for word, to the conversation between the fictitious characters Dr. Proctor and Bernie Amber in Bream's novel, *Negative Feedback*. You claim (but without adequate support) that the real-life conversation took place five months *after* the publication of the book, indicating that "Bream is perhaps the only novelist in history whose own life plagiarized his work. So cowed and mesmerized was his puppet doctor by the fame of the celebrated patient that he responded on cue, Charlie McCarthy-like, to Bream's leading questions and insults." Is it not possible, we submit, that you are mistaken about the date of the conversation? Might it not have occurred *prior* to the writing of the book, and been used as grist for the author's mill (a not uncommon practice among fiction writers)? Indeed, is it not an open secret in literary circles that Amber is the most transparently autobiographical character in the entire Bream *oeuvre*? Is not AMBER—as our crossword fanatic, Mr. Fenwick, says—a simple anagram for BREAM? For these several reasons, we counsel you to forgo this conversation.

Similarly troublesome is the first of the two footnotes on p. 492 (beginning "Freud, Jung and even Reich all agree . . ."). While it may be perfectly true that certain aspects of his life-style are indicators of "impotence or other sexual dysfunction" rather than the "prowess he publicly professes," there is no way you satisfactorily prove this, even by quoting the anonymous "Ms. X." Besides, here you are venturing into personal attack rather than professional criticism. We realize that you consider this an important insight into the "pathological sex episodes" of his work, which is the theme of this chapter, but we urge you to delete this footnote, as well as the parenthetical reference (in the body of the following page, 493) to what you call his "underendowment." The supportive Polaroid photograph which you indicate will appear on the "facing page" of the published book certainly must not be used. It is irrelevant that you obtained "the standard release form" signed by the photographer, his second ex-wife. What is required is a release from the subject, or model, Mr. Bream himself, and that, in our opinion, will be obtained only with the greatest difficulty. And surely the reference (same page) to his "*vain attempts at* solitary vice" (italics mine) is pure conjecture on your part?

(Before I forget it, allow me to backtrack and cover a couple of small spots I missed. In Chapter VIII, where you picture Bream's miscegenational first marriage, is it necessary to say "murderously jealous rages" and "where the body is buried," even though these expressions have a clearly metaphorical intent? They would not, perhaps, be problems were it not for the tragic sailing accident that took the life of the first Mrs. Bream, plus the fact that her body was never recovered. Some readers might interpret your figures of speech literally, as a monstrous accusation, and you would then be extremely vulnerable to the possibility of a lawsuit. Also inadvisable is the phrase, "Flowers die; rats live." You really must not call Bream a rat. And only this moment Mr. Fenwick calls my attention to the fact that the title of Bream's most famous novel is "rats live" in reverse—isn't that interesting?)

Now for the bad news. We must seriously question the wisdom of your lengthy (95 pages!) Appendix, in which you provide, verbatim and unexpurgated, letters written over the years by various editors, creditors, writers, literary agents, relatives, former fans and friends of Bream's, and so forth. The material, even if provably factual, is extremely damaging to Bream and was not originally intended by the letter writers for publication. In most cases, it seems unlikely that you have even secured proper permission. We strongly advise an appendectomy, that is to say removal of the entire Appendix.

Your revision of the above specified areas should protect you from litigation and, if I may so, result in a most valuable work of contemporary scholarship which I, for one, found to be brisk reading. May I look forward to receiving a personally inscribed copy of the first edition?

Yours truly,
For
WEST, FENWICK,
SCHLUSSELMANN,
KENNEY & VIECK
Arthur Lowell West

P.S. Our Mr. Schlusselmann points out the amusing coincidence that your name is the German equivalent of a well-known Bream character. Are you aware of this?

A Woman's Help

Henry Slesar

Arnold Bourdon was suffering from a progressive muscle disease, which, while debilitating and unpleasant, was neither painful nor imminently fatal. Arnold was suffering, that is, but it was his wife, Elizabeth, who had the illness. She robed herself in its symptoms like a queen, and from her bed and wheelchair ruled her subjects (Arnold, the three servants and her physician) with a tyranny that was sometimes overwhelming to Arnold's sensitive nature.

Arnold was a handsome, well-groomed man, kept younger-looking than his forty-three years through vigorous exercise and the health-giving benefits of an easy, moneyed existence. All his life, he had enjoyed the help of women. His mother, while poor and widowed, had devoted herself to his early care and feeding. His sister, sacrificing her own happiness for his sake, had supported him during his matriculation at one of the better Eastern colleges. Then he had met Elizabeth, who was rich, and partial to handsome, sensitive men.

Arnold's every feature was sensitive. His eyes were a tender blue. His nose was aristocratic. His lips fine and delicate. But most sensitive of all were his ears. Shrill complaining voices gave him headaches. The sound of petulant sobs was painful. The creak-creak of a wheelchair scudding overhead caused him to grit his teeth. But most of all, the clangor of a bedside bell, summoning him to the royal invalid presence, was excruciating agony.

When the bell sounded one Monday morning in late February, Arnold was in the kitchen supervising the precise timing of Elizabeth's two-and-a-half-minute egg. The pale blue eyes crinkled, the delicate mouth winced, and the elongated fingers closed about the handle of a butter knife in an oddly ferocious manner. He picked up the breakfast tray and carried it up the stairway to the second floor, trying to take comfort from the fact that he was performing the chore for the last time.

Elizabeth was sitting upright in bed when he entered. There was a satiny blue bolster behind her back, and magenta pillows behind her head. The background was all wrong for Elizabeth's graying hair and yellow skin. She had never been a pretty woman; now she was barely presentable. Arnold, as both esthete and husband, found her difficult to look upon.

"You certainly took your time," she grumbled, smoothing the sheet over her lap. "If this *woman* you hired doesn't do any better, I'll probably starve to death one of these days. Well, put it down, put it down!"

Arnold put the wicker tray in front of her, and glanced at his watch. "It's almost nine now. Her train will be here in ten minutes; perhaps I should start for the station."

"You seem awfully anxious," she said.

"I just don't want Miss Grecco to feel lost. You know that Hillfield station. I could send Ralph, of course, if you'd rather I stayed with you."

"Go ahead, go ahead," she said testily. "I'm anxious to meet your Miss Grecco. I suppose she's some frittery blonde with ten thumbs and a bad permanent."

"I'm sure she'll be fine. The employment service recommended her highly, and you saw her references. You need a woman's care, Elizabeth, you've said so yourself."

"Oh, stop yammering and go." She tapped the top of her egg violently with the back of a spoon. "And send her right up; I want a look at this creature."

The train, as usual, was late. Arnold, waiting at the wheel of the small foreign car that Elizabeth had given him on their anniversary, drummed his fingers impatiently on the dashboard. When the 9:05 lumbered into the suburban station at 9:15, only three passengers got off. Two were men; the other was a trim-figured young woman with a slouchy feathered hat covering her face. A conductor assisted her with the three shabby suitcases which accompanied her. Arnold couldn't determine much about her appearance from the distance, but he could see instantly that Miss Grecco had superb legs. Superb. He patted his thin, iron-gray moustache with one finger.

As he left the car to assist her, he saw that under her overcoat she wore a severe tweed suit that Elizabeth would have called Early Garbo. Something about the mannishness of the attire and the excellence of the legs made the woman's figure provocative. Arnold found himself anxious to see what was under the concealing hat.

"Hello," he said pleasantly. "I'm Arnold Bourdon, and I suppose you're Miss Grecco. Sorry about the train, but our service here isn't the best in the world."

She looked up from the feathery brim. She wore absolutely no make-up. If she had, if there had been crimson on her lips and blue on her eyelids, she would have been altogether too voluptuous an entry into the Bourdon household. As it was, Miss Grecco was a remarkably pretty woman, and Arnold experienced a tremor of doubt concerning his wife's reaction.

"I hope you'll be happy here," he said, smiling charmingly. "My wife's needed some female attention for some time, someone who can take care of her needs better than I. You understand about her ailment, I trust?"

"Yes, it was explained to me," Miss Grecco said shyly. "I've done practical nursing before, but I understand that your wife needs more of a—companion."

"You might say that. She requires all sorts of little attentions in addition to her medical care; you know how women are." He glanced at her briefly. "I certainly hope you'll like us, Miss Grecco."

"I'm sure I will," she murmured.

Arnold found Miss Grecco's interview with Elizabeth as anxiety-ridden as childbirth. In the living room, he paced the floor like an expectant father, waiting for the bedroom door to open on the second floor. When it did, Miss Grecco came downstairs on her remarkable legs, and her pale cheeks were flushed with the natural cosmetic of emotion. He questioned her briefly, but she offered nothing more than the information that his wife wished to see him upstairs.

Elizabeth was a thundercloud when he entered. She crossed over the lace bedjacket.

"Well, where did you get her?" she asked bitterly. "From the Folies Bergère?"

"Elizabeth, really—"

"That getup didn't fool me for a minute. I suppose you think you were being clever, don't you?"

"Nothing of the sort. You chose Miss Grecco yourself, from three résumés sent by the employment service. I've never seen the woman before today."

"But you admit she's pretty?"

"Miss Grecco's attractive, yes. But not pretty, no."

Elizabeth laughed briefly. Then she lowered her reading glasses and hid the intensity of her eyes. "Very well, we'll let her stay. It should be interesting watching you two. But make no mistake about it, Arnold. I'll be watching."

"Really, you're talking nonsense."

"I know you, Arnold, I know you inside out. I can hear your little romantic heart beating all the way over here."

"Elizabeth, please—"

"Well, go ahead, tell Miss Grecco that she's hired. No, never mind, I'll tell her myself." She picked up the bedside bell and rang it violently. The insistent clanging made Arnold grimace, but she didn't stop until Miss Grecco realized the summons was for her.

"Yes, Mrs. Bourdon?" Miss Grecco said, appearing in the doorway.

"I want to be wheeled outdoors this morning," Elizabeth said. "I'll need your help. Then I wish you'd see about Arnold's lunch; our cook has a tendency to fry everything, and Arnold has a delicate stomach. You see," she said slyly, "I'm not the only one here who needs attention. My husband deserves some, too."

"Yes, Mrs. Bourdon," Miss Grecco said, glancing at Arnold with a hint of panic in her lovely violet eyes.

It was two months before he kissed her. It had been a trying two months, in which Elizabeth's clanging bell had ripped through the house incessantly; not so much a summons as a warning. She was jealous, and she was enjoying her jealousy with a strange perverse pleasure. She hinted constantly about their burgeoning romance, and chuckled when the color rose in Miss Grecco's alabaster cheeks. To Arnold, she did more than hint—she accused. Eventually, as if weary of being damned for a crime he wasn't committing, Arnold kissed Miss Grecco.

It happened in the Bourdon kitchen, at midnight. Miss Grecco had come downstairs for a solitary cup of hot chocolate. When Arnold came in, he said nothing. Miss Grecco, in her housecoat, was especially feminine. Her auburn hair, normally tight-combed and pinned, was loose over her shoulders.

"Would you like some hot chocolate?" she whispered.

"Yes, thank you," Arnold said. Then he took her in his arms.

Half an hour later, Miss Grecco put her head on his shoulder and said:

"I love you, Arnold."

"I love you, too."

She sighed. "But it's hopeless, isn't it?"

"That depends on what you mean by hopeless."

"Why, I mean marriage, of course."

"Oh."

"That *is* what you meant, isn't it?"

"It would be, ordinarily," Arnold said ruefully. "But as you know, I'm well married."

"There are divorce courts."

"There are poorhouses, too."

Miss Grecco pulled away from him. "Then that's all there is to it, I suppose."

"We can't admit that—"

"What else can there be? I won't be a back-street wife, Arnold."

"That's a dreadful, romance-novel phrase. I prefer—lover."

"And I prefer—husband."

Now Arnold sighed.

They sat three feet apart at the kitchen table, their hands closed about the empty mugs of hot chocolate, waiting for an idea to occur. The thoughts that were finally expressed were no newcomers to either of them, especially Arnold.

"You know about the pentathalymine?" he said.

"That medicine I give her every night?"

"Yes."

"I know that it's a strong sedative. She's often so uncomfortable at night; it helps her."

"You know about the proper dosage, and all that?"

"I know that it's dangerous, that an overdose could affect the brain, possibly cause hemorrhaging."

"Naturally, you wouldn't make any mistakes about overdosing."

"Of course not."

"That would be foolish," Arnold said thoughtfully.

"Yes, it would," Miss Grecco said. "So easily detectable."

"However, isn't it true that an overdose wouldn't be detected if administered a bit at a time? That is, one extra c.c. per night would have the same effect, only not immediately."

"Yes, I believe that's true."

"She would become weaker every day."

"Nauseated. That's sure to be a symptom."

"Yes, but not necessarily ascribable to the drug. The difference in the bottle would be hardly discernible. How long do you think it would take before she—?"

"I'm not really sure."

"Just guess."

"Perhaps two months," Miss Grecco said.

"Why, that would be June," Arnold Bourdon said, smiling sentimentally.

When Dr. Ivey was called in two weeks later, he spent an hour behind the closed door of Elizabeth's bedroom, and emerged looking puzzled and unhappy. He asked to see Arnold privately, and being a man of integrity, admitted that he wasn't sure of the cause of Elizabeth's trouble.

"These nausea attacks she's been getting," he said. "They're not usual in such cases, and yet I can't seem to locate any other reason. She's extremely weak, but that's understandable, and her blood pressure is higher than it should be."

"Is there anything you can do for her?" Arnold said, sympathetically.

"I've told her to keep to her bed for the rest of the week; perhaps she's been overtiring herself lately. Also . . ." He paused and looked embarrassed. "Well, her mental state isn't exactly wholesome. She seems to have some strange notions about . . . well, about your Miss Grecco."

"What sort of notions?"

"Your wife's an imaginative woman. Confined the way she is, her mind is free to think up all sorts of things. You know what I mean. . . ."

"Miss Grecco has been absolutely loyal," Arnold said. "I'm sure that Elizabeth would admit that herself. Frankly, I don't see how we got along without her before."

"Er, yes. Well, it's something to be aware of, anyway. If you need me again before my regular visit next month, Mr. Bourdon, don't hesitate to call."

Arnold did call, four days later. Elizabeth had fainted suddenly while being wheeled about the garden. Miss Grecco did all the right things. She loosened her employer's clothes, held her head between her knees, and soon restored her to her senses. Dr. Ivey, arriving an hour later, complimented her on her prompt action, and suggested that she might wish to undertake a course of study as a registered nurse. Miss Grecco demurred, saying she had other plans for her future.

A week later, Elizabeth herself demanded the doctor's presence. She threatened to throw him off the case if he didn't improve her health, and worked herself into such a state that she was sick on her best oriental carpet in the living room.

"Nerves," the doctor told Arnold. "The woman is a bundle of them. You'll have to watch her very carefully, Mr. Bourdon; if her condition is no better by the end of the week, I think we should have her in the hospital for observation."

Arnold's blue eyes widened at the ominous statement.

"You can't," he stammered. "I mean, Elizabeth would never consent to it."

"She'll have to," Dr. Ivey said firmly. "I won't answer for the consequences if she doesn't."

That night, Arnold reported the threat to Miss Grecco. They had a serious decision to make over their midnight hot chocolate. If Elizabeth's condition was brought to the attention of probing clinical eyes, the overdose of sedative accumulating in her system might be detected.

"We could do this two ways," he said thoughtfully. "Either we could ease up on the amount we give her . . ."

"I've thought of that," Miss Grecco said.

"Or . . ."

"I've thought of that, too," Miss Grecco said.

They moved into each other's arms, with the easy grace of practiced lovers. They remained there for some five minutes, with Arnold murmuring into her ear and placing dry little kisses on the
white column of her neck. It was like all the other nights of their
romance, sweetened by affection, spiced by danger. Only this time
the moment became different. Arnold was aware of it first; his back
stiffened, and he sniffed the air. Miss Grecco's eyes rounded, and
then she looked over his shoulder at the doorway of the kitchen.
She made a gasping sound, and Arnold spun her about, as if for a
shield, and saw for himself the apparition that had intruded.

It was Elizabeth, in her night clothes. White faced, spectral in
the dim light, her hands skeletal on the doorframe, her eyes like
glowing charcoal.

"Don't let me interrupt," she said, feebly, but with venom. "Go
right on with it, Arnold. "

"Elizabeth, you shouldn't have come down here—"

"I couldn't find the bell. That damn fool doctor put my bell
somewhere. I had to walk down here . . ." She forced herself to
smile; her teeth were like tiny tombstones. "But I'm glad I did. I
wouldn't have missed this for the world, Arnold, this pretty picture . . ."

"Oh, Mrs. Bourdon," Miss Grecco sobbed. "Oh, you musn't think
that—"

"Quiet, you! I've had enough of *you*. Understand that, Arnold?
Quite enough!"

"You're mistaken, you know," Arnold said stoutly. "Miss Grecco
merely has something in her eyes . . ."

"I know," Elizabeth said. "You. But this is one woman you won't
lean on again, Arnold. I want her out of here. Tomorrow!"

Miss Grecco started to plead.

"That won't do any good!" Elizabeth said. "You're fired, Miss
Grecco. If Arnold were my employee instead of my husband, I'd
fire him, too. But he *is* my husband. Understand? *My* husband."

Miss Grecco turned and fled. Arnold, helpless, listened to the
rapid thumping of her low heels as she went up the carpeted stairway.

"Now you can help me," Elizabeth said, fatigued but with triumph. "You can carry me upstairs, Arnold. And tomorrow, you will

call the employment agency and see about a substitute for Miss Grecco. Only *this* time, I'll interview our candidates, personally."

"Yes, Elizabeth," Arnold said.

Ralph, the chauffeur, drove Miss Grecco to the station the next afternoon. She left the house in the tweed suit in which she had arrived, the slouchy feathered hat pulled down over her red-rimmed eyes. She didn't look back at Arnold, who watched her departure through the living-room window, his own expression pained and hopeless. It wasn't merely a lover that was being taken from him; it was a rescuer. As he watched her climb into the front seat of the car, he knew that Miss Grecco's appeal had been only partly romantic; that her help and understanding, her talented handling of the sedative that would someday release him from Elizabeth, were even more important than the attractive legs and pretty face. With a sigh, he turned from the window and saw Elizabeth in her wheelchair, watching him.

"Poor Arnold," she said, smiling maliciously. "There's always been a woman to help you, hasn't there? Only now she's gone, and you'll have to depend upon me. Poor, sick little me." She pushed the chair closer. "Have you done what I told you? Did you call the employment office?"

"Yes," he said wearily. "You'll have three candidates to choose from this afternoon. They've been instructed to arrive at alternate hours, beginning at two."

"Good."

"I think I'll go out to a movie," Arnold said. "If you don't think you'll need me."

"Go ahead," Elizabeth chuckled. "See a good romantic movie, Arnold, full of passion and pretty girls. Get it out of your system, Arnold, get it out for good."

She wheeled about sharply, and left him alone.

He returned home at five. From the moment the front door closed behind him, the bell began clanging upstairs. He threw his overcoat on the back of the sofa, and trudged up the steps. Elizabeth was in bed, tying her hair with paper curlers. She was almost affable.

"It's all settled, Arnold. I've found the perfect woman."

"I'm glad, Elizabeth. Did they all show up on time?"

"The first two were impossible," she said slyly. "They were so young. You know how you are around young women, Arnold. But

I'm sure you'll find the one I've hired most attractive. In a *mature* way. She's in the kitchen now. Why don't you go down there, and— look her over?" She giggled.

"You seem to find it amusing."

"Amusing? Why should I? Go down there, Arnold, give her the once-over. You might like her a great deal. Perhaps even more than you liked Miss Grecco. Go on!"

He frowned, and went out the door.

In the kitchen, the small, fat, dumpling of a woman was at the stove, watching a percolator. She turned when Arnold entered. She was in her mid-sixties, with stringy white hair, three chins and red cheeks.

"Does she want me?" she whispered. "Your Missus? I was just making some coffee."

Clang! Clang! went the bell above. Arnold, angrily, went to the stairway and looked up. His wife was in the doorway of her bed-room. "How do you like her?" Elizabeth shouted. "How do you like your new dream girl, Arnold?" She laughed wildly, and slammed the door.

Flushing, Arnold went back to the kitchen.

"My wife gets her sedative at nine o'clock," he said crisply. "You won't forget it?"

"No, of course not," the woman said. "You look pale. You don't look well at all."

"You understand about the dosage?"

"Yes, I understand. Just one c.c. above the normal."

"That's right. It shouldn't take long to finish her off now. God knows what's kept her going this long." He patted the red cheek affectionately. "I certainly appreciate this, mother."

She simpered happily, and went to answer the clanging bell on the second floor.